Where Eagles Fly Free

Where Eagles Fly Free

A Novel

❧ Book Two in The Courageous Series ❧

DAVID A. JACINTO

Where Eagles Fly Free

©2025 Meadow Vista Corporation, a California Corporation

All rights reserved. No part of this publication may be reproduced in any form or by any electronic or mechanical means, including information storage and retrieval systems, without permission in writing by the publisher, except by a reviewer who may quote brief passages in a review or as otherwise provided by USA copyright law.

Published by Meadow Vista Corporation

Print ISBN: 979-8-2184977-2-9
Ebook ISBN: 979-8-218-63272-4

Cover design by Claudine Mansour Design
Interior design by Liz Schreiter
Produced by Reading List Editorial
ReadingListEditorial.com

Printed in Canada

MEADOW VISTA
CORPORATION

This book is dedicated to my family, past and present, but especially my wife Anne, also an immigrant and from a long line of Welsh coal miners.

I also want to dedicate this book to my four wonderful children and their spouses: Michael and Sandra; Paul and Elizabeth; Rachel and Jason; Daniel and Christie. And, of course, to my near-perfect grandchildren—all thirteen of them: Alan, Kara, Clark, Cole, Jack, Miles, Eden, Parker, Cooper, Kalani, Elayna, Gionni, and Xenaya.

Family Tree

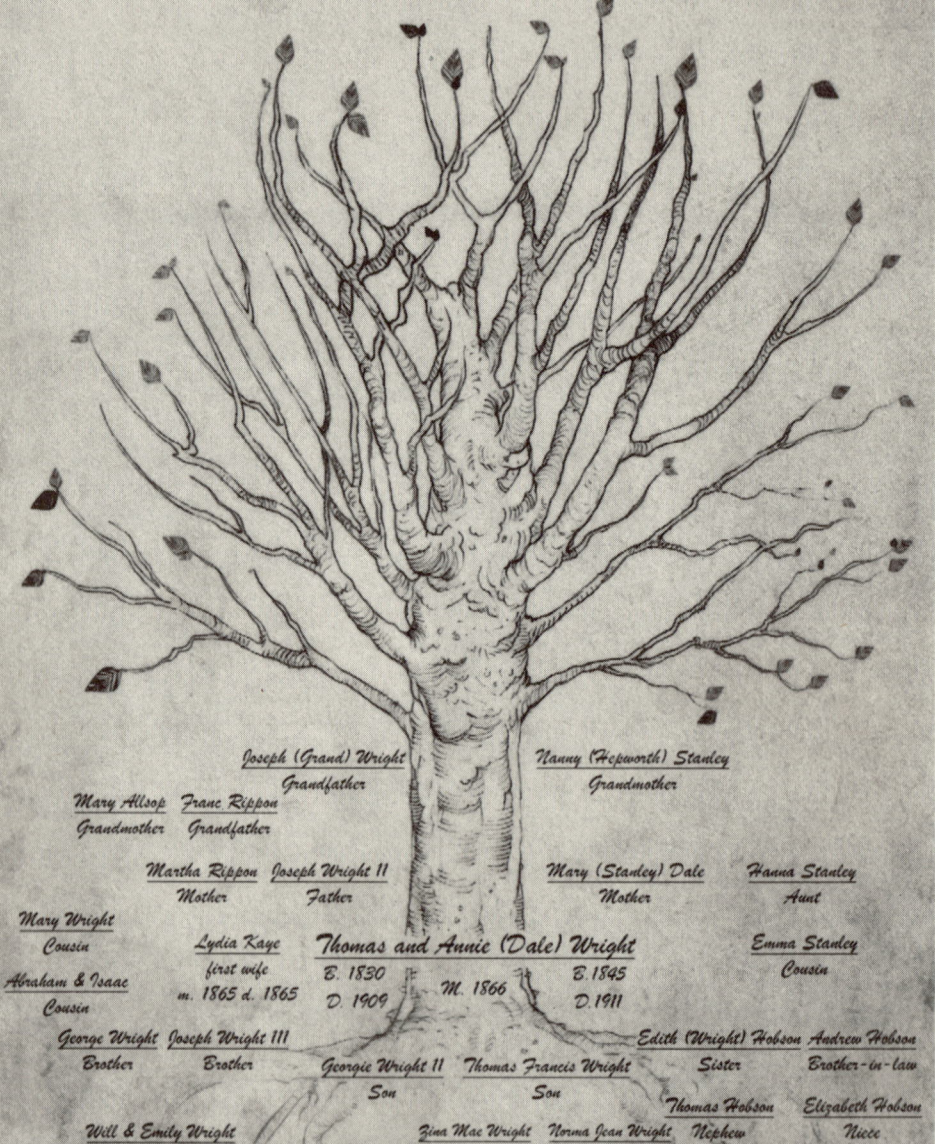

<u>Joseph (Grand) Wright</u>
Grandfather

<u>Nanny (Hepworth) Stanley</u>
Grandmother

<u>Mary Allsop</u>   <u>Franc Rippon</u>
Grandmother   Grandfather

<u>Martha Rippon</u>   <u>Joseph Wright II</u>
Mother   Father

<u>Mary (Stanley) Dale</u>   <u>Hanna Stanley</u>
Mother   Aunt

<u>Mary Wright</u>
Cousin

<u>Lydia Kaye</u>
first wife
m. 1865 d. 1865

<u>Thomas and Annie (Dale) Wright</u>
B. 1830   B. 1845
D. 1909   M. 1866   D. 1911

<u>Emma Stanley</u>
Cousin

<u>Abraham & Isaac</u>
Cousin

<u>George Wright</u>   <u>Joseph Wright III</u>
Brother   Brother

<u>Edith (Wright) Hobson</u>   <u>Andrew Hobson</u>
Sister   Brother-in-law

<u>Georgie Wright II</u>   <u>Thomas Francis Wright</u>
Son   Son

<u>Thomas Hobson</u>   <u>Elizabeth Hobson</u>
Nephew   Niece

<u>Will & Emily Wright</u>
Cousins

<u>Zinn Mae Wright</u>   <u>Norma Jean Wright</u>
Grand daughter   Grand daughter

<u>Eileen Wright</u>
Great grand daughter

<u>David Jacinto</u>
Great. Great grand son

PART I

June 1868

Chapter 1

⥤ • ⥢

THE BRIGANTINE *COLORADO*, SAILING UNDER a light breeze, prepared to turn westward from the placid blue-green waters of the Irish Sea toward the brutal cold of the North Atlantic. Under billowy clouds drifting lazily across a deep-blue summer sky, Tom leaned out over the railing for one last nostalgic look at the vibrant green mountains of England. It was breathtaking, the last of his homeland he would ever see.

Tom, his young and very pregnant wife Annie, his little brother Joey, and his sister Edie with her husband Andrew and five young children were on their way to America. With clenched jaw and resentment churning in his stomach, he was haunted by the thoughts that swirled in his mind. Their home had been burned to the ground, and they'd been driven from the British Isles by the industrial might of an aristocratic class hell-bent on subduing the common man. They carried with them all that remained of their old life in the two small trunks Tom's mam Martha had given them along with all the money she had. In her final sacrifice for her family, Martha, now homeless, remained in Liverpool to care for Papa, who'd been ravaged by black lung. Tom would never forget the look in Mam's eyes, as she stood on the dock watching the *Colorado* carry away all she loved in this life, never to return. It near tore his heart out. He had wiped at his runny nose before waving his final farewell to her. Tom would take nothing else with him to America but memories—his boyhood in the mines, the education Mam had sacrificed everything to give him, and the disasters caused by uncaring industrial aristocrats that had taken his Grand, Tigger, Mica, and of course, Lydia, the soulmate he'd adored beyond all else on earth.

⊱ • ⊰

"Ladies and gents!" thundered the voice from the quarterdeck of the brigantine *Colorado*.

Tom and Annie, uncomfortably heavy with child, halted their conversation midsentence. To hear their rugged American captain speak, they eased over to join the rest of their family.

"I'm Captain William Preston, and this here's my ship, the *Colorado*!" A man of medium height in his mid-forties, the captain had a hardened look about him, with muscular forearms, brooding eyes, and a bushy, sun-bleached beard that framed his face from his ears to below his chin. "If ya ain't bound for New York Harbor, you're on the wrong boat."

The throng of passengers shifted closer to listen.

Annie leaned over and whispered into Tom's ear, "He looks like a mischievous rascal peering through a hedge, considerin' mischief!"

Tom frowned. "Hmm." He furrowed his brow.

"Just sayin'." She smiled, holding his arm tighter.

Captain Preston's voice was stern. "There's only one hard-and-fast rule on board this ship to concern yerself with." He paused for effect and the passengers fell silent. They were from all over Europe, most strangers to one another. Standing clustered in families, the groups maintained an uneasy separation. It was clear to Tom that many were concerned for the seaworthiness of this bucket of soggy timbers.

"While yer on my ship, you'll be under my rule and mine alone." Squinting in the morning sunshine, Captain Preston's steely eyes looked squarely into those of each man and woman. "On board this brig, my word is like the iron rule of God Almighty. You'll obey it, or suffer the consequences." He paused again, this time to spit out a chaw of tobacco that slid across the deck. "On the length and breadth of this little brig, I lay down the law, to be brutally enforced with the power to cast judgment over life and death."

"There's yer mischievous rascal," Tom echoed back Annie's words. "I wouldn't suggest testing his resolve."

"You're free to inspect the ship with me if ya like." The captain turned and pointed to a tall, burly sailor with a four-day growth covering his leathery face. "Or, if ya wish, ya can join my first mate Mr. Jenkins here for a tour belowdecks."

There was a gleam of unyielding determination in Captain Preston's life-hardened eyes. "He clearly intends to remind us he holds our lives in his hands for the next two fortnights," Tom said. He reached for Annie's arm to help steady her as they walked the rolling deck. "I'm thinking he's gonna be a force to be reckoned with. I pray to God it's a force for good."

Tom's family of ten souls followed the captain across the deck to an open hatchway that led to the hold below. "How are you feeling?" Tom asked Annie, his arm still entwined with hers.

"A bit like a beached whale, but I'm fine." She held tight to his arm, trying to adjust to the undulating sea below their feet. "Thank you, Thomas."

"For what?"

With her hand resting on her belly, she gave him a serious look. "For everything. For marrying me. For being the good man you are. For taking me to America."

The captain turned to those following him and pointed. "This here's the aft hatchway ta get ta yer quarters. This be the midship quarterdeck hatch to the hold, where you're welcome ta store yer trunks. But . . ." His tone grew grave. "Once they're stored, you're forbidden to touch those trunks until we dock in New York."

Captain Preston ducked into the hatch. He beckoned for the others to follow down the steep, narrow stairway. Tom clung to the damp railing with one hand, and with his opposite arm, he cautiously steadied his expectant wife as they descended the creaky steps into the musty shadows of the galley below. Both were eager to see their home for the next two fortnights.

"Watch yer head, gents, or ya might lose it. It's a bit dodgy in these shadows down here." Captain Preston pointed to the grimy, dilapidated dungeon ahead. It measured just ten by fifteen feet. "This be the galley and the common."

Tom's senses were assaulted by the smell of mold, mildew, and decaying fish, by the taste of salt in the humid air. He felt a tightening in his chest and found it difficult to breathe in the stuffy warmth of the close quarters.

Captain Preston gestured toward the bulky, rolled-up sail and mast on the galley floor. "Once the storms rip away the main mast, we'll use this spare one here in front of the portholes. Should be more light down here after that."

Keeping his head down, Tom stared numbly at the tight quarters, his eyes slowly adjusting to the darkness. The small space included a cook's galley, latrine, and two large teak tables. He wondered how all the strangers lodged here would manage to live and eat together. But real astonishment hit when Captain Preston pulled back a canvas curtain and announced, "This here will be the stateroom for the Hobson family."

The captain stepped aside, allowing Edie and her husband Andrew to see into the cramped quarters. The sleeping bunks looked like they were built for dwarfs.

Tom peered over his sister's shoulder. The term "stateroom" had rolled so luxuriously off the tongue when he had first read it. The reality was five feet wide by five and a half long, with no windows, no ventilation, and a ceiling that, like the common room's, was not high enough for Andrew or Tom to stand erect.

"Don't fret yer choice of staterooms, folks. They're all the same."

Tom noted that two boxed-in bunks had been crammed against the wall facing the canvas-covered opening. Each was shoulder width, one atop the other, just long enough for a man to sleep in the fetal position, with the occupant's nose nearly touching the bunk above or the ceiling. A grown man wouldn't even have the space to turn over.

"It's gonna be difficult to fit our whole family in here without knocking elbows," Edie said anxiously to the captain. "And how will we fit all our things?"

"Oh no, Mr. and Mrs. Thomas Wright will be joinin' ya as well. Be quite cozy," Captain Preston said in an encouraging tone. He pointed to the floor. "Stow the things you can't do without right down here between the bunks. Pile 'em up to the first bunk. Don't worry about havin' space ta stand. You'll be surprised how grateful you'll be ta have yer things close. And when yer rollin' around on your bunk, pukin' yer guts out in the heavy seas, at least ya won't have far to fall." Captain Preston turned to go. "I'll leave you folks to sort out the details while I show the rest their rooms."

Tom, Annie, and the rest of the family were left staring at each other.

"Excuse me, pardon me, Captain." A primly dressed lady standing behind Captain Preston tapped him impatiently with a silk-gloved hand.

The captain spun around to face the woman. "Ma'am?" Her interruption brought a cold, sharp edge to his voice. "I don't believe we've had the pleasure."

Annie had never seen a woman dressed like this before. Near Annie's height and just a bit older, the passenger had a style and elegance that seemed ageless. Her auburn hair was combed back, held in place with a stunning whalebone barrette. She had rouged cheeks that highlighted her flawless pale skin. She was dressed in a trim, fitted blue dress with black silk buttons marching up her neck as well as a long matching coat. A paisley shawl hung about her shoulders, and the ensemble was accented by silk gloves. Her voice indicated she was well taken care of and educated, blessed with an upper-class upbringing, in stark contrast to the other passengers. But it was her self-assured boldness that really set her apart.

One brow raised, the woman's gray-green eyes narrowed to an impertinent gaze that swept the captain from head to foot. "You're American!"

"Yes, ma'am," answered Captain Preston with an untampered grin. "Born and bred on the docks of New England. Me pap's a longshoreman and Ma's a barmaid. Been at sea since twelve. We do things a bit different where I come from, ma'am."

"Really!" The woman pulled off her gloves and put a hand with polished, bright red fingernails on her hip. "My name is Mrs. Rachel Rollins Stone," she replied haughtily to the captain's brash, unfiltered comments. "My husband, Gabriel Stone, and I have just arrived from London. I'm sorry we missed your introduction. It was delightful and enlightening, I'm sure." There was an edge of condescension in her voice. "Mr. Stone is still busy taking care of some luggage business with your bosun."

Annie leaned over and whispered into Tom's ear, "Isn't Gabriel Stone your new benefactor in the Comstock Silver Mine?"

Tom, arms folded, pulled his brows together and frowned. A dour cast in his eyes, he looked down at the woman in silence.

Mrs. Stone pointed to an alert, freckle-faced young girl. "This is my daughter, Abigail."

Twelve-year-old Abigail, with her flaming-red hair in pigtails, politely curtsied, tipped her head, then stood quietly beside her mam, paying rapt attention to Captain Preston's words.

"What can I do for you, Mrs. Stone?" the captain asked with cool amusement.

"I don't think there is enough room in here for my husband to even stand up," a perturbed Mrs. Stone replied.

"Is there anything else, ma'am?"

"I heard your comment about rolling around in bunks and such. I was wondering if we might get seasick on this voyage?" Mrs. Stone asked, apprehension creeping into her voice.

"Well, Mrs. Rachel Rollins Stone, I suspect even before we're out of sight of land, you and most all the passengers will be seasick." The captain spoke loudly enough for all to hear. "And for many, that'll just be the beginning. That first rough patch after we leave the warm waters of the Gulf Stream is followed by the North Atlantic. Ya can expect ta see some real weather in those icy waters. And all bets are off if we run into a bad nor'easter, or God forbid, a hurricane. 'Tis the season in the straits of Nova Scotia." Preston raised a brow. "If we do, all hell will break loose." The captain paused to let his comments sink in.

"Ma'am, what do you weigh right now?" he asked, the question harboring such command that Mrs. Stone's confidence seemed to crack, and she had no choice but to answer honestly. "About nine stone," she whispered, her brows raised, trying to appear self-assured. Clearly, she was rattled waiting for the captain's point to be made.

"That's about a hundred and twenty-five pounds," the captain estimated with a wry smile. "My guess, Mrs. Rachel Rollins Stone, you'll be so seasick in yer little stateroom, you'll be lucky to arrive in New York weighing over a hundred pounds. And your husband, ma'am, I wouldn't worry about his head hitting the ceiling. I suspect he'll be spending most of the voyage lyin' flat on his back in his berth, begging to be back in Westminster."

The captain, calm and confident, locked his gaze on her, a hint of green mirth flashing in his steely gray eyes. "Have a nice day, ma'am." He tapped his hat, and with that he was on to the next room.

The rest of the passengers stood in stunned silence, eyes wide, mouths agape, joining Mrs. Stone in staring after the unrepentant captain as he walked off. Many looked as if they were already seasick, despite still being in the calm waters of the Irish Sea.

Tom chuckled, leaning down to whisper in Annie's ear, "I think I might like this captain."

"If they're friends of Bishop Walker, I'm sure the Stones will be very nice," Annie murmured, hopeful.

"I'm not bettin' on it." Tom frowned, consternation showing in his furrowed brows. "And for heaven's sake, Annie," he pleaded, "please don't fuss over this lord and his lady, especially in your condition. They can take care of themselves." But Tom knew Annie would ignore his request. "I'll be spending my days on deck working with the crew. Some nights, too, I suspect. I'll not be much help to you and the family belowdecks. Joey is already eating and sleeping in the crew's quarters. So, please, Annie . . ."

"I'll be fine, Thomas, but thank you for worrying about me."

"Right!" Tom shook his head and rolled his eyes.

≻ • ≺

Annie, exhausted, sat alone on deck alongside her family's luggage, taking a moment to rest her feet while Tom checked on his work assignments with the first mate, Mr. Jenkins.

"You be Mrs. Wright?"

Annie looked up, raising her hand to shade her eyes from the sun. The sailor's foul smell made her recoil. "I am." She nodded, a vague recollection of the man who stood before her returning, but from where? There was something in his demeanor that sent a chill skittering down her spine.

He was tall, wiry, with a well-worn body and sparse, stringy hair sticking out from under his cap. The shadow of the bill kept his face partially hidden from her. Still, she could see he was agitated, suspiciously scanning the deck for observers. An open frown contorting a long scar running across his weathered face revealed a graveyard of broken, rotting, and missing teeth.

Concentrating hard, her body tense, she pulled her brows together. "Can I help you, sir?"

"I'll help ya with 'em trunks down ta da hold."

"That is very kind of you, sir." She wasn't about to go anywhere with him.

He didn't respond. He wasn't looking at her; he was staring at Tom and Joey, who were talking to Mr. Jenkins in the distance.

"May I have your name, sir?"

Peering down at her, he considered her question with a scowl. She could see his eyes now. They were vacant, leering, and they kindled a spark in her memory. They were eyes she would never forget. The fire—Boo Black. This man had been one of Boo's thugs, standing in the background when Boo burned their house and all those in it to the ground that night.

"Name's Jacque," he muttered. "Jacque Croquet."

Annie's hand flew up to cover her face. To extinguish the shock in her expression. She turned away.

"Ya want dat help or not, lady?"

The blood drained from her face. "Thank you, but no," she whispered with an uneasy frown.

"Suit yerself, lady," he sneered, turning and walking away.

Annie felt dizzy, but didn't she often feel that way in her expectant state? She turned back to watch him disappear into the shadows, clenching her shaking hands tighter on the two trunk handles.

"Oh, Thomas, be careful." Her lower lip quivered. "I must warn him!"

Chapter 2

Two days out of port and as promised the weather had turned after leaving the warm waters of the Gulf Stream. Annie, bundled in her coat, stood at the rail, arm in arm with Thomas on the biting cold morning.

"Tell me again how it's going to be," Annie begged as she looked up into Thomas's eyes. "I love to see your face light up when you talk about our future on our own land, where we're gonna raise our children in the Sierra Nevada mountains of California." She put a comforting hand on her swelling belly.

Tom looked down with a heartfelt smile. His imagination came to life. Eyes dancing, he shared dreams that had held him hostage for as long as he could remember. "In America, a man is only limited by his own ambition, imagination, and willingness to work hard. Judged solely by character, what he can do with his own two hands and the mind the good Lord gave him." He paused. "People aren't owned by aristocrats, the company store, nor are they subject to a tyrannical government. Folks are free to pursue the life of their own choosing."

For better or worse, Annie knew she was destined to spend the rest of her life in love with this man and his dreams.

Tom turned to look out to sea, across the bleak, fog-covered North Atlantic, which seamlessly blended with the dark-gray skies overhead. His visionary eyes alighted with excitement on their future home, which shimmered in his mind. His thoughts ran free, allowing dazzling prospects to capture his imagination. "Can you imagine it—to live your life on your own land with no one to tell you what you must do? How you must raise your family. No one to take your leave of."

"I can't wait." Annie sighed, hopelessly under his spell. She slid closer beside him, her arms intertwined in his, leaning her head against his shoulder. "Tell me more, Thomas."

Tom filled his lungs with the sweet ocean air. He focused intently on the adventure that lay before them. "Out west in California, they have unsettled land as far as the eye can see. Mountains, fertile valleys, long, empty shorelines. It's just there for the taking. I hear tell they've got gold nuggets in the streams that a man can pick up when he has a mind to."

Annie, maybe a bit skeptical, was nevertheless caught up in the longing she sensed in her husband's vision of America.

"I want land, acres of it, with a crystal-clear stream running right through it. Land is the only thing that lasts. It's not just the symbol of wealth—land *is* wealth."

"I suppose it is."

"We'll grow our own vegetables, alfalfa, maybe even have a fruit orchard. And pigs. Yes—big, fat, noisy ones that roll around in the mud."

Annie crinkled up her nose. "What is it with you and your pigs!" Her brows pulled together in a frown. "You have an obsession with that animal."

"I want to go fishing in my own brook." Tom was too distracted by his dream to respond to her complaint. "I want to catch trout with a pole." He had been captivated by the wonderful fluorescent colors of the trout in the pooling pond of Spring Hollow, their muscular, torsional beauty and iridescent patterns glistening in the sun like an imprinted code of life left by God's own hand. They had seemed so close, with their white-tipped fins wimpling in the water. It was almost like he could reach out and touch them. "Can you imagine?"

Annie, as always, couldn't help but catch Thomas's enthusiasm when he lost himself in sharing his daydreams of life in America. "I could send you and our boys out to catch our evening dinner while I play with our little ones on the floor in front of the fire in our own home."

"Trout for dinner, just as nice as you please. Streams so clear you can drink from 'em. Clear as icicles. None of that black water thick with coal tailings."

"Edie and her family could have a cabin just across the pasture." Annie paused, her own eyes now filled with the wonder of it all. "The whole family could join us for dinner on Sundays, Joey and his new wife too."

"Gotta find that boy a wife."

Annie giggled. "Maybe there's a squaw out there in the Wild West?"

"Livin' off the land, just 'cause we have a mind to." Tom gazed out across the ocean pathway to their future. "Aye, I 'spect it'll be heaven on earth."

"All of our friends and family living nearby."

"No friends." Tom frowned, shaking his head, pulling his brows together in discontent. "Nobody outside of family around to bother us with their problems."

"Oh, Thomas. Don't be an old prude." She rolled her eyes and frowned. "We gotta have friends and a church nearby where we can visit, have picnics. You may be a handsome brute, but I still have some work to do with your misguided thinking."

Tom shrugged, lifted his brows, and said with tight lips, "No church."

"Well, aren't you the cynical one, Thomas Wright! Could there be anything more American than family, friends, and faith in the Almighty?" Annie's brows knitted together. She looked thoughtfully at her husband. He still had his demons; he was still fighting the dragon. Annie wondered if she would ever have sway over him . . . like Lydia had. The thought pained her, but she was determined to at least be a force for good in his life.

"I can't wait to have my children with you, Thomas. A family of our own, living on our own land in the California mountains. I want to watch them play in the meadows. Run down to that stream of yours. No more filthy alleyways, sewage running in front of our coal miner's shanty, smoke filling the sky overhead, or living with rats. Just meadows, brooks, fresh air, and mountains to climb."

Tom gazed down at her. She was leaning against his shoulder, looking out to sea, sharing in the wonder. He smiled.

"You know, I promised Mam I'd find out what happened to my brother George."

"You're a good son!"

"I can imagine he stood right here looking back at this same scene when he left us those many years ago. After losing both his wife and baby . . . to think of him going all alone on his great adventure . . ." Tom looked down at Annie. "I'm so glad I have you as my traveling companion."

Glancing up at him, Annie smiled. *His traveling companion*, she thought. A feather stirred in her stomach. She balled up her hands against the turbulence rising in her chest. For a few moments she had forgotten—forgotten she would never be first in his heart.

Tenderly, she ran her fingertips over the boyhood scars on the back of Tom's callused hands. She traced the memories of his heartbreaking losses. Her heart bled for him. So much pain and suffering. In the wake of these tragedies, the burden of caring for his entire family when he was only a boy himself, the loss of his soulmate, he had been left with anger, distrust, and a tremendous drive to succeed. His determined hands revealed the promise that every hurt could be healed and every dream reached if given the opportunity. She lifted her head off his shoulder, gazing up at him. His unalterable determination was one of the things she admired most about him, but it scared her too. What she wanted, but dare not say, was not financial success or even a home on their own land. What she wanted was to be a mother, have her own family surrounding her. What she wanted was her husband's heart. She knew she would never be the great love Lydia was. Nor would his love for her ever match hers for him. What Annie hoped for beyond all else was to be loved and cherished by her husband and to be a mother surrounded by a loving family.

⇝ • ⇜

"Mr. Stone, Mrs. Stone? I'm Tom Wright. And this is my wife Annie."

Gabriel Stone seemed preoccupied, responding with a perfunctory touch of his hat. "Nice to meet you, Wright." He looked uninterested, being only as polite as good breeding demanded. "Mrs. Wright." He looked past Tom, glancing around the deck.

Annie offered a warm smile. "Pleased to meet you both."

But Mrs. Stone, too, proffered a disinterested reception.

"It's Rachel, isn't it?" Annie asked.

"Why yes," she answered, glancing in her direction, seeming as distracted as her husband.

Annie continued pursuing a conversation. "I understand your daughter has already met our niece Elizabeth, and like twelve-year-olds do, they've decided to be new best friends."

"Oh, is that so?" With wide eyes, Mrs. Stone looked down her nose, offering the obligatory nod of acknowledgment. "Abigail certainly has a lot of friends."

Tom glanced at Annie, his brows furrowed, his mouth curling down. He'd experienced this kind of discourteous reception before from the upper classes and didn't much like it.

Gabriel, catching sight of the captain, excused himself with an abrupt wave of his hand. "I'm sorry, but I must speak with the captain."

Rachel, looking upset, followed suit, excusing herself with a cool but courteous nod.

"That went well. And I thought they might be snobbish." Tom shrugged, attempting to shed his annoyance. "I hope I don't end up punching this son of a match factory owner in the nose before we get to New York."

"That'd go over well with your benefactor." Annie sighed. "Give 'em a chance, Thomas. Maybe he had live frogs for breakfast?"

"What?" Tom laughed. "Can't you at least let me have my petty irritation in peace."

Chapter 3

❖ • ❖

BY THE MORNING OF THE fourth day, the warm waters of the Irish Sea had been eclipsed by the icy cold of the North Atlantic. A translucent fog hovered over the surface of the vast ocean, enveloping the *Colorado*, floating silent on the placid beauty of the water. With her light-air sails ballooning aloft from the ends of the spars, the ship had the eerie appearance of lace ruffling in the indiscernible wind.

Annie, on break for a bit of fresh air topside, smiled at Tom and Joey, still new to the work of mopping the deck. "You two are going to need to get a lot better at this if I'm gonna be able to hire you out when we get into port."

Tom laughed. "That's not gonna happen."

Flashes of light appeared on the distant horizon above the gray line of the ocean.

"What was that?" Joey stopped to look up. "Did you see it?"

Tom, his brows knitted together in concentration, looked into the distance. "There it is again."

Annie, with her hand shading her eyes, frowned. "I saw it."

"It looks like lightning." Tom's eyes went round. "Wow! That was a big one." Then came the faint sound of thunder.

"Squall!" yelled the captain as he ran from the deck to the bridge. "Prepare to meet the gale, Mr. Jenkins."

"Aye, sir." Mr. Jenkins turned to the crew, shouting out instructions. "Batten down the hatches; lower the main, stanchions, and topgallant sails, bow and aft; tie off all on deck we don't want goin' ta the bottom." The lightning, coming faster now, electrified the sky. A clap of thunder followed close behind.

"You there." Captain Preston pointed to Tom and Joey, who were standing wide-eyed in confusion. "Help those men secure the animals and food crates," he blared, pointing to the reel of line on the bulkhead. "Tie 'em down before they're washed into the sea. And damn it, get those passengers belowdecks."

"Go down Annie, now."

Her worried eyes ablaze, Annie cautioned, "Be safe, you two." Within moments the morning fog enveloping the *Colorado* had been swept away by cold, whistling winds, driving Annie and the few beleaguered passengers belowdecks.

Tom, confused in the swirling chaos, yelled at Joey over the din of the storm, "Help me with this crate."

Joey froze, staring at the crate.

With an anxious frown, Tom wrapped a rope around the crate, threw the loose end to Joey, and instructed him to tie it to the bulkhead. Then he moved on to the next.

The funnel of the spinning cyclone was coming right at them, moving fast. It extended high into the clouds. Like a furious monster rising out of the sea with outstretched arms, the storm lorded over the little brig.

It was almost impossible to stand upright in the driving wind and rain. Captain Preston spun around on Tom. His steely gray eyes bore into him. "Leave the rest of the cargo and lash yerselves down," he growled, pointing to the main mast pole just behind Tom.

But Tom and Joey hesitated in the whiplash of the storm; a lightning strike nearly hit the deck.

"By God, man, that's an order. Both of ya!" the captain boomed. "If ya get washed overboard, we ain't comin' after ya."

"Come on." Tom grabbed Joey by the arm, pulled him to the mast, and with fumbling fingers, quickly did as ordered. But even as Tom finished lashing himself and his brother, he could tell the gale was about to tear the sails right off the rigging. Tom's pounding heart was caught in his throat, his face blasted by furious wind and rain. He could hardly breathe, and powerless to move, he was just trying to save himself.

The storm had come so fast. The *Colorado*, now completely engulfed in vicious winds and drenching rain, was seemingly entirely at the mercy of the cyclone. Lightning struck with a flash that lit up the skies like noonday, then quickly all went dark again in the deafening thunder that shook the little ship.

In the disorienting gusts, Captain Preston stood alone, tethered to the forward bridge and firing out commands to save his ship. But despite the desperation of the sailors to do as ordered, the winds blew too hard to lower the sails further. Driving rains pummeling the deck made it almost impossible for Tom to see sailors as they were blown off their feet while scurrying for safety. Wide-eyed, his heart pounding, cold hands shaking, he watched sailors trying to save themselves. They slid across the deck grabbing at masts, bulkheads, anything tethered against the furious rush of water.

There was no one left to defend the *Colorado* in the seventy-knot howling winds whipping the sea into a frenzy and tearing through the mainsail. With the crack of splintering wood just above his head, Tom saw the center mast split to half its length. Tom's heart and breathing stopped. His eyes were wide with fear. The thousand-pound mast beam slammed onto the deck in a thunderous crash that shook the rivets right out of the hull. Tom leaped in his traces, and with his heart in his throat, he thought for a moment that they were heading to the bottom. The little brig shuddered, lurched, and dipped to one side as a swell that was tall as a three-story building rushed over the deck, into every nook and cranny, lifting hoists, crates, and everything else not securely tied down, sweeping it away into the sea. Tom watched in horror as sheep, chickens, and other livestock slid by him, eyes wild and frightened as they washed overboard through wide openings between the railings. Lost forever.

Then, quick as she had arrived, the cyclone was gone. But her damage was done. There was devastation everywhere. Animals and cargo crates of fresh vegetables gone; equipment destroyed; the broken main mast lying in a mountainous shamble of shrouds and splintered wood on the deck. And the *Colorado* was still three thousand miles from her destination.

※ • ※

Only two weeks out of Liverpool and rough seas had made it necessary to keep the hatchways closed most of the time. Fresh air no longer swept through the dank confines of the staterooms. The smell of sickness, sweat, mold, and vomit permeated everywhere belowdecks, an ideal breeding ground for disease. Gripping biliousness led to more sickness, boredom, anxiety, and depression. Passengers and crew alike were plagued by lice, fleas, and all manner of what the sailors called "arithmetic bugs" because they added to their troubles, subtracted from their pleasures, divided their attention, and multiplied like hell. Most all in the family had fallen dreadfully ill. To make matters worse, because of the losses from the storm, the remaining food was rationed.

With so many sick, Tom was needed topside. He worked long days and slept in the crew's quarters, leaving Annie to care for the rest of the family by herself. Only Elizabeth and Abigail Stone were able to help. The three Good Samaritans flitted from one sickbed to the next, cleaning up foul messes, offering food, water, and any help they could. But they could do little more than comfort the sick and bandage injuries.

Each night Annie fell into bed exhausted only to arise before dawn the next morning. She struggled to stay on her feet, doing her best to aid as many people as she could in her compromised condition. All her days and nights seemed to run together.

"I don't know what to do, Annie." A very sick Edie was beside herself with worry, her two-year-old Tommy laying across her breasts so dreadfully ill. "He just lies in my arms staring at me, eyes wide, whimpering." Tears of frustration flowed down her cheeks. "I can do nothing to get him to eat!"

"Here, let me take him for a while." Annie leaned down and slid her arms under the fragile, defenseless little boy.

"Auntie Annie, I hurt."

Smiling and singing a lullaby, Annie rocked him in her arms. Sweat beaded on his weary little brow; his heart pounded fast as Annie held him. His face was pale and drawn, and he struggled for air through lips tinged blue.

As much as she could, Annie tried to ease Edie's burden, but Edie's fearful worry and little sleep had only made things worse for mother and child.

"I know he's hungry, but what am I to do? I cannot get him to eat anything," Edie lamented. "He can't seem to find the strength."

"I'm so sorry, honey," Annie said, trying to comfort her. But like her own little Henry, without nourishing food Tommy would become too exhausted to fight, and then no one would be able to forestall the inevitable. And so would go the light of joy from this young mother's heart. "Let me see what we can do."

"Oh, please, Annie," Edie pleaded in a panic, hope in her eyes. "I don't know what I'll do if . . ." She heaved great, ragged sobs between her hacking coughs.

Annie leaned down and put a hand on her sister-in-law's shoulder. "You're a wonderful mother." Her heart broke for her. Even if they didn't talk of their love or share their feelings openly, Annie knew the bond would always be there. "You've done all you can."

※ • ※

The cuisine on board the *Colorado* had been disappointing from the beginning, but after the storm, the food became downright inedible. Mr. Bunnings, the cook—though it seemed a travesty to call him that, for he knew little of the art—was a pudgy, miserable little man, with greasy black hair, rotting teeth, thick spectacles, and the temperament of a troll. He clearly despised his work and didn't seem to care a whit about what he served his patrons, nor the difficulty they had in keeping it down. Annie and her two helpers did what they could, but it was clear some passengers would not survive the voyage, and she considered Mr. Bunnings a despicable accomplice to their demise. He seemed to ignore all complaints, serving rotten tomatoes with every meal. Rotten tomatoes with hard tack, with festering cheese, with moldy breaded stew.

"This is disgusting!" Rachel complained, then proceeded to heave up what she had just choked down. This only served as a catalyst for her husband to unleash his meal.

Acting upon her promise to Edie and concern for little Tommy, Annie confronted Mr. Bunnings. "What is this you're serving these poor folks?" She glared at the cook. "We might rather starve.

You're doing more to kill off those you're charged to nourish than the pestilence they're suffering from."

"Take it or leave it. 'Tis a good bit of fruit salad for the scurvy," Mr. Bunnings growled.

"Oh, please, Mr. Bunnings." Annie looked at him in disgust. "Tomatoes may be a fruit, but even the simplest of fools knows a bowl of rotting tomatoes don't make fruit salad."

"There ain't nothin' wrong with 'em," retorted Mr. Bunnings in his hard, nasally Brooklyn accent.

"That's enough, Mr. Bunnings. These folks need nourishment, not poisoning!" Annie insisted. "No more rotten tomatoes—please!"

While all watched, he tipped back his head and dropped in a moldy, rotten tomato, gulping it down like a rabid animal, putrid juices dripping off his chin. All the while, he was laughing at a pale-faced Annie, who could do nothing but retch. "No, lady," he added, as Annie turned away in disgust, "it's delicious!"

"Oh, Mr. Bunnings." Rachel's eyes narrowed in revulsion. The mere sight was enough to dislodge what little nourishment she had left in her stomach.

"Under pain of death, we will not down another rotten tomato," Annie announced. "I'm talking about *your* death, mister."

Chapter 4

⇘ • ⇙

DESPITE ANNIE'S BEST EFFORTS DURING the first weeks at sea, most of the passengers remained sick. Most were forced to lie in cold, wet berths, fighting the persistent rolling of the sea, beset by bloody elbows, knees, ankles, and bed sores from bumping in the cramped bunk. Rachel Stone hardly spoke, and a feeble Gabriel moaned in the bunk beside her.

"Abby, I am fearfully cold," whimpered a despondent Rachel. "I'm going to be sick!"

"I've a bowl for you, Mam." But before Abby could strategically place the bowl, the brig lurched forward, and Rachel vomited from one end of their stateroom to the other.

Tears welled up in Abby's eyes, but without a word she began scrubbing the floor and cleaning their belongings yet again.

"I am so sorry, Abby."

Hearing Rachel's discouraged cries, Annie stepped into the Stones' stateroom.

"How can I help?"

"I've made such a mess of things for Abigail," Rachel cried, wiping the tears from her eyes. "I'm such a nuisance."

"Nonsense. It's not your fault," Annie said softly. "We're here to help, and if not for you, we'd be in with cranky old Mrs. Blanchet. Right, Abby?"

Abby tried to laugh without crying.

Rachel raised her hand weakly. "Thank you, Annie."

"Let's clean up those elbows, shall we? They're all bloody." Annie began to unroll a cotton bandage from her pocket. "And let's make you a little more comfortable." Annie propped Rachel up and gently washed and dressed each elbow, speaking soft, encouraging words. "You'll feel better when you're clean and have dry bedding—fair enough?"

"Oh, Annie. You are an angel sent from heaven. How will I ever be able to repay your kindness?"

"I'm sure you'd do the same for me."

"No, I wouldn't. And I'm ashamed to admit it."

Annie gave a faint smile to Rachel's confession, then turned to face Mr. Stone.

"How are you feeling this morning?"

He gave a weak smile. "I'm a bit better thanks to you, Annie. And please, call me Gabriel. I think we can dispense with Mr. Stone now that you've seen me at my worst. We'll never forget what you've done here."

"I'll send Thomas down when he gets a break to help you get cleaned up and changed into fresh clothes. The girls can change your bedding too." Before leaving, Annie offered a compassionate smile to both.

"You're doing the work of two, Annie," said Gabriel feebly. "And in your condition. God bless you."

"You can thank your very capable daughter."

"And if you don't mind, you very capable young lady," he said, smiling at his daughter. "I'd appreciate it if you could help me get to the loo?"

"Please, Gabriel, show a little class," Rachel chimed in.

"It comes when I least expect it," Gabriel added shakily as Abby helped her papa out of the room.

Rachel looked weakly at Annie. "You're remarkable. And I apologize for not telling you that earlier."

"Thank you." Annie reached out to give Rachel's arm a comforting touch. "Well, I'd like to stay and talk, but I need to check on my sister's two-year-old before I run out of steam."

"How is Tommy?"

Annie was quiet. She wiped her forehead with the back of her hand. "Tommy's very sick," she said with a sigh. "It breaks my heart to see him like this. Edie is beside herself with worry, poor thing." Annie looked on gravely, not wanting to drag Rachel through the whole of it. It broke Annie's heart to see Edie, the lines etched into her brow, trying to comfort Tommy. "The whole family feels helpless, praying for a miracle. No one in the family can keep their meals down. All look like the walking dead, except Elizabeth, of course. She spends much of her day waiting on the rest."

"Of course, Mr. Bunning's meals are horrific, but Elizabeth and Abby seem to have iron stomachs." Rachel paused, looking at Annie. "Are there many like Tommy on board?"

"Captain Preston says he suspects there will be deaths before we arrive in Castle Garden; unfortunately, some will be little children."

Rachel, lost in thought, nodded wearily.

Annie wrung her hands and took a deep breath to help control her emotions. "I'm scared for these little ones." She couldn't help but think of her own little Henry, her nephew Tommy, and the other terribly sick children and their desperate families.

"It must be so hard to lose a child," Rachel whispered. "Abigail was our miracle baby after the frustration of trying for years. I thank the Lord every day for her. I don't think I could go on if I lost her."

Annie swallowed. "It's hard . . ." she trailed off, looking away, her thoughts far off in heart-wrenching memory.

"I'm so sorry, Annie." Rachel reached out and took her hand. "That was thoughtless of me."

Annie stared at the floor without a word. Pushing back the memories of loss—her own last visit to her little Henry's gravesite.

"How is it," Annie questioned, "that we can love a child so deeply we willingly give up a portion of our lives, and even risk death for them? How can our love be so strong that we voluntarily subject ourselves to the pain, vulnerability, and the heartache? And when we lose them, our hearts seem broken beyond repair."

"Children seem to leave us mothers teetering between transcendent joy and unfathomable pain."

"Yet we keep coming back for more of the same?" Annie looked up with a soft smile.

Rachel glanced at Annie's burgeoning belly. "God bless you, Annie." She paused. "When I consider my feelings for Abigail, I sometimes think maternal love is as close to divine love as it gets. No one will ever love your Henry as much as you do. It's your contribution to eternity."

Annie nodded. "Thank you." She squeezed Rachel's hand. "I think your friendship is going to be a blessing to me."

"To us both. You have a giving heart, Annie. I was so wrong to think of you in any other way when first we met. You're showing me what selfless charity looks like." Rachel paused again. "I don't know if time heals all wounds, but I hope this new baby helps to ease the pain of your loss."

Annie placed a hand on her belly, so close to the miracle growing inside her. She felt a kick, which brought a shy smile as she looked up at a wide-eyed Rachel. "Despite it all, some things about being with child are downright wonderous, aren't they?" She sighed.

Rachel offered a comforting pat on Annie's belly and smiled. "They are. Carrying and bearing Abigail was without question the most miraculous time of my life."

Annie pulled in a deep breath. "When Henry died, I was crushed—no, demolished. I tried to put on my most confident face for everyone around me, but inside, my whole being was in turmoil." Annie stared into the empty space. "He died as babies often do, gently and without complaint."

"Maybe they hang on to life so weakly because they've spent such little time here with us, the memory of heaven still living fresh within them," Rachel responded, solemn. "They don't seem to fear death as we do."

"Thomas doesn't talk to me about it. Oh, how I wish he would. I suppose he thinks he's being strong for me. I can't bear to tell him it isn't working."

"Well, I'm excited for you, Annie," Rachel said, upbeat. "You're healthy, and I'm betting this will be a gorgeous baby."

※ · ※

Annie stood beside Thomas feeling the weight of tension as they watched a mother and child, wrapped in a single sheet, cast overboard. With her broken heart lodged in her throat, Annie observed the two bodies bobbing on the rolling swells until they were finally claimed by the sea. The poor father stood silent at the railing, gripping it hard, nothing left but his grief, tears running down his cheeks.

Overwhelmed, the dam in Annie's heart broke, unleashing a wave of suffocating despair. "I couldn't help them," she whispered, recalling the hopeless feeling in her shattered soul as she had watched the baby's eyes close for the last time, his tiny veins pulsing beneath porcelain skin . . . once . . . twice . . . then no more. And as his life had slipped away, so went the light of life from this young mother's heart. "I just sat there . . . useless. Please, God, forgive me!"

Thomas turned to her, wide-eyed. "Annie, look at you. You're exhausted, chalky pale. Your hands are shaking." He paused, brows pulled together. "You can't do this any longer. You can't get so involved with these people's lives, especially in your condition."

She turned on him in anger. She was scared, confused. "What is wrong with you, Thomas?" She lashed out in frustration. "Do you have no heart?"

"They're not your problem, Annie."

"This could be our little Tommy in a few days and . . ." Not wanting to say something she'd regret, Annie stormed off.

※ • ※

Having sent Elizabeth to Mr. Bunnings for a bit of meat broth and mashed potato soup, Annie sat beside an exhausted Edie, patting a cool cloth on Tommy's forehead. It tore at her already broken heart to watch this desperate mother holding her very sick little boy's despondent gaze as he lay deathly quiet in her arms.

"Oh Annie, I feel so helpless. What can I do?" Edie repeated, heartsick, disillusioned. "He doesn't even cry. He just stares at me. I can't get him to eat." She cried, tears rolling down her cheeks. "What kind of mother am I?"

For three long days and three desperately long nights, Edie had held her little boy, trying to comfort him, to encourage his will to live, to coax him into eating something. Tommy was so exhausted and weak that Annie was not sure how much longer he could fight. She feared no one could forestall the inevitable.

"Aunt Annie?" Elizabeth handed Annie a bowl. "This is all Mr. Bunnings said he could spare."

Annie looked down at the watery, rotting tomatoes, green mold growing along the edges. The heat of anger rose to her face. "Where is he?"

"Up on deck taking a smoke."

"Thank you, Elizabeth," Annie whispered, dumping the contents of the bowl in the trash can. She'd lost one little one. She wasn't about to lose another. "I'll be back."

※ • ※

Both crew and passengers alike were lounging on deck when Annie climbed the stairs from the hold with a gunnysack full of rotten tomatoes in one hand and a broom handle in the other. In long, determined strides, with teeth gritted, eyes fierce, she pushed through the crowd of lesser creatures, crossing the deck to where the cook leaned against the mast, smoke drifting upward from a rolled cigarette dangling from his fingertips.

"Whadda ya want, lady?" Mr. Bunnings sneered when he saw her frown, raised brows, and pursed lips.

Passengers and curious deckhands alike stood silent, watching the unfolding scene.

Annie slammed the broom handle against the bulkhead so hard it sent a *whack* echoing the length of the little ship. Bunnings jumped, raising his hands to protect his face. "Watch out with dat there stick."

"Ah, good, I have your attention." Annie spit out her words with cold contempt.

If anyone on deck had not been paying attention before, they certainly were now.

"You have bullied and abused those under your care, Mr. Bunnings. You've little skill in the art of cooking, using rancid oil, dirty pots, and pathetic fare." She paused and stared. "I might even be able to abide your incompetence, if it were not for your arrogant lack of concern for those you serve."

He cringed at this crazy woman, raising his hands for protection.

"I am a good judge of character, sir, and yours is sorely lacking. God never intended for sick folks to eat so miserably." She put out her hand. "Give me the key to your private food stores, Mr. Bunnings. Oh yes, I know you have them."

"I'm not giving you nothin'."

Without another word, Annie, fuming now, swung the broom handle in a cross hook at his head. He ducked, and the handle gave a loud *thwack* as it hit the mast pole he'd been leaning against. "The key." She reached out her hand.

"Okay, lady!" Mr. Bunnings screeched in fear, frantically reaching into his pocket for the key with one hand while he held up the other for protection

With key in hand, Annie left Mr. Bunnings smarting from the rebuke, and while all else on deck watched her, mouths hanging open, she proceeded to the railing. One by one, Annie threw the rotten tomatoes as far out into the sea as she could.

Tom stood on the bridge with Captain Preston, both watching the scene play out. When Annie had finished throwing all the tomatoes overboard, all eyes on deck shifted to the captain.

The captain's red face was without expression. But then his eyes crinkled into bright gray-blue slits and he burst out in strangled laughter, slapping his thigh. He bent in such mirth that despite all the discipline on board, passengers and crew alike delighted in the amusement and gave Annie a standing ovation.

"Well, Mr. Wright, that's one hell of a woman ya got there." Preston grinned. "I wouldn't cross her!" Continuing to laugh, he turned to walk back to his cabin. "Yep, ya best be mindin' yer p's and q's."

Tom stood at the door of Captain Preston's cabin. He knocked twice.

"Who is it?"

"Tom Wright, sir. Hoping I might have a word?"

"Come in, Mr. Wright." Captain Preston opened the door, and stepping aside, he ushered Tom into his inner sanctum.

It was a different world within the walls of the captain's cabin. Polished walnut bookcases lined the aft wall, holding books on every subject imaginable. Navigation maps lined the forward and port walls, with mementos of every kind scattered around the well-organized cabin. Artifacts from ports all over the world were displayed on his African walnut desk.

The captain gestured toward a large, cushioned mahogany chair. Tom sat, and the captain took his chair behind the desk on the starboard wall below a brass porthole open to allow a fresh breeze and a little sunshine.

"What can I do for you, Mr. Wright?" With an intelligent, quizzical look in his eyes, which peered out from a forest of whiskers, the captain folded his hands and placed them in front of an open book on his desk.

"Sorry for interrupting, sir." Tom put aside any further formalities. As always, the captain seemed interested in getting to the point. "As you well know, we have some very sick children below who need fruit, fresh vegetables, and quality meat." Tom paused. "Understand you have some private food stores. Hoping you might part with some under the circumstances, sir," Tom requested firmly.

Captain Preston frowned. Folding his fists together under his chin, he looked at Tom for a long moment, seeming to judge the depth of his resolve. "Is it necessary?"

Tom returned his steady gaze. "Essential, sir!"

With a slight chuckle, he responded, "You certainly seem determined, Mr. Wright."

"It's my wife, sir. On this subject she has very strong opinions. Unbendable, really!"

"Oh yes, Mrs. Wright." He smiled knowingly. "I would venture ta say yer wife's sentiments about Mr. Bunnings's cooking skills and the fare he serves are widely held," the captain answered matter-of-factly. "I've also heard your wife is well acquainted with that particular skill—ran a butcher shop, I hear, servin' meals?" He paused, waiting for a response to the compliment, but without response, Tom continued to look the captain in the eye.

"Hmm!" Captain Preston sat up, put his elbows on the desk, rubbed his whiskered chin, then said in a respectful tone, "Let me see what I can do."

❧ • ❦

"Aunt Annie?" Elizabeth whispered, anxious.

Annie, sitting beside a sleeping Edie after eating her first good meal in days, pressed a cool, wet cloth on a very sick little Tommy's forehead. She spun around. "Yes, honey," she whispered.

"Uncle Thomas." She paused. "He's in the galley asking if you might please join him for a minute?"

"Sure." Annie tiptoed out of their stateroom.

Standing in the middle of the empty galley was her husband, holding two live chickens, one dangling upside down from each hand.

"What is this?" She looked on, wide-eyed. "Where did you get those?"

"Apparently, Captain Preston has been through storms before. He had a few private crates of his own stashed away."

"Really, and how did you commandeer them from our captain?"

"Well, he decided he best not risk your wrath."

"That's not funny, Thomas."

"You're right. I figured we needed some good chicken soup for my namesake and the rest of the family. I have a bit of fruit and some vegetables as well."

"Really?" Annie gave him a sly, questioning look.

"I suppose, you being a butcher and all, you know what to do with these."

"I do!"

"And do you think this may return me to your good graces?"

"Maybe." Annie reached out to take the two chickens, trying her best to keep her stern composure.

"You've got full kitchen privileges now." He paused, admiring her determination. "A small conciliation from our captain after your dressing down of Mr. Bunnings."

"Trust me, Bunnings is not touching these two little darlings."

"Now don't go sharing my chickens with them other sick folks." He squinted at her, knowing Annie would ignore him.

Heading toward the preparation quarter, she turned and looked over her shoulder. "Thank you, Thomas!" A warm smile swept across her face.

Chapter 5

❧ · ❧

"Rachel, I've brought you and Gabriel a little dinner." Annie helped Rachel sit up in her bed, handing them each a bowl of chicken soup.

"Thank you." Gabriel breathed in the enticing aroma. "This doesn't seem like Mr. Bunnings's usual fare. Do I taste a bit of real chicken?"

"Hmm! Mostly broth." Annie smiled softly, not revealing her culinary secrets. "You look much better all cleaned up."

"I feel much better, thank you," a grateful Gabriel responded. "Thomas, is he doing well?"

"Well enough. So many sailors are sick that both Thomas and Joey are working double shifts. I'll be able to hire 'em out as deckhands by the time we get to New York."

Rachel's eyes flickered with a smile.

"Maybe I'll get some fresh air, topside." Gabriel dragged himself out of bed and shuffled his way out of the room.

"Have you spent much time on deck, Annie?" Rachel asked.

"This morning with Thomas. He spends every day and most nights working now. He sleeps with the crew to give the rest of the family more room."

"I'm sorry you're stuck down here taking care of us." Rachel frowned. "What's the weather like?"

"Balmy. Sea pigs jumping everywhere. The crew caught several big ones. We'll be having sea pig for dinner tonight. A nice respite from . . . whatever it is Mr. Bunnings has been serving these past three weeks."

"What are sea pigs?"

"That's what the sailors call 'em. I suspect they have another name. The most odd-looking fish with stubby pink noses." Annie's eyes sparkled with a smile. "Interesting creatures! They swim in schools pacing the ship, and sail right out of the water."

"I'd love to see them," Rachel said. "I need to get out of this bed. I'm missing it all."

Annie smiled as she worked to clean up and bandage elbows. "How did you first meet Mr. Stone?"

Rachel returned the smile. "Believe it or not, we met at Oxford. I was a secretary in the English Department and fell in love with this handsome student who wanted to be an English professor." Rachel frowned again. "But Gabriel's father wouldn't have it. He joined the family business, planted behind a desk in London's financial district, until . . ."

Annie waited for her to continue.

"When the market collapsed, we lost everything—the maids, the London flat, the horses, the carriage. It all went to auction. All we own now is in those two trunks."

"I'm so sorry."

Rachel's eyes grew cloudy. "My father-in-law swooped in, insisting Gabriel take this position in Virginia City in his newly acquired Comstock Silver Mine. 'I acquired this company in the colonies to toughen you up,' he said. 'Get your thinking right. Take over for me here someday.' Of course, desperate for anything, we agreed. We actually relished the idea. On our own, away from his overbearing father lording over us."

Annie was silent for a moment. "It must have been difficult to lose all that," she replied before looking away.

"Oh, Annie. I'm so sorry. I wasn't thinking. I must sound thoughtless, after all the struggles you and Thomas have had to endure."

Annie forced a smile, thinking of her little Henry. "I suppose it's all relative. We're looking forward to our new life."

"You always seem to make the best of every situation, Annie. I hope we have many long years of friendship ahead of us."

"I do too." Annie returned Rachel's smile.

⊱ • ⊰

Benjamin Dreyfus was a small man who took small steps. His green eyes sparkled with intelligence under his tufts of gray brows. He had big ears, a prominent nose, and sparse silver hair that crinkled and spilled over his forehead. It seemed that, if at any moment a strong breeze were to pass through his stateroom, it might whisk him up out of the hold and into the clouds. And although his teeth were crooked, slanting this way and that, Annie couldn't help but reciprocate her favorite patient's contagious enthusiasm for life.

She often rushed through her rounds just to get to him. She wasn't sure why the bright, welcoming smile of this kindly old gentleman brought such warmth to her, but it always seemed to, starting with the moment she walked into his room. He inspired her. And some days, Annie felt awkward, as though Benjamin were the parent and she the child. He often scolded her for wasting her time with an old man instead of being with her family. She didn't dare tell Tom.

"I married my Jenny when I was eighteen," he whispered in Annie's ear. "She, only fifteen." His whole face lit up when he talked of her. "She was the most beautiful girl in the entire village. But after we lost our home and we had to leave our village, my Jenny passed of a broken heart . . ." As he sat on the edge of his bed, his sallow eyes looked up nostalgically. "It was then I knew I had to bring our youngest to America to join his older brother."

"It must have been devastating after your daughter . . ." Annie couldn't bear to say the words. His teenage daughter had been raped and murdered by the Prussian troops after their home was burned to the ground. All because they were Jewish.

"My Abraham lives in Brooklyn, ya know. He's got a good job working for family and a beautiful wife. And I've got a photograph of my four near-perfect grandchildren." Benjamin refused to let his troubles dampen his spirit. "I'm very fortunate to have such good boys." Despite all his troubles, his struggle with age and sickness, Benjamin was always delightful. He refused to wither. He was determined to go on for his youngest son Isaac.

One morning, Annie was feeling sorry for herself, burdened by her struggles—wanting more from Tom. Heavy with child, every part of her body seemed to ache. She was impatient for a family, a home of her own, the love of her husband. And in a weak moment, she shared her concerns with Benjamin.

"The pushes and pulls of life." He frowned. "You want one thing, but you have been given another. Something hurts inside, and you can't seem to get over it. Is that it, Annie?" He paused, seeming to ponder the thought.

"It sounds so inconsequential, after all you . . ."

"Of course it's not." He gave her a smile that melted her heart. "It's the tensions of life?"

She gave a lopsided grin. "It's like a wrestling match, isn't it?"

He chuckled. "It kinda is. And most of us live in the middle between what we want and what we get. The trick is to be thankful for our blessings." Benjamin's face brightened. "Even when you look like a pathetic old man, there is always something to be grateful for. Sometimes we take our blessings for granted even when we know we shouldn't."

Annie wiped at the moisture in her eye. "I can see how useful it might be to put a limit on my self-pity—maybe keep it under a minute each day."

"My only advice: Just try not to chase the wrong things, focus on what is important; be grateful for the blessings God has given you." Benjamin looked into Annie's eyes. "Learn how to give out love, then to let it come in when it's returned." His eyes crinkled around their edges. "And remember this, my dear beautiful young lady: There is nothing more important in life than family." He smiled. "Families are forever."

Benjamin Dreyfus was determined to bravely cross that final bridge between life and death with dignity. And no matter how burdensome Annie's day was, his heartwarming smile lifted her spirits. He was a humble man who lived with courage, with humor, with composure. And his optimism filled his life like an overflowing soup bowl, and Annie's too.

Annie leaned over and kissed his cheek. And as always, she left him with a little more warmth in her heart and lift in her step.

⸻ • ⸻

On an early evening four weeks out of Liverpool, upon calm, languorous seas, a strange, magnificent ship approached. Its cluster of enormous sails billowed brilliantly in the blood-red sunset. It dwarfed the *Colorado*, with markings suggesting it was out of Africa, heading toward London.

"Mr. Wright, please collect letters from the passengers that they'd like to send home. We'll be boarding this ship, exchanging mail," Captain Preston called out. "Maybe join them in a bit of prayer."

"Aye, Captain."

Tom hurried belowdecks to share the news with Annie, but when he found her on her hands and knees cleaning up the remains of a passenger's unleashed breakfast, a frustrated worry eclipsed his better judgment. "Ah, Annie, get off that floor." He reached down and helped her up.

"Thank you, Thomas." The look in her tired eyes, her trembling hand atop her swelling belly, her full breasts, hard hips, and frazzled countenance told the story. The long hours of caring for the sick and needy belowdecks in the dank, bilious air, with the boat rocking and rolling on rough seas, had taken its toll on his very pregnant wife.

"Annie, why do you overtax yourself so?" he whispered in irritation. "I don't understand. Why do you care so much about these people? You're with child, for heaven's sake. Don't you have enough to concern yourself without looking after . . . You are not your brother's keeper."

"Don't be such a curmudgeon, Thomas. I want to help where I can," she replied. "I feel better when I can help."

Tom frowned in frustration, knowing his advice would go unheeded. "I'm worried about you."

"I'm sorry, Thomas. I'd agree with you, but then we'd both be wrong!"

"What am I to do with you?" He shook his head. "You seem to have compassion for everyone but yourself."

"Just like your mother." She smiled. "Think of us as limited editions."

"You're right there." Tom frowned again. "Well, I don't want you on your knees cleaning up someone else's messes anymore today. I'll finish cleaning up this mess, after I collect the letters. Now go topside, please! I'll join you when I'm done here."

Annie nodded her acquiescence. "Thank you, Thomas!"

※ · ※

Annie helped Rachel out of bed. And together, they made their way up the stairs to the upper deck. It was a welcome respite from the cloistered space below. She pulled in her first deep breath of fresh air in three days.

The enormous ship looked magnificent, glistening golden in the setting sun, rising tall out of a placid sea.

"Mr. Wright, do you have those letters?" Captain Preston called out as Tom came up the stairs.

"Aye, Captain."

"Like to join us, Mr. Wright? Deliver the letters yerself?"

"I would, sir." Tom fell in beside Captain Preston, grateful for a change of scenery.

Annie stood beside Rachel at the railing, watching her husband and the others climb aboard the longboat. The bosun lowered them into the sea and she fixed her eyes on the skiff as the crewmen rowed the distance over the glassy surface reflecting the magnificent ship.

Out of bed for the first time in weeks, Rachel stood enthralled. "This has to be one of the most beautiful pictures God has ever painted."

"Yes," Annie agreed.

"How is Edie's little Tommy doing?"

"Much better. Thank you for asking. We thought we were going to lose him, then miraculously he made a turn for the better. Poor Edie and Andrew are still very sick in bed, but Tommy's improvement has seemed to help them as well."

"That is wonderful."

As the longboat reached the great ship, Rachel turned her gaze toward her daughter and Elizabeth standing at the bow, both watching the scene, intent upon not missing a thing. They were holding hands, giggling in delight, Elizabeth's blond hair whipping in a whisp of breeze. Abigail's bright red curls danced in her excitement as they chatted.

Seeing the love in Rachel's eyes, Annie smiled. "They make a striking pair, don't they?"

Rachel nodded. "They've grown close in these past weeks."

"Separated only long enough to sleep!"

The friendship between a coal miner's daughter and a well-to-do West Londoner was an enigma. Admirably, both had overlooked class distinction and the darkness of misunderstanding to break the bonds of prejudice. In their innocence, both ignored culture, class, age, religion, and their inability to speak French, German, Italian, Portuguese, or even Welsh. Instead, they shared a common language that all on board seemed to understand—loving kindness and respect for others.

"You know, Annie," Rachel began, grabbing hold of Annie's arm for support. "All three of you have become respected by passengers and crew alike. We're forever indebted to you." Then with a sober smile and a squeeze of Annie's arm, Rachel added, "God bless you for opening my eyes!"

Annie smiled back, appreciative of Rachel's sentiment.

They continued watching Abigail and Elizabeth, arm in arm, wearing exhausted, teary-eyed smiles, fixated on the unfolding scene. Seeing them giggle with each other, reminding Annie they were still young girls. Annie tried to imagine what future lay in store for them beyond the beautiful ship, whose shadowed silhouette loomed ominous on the evening glass of this languid sea.

The mood quickly changed when the longboat returned to the *Colorado*, after only a brief absence, and the tall ship resumed its course eastward into the darkening evening. The normally loquacious sailors were quiet, sullen, and brooding. They filed off the longboat, their heads hung down. Annie noticed the lines of distress on Tom's face as he climbed aboard the *Colorado* still holding the stack of letters.

Gabriel approached him, but Tom put up a warning hand, waving him off as he headed toward the stern. Gabriel, seeing his letter still in Tom's hand, ignored him.

"What the hell, you didn't deliver it," Gabriel blurted angrily. "That was an important letter to my father."

Tom spun to face him. His lips were turned down in anger. "To hell with your letter," he said coldly, his eyes blazing. He spoke loud enough for all on deck to hear, throwing down the stack of bound letters. They skidded across the deck toward the captain, who was the last to step aboard.

"You had no right. That letter to my father was important."

"Your letter, humph. You damn aristocrat. Your father, who condones the abuse of young girls, sending them to their death in his match factories. Not much better than them damn slavers in their big ship." Tom was standing eye to eye with Gabriel as he coldly made his point. "I wouldn't give them anything of ours. Yes, they were on their way back to London—after delivering their human cargo in Brazil and trading their filthy lucre in our new country. I only wish we'd been armed. I wish to God Almighty we could have sent that foul ship to the bottom."

Tom turned and continued to the stern, where he stood alone, looking out to sea. His mind was reeling at what he had seen. He could still hear the clanking chains against the hull, see them swinging in the swell, with dried blood, excrement, and rotting flesh stuck to the sides of the hold. The evidence of debauchery, death, and destruction of those poor souls. The villainy of the crew seemed to be everywhere. Tom was sick to his stomach just thinking of the men, women, and children facing certain death or even worse.

Tom gagged, then vomited over the railing.

The captain, without saying a further word to passenger or crew, joined Tom at the railing. He stood quiet beside him and put his hand on Tom's shoulder in an unusual expression of comfort. His stern countenance and riveted jaw, set like cold, hard steel, conveyed a message that the rest on board should keep their distance.

For a time Annie stayed away, allowing Tom to be by himself. But as the sun set in the west and the light of a rising moon shimmered on the sea, she came to stand beside her husband.

"How are you feeling?" she asked. Tom's pale, blood-drained face reflected the awful sight he had seen.

"I'm not sure. I know what I've seen and heard and felt today will be imprinted on my mind forever."

As the *Colorado* sailed silent into the setting sun, Tom leaned onto the bowsprit, unaware of Annie's arm intertwined with his. He stared down at the foaming water being sliced and peeled off the bow to reveal the deep undercoat of blue-green sea glass sparkling in the soft light. The undulations of the sea beneath their hull brought a weightlessness to the deck, rising and falling away again like a ballasted balloon beneath their feet. The endless graying sky above and deep darkness of the ocean below blended without edges. It seemed so immense that Tom's mind was unable to take in the vastness. His lungs could not breathe it in. He felt small, insignificant, inconsequential.

"The smell was awful," Tom shared as though he must. "The taste of death was in the air, even before we stepped on the deck of that awful ship."

"Oh, Thomas."

"They had not secured the chains in the hold. And the sounds of their clanging sent a chill through me. The heaviness in the air. Then I saw . . ." Tom gagged.

"It must have been horrific."

Tom knew that without seeing it, Annie couldn't really fathom it. He rubbed his hands on his shirt to erase any trace of the ship he had touched, but it didn't seem to leave him. "It was a dark ship, an evil ship! There were no prayers to be said for those sailors or their godforsaken souls." Tom paused. "I wanted them all to pay, but I did nothing." With his elbows on the railing, he put his head in his hands. His heart in his throat, he felt panic. "I wanted to."

"But what could you have done?"

"Something! I just stood there looking to the others for retribution." Tom paused again. "And I'm so ashamed to admit it, but when I first recognized what had happened there, I felt a tinge of relief it wasn't done to me."

"Oh, Thomas . . ."

"We all just stood there as if it wasn't our place to do anything about it. After all, we weren't black slaves, from their villages, or responsible, were we? I didn't even protest the debauchery, the injustice." His mind was a swirl. His hands in tight fists. He grimaced. "Why is it so hard for men to stand up for truth and justice, to push back on the dark underbelly of human nature, the sickness, the evil, when we aren't the subject of the persecutors' villainous acts?"

"I don't know." Annie stared out to sea.

"I pray I will always remember the sound of the swinging chains. The smell of the filth, the taste of the rotting flesh in the air, the sight of the carnage, and the touch of these evil men when they shook my hand."

"I suppose all those slaves had beautiful African names. They must have each had families who will miss them. God made men equal, didn't he—all men?"

Tom knew one thing for certain: that slaver had shocked him into seeing his own flaws starkly. His own failings. The slaver had made him recognize he, and all good men, had some kind of obligation to spit out the abuse of his fellow man. If it left a bad taste in his mouth, then he must have the courage not to swallow it back and go on his way. Tom felt embarrassed in front of his wife, who had always been such an example of charity and human kindness.

"I love you, Thomas."

Looking out to sea toward America, Tom pleaded in anguish, "God, give me strength to never stand by again without a fight, to never again watch man's inhumanity to man play out and do nothing." He paused in thought, wishing to never forget the sacrifice of hundreds of thousands of young lives in a civil war to set right the American covenant, to remedy man's injustice to God's gift of a promised land.

Chapter 6

❧ • ❦

FIVE WEEKS OUT OF PORT, the *Colorado* floated silently off Nova Scotia in an indiscernible wind over the placid beauty of the North Atlantic. Tom had taken a break from his work to join Annie at the railing as passengers and sailors alike watched a family of humpback whales at play in the early morning mist.

Annie's eyes were wide with excitement. "Look at that rambunctious calf weaving in and out around her mam."

"And the bigger whales surrounding them," Tom added, referring to the enormous male protectors who gracefully split the glassy surface, encircling mother and calf on their family trek north to their summer feeding grounds in the North Sea.

"It's breathtaking," Annie whispered in awe. "Absolutely amazing creatures."

"The sailors tell me it's Neptune, god of the sea, who fills the ocean with the magnificent abundance of life to entice the goddess, Calypso."

"How fascinating," Annie said as she looked on, enthralled. "I've never been to the London Palladium, but I can't imagine a more impressive spectacle than watching a whale as big as the *Colorado* pirouetting in the air, then crashing back down into the ocean while slapping her long flukes in a thunderclap."

The calm waters of the North Atlantic, filled with the wonders of life, seemed to have lulled all on board into complacency. But just as easily as the sea could bring forth life, it could take it away. Superstitious sailors who roamed the sea knew Calypso also had a jealous temper. Calypso had been responsible for sinking hundreds of ships just like theirs. And unbeknownst to these complacent travelers, Calypso was preparing a heart-stopping surprise. Two thousand miles to the south in Panama, off the narrow neck of land where continents join, Calypso had conjured up a Caribbean tempest. After gaining strength in its Panamanian birthplace, the avenging angel's hurricane went forth throughout the Caribbean, laying waste to the islands of Jamaica, Haiti, The Bahamas, Turks and Caicos, and Cuba. Then turning north, up the Eastern Seaboard of North America, she left death and destruction all along her path through Florida, the Carolinas, Georgia, and Virginia. After leaving New Jersey in a shambles, the hurricane Calypso spun toward Nova Scotia, preparing to introduce herself to the *Colorado* as it sailed on a blissful circumnavigational arc through the North Atlantic just a few dozen miles southeast of Cape Breton.

Powerful, deep ocean swells rolled beneath the calm surface of the sea, lifting and plunging the bow of the *Colorado* into the rolling waves, ever closer to the oncoming hurricane.

The slight increase in the northeasterly winds might have been a welcome change to the inexperienced young sailor, after seeing the *Colorado* had made little forward progress over the last few days. But Captain Preston was not fooled. He knew full well that Calypso was not to be trusted during the late summer months, when she was most apt to lose her temper.

The wind increased. Still Captain Preston stood calm at the helm, with seemingly no more emotion than last year's bird's nest.

Monitoring the falling barometric pressure, the dark-gray skies looming in the distance, and the deepening swells exerting greater power beneath the hull of the *Colorado*, he was sorting out the warning signs of things to come. He'd hoped his little brig might slip into the protection of Halifax Harbour before they met the hurricane, but now he knew it was not to be. Despite his best efforts to push the advantage, he could not make the *Colorado* move any faster. The vigilant captain searched the horizon for an alternate escape from Calypso's pending wrath.

Heavy gray clouds moved in to cast shadows over an increasingly angry sea. Tensions among the sailors rose high. Weak stomachs turned queasy, and a fractious fear gripped each crewman as they went about their business, completing tasks with disquiet. Each sailor took his turn casting stolen glances in the captain's direction, checking for changes in the concern etched onto his face. These were anxious looks intended to linger only briefly, so as to go unnoticed. Each sailor was careful not to reveal his own rising superstitious fears. For all sailors knew, their stolen glances, if detected by the captain, could curse their fate.

By afternoon, the warm reassurance of the smoldering sun had been entirely blocked out by dark, foreboding clouds. The calm seas beneath the little brig had given way to powerful rolling swells of twenty feet or more. The ship's bow dipped perilously through the great, cresting waves. Turbulent winds began to drive the *Colorado* ever closer to the ragged coastline despite the captain's effort to maintain a northwesterly tack away from the impending danger. With the full force of her brutal vengeance, Calypso was about to turn the beauty of Neptune's paradise into a living hell at sea.

Captain Preston leaned into the binnacle, spyglass in hand, searching the horizon with an almost hypnotic intensity to find a port of safety off Cape Breton before the full wrath of the storm was upon them. He knew now they could not survive the force of the hurricane if they were caught in the open ocean or strayed too close to the jagged rocks. They must reach the Strait of Canso—and soon—if there was any hope of survival.

"There she is, Mr. Jenkins," Captain Preston barked to his first mate loud enough for the rest of the crew to hear. "Chedabucto Bay and the straits beyond, off the starboard bow. This be our openin'. Make all preparations to meet the gale."

"Aye, aye, sir," Mr. Jenkins confirmed before turning to the crew. "We'll be makin' a run for the bay ahead o' da storm!" Jenkins shouted out his commands. "Batten down the hatches, tie off all we must not lose, and everythin' else push overboard. We'll need ta make her lighter if we're gonna outrun her! Bring 'er around, two points starboard."

Tom joined the other sailors in following the commands. He wouldn't be caught flatfooted this time. He'd learned his lesson from the earlier storm and moved quickly into action as a lightning strike nearly hit the deck.

"Mr. Jenkins, maintain full sail! Raise the stanchion topsails!" the captain ordered. "By God, we're gonna make Chedabucto Bay by darkfall or drown tryin'!"

"Aye, aye, Captain."

As afternoon melted into dusk, a great sweep of powerful wind with nothing to inhibit it for hundreds of miles rushed toward them, breathing fear into Tom and every other sailor on board. Swirling gusts of fifty-knot winds and blinding rains pummeled the ship. There was no doubt who was in charge of Mother Nature on this day. Calypso's hurricane had arrived. Even the most reckless, irreverent of sailors would seek shelter from this storm threatening to tear the sails right off their crossbeams.

"Can we outrun the storm and avoid the rocks, Mr. Jenkins?"

Captain Preston barked above the chaos of howling wind, ferocious rain, and raging seas. Both knew it was an unfair question intended only as a warning call to all the other sailors on board. The ship was increasingly being pushed toward Sable Island, the graveyard of more than a hundred lost ships along Nova Scotia's coastline. Their only hope was to fight the wind up the coast, around the point of Cape Breton, and sail into the protective straits off Chedabucto Bay.

Captain Preston stood alone on the forward bridge in the midst of the furious storm. To Tom, it seemed the captain was in his element, doing what he was born to do! Tom paid rapt attention to every word and gesture from the hand of their master and commander as he fired off orders in a Gatling-gun cadence. "Lower the stanchion staysails. The gallant topsails, bow and aft, turn another point starboard. Mind the swells comin' port. Make haste, gentlemen, or there'll be hell to pay. Prepare fer the worst. And pray ta God fer mercy!" The captain barked out from the bridge, the driving rain soaking him, the wind whipping at his bold face, as he stared fearless into the storm.

☙ • ❧

A giant wave crashed over the bow, flooding over everything on deck. "Tether yourselves down!" the captain called out.

Tom reached for a rope to lash himself and his brother to the foremast. But just then, with a chilling blaze in his eyes, Jacque Croquet pushed Joey away and slid in beside Tom. Ignoring the protests, Jacque quickly tied himself and Tom to the mast using a double-hitch seaman's slipknot, known by experienced sailors as an instrument of death to adjoining partners.

"You there, Wright, Croquet," Captain Preston blared. "Secure the braces and steady the halyard rigging from yer station."

The tendrils of Calypso's angry tempest lifted the *Colorado* high into the air, then slammed her down to drown in a swirling whirlpool of riptides. Her port beam nearly buckled, and timbers screeched, squealed, and strained to the limit with every thrashing blow.

Tom, wide-eyed, sucking in every breath as if it were his last in the frothing surf, was a front-row witness to the chaos as another gigantic wave broke over the bowsprit. The concussion split the air like an artillery shell, vibrating everything on deck with such terrifying ferocity that it blurred Tom's vision of the horizon. The unbridled fury of the crashing wave swept across the deck in sheets of flooding water, attacking men and the ship like treacherous crashing surf buffeting shoreline rocks. The rushing water ricocheted off the bridge and frothed wildly around the foremast. No man, beast, or object not well anchored or lashed securely could avoid being washed into the tumultuous sea and lost forever.

All the while the *Colorado* was being pushed closer to the rocky shoals off Cape Breton by the maelstrom of waves from the angry tempest. It was clear to all they were in trouble. Most likely to be thrown onto the reef, joining the hundreds of ships who had gone before. All on deck looked to their fearless captain, anchored atop the forward bridge like Poseidon himself facing up to Calypso's rage of gale-force winds. Drenched by the rain and crashing seas, the implacable tyrant at the helm spat out his commands, composed and confident, as if sailing a pleasure craft on a calm summer's afternoon.

"Do you keep your eye on our course, Mr. Jenkins?" shouted the captain to his first mate through the torrential rain whipping at his face.

"Aye, sir."

"Can we take more seas without breaking up, Mr. Jenkins?"

"No sir, we cannot."

Chapter 7

❧ • ❦

"It's now or never, Mr. Jenkins!" Captain Preston shouted above the hammering tumult. "We're gonna make this ole tub earn her keep! Prepare to bear away to a broad reach and hold course down the face of the cresting wave. We'll run her out, using the power of the wave to push our advantage."

"Aye, sir." Mr. Jenkins prepared to turn into an approaching wave, shouting out commands to whip the brig around astride the thirty-foot monster, then ride down the face of it as its crest peeled off behind them.

Tom hung on his every word, straining to hear and execute his orders exactly as delivered by the first mate. Though their lives were in the hands of the notoriously competent Captain Preston, only God knew if he was mean enough to face down the mighty Calypso.

"Do it now, Mr. Jenkins. Slam the tiller hard portside, turn the bow starboard three points to the beam, and let the sheets fly."

"Aye, Captain."

Tom did his duty and the little craft turned her beam on end, pivoted on her stern, and dropped into the trough of the monstrous swelling wave, gaining speed as it hurtled down the precipitous face in a wild ride.

He, like every other sailor on deck, held on with white knuckles, leaning back into the wind as they fell, holding his breath and gripping the assigned rigging with all the strength God had given him. In fear for his life, Tom felt his heart rise into his throat until it stopped beating. The brigantine knifed her way down the steep, gleaming face, wind whistling from behind to push her even faster. Only her keel, caught in the sheer face of the fifty-foot monster, held the little ship from slipping into the vast crevasse of the barreling, explosive confusion of whitewater chasing after her.

The raucous ride threw blinding ocean spray into the captain's face, but he was fearless. Holding his ground, he was anchored in the bow like an Olympian god. His right arm was pumping high into the air as he cried out in defiance of Calypso's hurricane, "You will not defeat us!"

The *Colorado* raced down the undulating hollow of the enormous wave into its cavernous barrel in a great sweep of speed. But she held fast, staying just ahead of the collapsing wave chasing her from behind with a crashing thunder.

"We'll not be defeated, by God!" the captain shouted, his eyes wild, blazing in a frenzy, his fist pumping through the air to punctuate his resolve and make clear his determination would prevail. Under the sheer power of the captain's will, the little brig dared not flounder. She sped down the cavernous face like a seal under chase by the vicious, gaping jaws of the storm's oncoming fury.

At the end of the wild ride, the creaking timbers of the *Colorado* seemed on the verge of breaking apart to plunge into a watery grave of surging, foaming whitewater that would surely engulf her. But Tom, in absolute terror, like every other sailor on board, was intent upon keeping his head—to execute Preston's next orders precisely, that their lives might be saved by the iron will of this captain of the sea.

Captain Preston ordered, "Mr. Jenkins, pull the tiller hard portside." The craft spun on her beam, pulling out of the wave just before the raging giant could devour them in a crashing roar of mountainous foaming water and bury them all in Davy Jones's locker.

Tom, his stomach turned inside out, sputtered out the breath he'd been holding. He was still alive, and the *Colorado* had made significant progress.

"Hooyah!" came the relieved cry of the sailors, eyes bulging, fists pumping. Captain Preston, their exalted savior, still stood at the helm, and in the minds of all on deck, he had outwitted Calypso herself.

Tom, holding on to his traces for life, believed only God knew how the little ship of gum and timber had held together under the torturous pounding. Entirely undone, his eyes were wild, his grimace fixed, his breath alternately held then panting, heart seeming to pound out of his chest. Most of the time frozen in fear, he was barely able to engage his muscles. In that moment, there was not a more religious man in all the Western Hemisphere.

"Lord, please help us through this horrific, torrential thrashing," he prayed fervently, "and I'll be yours forever."

"Mr. Jenkins, are we still slipping toward the rocks?" the captain knowingly questioned his first mate.

"That we are, sir, steadily closing in on 'em."

Without breaking concentration, Captain Preston ordered the brig to come about, head back out to sea, and prepare to do it all again.

≻ • ≺

To Annie and the rest of the passengers trapped below in the darkness, the howling winds, driving rain beating on the deck above, and thundering waves seemed to be tearing the ship apart. Though her hands were shaking and she found it difficult to breathe in the foul-smelling confinement, Annie went from room to room encouraging calm as the sea streamed in through a rattling hatch and sloshed into their staterooms. Pots, pans, dishes, and all else in the galley clattered and crashed to the floor.

Elizabeth wrapped her arms around her trembling little brother and sisters, whose hands were clasped over their ears against the angry sound of the storm. She cried out for her mam, but Edie, prostrate on her berth, deathly ill and holding on for dear life, was unable to offer any help. And Papa, wedged into his berth to prevent spilling onto the floor, was so sick and delirious that he made little sense.

The straining timbers shuddered and creaked, spawning wild imaginings of an uproar of furious threats being hurled at them from all directions.

Elizabeth began to cry in the darkness as she held on to her screaming little brother and sisters. "I need to get out of here." Panic stricken and unable to catch her breath, she frantically pulled away from the screaming children and fumbled in the darkness for the doorway. "Annie, I'm scared!" she cried out, her eyes straining, darting this way and that. "I can't do this anymore. I want out of this awful, smelly place. I can't breathe. I'm scared. This storm is going to tear us apart!"

Annie was suddenly there. "Oh, honey," she whispered, soft and calming in the girl's ear. "It's just the storm playing tricks on your mind," she soothed, wrapping her arms around the teary-eyed girl and her younger siblings. "I'm with you now. It will be all right."

"Please help us, Annie! Please help Mam."

"Shush, honey. It'll be all right."

"The storm is rushing in to meet us," the cook blurted out from the galley, above the din of another enormous wave hitting the timbered portside hull. "There ain't no gettin' outta this watery tomb alive if we hit the reef."

"Oh, Mr. Bunnings, please! You're scaring the children," Annie called out in a buoyant voice for the benefit of passengers and fearful children alike. "We must have confidence in the captain, and the Lord."

"Are we sinking?" A plaintive cry arose from another passenger. "Please, God, don't let my children drown!" Even in this disembodied voice, the terror was clear.

Still holding Elizabeth and the children in her arms, Annie took command over the chaos. "God is with us and this ship. He will not abandon us, not see us drown here! All will be well!" Her voice rang clear, calm, and comforting amid the clamor of the storm.

Another giant wave slammed into the bulkhead and rushed across the deck, snapping the latch on the hatch cover, flooding into the galley, and sloshing into the staterooms to put out the remaining candles.

"Elizabeth, please take care of your mam and the children," Annie whispered calmly. "I'm going to close the hatch and relight the candles. I'll be right back."

Annie, holding her swollen belly in her hands, could tell her time was not far off as she sloshed her way through the dark shadows and into the galley. Her soft, round face strained with exhaustion, her body near collapse, but still she pushed on, resolute.

"Mr. Bunnings, please secure the hatch," Annie called out as she fumbled with wet matches. Another thunderous wave collided portside, the ship's bow plunging beneath the tumult of the crashing wave and sending water rushing across the deck and through the open hatch. Torrents of cold gray water cascaded in, flooding the galley and knocking Annie off her feet. Tumbling with everything else in the galley, Annie slid across the dark room in a rush of water.

Her heart pounded in her throat. Her arms flailed, searching for safety in the darkness, grasping for anything to stop her.

"Help me!" she screamed, slamming into the bulkhead in a wash of debris, every wisp of air knocked from her lungs, leaving her breathless, unable to inhale. Then, with a smashing thud, the heavy teak table crushed her against the bulkhead like a fireman's sledgehammer. A wrenching pain stabbing deep in her abdomen bent her over. Warm, sticky blood splattered across her face. The table careened off into the darkness, and she was left convulsing. Cold, disordered, in a tangled heap of blackness, her scream came out in a whisper. "My baby?"

≻ • ≺

A bolt of lightning cracked open the sky to light up the cape, so close Tom felt he could almost reach out and touch the treacherous rocks off their starboard bow. He watched Captain Preston, calmly staring down the throat of the hurricane, calculating in his head the bearing of the wind, catchment of the waves, proximity of the rocks, and advantage to be maintained by his intense, indomitable will.

Drenched in heavy rain and hurricane spray, he turned to his first mate, sputtering words for his ears only. "Absent a miracle, we'll be lost on the rocks!"

The finality of his words hit Tom like a steel ball to the stomach. His heart pounded in his throat. He could hardly breathe. *Death often comes as an intruder,* he thought. *Sometimes when we least expect it, when we're least ready for it.* He had come to the borders of hell in the midst of life's bloom. A flash of memories crossed his mind: Mam patiently teaching him to read; the smell of bacon cooking on the hearth; the awe of holding the bow Grand had made for him for the first time; Tigger's infectious grin; freckles filling every facet of

Fidget's face. Lydia, the love his life, standing in her summer dress in a meadow filled with wildflowers. Spring Hollow's honeybees flitting from flower to flower on a radiant spring morning; the sweet taste of wild blackberries by the pooling pond dappled with a steady autumn rain; and Annie's smiling face on the road to Liverpool.

The wind blew. The rain pounded hard and cold. It stung his face. And the memories blurred together.

"Mr. Jenkins, shall we risk raising the gallant full into the wind?" Captain Preston asked. Both knew that although raising the gallant topsail to the top of the mast might leverage the power of the mighty hurricane winds, it would almost certainly be torn away, and most probably the mast would be broken. But slim as it was, it was their last hope.

"Yes, sir, we must risk it."

"Then do it, Mr. Jenkins. Do it now!"

The captain's first mate whipped around, shouting out instructions. Hearing the anxiousness in the voice of the otherwise stoic first mate, the sailors unlashed and hoisted the halyard and with all dispatch, hauled the topsail into the furious wind. But the rigging snagged on the masthead spreader before the gallant reached its full height, tangling in the storm, and the sail lost the wind altogether.

Captain Preston pointed to Jacque Croquet. "You there," he boomed in a voice of thunder, "get up that mast, slide the rigging clear of the beam and top block."

In the pounding rain and the furious wind strafing his face, Jacque looked into Tom's eyes. A crack of thunder and flash of lightning lit up the sky. And in that instant Tom saw Jacque's fierce cobalt eyes ablaze with evil.

Jacque donned the safety harness, and with a single pull he released the rope securing both his life and Tom's, with a glare in his eyes and scowl of malicious intent. It sent a chill skittering down

Tom's spine as Jacque swung himself into the safety of the shrouds. Looking down at Tom no longer tethered to the mast, Jacque threw the loose end of the rope into the darkness, well out of Tom's sight.

"Ya didn't really think ya'd escape Lord Fitz wit yer life, did ya?"

Jacque turned, and with an evil grin, he scrambled up the rack lines. Panicking, Tom fell to his knees, fumbling in the darkness.

"Mr. Wright," Captain Preston yelled, "jump to it, man. Help Wiggins with that climbin' line!"

Struggling to find his footing, hands trembling, Tom stumbled over to Wiggins, slid down the mast pole, and wrapped his legs around the pole as best he could. Then he joined Wiggins in keeping tension on Jacque's safety line. The near-frozen rope tore at his hands, but he kept his eyes on Jacque's silhouette scrambling up the rigging like a monkey.

Jacque disappeared into the shadowy darkness. Then came a jagged knife of lightning, tearing open the sky, illuminating his body, wrenched-up face, and round blazing eyes. A cannon fire of thunder followed right behind, vibrating the standing water on deck into glistening diamonds.

Tom shuddered, his eyes locked on Jacque, willing him to go on. For this villainous sailor held their lives in his hands. Only he had the power to parole all on board the *Colorado* from certain death.

The ship pitched and yawed. Again, lightning lit up the sky, freezing Jacque's climbing form as he sped up rack lines strung from crosstrees. Over the straining shrouds he inched. With the agile athleticism of a circus performer, he pulled himself up and over the trestle trees heading toward the lover's hole, well over a hundred feet above the deck. The main mast swayed violently as the little ship rode up and over the powerful ocean swells in the hurricane's strengthening winds. It rolled and heeled from one beam to the other. At each extremity of swing, the tall mast seemed like it would lean into the sea, but then it whipped back in the angry sky, determined to dislodge this pestering sailor from the rigging.

Jacque hooked an arm on the aft tree and pulled with all his might. But he could go no farther. The climbing-safety rope had stretched to its maximum length, but still Jacque could not reach the top of the stanchion. Desperate to get higher up the mast, he unleashed his safety harness. The rope went slack in Tom's hands. Free of the impinging restraint, Jacque stretched his body and reached his arm high overhead for the rigging.

Another flash of lightning froze Jacque, the deep furrowed brows, the lines of determination etched into the sailor's twisted face. Every muscle, every tendon of his wiry frame strained to near breaking point. He reached his sinewy arm up to the jib boom to unsnag the shrouds of the gallant topsail waving wildly in the storm. The rigging snapped free, letting the full force of the wind unfurl the gallant. The topsail ripped open, and in that instant, it strained the canvas shroud far beyond its limits. The tall mast swung madly in reaction to the gale-force wind. And in the space of a heartbeat, the violent whiplash jolted the sailor free of the mast, flinging him from his precarious perch far out into the night. Grabbing wildly at the air, Jacque fell toward the deck, hitting the crossbeams on the way down. Spinning in the air like a circus cartwheel artist, he slammed into the railing and careened off into the icy waters to be lost forever in the darkness of the sea.

Tom sat stunned, unable to breathe. The silhouetted image of Jacque falling to his death seared into his memory. Then in a flash of lightning, he saw it. The safety lashing Jacque had thrown to the side. Tom released his tenuous mooring, uncurling his legs from around the mast, and scrambled toward the lifeline lying loose across the deck just as another giant wave crashed over the bow. The flooding water raced toward him, ricocheting off the bulkhead. Frothing wildly, the rush of water swept him up, his arms flailing helpless in the darkness. His eyes bulging in fear, his heart pounding, his hands outstretched, Tom grasped at the air, seeking anything that might stop him from cascading overboard.

"Help me!" he cried out, but there was no one. His stomach churning, heart lodged in his throat, he slid toward the opening between railings like a seal diving into the tumultuous sea. "Annie!"

Chapter 8

⊱ • ⊰

Tom slammed into the rail post. Pain ripped through his jaw, his shoulder. The world spinning, he wrapped both arms around the post and clung for dear life. When the rush of water receded, he was stranded on deck like a thrashing fish trying to catch his breath. Heart pounding, he slowly and woozily unclasped his limbs and stumbled through the darkness, sputtering out saltwater, gasping for air and seeking safety. With fumbling hands, he tethered himself to the mast as the hurricane raged on.

A great burst of wind stretched the rigging taut, taxing the sails and masts well beyond their breaking point. It was clear the gallant topsail could not withstand the onslaught. The riggings must surely break free, and yet . . . they held. The mainsail, staysails, topsails, squared fore and aft, masts and rigging all trimmed out to best catch the wind. For reasons only known to the great Almighty, the *Colorado* held together.

"Has she stopped her sliding toward the rocks, Mr. Jenkins?" the captain shouted.

"That she has, sir," the first mate confirmed with a catch in his throat.

"God only knows how," Tom whispered in awe as they pulled

steadily away from the dangerous shoals. The little ship had cheated death, avoiding the watery grave of hundreds of other vessels that had been lost on this reef over the centuries. The cape was clearly visible now on the starboard bow. The storm continued to pound its angry fists in fury, but the *Colorado* pulled even with and then around the point of Cape Breton.

While the ship raced through the bay toward the Strait of Canso, Captain Preston's eyes ceaselessly sought the inlet that would guide them to the protection of the mountains. With each passing moment, the storm loosened its grip on the *Colorado*. A flash of lightning lit up land, sea, and sky. "There it is, Mr. Jenkins."

When he heard the words, Tom's heart leapt.

≻ • ≺

Dusk melted into the stormy evening, and the last frightening blasts of the hurricane's fury passed into memory as the *Colorado* navigated the throat of the natural cove, then slid unmolested into the strait tucked among the mountains of the Inverness forest.

"Prepare 'er for port, Mr. Jenkins," the captain ordered.

"Aye, sir."

The *Colorado* threaded her way through the narrow strait, cascading mountains rising steep and protective from either shoreline. Ship Harbour lay just ahead in the placid waters of St. George's Bay.

Tom watched in wonder as the sailors caught their breath, unlashed their safety lines, and thanked the Almighty for their deliverance. Some took a moment to mourn the loss of one of their own. Then all was jubilation, and the sailors resumed their raucous engagement with life, congratulating one another, patting their closest mate on the back, and sharing irreverent asides as they prepared for landing in the pounding rain.

A great weight had been lifted from Tom's chest. For the first time in days, he could breathe freely. He shared in the exhilaration, knowing he, his family, and all else on board would live another day. But although he had earned the right to celebrate, he remained quiet. Reverently, he cast his eyes over the battered little ship. How had it withstood the impassable storm? The sheer improbability of their survival moved him deeply. They had battled the elements, heading into the heart of the storm, with unimaginable winds and monstrous seas driving them toward treacherous reefs that had claimed thousands of lives over the centuries.

It seemed they'd avoided disaster by a precise margin that was unexplainable by simple seamanship. Tom didn't understand the mechanics, the tactics, or the techniques of fighting the storm, but he thought he better understood this American captain. He better understood the draw of the sea for these men, the intractable need to live their lives unshackled. These were rough, rugged, fiercely independent men who would give their lives for their mates. This near disaster filled Tom with appreciation of the precious cords of life that bound men together. He understood more men's desire to be free. He understood more about himself. *The human spirit might be the greatest force in nature*, Tom mused as he looked at these men in wonder.

"Cut her back on a nor'easterly tack, Mr. Jenkins," Captain Preston thundered, yielding the bridge to his first mate with a parting order. "Find a good place to drop anchor, lower the sails, uncleat the hatches to below, and shut 'er down for the evenin'. We'll be stayin' in port a few days ta ride out the storm and make repairs before our run into Halifax and on to New York. The crew can expect alternating shore leave beginning tomorrow afternoon."

"Aye, sir."

Without another word, the captain turned on his heel and

walked toward his cabin, head down. The sailors, doffing their hats in respect despite the wind and rain, quietly looked on with reverence as he passed. While all on board had faced the storm and reckoned with their own mortality, Captain William Preston's performance had revealed one of America's greatest strengths: Men achieved positions of authority based on merit and proven ability, not because of class or heritage. Once again, Captain Preston had proven his mettle to take on the hallowed responsibility of captaining this ship.

Mr. Jenkins brought the *Colorado* around in the calmer waters of Ship Harbour in the rapidly gathering darkness. And with the skill of a seasoned sailor, he anchored her adjacent to the landing wharf as soft and gentle as a first kiss.

Chapter 9

❖ • ❖

Tom stood impatient as the sailor removed the cleated nails securing the hatch to the stuffy, foul-smelling confines of the living quarters below.

Edie was the first to reach the deck, pulling into her collar against the blustery wind and pounding rain. She took in a deep breath of the cold, fresh air, reluctant to look into Tom's eyes as the long line of passengers who had been locked below during the raging storm boiled out from the bowels of the *Colorado* like drowned rats escaping a sinking ship. But Annie was not among them.

"Where's Annie?" He could feel Edie's hesitancy and see the concern written on her face. "What is it, Edie?" His eyes were wide with alarm.

Edie frowned, her brows pulled together. "She's in Rachel's stateroom." She hesitated. "Rachel and I just finished cleaning it up."

"What's wrong?" His anxious voice rose against the wind.

"Just go to her, Tommy." Edie's voice quivered, her eyes locked on his as she wiped at the rain splattering on her face. "Be kind, brother. She needs your patience right now."

Not waiting to coax more information out of his sister, Tom turned away and pushed through the last of the passengers exiting the open hatch. With his hand on the railing, he eased down the creaky steps, his eyes adjusting to the eerie darkness. The galley was a shambles. The air was filled with the acrid odor of festering mold, musty smells of the unbathed, and the taste of rotting food. With every step the sinking feeling in his gut intensified. All was quiet but for the scraping sound coming from Rachel's stateroom.

Tom pulled aside the canvas door covering and stepped into the shadows of the freshly cleaned, candlelit room. Annie was on her hands and knees feverishly scouring the rough-hewn timber floor with violent jabs of a heavy wire brush. Her desolate eyes focused intently on the job at hand. She didn't appear to even notice he'd entered the room.

"What are you doing, Annie?" he whispered with concern, frowning, his brows scrunched together. He leaned down and put a gentle hand under her elbow to help her up, only to have her pull away. "Annie, what is it?"

"I can't get the blood out of this floor!" She sobbed. "No matter how hard I try, it won't come out."

"Please, Annie, stop. Talk to me."

She sat back on her haunches in the flickering light, her tangled, sweaty hair hanging over a scarlet face covered in beads of perspiration. "Where were you? I needed you."

"I was fighting the storm," he fumbled. "I—"

"I lost our baby, Thomas." Her voice had a hollowness that seemed to reach the very depths of her soul in unfathomable grief. It was as though she were drowning in great sobs and ragged heaves.

"What?" His voice cracked as he blankly looked down at her. Slowly, he comprehended her declaration and depth of anguish. She wore a fresh dress of faded blue. The swell in her belly was no more. Sweat mixed with a trace of blood was smeared across her cheek, and there was deep hurt in her crimson-rimmed eyes. Her pale, chalky complexion and listless expression told of the long night.

"Oh Annie, please let me help you," he said in a fog, kneeling down to try and comfort her, but she would have none of it. "Please, tell me what happened?"

"What happened?" she cried out in anguish, the heavy liquor of heartache in her voice. "You told me to be careful, not to take risks with our baby, but no . . . How could I have been so foolish?" Annie's lips curled down in quivering anguish. "Is that what you want to hear? I . . ." Her voice trailed off.

"No, Annie. I'm so very sorry." He tried to hold her, but again she pulled away, her eyes fixed on the floor.

"I lost our baby and I needed you, but you weren't here."

"Oh, Annie." Tom sighed, pale and drawn with shock. Gently, he slid his hands under her arms, slowly pulling his fragile, broken wife closer. This time she didn't resist. She leaned into his touch, clearly taking strength and comfort from it. Sagging against him, arms limp, the scrub brush dangling loose from her hand, she wept.

"I'm so sorry," she whimpered.

"It's not your fault." He sighed. "It'll be okay."

"How can you ever forgive me?" Pain wrenched her face. "Why did you ever marry such a foolish, worthless girl? What kind of wife am I?"

"You're my wife!" He wrapped his arms around her, his own insides churning. "And you'll always be my wife," he whispered reassuringly, still digesting this horrific revelation himself. "You have every reason to feel broken, but please let me help."

"My one purpose on earth is to have children," she sobbed. "And I've failed, again."

Tom stroked her hair tenderly. "You're a remarkable woman, Annie." He traced her cheek with his fingertips. "You've endured hardship without complaint."

Tom, who had not slept in three days, was tired, confused, heartbroken. It was their first time alone together since leaving Liverpool. He tipped her chin up, trying to look into her eyes, placing his warm palm on her cheek. "You've shouldered everyone's troubles but your own these past weeks, and I've neglected you. For that I am so sorry, Annie, but you're not alone."

With solemn eyes, she queried, "What if we never have children? What if you're never a father?"

"Well then, I guess children are not in our destiny. It was you I married. We get what life gives us. If it's just you and me, that will be enough for me."

"Really, Thomas?"

"I chose you. If I've seemed to take you for granted . . ." His voice cracked. "If I made you feel any less than a caring, thoughtful, wonderful wife, then I beg of you to please forgive me. You deserve better."

"Oh, Thomas." Even in the dim room, she could see the flecks of green in his dark brown eyes, feel that his heart was broken too. He searched her face for hope. And despite his own pain, he'd offered what comfort he could. He was a good man. A warmth filled her. A warmth she had not felt in a long time.

"We will get through this. You are a part of me now!" he said. With a gentle touch, he wiped a tear from her cheek. Tenderly he brushed her hair back from her face; it fell loose over her shoulders. "I'm so sorry about the baby, Annie." He paused for a long moment. "I can imagine my life without a child, but not without you in it. You have grown to be my dependable rudder. The stable tiller I didn't know I was missing."

"Oh Thomas . . ." She desperately wanted him to love her. Tears came again to her burning eyes. She rocked on her toes, kissed him sweetly, then leaned her head across his shoulder.

He kissed her softly on the cheek and rose, gently lifting her up in his strong arms and setting her down on the narrow bed that smelled of washed linen. He lay beside her. She could feel his heart beating. In her helplessness, she melted into him, yielding to the surging tide of his warmth. The trials, the suffering, the loss of their baby—all malignant thoughts of the past few weeks blurred. For a long time, he just held her in his arms, as sure and powerful as an ocean storm. She clung to him as if he were the only solid thing in her uncertain world. Even when she was afraid, when he held her in his arms, she felt comforted. There, curled up together, both slipped into a well-deserved sleep. And for a time, at least, there was peace in their bruised souls, as if they were floating on a tranquil sea under a windless summer sky.

✢ • ✢

It would be a simple service for their little girl, taking place under a great, spreading oak in the cemetery of the quaint fishing village of Port Hawkesbury. On this blustery morning, Tom stood sullen by Annie's side, their collars pulled up against the rain, looking down on their little girl's final resting place. Family, a precious few of the beneficiaries of Annie's tender loving care, and a respectful captain all gathered around them to watch the shoebox coffin lowered into the shallow grave.

Balancing on shaky sea legs, Tom took the quiet moment while the coffin was being lowered, the flowers placed and organized, to try and regain his composure, to control the ache in his grief-shackled heart before beginning his eulogy. He considered how his daughter's tiny burial plot looked in the dark shadow of this enormous oak tree. It appeared almost inconsequential under the canopy of great recumbent limbs stretching out over the graveyard. Its ancient roots jutted out ominously, like giant knuckled fingers clawing at the ground, dark and powerful enough to split rock.

His thoughts drifted back to a great beast of a tree he'd often passed as a young boy walking with Grand. On the edge of the forbidden forest, he had often envisioned dungeons, dragons, and the like living inside the tree's great trunk. He had feared the gnarled roots would reach out and grab him, take him inside to live chained up in the darkness. Grand, noticing his shyness, had one day taken him by the hand, and together they stroked the bark, touching the great tree's roots, its branches, its leaves.

"Don't be afraid, Tommy," he'd said. "'Tis only yer imagination that brings on the fear of the unknown. And it can take it away just as well. 'Tis no monster, but a humble, kind, and forgiving old fellow who loves little children. And maybe, if ya be caring and respectful, that courtesy might just cause the kindhearted old gentleman ta wave in appreciation." So, for years after, even when he was far too old to believe in dungeons and dragons, Tom would tip his hat when he passed the great tree, and the gentlemanly old giant would wave back with its branches on the fickle whim of the breeze. This reminder not to fear the unknown brought a smile of wonder to Tom's face.

❧ • ☙

Annie looked up at her husband. How could he be smiling? The look she saw in his dark eyes broke her heart again. It was clear to her he had withdrawn into the world he'd left behind, a world filled with the love of another. How could he be thinking of her at the graveside of their little girl? God help her with this bottomless pit of doomed love. She was confused, distraught, feeling inadequate, her heart torn in two. She needed him, body and soul, to soothe and help her mend that tear. The words burned in her throat, but she was not brave enough to express her innermost fears to this handsome, confident man she'd married. So, she would do what she had always done: hold her tongue, disappear into her private world of helping others in need, write to Emma, or share her grief with her newfound friend Rachel. She would just wait. Wait in the hope she might learn to endure living with Lydia's ghost between them.

Tom bowed his head, concealing his spilling emotions, and began the eulogy for their daughter.

"Death claims the aged, the weary, and the worn. It is the destiny of all mankind. Frequently it comes as an intruder. Sometimes it seems an enemy of all human happiness. Today, death has silenced our baby, taken our Nannie through the veil and into the realm of God Almighty. We send our precious little Nannie back to you, oh Lord. Please look after her for us.

"All must pass through death's portals, for as the apostle Paul said, 'We are all appointed only once to die!' And that would be the end of it, if it were not for our savior, Jesus Christ. 'For God so loved the world that he gave his only begotten son, that whosoever believeth in him should not perish, but have everlasting life.'"

Annie stared down at the shoebox containing her little girl resting at the bottom of the shallow grave. Nannie had seemed so vulnerable in death, utterly defenseless, but she was past harm now. Still, Annie could not defeat the twisting blade jammed into her broken heart. She would never again see her little girl's angelic face, her apple cheeks, her perfectly formed body with her long, delicate fingers. Annie pondered the future they would never have. *I will never dry a tear from your eye, never care for your first skinned knee, or hold you in my arms when you're afraid. Never give you a sweet good-night kiss to make your hurts all better. I will never play dolls on the floor with my little girl. There will be no walking you to school on your first day, no talks about your first crush, your first kiss. There will be no wedding day, no lunches in the park, no grandchildren to spoil. It might have been, but now will never be.*

Chapter 10

❧ • ❧

THE *COLORADO* HAD BEEN IN Ship Harbour for several days. The storm had passed, food stores were replaced, and repairs were near complete. Captain Preston announced they would be leaving with the tide on the following morning for their final week-long leg into New York. This pause had been a welcome respite after the rough seas. The sick passengers had surfaced from dreary life belowdecks to revive in the warm, peaceful sunshine that had settled over Ship Harbour. But Annie had remained a recluse in her room.

Finally, on this morning, with a light sea breeze in her face, Annie stood on deck and took in a deep breath of the fresh salt air. Her heart lodged in her throat, she pushed back on the raging emotions, raised her chin high, and smiled at Rachel and Edie. "Good morning."

"Thank you for coming, Annie," Rachel said, smiling warmly. "Getting out of that stuffy hold will do you good!" She gave Annie a warm hug. Edie did the same.

"Port Hawkesbury is a beautiful little village," Edie said, trying her cheerful best to bring Annie out of her shell as the three strolled up the main street. Charming cottages and quaint shops cascaded down the craggy hillsides of the forested portside village.

"I found this wonderful little bathhouse," Rachel added, "when I was wandering around the village yesterday."

Annie frowned.

"Please hear me out. Edie and I have arranged a bath, for just the three of us."

"None of us have had a decent bath in weeks." Edie's eyes were alight.

Annie, not wanting to disappoint, thanked them both. "You're very kind, but I'm sorry, I don't think I'm up to it."

"Oh, Annie, please let us do this for you," Edie encouraged. "When I look at my little Tommy . . ." She wiped a tear from her eye. "I can't help but think he wouldn't even be here if it hadn't been for you. Please let us do this, for us if not for you."

"I'm in a very dark place right now. I don't know."

"I'm sure it must seem like the darkest of forests," Rachel empathized. "But over these past weeks, you have shown me what real compassion and kindness are. Let us help you try to find a path through the darkness?"

"Hmm." Annie looked at these two women she loved. As much as she wanted to curl up in her room, hide away from the world, she knew they just wanted to help.

"At least come see the place with us," Rachel requested, offering a middle ground.

⊱ • ⊰

Annie felt fragile, lightheaded, and even a bit afraid of stumbling as she took the steps up to the bathhouse on shaky legs. She inhaled deeply to help steel her nerves as Rachel knocked on the bathhouse door.

"Welcome, ladies." The matron of the quaint establishment

invited them into the freshly cleaned, beautifully appointed bathhouse. "All arrangements have been made per your very specific instructions!"

Annie looked inside and raised her brows at her two companions. "You've been busy."

Three tubs filled with steaming-hot fresh mountain water sat together in front of a very large window, shades drawn back to allow the room to flood with light. The view was spectacular. Craggy cliffs cascading down hundreds of feet, the vibrant blue of St. George's Bay in the distance, set in the emerald Inverness forest.

Bouquets of fresh-cut, sweet-smelling flowers were strategically placed around the tubs. "Primrose," Annie commented, a soft, nostalgic smile brightening her face. "My favorite!" she whispered, wiping at her eyes. "Thank you, Edie!" Then looking at Rachel, she added, "This has to be expensive?"

"You're worth it."

Annie frowned, but her wide eyes filled with gratitude for these women who had become closer than any two sisters. "What can I say? I've never seen anything . . ." She paused. "What's that next to the tea set?"

"Ahh!" Rachel smiled. "That's Cadbury milk chocolate from London. And you're gonna love it. Without question, one of the few things I miss most from London: a decent bath and chocolate!"

"Oh, Annie. You deserve this." Edie was smiling, too, her eyes pleading. "We can't hope to repair the tear in your heart, but please let us at least do this for you?"

"Okay, you win." Annie undressed and slipped into the hot bath one inch at a time. Then she sank to her chin in steaming, fresh water, the pinnacle of indulgence. "I have to agree with you, Rachel, this is decadent. I could spend my whole morning in this tub."

"Here, try a little of this." Rachel handed her a jar. "It's called

Parisian shampoo. It has been wasting away in my trunk."

"I suppose my resident family of lice might not appreciate it, but I'm sure I will." Annie thought for a moment. "I'm already afraid most of my arithmetic bugs are struggling to find safe harbor."

"Wait till you taste the chocolate."

Annie smiled. For a moment at least, she would try to set aside her heartbreaking troubles. She'd languish in this luxurious bath, share conversation with friends, and appreciate nature's beauty. She felt clean for the first time in a long time.

"I've decided it's about time for a revitalization of my husband's good impressions of me," Rachel declared. "I'm dressing up on this, our last day in port."

"That'll be nice," Annie said softly, eyes closed to the world.

"I figure Gabriel deserves it, for he has seen me at my worst these past weeks." Rachel's nose crinkled. "Who knows what benefits that might bring?"

Annie remained silent, soaking up the ambiance and not wanting to think of such things.

"In fact, Annie, it would do you wonders to put on a nice dress. We can have our lunch in the village after we're done here. Just the three of us." Rachel turned and whispered with a gentle smile, "In hard times, I find anything that can make me feel pretty is worth its weight in gold."

"Hmm." Annie, her eyes still closed, wasn't really listening.

"It might just lift her spirits—don't you think, Edie?"

"This is enough for me!" Annie smiled gently, her arms on the edge of the tub.

"Nonsense!" Rachel turned to her. "People who *think* they know everything about fashion and its benefits to the soul are a great annoyance to those of us who actually do." She frowned. "I have your perfect dress for our luncheon."

Annie opened her eyes in confusion. "Oh no, Rachel, please don't?" She looked at Edie, clearly an accomplice in Rachel's clandestine scheme. Then she raised her brows and glanced at the dress hanging in the closet behind them. "I've never worn anything beautiful in my life. Your dress wouldn't fit anyway."

Outnumbered, Annie sank deeper into her tub, dipping below the waterline. When she broke the surface, Rachel caught her arm. "You will fit into my dress nicely," she whispered. "I only wish I could fit into the beautiful thing. Unfortunately, this voyage has stolen my voluptuous figure. I'm sure in time it will return. But I insist."

"If not for you, then do it for us," Edie added.

Annie turned to look at the simple but elegant lines of the dress hanging behind her. The sheer silken fabric with hidden seams shimmered softly in the light coming through the window. It was unpretentious but beautiful. "I don't know, Rachel; your beautiful things are wasted on me."

Rachel gave Annie a stern, caring look. "It is the least I can do for such a friend as you have become. You need to feel like the beautiful woman you are. That work of art complements the inner beauty you radiate to everyone around you."

"I only wish Thomas could see me in that way." As soon as the words had slipped from her mouth, Annie wished she could retrieve them. A woman had taken the place of that girl he'd first met. She was mother of two lost children now. And she wondered if he would ever fully acknowledge who she had become.

"This is for us, not our husbands," Rachel responded. "Although, they may be the lucky beneficiaries of our selfish desires!"

Edie reached out for Annie's hand, whispering in her ear, "I love you, sister. You really are lovely, inside and out—a remarkable woman." She smiled. "Thomas would be a fool not to recognize he is on the threshold of a great love affair—and my brother is no fool."

Chapter 11

⤜ • ⤛

THE *COLORADO* GLIDED INTO UPPER New York Harbor in the wee hours of a summer morning. The pearly lights of the city arced through the foggy darkness, a deafening quiet pervading the air. Below, in the sleepless bowels of this little ship, darkness likewise gave shape and sheen to the private imaginings of a hundred minds' eyes.

One by one, passengers came on deck to see their new homeland. The remains of the cool night air melted into the hazy light of daybreak, and through the fleeing mists, the gateway to America was unveiled. The City of New York!

"It is so beautiful," Annie whispered to Tom, tears coursing down her cheeks.

Everybody was crying as the American flag unfurled and flew resiliently from the ship's center mast in the early morning breeze. The sun reflecting off the textured surface of the bay sparkled like diamonds scattered upon glass in this new land of promise.

The brigantine *Colorado* pulled up to the dock at Castle Garden, a collection of dilapidated buildings soon to be replaced by a more modern Ellis Island. The mainsail was collapsed, the anchor chains groaned and clattered. For most, this sound was like the ravaged bones of Europe rattling one last time. They were released. Tom and Annie, like so many of the passengers, wept remembering all that had gone before, with visions of the opportunities that lay ahead.

Tom leaned against the railing of the little brig, Annie by his side. Both gazed upon the horizon of their new homeland.

"Annie, I may be a coal miner and you a butcher's helper, but in America, where anything is possible, someday our children can become wealthy engineers or builders in a city like this one. So, our grandchildren can become . . . sculptors, painters, or musicians."

"Yeah, so we can move in with 'em!" Annie smiled.

≽ • ≼

Tom, Annie, and the rest of the beleaguered immigrants stepped off the *Colorado* with hearts lodged in their throats. Gingerly they traversed the gangplank through the arched gateway into Castle Garden, the golden doorway into America. Most were full of hope tinged with anxious uncertainty. For not all were welcome; some would be casualties of the growing pains of this young nation.

Annie stood silent beside Tom in the long line of families, each waiting their turn for their fate to be decided in the examination center. She and her family had passed the all-important medical test. She saw Benjamin Dreyfus, his youngest son by his side, in the next line over. He had apparently failed the medical examination. She was only a few feet away when this father and son were ushered into the deportation area. She heard Benjamin tell the examiner, "I'm a tailor; my son's a student."

A frown crept onto the examiner's face. "I'm sorry, Mr. Dreyfus, but the doctor says you are very sick." He paused. "You may not enter our country."

Annie gasped.

"Are you willing to be separated?" asked the examiner. "Your son to stay here, and you to go back to Prussia?"

This aged father and his youngest son looked at each other. There was no emotion yet visible in the boy—the question came so suddenly that its implications had not settled into understanding.

Annie followed Benjamin's eyes to his eldest son, waiting for them just a few steps away at the building's kissing post, the scene of happy reunions. She looked to the son's wife, and all the rest of his family, including Benjamin's four grandchildren, whom he'd never met. They were all smiling, clearly excited, waiting. Benjamin answered the examiner. "Of course! This is the land of promise, is it not? The land Mr. Lincoln has called the last best hope of man on earth." Benjamin paused as he looked upon his youngest son, and then again, his eldest with his beautiful family. "How could I deny my son these blessings?"

For a moment, Annie locked eyes with Benjamin in desperate understanding. Her heart sank. Her voice caught in her throat for this father she had come to so greatly admire. His words from weeks before echoed in her mind: "I would do anything for my family."

"Nooo!" Annie screamed, stepping out of line to come to Benjamin's aid. "You can't do this." But Tom grabbed her arm, pulling her back.

"Annie, it's not your business." Tom held her tight while everyone around them looked on in curiosity. "Do you want them to send us back too?"

Annie struggled, her eyes still locked with Benjamin's as he was being ushered away to almost certain death. He raised his hand, and in a solemn whisper, mouthed, "Family first!"

The one shall be taken . . . the other left behind, Annie thought, recalling the words from scripture. This was Benjamin Dreyfus's judgment day. He would never know that his niece, poetess Emma

Lazarus, would someday be immortalized for her words written on the bottom of the Statue of Liberty: "Give me your tired, your poor, your huddled masses yearning to breathe free, the wretched refuse of your teeming shore, send these, the homeless, tempest-tost to me."

※ · ※

Tom and Annie stepped out of the immigration center into a warm summer afternoon and a raucous, shoulder-to-shoulder crowd on the wharf. They were greeted with an outstretched hand, an infectious smile, and a "Welcome to America."

New York City was filled with immigrants from all over the world, there to make a new life for themselves and their families—some honestly, and others under somewhat less scrupulous circumstances. The shock of this new land was magnified by the city itself—the pumping heart of capitalism, where the shackles had been thrown off, men and women were masters of their own lives, government the servant to the human spirit.

Tom was captivated by the sights, sounds, bustling industry, and commerce of every kind in this burgeoning city, by the dark and nameless alleyways of the Manhattan tenements. This city was the symbol of America's resurrection from the devastation of civil war. Construction was flourishing everywhere; tall buildings rose out of the ground, and an elevated railway was under construction. Grand Central Station, Madison Square Garden, and Greenwich Village sat near Central Park. The ingenious caissons of Brooklyn's suspension bridge were being sunk. And the Statue of Liberty, with its invitation to all the world, was on sculptor Bartholdi's drawing board.

Tom stood in awe, witness to the fruits of freedom in this new land of architectural wonders, music, and arts that would transform New York City into the urban center of the Gilded Age. He could feel the vibrant rumble and hear the murmuring of the beast of industry and smell and taste in the air foods from all around the world. As far as his eye could reach, everything was in motion.

Human struggle—massed, stacked, and multiplied. New York City's youthful generation of Rockefeller, J. P. Morgan, Vanderbilt, Carnegie, and Edison were all shifting their careers into full gear to become the world's wealthiest self-made titans of industry. And in the arts, Walt Whitman, Ralph Waldo Emerson, Mark Twain, and Emily Dickinson all called New York City home, and they were producing their very best work.

Across the East River, chimneys as tall as the tallest of buildings seemed to touch the very sky, belching and pulsing from the dark heart of the city. Thick columns of oily soot, black as coal, rose high into the air. Curling clouds of smoke uniting into ashen rivers streamed west on the sea breeze, away from the city toward the vast landscape of open America beyond.

With his feet wide apart, his hands on his hips, Tom took in a deep breath and blew it out. "Doesn't look much like our village, does it?" He felt young, full of life, all his senses triggered by the intoxication of the city—the sights, sounds, and smells—leaving him to think he could almost taste the adventure that was about to unfold.

Annie, eyes round, was stunned silent by the enormity of it all. They could now be counted as two of the courageous few who had come to this unknown land where the desperate, hardy, and adventurous would risk it all, rising or falling based on their own self-determination, their cunning wit, and the strength of their arms. This was a new nation, not of birthright, but of choice. This was a country where men and women would not be judged by their parentage, aristocratic lineage, religion, or native language, but by the content of their character.

"Never seen anything like it!" Gabriel muttered.

"Hmm." Tom studied him, noting even London aristocrats were overwhelmed by New York City.

"Our thought," Tom shared, "is to catch a steamer up the Hudson River to Albany. A ferry to Niagara Falls, Chicago by rail, a steamboat down the Mississippi to Nebraska to catch the railway under construction west to Wyoming. Our last leg, a wagon train to California, getting off at Virginia City to rendezvous with you by early autumn."

"Are you suggesting we join your family going west?" Rachel asked.

"I thought you'd be traveling first class and we . . ." Tom could see Annie was crestfallen.

Andrew turned to Gabriel. "Family would have my head on a platter if we didn't ask."

"Fair enough!" Gabriel replied. "What if we chip in our extra per diem?"

"Great!"

All seemed to agree to the Stones joining them going west, except for a defeated Tom, who remained silent.

The first three vessels in the impressive array of steamboats, ferries, and lacy sailboats were booked and ready to set forth. But when the group reached a hotel-size steamboat with an enormous paddle wheel, a sailor standing at an on-deck podium called out.

"Hello, folks, where're ya headin'?" The sailor engaged them with a congenial tip of his hat. The *Lexington*, a gaudy affair, looked like a four-layer wedding cake. On all sides, thin white columns spread along the stacked decks to hold up a porch covered with a blue-and-white awning.

"California!" Tom called up from the dock. "Eventually," he whispered to himself.

"Well, you're in luck. We've got a few spots left to get you folks as far as Albany." With a smile, the sailor motioned for Tom to come aboard and begin the requisite haggling over a group fare for the passage upriver. While Tom and Gabriel negotiated, Joey and Andrew gathered up the trunks and belongings.

"California?" The voice came from a beautiful lady in a white summer dress leaning over the railing four stories up, gazing with interest at the busy scene on the docks. "Where're you coming from?" she questioned through cupped hands, seeming uninhibited in her interruption.

"England, ma'am," Annie called back.

Annie and Rachel lifted their skirts to board the garish *Lexington*. Edie and the children followed close behind as the beautiful lady made her way down and over to introduce herself.

"Hello, I'm Mrs. Constance Cohen, and this is my friend Josephine Stephenson," she said, gesturing to her equally elegant companion.

A short but entertaining conversation ensued, where all the women found interests in common and soon were laughing and flattering one another. The two Americans, enthralled by the immigration story, quickly became fast friends with these English women, as only curious and interesting women can.

"You must be hungry?" Constance inquired. "We would be pleased if you folks would join us upstairs for lunch." She smiled. "We'd love to hear more of your adventures, your plans, and lunch would be on us—right, Josephine?"

"Absolutely!"

Rachel looked at Annie, and Annie at Edith. All three were clearly eager to accept, for even Rachel had not seen such luxury as she spied on the upper decks of this floating casino.

"We would be delighted!" Rachel turned to appeal to Gabriel. "We're hungry and—"

Gabriel cut her off. "We have all the arrangements still to be made, our baggage to bring on board and stored in our steerage quarters." He turned back to his haggling but then paused, catching himself, seeming to remember to tread cautiously with his wife. "Rachel, this is not our decision."

"You don't want to leave these fine ladies hungry and cranky, do you, honey?" Rachel pointed to Annie, Edie, and the children with a sly smile. "It would make for an appalling afternoon for you gentlemen and an even worse evening. And besides, you're not paying."

Catching on, Tom chimed in. "There's ten of us," he said, his cynical brows curling down. He didn't want to be bought, paid for, and put on display as a novelty for a bunch of rich folks to gawk at. "It's not possible!" he concluded with finality.

"I'll tell you what, gentlemen," Constance continued. "You stay here and take care of all the lodging arrangements, and Josephine and I will take Annie, Edith, Rachel, and the children with us. When you're done with your business, you can join us. And we'd be thrilled to make arrangements for the children's entertainment while we talk. How does that sound?"

Tom, irritated at being bullied by American aristocrats for their afternoon entertainment, curtly responded, "I don't think so, but thank you." He looked at the other two men for confirmation. But they seemed to have recognized the argument was lost before it began.

"This is how we do it here in America," Josephine interjected. "I don't see you gentlemen have a choice. We have a saying in this country: 'Happy wife, happy life.' Besides, if you don't agree, Constance will pester you until you do! I can tell you from experience, it is a battle you gentlemen can't win!"

Rachel issued the coup de grâce. "Annie and Edie need the break from the children, and these fine ladies are making that possible at no expense to you. It's an offer you can't refuse, gentlemen!"

Tom frowned angrily at Annie, who had kept silent through the entire affair. He could see the negotiations had been concluded, a settlement reached, and the husbands were expected to shrug their shoulders in defeat. There seemed no avenue of retreat left to him. In irritation, he turned away from the argument without further word.

Gabriel nodded to Rachel, ratifying the treaty. "If I didn't say yes, I'd have hell to pay."

This only further irritated Tom. "Maybe we should let them negotiate our boat passage."

Chapter 12

☙ • ❧

AT THE DOORWAY TO THE first-class dining room, Constance and Josephine stood aside to let their guests take in the expanse of white linen, glistening silverware, elaborate place settings, and sparkling glasses—three for each setting. Summer flowers were everywhere in the grand Crystal Ballroom dining area. Windows opened onto views of men in gray suits and well-dressed ladies with parasols lounging on the sundeck.

Annie was overwhelmed, but she didn't miss the sign on the door: "WHITES ONLY." She had seen those signs in New York City, at restaurants, hotels, and markets. She felt a knot of disappointment in her stomach.

Before she knew what was happening, Annie was whisked into the dining room with the rest of the party, where waiters fussed about rearranging tables and resetting them to accommodate the enlarged party. The two American women's waiting husbands began asking questions, clearly prepared to enjoy the afternoon's entertainment.

Annie picked up a menu, which was folded and decorated with blue, pink, and soft salmon flowers painted on the cover. She shared it with Rachel and Edie, and they perused the staggering list of dishes, almost none of which the cadre of foreigners had even heard of.

"They have all this food on board?" Rachel asked.

"Just waiting for you to order it." Constance relished the astonishment on the faces of her guests.

Annie leaned over to Rachel to whisper, "We can't ask them to pay for this. It must cost a fortune."

Constance was quick to interrupt. "Ladies, as promised, you're our guests. In return, you must promise to regale us with your adventures."

While the waiters continued their reorganization efforts, the American women turned their attention to the children. Fascinated by their accents, they listened enthralled to Abigail and Elizabeth's story of their harrowing experience across the Atlantic, including the near death of little Tommy.

"You are very bright young ladies! How old are you?"

"Twelve, going on thirteen," Abigail replied, exchanging smiles with Elizabeth.

"Ah, yes." The fashionably dressed Josephine leaned toward Edie and Rachel, whispering, "Your children are charming."

Constance smiled, brushing an admiring hand over Abby's red hair, then sprang into action. "All right, everyone, time to ante up. I have one dollar to contribute toward these two beautiful young ladies for their impending thirteenth birthdays. Ladies, these girls and their younger charges must go get some treats while the rest of us have a leisurely lunch. That is, of course, if it's okay with Edith and Rachel?" Waiting only a moment for a nod of confirmation, Constance began collecting money.

She handed half the five dollars collected to each girl. "Now, this is just for you. It's not to be spent on anything but fun for you and the rest of your charges."

"Oh, thank you so much," both Abigail and Elizabeth gushed in sync. "We will use it wisely."

"Wisely is not requisite." Josephine winked. "In fact, the order of the day is to just have fun!"

With that, the children scampered off, shouting, "Thank you!" over their shoulders. Shaved ice, popcorn, frankfurters, and candy awaited them, as did an exploration of the wonderous first-class surroundings on the beautiful fairyland steamboat with its giant paddle wheel and novel sights just begging to be explored.

≻ • ≺

Tom, Andrew, Gabriel, and Joey arrived, and introductions were made all around. Everyone took their places at the tables, the women grouped together in a covey to carry on their conversation. The American contingent leaned in, eager to hear the story of these immigrants: England, coal mining, and brushes with death on their voyage.

The chief steward, a stately black man with white hair, quietly bent over Annie's shoulder to take her order.

"And what would madam desire?"

Annie was powerless to choose from the vast menu, looking up at her waiter in desperate bewilderment, her eyes wide with questions. Not wanting to commit some act of incivility through ignorance of what seemed common knowledge at this table, she said nothing.

The steward hesitated just long enough to be polite, then whispered, "May I suggest the terrine of duck? It is superb the way our chef prepares it."

"Oh, I love duck," Annie cried in delight, relieved she didn't have to make the decision herself. "That's what I'll have." Then she whispered back, "At least I know what a duck is."

Turning to Rachel, she whispered in her ear, "My cousin Emma used to tell me, 'When in doubt, just look intelligent.'"

That brought a smile.

Annie allowed the steward to fill in the rest of the order, including unusual vegetables, soup, and mashed potatoes with gravy, none of which she had eaten before. "Would madam be interested in a terrine of pâté de jour hors d'oeuvre?" he asked.

Annie shot him another blank look.

Constance, seeing Annie's confusion, passed over a sample on a fork.

"Oh . . . just a bit of chopped liver on a cracker." Annie's eyebrows raised and she smiled. "I thought maybe this handsome man was making advances in French!"

Constance and Josephine took in the whole affair in amused delight, pleased that they could introduce their new friends to the best of what their new country had to offer.

Annie couldn't help but watch the sophisticated black waiter, weaving through the guests, seen but not seen, as he deftly went about his work with grace. She thought it strange that he was permitted to serve her but for the warm copper color of his skin would never be allowed to dine with her.

Mr. Cohen, a diminutive, elderly Jewish financier with intelligent eyes, had been quietly observing Annie's interaction. He leaned over and whispered, "As the renowned Fredrick Douglass has put it, now that slavery has been abolished, the real work begins to liberate the human spirit and tame our own natural proclivity toward self-centered prejudice."

"Hmm." She felt a tinge of sadness. Clearly all was not right in Camelot.

"The array of food is wonderful." Gabriel beamed. "There is nothing like this even in London's finest restaurants."

Tom glowered at Gabriel. He could feel the anger rising. *London's finest restaurants. What does he know about the "array of food" for the families working in his father's sweatshops?* he thought. Match girls suffering from malnutrition. Young mothers working fourteen-hour days for a pittance, and when they become disabled under the horrific working conditions, their children were left to starve in the streets. Bloated bellies, yellow pallor, drooping shoulders, and heartbreaking hopelessness in their eyes. And when the match girls died, as most did, including Lydia, their loved ones were left behind to watch in horror.

After the rest of the orders were taken and everyone was sipping their drinks, the other members of the party began with questions. "What made you decide to emigrate to America? Why out in the Wild West, Mr. Wright?" asked Mr. Stephenson, a tall, middle-aged, well-fed New York City banker.

Tom cleared his throat, a sober expression on his face. "I've wanted to come to America my entire life. Make my own way, living in fresh air, growing my own food, on my own land with crystal-clean water. Maybe California, where they've got gold in the creeks." He lost himself for a moment in the telling, but then his eyes narrowed as he looked around the table. "Beholden to no one."

"Dear God, when I left home last week," offered Mr. Stephenson, "I fancied I was taking this tremendous journey to another land, all the way upstate to Niagara Falls. These folks are planning to go all the way to the Wild West to pan for gold."

All laughed. "Do you know how far that is?" Mr. Stephenson added.

"About twice the distance across all of Europe," Annie replied. "When we left our village in Yorkshire to sail across the Atlantic, no one in our family had been more than twenty-five miles from home. Except in books, of course!"

"Why America?" Josephine asked. "Why not another part of Europe, Canada, Australia?"

"It seems most everyone in Europe wants to come to here,"

Annie responded. "Look at you fine ladies and gentlemen, speaking to us without airs, polite, interested and making us feel welcome." Annie paused for impact. "This would never happen in Europe."

The Americans smiled in their delight.

"In England, proper ladies and gentlemen of your station might let us serve you, but certainly not dine with you." Annie frowned, watching Tom's cold eyes looking on his future employer. "That alone is unique in all the world!"

"I'll take that as a compliment," Constance chimed in. "Your willingness to give up everything to make an entirely new life here in an unknown land shows real character."

Mr. Stephenson added, "For most of us, our families have been here a generation or more. My family's from Denmark, Josephine's from France, Mr. and Mrs. Cohen from Prussia and Belgium."

"After a generation as citizens, we've all joined America's great melting pot with different religions and cultures," said Josephine. "No other country in the world can say that."

"What America has invented that makes us different from all other societies," Mr. Cohen interjected, "is a government intent on individual liberty for all peoples, regardless of national origin! It's a way to channel individual self-interest for the benefit of all. Frankly, we seldom have an opportunity to speak candidly with newly arrived immigrants like yourselves, the lifeblood of this American experiment."

"My brother George was the first to come," said Tom. "Just before the Civil War." He frowned. "Fascinated by his stories of life across the ocean, we sat in front of the fire in our ten-by-twelve-foot miner's shanty, my mam Martha reading us his war letters—terrifying, but inspiring."

"Where is George now?" Constance asked.

"Don't know. He spent some time at the *Chicago Tribune*." Tom looked back at Constance. "Hoping I might find out more when we pass through there later this week. We lost contact with him."

"I'm so sorry," Constance offered.

"Hmm." Tom was momentarily lost in remembrance.

"We sometimes forget the great sacrifices people around the world make to come here," Constance added. "My family came to escape Jewish persecution in Europe before I was born. My husband was an orphaned immigrant." She glanced at him. "His family killed in Prussia."

Annie couldn't help but think of her friend Benjamin Dreyfus.

Tom nodded. "It's more difficult for some than others. Trading in our old lives owned by upper-class aristocrats for hope in a better life here." He sighed. "Not a bad trade."

Constance nodded.

"They tried that aristocratic rule over here." Mr. Stephenson chuckled. "It didn't take. But it took a revolution to get rid of those bloody rascals." He smiled. "Thomas Jefferson in his declaration argued we're all equal under the eyes of God, and we'd like to keep it that way."

"There is no question, freedom is intoxicating," Andrew said. "It's a draw that folks like us all around the world find hard to resist. No matter where we come from."

"Came here to get away from those greedy aristocrats." Tom glanced again at an uncomfortable Gabriel.

Mr. Cohen smiled. "The world runs on greed, Tom. We all pursue our own self-interest."

"That's why we've come to America," Tom countered, cold irritation in his eyes, remembering how he, his mam, and the rest of his family had struggled just to survive. To escape greedy, grasping, clawing aristocrats who wanted it all and were willing to grind families like theirs into the ground to get it. "I've come here to get my own, to make my own way, no matter what it takes."

Mr. Cohen looked at Tom openly. "And that's not being greedy?" He gave Tom a moment for the question to sink in. "What is greed, Tom? Of course, none of us sitting around this table want to consider ourselves greedy. It's always the other guy. But aren't you, like the rest of us, seeking your own self-interest?" He paused again and then turned Tom's own words against him. "Not so unlike the aristocrat in Europe, you have come to America to seek your fortune, your own land, gold in the creeks. Your greedy self-interest."

Tom bit his lip, forced to ponder Mr. Cohen's point.

"But can't we have a government that helps the poor?" Edie asked, intervening to calm the harsh edge to the discussion. "The less fortunate? Rather than being a shill for the wealthy?" She caught the glint in her brother's eyes. "To ensure the virtuous get their fair share."

"Aren't you being a bit naïve, Edie?" Mr. Cohen inquired. "Where do we find these angels in government who are willing to sacrifice their own self-interests for the betterment of the virtuous? Is political self-interest, greed for power if you will, more noble than economic self-interest?" He paused. "I wouldn't even trust you to make the decisions for my family."

Some at the table laughed, uncomfortable at the turn of the conversation but fascinated by Mr. Cohen's argument.

"Limited government is what our founding fathers had in mind; let the individual be master of his own fate and allow free trade amongst all people without preference, as long as the two parties exchanging goods reach a mutual agreement," Mr. Stephenson interjected. "Capitalism is the freedom to pursue each man's own personal interest, greed if you will. It is a system that has made life better for all of us here."

Tom, still brooding, grew surly. "Call it what you want. All I know is I will become successful here. I've come too far, overcome too much, not to be." His eyes ablaze, face flushed, he glanced around the table at Mr. Cohen, Mr. Stephenson, the others, again settling on Gabriel. "And I don't need anyone else to get me there." He paused, his breathing slow, lips tight, eyes narrowed. "I suspect the West is a place where the strong survive and the weak are crushed underfoot. I'll make my own luck. Hack my life out of the wilderness with the strength of my back, if necessary. Using my wits and my own two arms."

"Rather brutally put, Mr. Wright," responded Mr. Cohen, coolly. "But you know—"

"The magnanimous founding fathers. Hmm!" Tom interrupted. "If they cared so much about the rest of the world, they wouldn't have declared their independence from it."

"You know," Mr. Cohen continued with a smile, "in some ways I envy you, Tom. Some men are born into it. Raised their whole life for success, feel entitled, expecting the sweetness of illusion rather than the harshness of reality."

Around the table, the smiles had faded. All sat tense, closely following the conversation.

"But you, Tom, like so many other immigrants—like Ishmael of old in the Torah—have no other choice but to succeed. That's an asset here."

Tom's eyes blazed defensive. "I don't plan to concern myself with other people's business. We've enough trouble with our own, trying to keep our boat afloat." He fidgeted, not wanting to look at either the Cohens or Annie. "Look out for myself and let others do the same. Dump overboard those cultural niceties, until I can afford the luxury."

Constance Cohen locked eyes with Tom, who sat across from her. "I might warn you, Mr. Wright, it is sometimes hard to salvage jettisoned cargo, and if it is retrieved, it's usually irreparably damaged." She smiled, cool and controlled. "And I fear, if you're not careful, when you can afford to dredge up what you have thrown overboard . . . those niceties, as you call them—kindness, consideration for your fellow man, your family—you might find they have grown a bit soggy after swimming with the fishes."

All were quiet. Tom sat looking down at his hands stretched out in front of him on the table. Frowning with tight lips, he pushed back his temper as Annie put a calming hand over his.

Constance continued with a wry smile. "You might have noticed on our coinage the words *liberty, in God we trust,* and *e pluribus unum.* It's called the American trinity. These supremely important values are also displayed prominently in the halls of Congress. Do you know what Pythagoras's Latin phrase, *e pluribus unum,* means?" she asked politely.

"No idea."

"America's strength, unlike any other nation in the world, comes from accepting all peoples of good faith as citizens, no matter their origin," she answered without dropping her gaze. "As our beloved President Lincoln shared, when each person loves and accepts the other as much as himself, it makes—out of the many individuals—one powerful nation."

Tom stared at her silently as everyone waited for her to drive home her point.

"Mr. Wright, I believe in my heart you will find your land and probably financial success, too, but may I caution you, sir: If you don't take the time to listen to the better angels of your nature on your climb to the top, to reach down and help others up that ladder of success along your way, you may find it rather lonely up there."

All sat uncomfortably quiet.

"Right, then!" Mr. Stephenson cried, raising his glass in a toast to ease the tension. "To our travelers west." His eyes brightened when the whole table enthusiastically raised their glasses to his. The smiles returned. "Welcome to America. Where not even the majority rules. Where you're free to shape your own life without other folks sticking their noses into your business." He laughed. "And as Mr. Jefferson put it, when the gov'ment gets too big for its britches and starts tellin' us what to think and what to do with our lives, it's time for another revolution."

The food arrived, dispelling the last of the uneasy feelings.

"Oh my goodness," Annie whispered into Tom's ear, astounded by such seductive abundance. The duck was delivered resting in its dish, with asparagus, potatoes, fresh fruit, breads, and jellies.

"We who have been born in this country all need to spend time with immigrant families like yours." Mr. Cohen grinned at his new friends from abroad. "You make us appreciate how much we have to be thankful for."

"Thank you all." Annie nodded. "It certainly has been a delightful time. A welcome respite for us."

"Mr. Wright, I've thoroughly enjoyed our conversation," said Mr. Stephenson. "You know, our bank has done quite a bit of business with the *Chicago Tribune*. I am personal friends with the editor. I'll send Mr. Dinkins a telegram. With a little luck, he can help you find out about your brother."

"Thank you." Tom nodded his appreciation.

⁕ • ⁕

At the end of a long evening, most headed off to bed. The hosts to their first-class accommodations, and the rest down the stairs to steerage quarters.

Tom and Annie decided to take in a little air on the stunning summer night before retiring. They stepped out onto the terrace overlooking the river far below. The enchanting full moon was shining bright over the wide expanse of water. Both stood transfixed at the end of the long shimmering trail left by the luminescent orb, like sparkling glints of light on broken glass.

"Breathtaking!" Annie whispered in quiet reverence. "It seems as though I could almost reach out and touch it."

"Hmm . . . It is beautiful!" But Tom was lost in thought.

"I've never had such an incredible dinner in all my life."

Stored dormant in the dark corners of Tom's mind, a vision of a dinner on another warm summer's evening beckoned. A long-ago meal on another river, in another time and place. Feeling guilty, he tried to push aside the memory, but it remained resistant. The breathtaking beauty of it. Lydia had taken him to her secret place in the forbidden forest. She'd spread out a picnic blanket on the bank of the placid River Rother, lit a prepared campfire, and cooked an unforgettable meal over the open fire—freshly caught trout covered in herbs and spices, wild onion and mushroom sauce, turnip greens and mashed potatoes. And as dessert, wild raspberries and fresh cream. He could still taste the sweet tartness that had exploded across his tongue.

On that enchanting evening when Tom was young and in love, Lydia had been breathtakingly beautiful. He felt a twinge of guilt as he recalled sitting with her in the verdant meadow filled with the fragrance of wildflowers. They'd eaten until they could eat no more. Then they lay back on their blanket as the moon rose and lilac and yellow-gold tulips began to close for the night. The sun dipped behind the rolling hills of scattered oak, seamless birch, and evergreens. The underside of clouds overhead blazed in crimson, orange, and gold. Those colors were mirrored upon the swirling surface of the gently flowing river to the music of the water's rushing, the only sound that broke the silence on that warm summer evening.

Even with all its glitter of polished silverware, fine china from London, and French cuisine from the *Lexington*'s kitchen, tonight's dinner had paled by comparison.

"Thomas, do you think we should?"

Tom broke from his reverie. "I'm so sorry, Annie. Do you think we should what?"

"Do you think we should go down to settle in before it gets too late?"

"Oh . . . Oh, yes. Of course, you're right."

Chapter 13

⇝ • ⇜

BY EARLY THE NEXT MORNING, the *Lexington* was well up the Hudson River on its way to Albany. Tom and Annie stood next to Mr. and Mrs. Cohen at the railing, soaking in the sights, sounds, and smells of the majestic river winding through the wilderness of this new land.

"I've heard New York is the richest state in the country," remarked Annie.

"It is, but Manhattan holds its only financial wealth," explained Mr. Cohen. "Up the Hudson, the riches are far different. To the east lies the uninhabited forests of the Catskills, raw wilderness with trees coming right to the shoreline. On the west are the wild Taconic Mountains, green meadows, the finest homes in all of New York. In my mind this is the richest part of the state, maybe the entire country."

"Early mornings like these in late summer are beautiful in most every part of this country," Constance offered, "but those of the Hudson in upstate New York are preeminently so. Nothing can match the vast wilderness, the beauty of the sky nor sweet smell of evergreens in this temperate climate. No charm of scenery can surpass the world through which we are now sailing on this cool, crisp morning."

The wide, reflective sandbars stretched for miles, bathed in the almost imperceptible swirling of the glassy blue-green water. Still and blissful, the beauty of the river seemed to complement the silence of the ancient virgin forests that the ax had not yet despoiled. Only the occasional flocks of wild geese, swans, sandhill cranes, and pelicans stocking the shorelines pierced the quiet. The earth and the crisp blue sky above rendered the broad Hudson the thread of life stitching through this great land, bringing it all together. To Annie, all of it was magnificent.

"Is that West Point?" Annie pointed to the structures jutting out into the river. "Where Washington beat back our British forces?"

"It is," Mr. Cohen answered.

"How do you know that?" Tom whispered in her ear, marveling as the steamboat slid past the scene of infamy.

"I told you, silly, I lived a boring life before you—I read a lot and tried never to miss a good chance to shut up and listen." Annie snickered.

"It seems every day I discover new and interesting things about you," he said in admiration mixed with a twinge of unexpected guilt. "You're amazing!"

"It's always been my intention to astonish you, sir!"

⁌ • ⁍

After bidding farewell to their generous new friends in Albany, Tom, Annie, and the rest of their contingent boarded the Great Western Railroad to Chicago, Illinois. Arriving on a Monday morning, Tom had just enough time for a quick bath and shave before putting on his Sunday best and hightailing it downtown to meet Mr. Dinkins for lunch at the Tremont House Hotel, across the street from the *Chicago Tribune*. There was only a brief window before the next leg of the family's journey, which involved catching the train to Quincy to board a steamer down the mighty Mississippi, bound for Florence, Nebraska.

"Welcome, Mr. Wright, it's a pleasure to meet you." Mr. Dinkins reached out to shake Tom's hand. "Mr. Stephenson tells me you have quite an interest in Abraham Lincoln. So, I thought it might interest you to see the Tremont. Mr. Lincoln and Stephen Douglas started their Senate campaigns here with a three-day debate. And Lincoln and his family were frequent visitors here while he was president. His wife Mary and her family stayed for a month after President Lincoln's assassination."

"Thank you, sir. Have to tell my wife Annie." Tom paused, in awe of the hotel and the crush of impressive buildings surrounding it. "Chicago seems a city on the move."

"Some say Chicago became the center of American values after the great war. The home of rugged individualism and modern industry, where almost anything is possible. We're already planning the Chicago World's Fair two years from now—it will shock and amaze."

"I bet it will!"

Mr. Dinkins took a moment to look at Tom as they waited to be seated for lunch. "Mr. Wright, tell me, what can I do for you?"

Tom cleared his throat. "Hoping you might be able to shed some light on the mystery of my brother's whereabouts?"

"Mr. Stephenson told me the sad news about George's disappearance. We all grew to like George while he was with us. He had the makings of a fine journalist," Mr. Dinkins offered. "George had more energy and thirst for adventure than any two of my other young reporters. We were sorry to see him go, but George was a restless soul. I've found when a young man like George gets the bug for adventure, it's hard to hold him down."

"Sounds like George. We looked forward to his letters." Tom

smiled. "Always the adventuresome one in the family."

"A born newspaperman. The firing of cannons on Fort Sumter happened just a month after he headed west. My guess, he would have been right in the thick of things had he stayed."

"Do you have any idea where he might have gone from here?" Tom inquired.

"He headed out west from here—an exciting adventure after the Gold Rush. He was fascinated by the transcontinental railway and wanted to be a part of it. That's all we know."

"Anyone I might talk to who might know more?"

"I'm sorry, son. I wish I could be more helpful. I tried to ask around, but what I have told you is all I could find out. Like so many, as far as anyone knows, he was swallowed up by the vast wildlands west of the Mississippi."

Tom reached out and shook Mr. Dinkins's hand. "Thank you for your help," Tom said, disappointed. "And for lunch. It's a beautiful hotel. My wife will be sorely disappointed she missed it."

"Godspeed and good luck, son!"

Chapter 14

⊱ • ⊰

Tom and his traveling companions stepped into Union Pacific's Florence, Nebraska, train station expecting a comfortable ride on the transcontinental railway to Benton, Wyoming—the end of the uncompleted line. Hurtling down the track at nearly thirty-five miles per hour, they marveled at the passing Platte River through plate glass windows. The landscape was mostly open prairie filled with wild sunflowers skirting the heavens as far as the eye could see. A world without feature, an unbroken horizon of empty sky.

"The millennial marvel," said the gentleman sitting in the aisle seat next to Tom. "It lives up to its name, doesn't it?" The tall, middle-aged man was wearing a big Stetson hat, a red flannel shirt with studded buttons, rugged pants, and cowboy boots. His leathery face was tanned below his hat line from long hours in the sun.

"It certainly is a marvel," Tom answered.

"For decades folks have drug barges, handcarts, wagons, and rode mules over these prairies, crossin' rivers, mountains, through the snow, ice, blazin' summers, in sickness and near starvation fightin' Indians and wild animals ta get ta the California gold fields. Now they tell me when finished, this transcontinental can make the entire three thousand miles from New York City to San Francisco in a week."

"Near impossible to imagine!" Tom shrugged, raising his brows. "Where you heading?"

"Benton, then on to Fort Laramie."

"Business there?"

"Yup. Rancher from Abilene, Texas. Name's John Meyers."

"Tom Wright." Pointing to the window seat, he said, "My wife Annie."

John Meyers tipped his big Stetson hat. "Nice ta meet ya folks."

"We're on our way to Benton ourselves. To catch a wagon train west," Tom offered. "Long way from home, aren't you, Mr. Meyers?"

"Have a contract with the gov'ment in Washington, DC, ta deliver longhorns ta the US Cavalry."

"Longhorns?" Annie asked.

"I suppose with those accents you folks aren't from around these parts." The cowboy chuckled. "Beef cows. Just completed a cattle drive—Abilene to Fort Laramie."

"You must know quite a bit about this area?"

"A bit. I have a lot of cattle to deliver and men depending on me, including my son, who is ramrodding this outfit through Indian territory. I'm meetin' up with the general ta settle up and arrange another drive in the spring."

"Only in America," Annie reasoned. "You must have a big ranch if you came all the way to Washington, DC, to sell cows."

"Cattle!" the cowboy qualified. "Thirty thousand acres."

"Wow!" Eyes wide, Tom put his hands on the top of his head. "Twice the size of Lord Fitzwilliam's entire estate."

"We do things big in Texas."

"That's an understatement."

"Should be pretty busy in Benton this week," Mr. Meyers added.

"Oh, why's that?"

"Soon-ta-be president Ulysses S. Grant, General Sherman, Doc

Durant, and a bunch more fellas headin' to Benton City. Most of 'em on the train right behind us. Course they gots a whole cavalry escort on board."

"Why Benton?" asked Tom with a frown.

"They're meetin' Brigham Young and the folks comin' east from the Central Pacific at Fort Laramie to talk about the progress of the railroad."

"What does Brigham Young have to do with it?"

"Railway alignment negotiations, I hear." Mr. Meyers paused. "It seems wherever Doc Durant is, there's always a bit o' trouble. A New York City slicker, and as I hear it, he's all hat and no cattle when it comes to keepin' his word."

"What do you mean?"

"The two railroads are joinin' up near Salt Lake City. The Central Pacific coming from Sacramento and the Union Pacific from the east in a race to the finish line. There's a lot of strong-minded folks vyin' for a lot of money, land, and power. It's the American way."

"Sounds like Benton's going to be a busy place."

"Always, but with a future president and all them prideful folks, I'm sure it'll hold up its reputation as a Hell on Wheels town."

"A Hell on Wheels town?" Annie chimed in.

"Benton, a town of three thousand souls, was set up in a week, just two months ago. It was even before the railroad arrived. Canvas shebangs, big tents full of shufflin' cards and rattlin' dice to the sound of hurdy-gurdies, banjos, shouts, and mingling of glasses. All tryin' to drink themselves six feet under before turnin' thirty," Mr. Meyers lamented with tight lips and a look of disgust.

"Don't they have lawmen?" asked Annie.

"The only law in Benton is the barrel of the pistol and blade of the bowie knife," Mr. Meyers sneered as he sat watching the spellbound faces of his new friends. "They elected a mayor last June to civilize the place, but I hear tell someone shot 'im dead."

"Doesn't sound like a place I want to raise my family." Annie chuckled.

"Hardly!" Meyers laughed. "Most came to the work fresh off the battlefields—Southerners and Northerners alike. Young, hostile, hard-drinkin', fightin' men, bent on continuin' their destruction to the very end. Benton, like most all Hell on Wheels towns, will last as long as the workin' men are there. Not a moment longer, leavin' nothin' behind but a few tin cans and a whole lot of unmarked graves."

⇾ • ⇽

Abigail was the first to see the Shoshoni war party appear along the ridgeline—dozens of them. They spurred their painted ponies into a dead run and rushed across the prairie like waves rolling and crashing toward the shore.

"Here they come!" Abby said in wonder. "Look at 'em!"

Both girls stared transfixed out the window. Elizabeth, her eyes wide, was fearful the Shoshoni would burst through the glass at any moment, and she turned away. But not Abigail—she was enthralled and couldn't take her eyes off them.

Most of the passengers crushed up against the west-side windows to get a better look. There was more than a bit of fear in their eyes, too, yet there was a curious awe. It was an incredible sight: the war party racing alongside the speeding train.

"Look at 'em ride, Elizabeth," Abby said raptly. "Like the wind."

Elizabeth, in nervous astonishment, saw the Shoshoni's powerful arms, rippling chests, and naked thighs moving in complete sync with their ponies. "I don't like them!"

"Well, I think they're fascinating!"

It was clear to all on board these were true horsemen. At the forefront of the war party rode the chief, resplendent in a costume so foreign to many of the passengers that their mouths hung open. Powerful, terrifying, yet magnificent with head feathers trailing in the wind, strings of beads around his neck, long strands of elk bones falling from his temples, and a breastplate with beaded furs.

Behind him the braves rode, fierce and frightening, lances or guns held ready by their sides. They appeared to be on a serious mission, still keeping pace with the train, which was now speeding at forty miles per hour. The train surged even faster, belching heavy black smoke from its stack.

Abby, lost in the fascination of it all, held tight to Elizabeth's arm with one hand, her other flat against the windowpane, her face alight.

"They're every bit as magnificent as the penny novelettes say they are," Abby shouted out, lost in the enthusiasm of it all. "I can't pull my eyes off them."

Elizabeth turned to her best friend. "They look ferocious!"

"But handsome, don't you think?"

"No! Can't we go any faster?" Elizabeth closed her eyes and held her hands over her ears; she was frantic. "I don't want any part of them."

The train was pulling away now, but suddenly, at the chief's signal, the band of braves broke from the rear and thundered to the fore. There were maybe thirty or more, almost naked, riding their ponies alongside the train. The Shoshoni grandeur lay in the fierce insolence with which they pursued their adversary. Several Indian braves, keeping one leg wrapped around the saddle tree, leaned far down on the right flank of their galloping ponies and swung under the animals' necks to fire flintlock rifles at the racing train.

Passengers screamed, ducking down behind their seats as bullets ricocheted off the side of the train, breaking several of the windowpanes on the passenger cars. But not Abby; Elizabeth had to grab her arm and pull her down below the broken window.

"What are you thinking, Abby?"

"Sorry! It's just so . . ." She stopped to listen. But as quickly as it had started, the shooting stopped. Abby peeked out the window to see what was coming next, but all the Indians were gone. Disappeared into thin air like magic marauders, leaving a ghostly feeling.

A shiver ran down Elizabeth's spine. The train was left to speed down the track alone, at more than forty-five miles per hour.

Women were shaking, children were crying, and men were questioning each other and the conductor.

"What just happened?"

"Will they be back?"

"Have you ever had this happen before?"

But there were no real answers. The train kept moving toward Benton, away from the Indians, away from the open plains.

"Those were Shoshoni," drawled the cowboy. "They're—"

"They're just savages," interrupted the conductor, trying to calm down the passengers and share what little he knew.

"Why are the Indians so upset?" asked Annie.

"Who knows with these savages."

"That's it, then, just savages?" Tom echoed the conductor's response.

"That's it," the conductor confirmed. "These Indians, unprovoked and sadistic, are attacking good men who have done nothing to them." The conductor contorted his face into a sneer. "Some say they're after Doc Durant and the UP. No tellin' why these beasts do the things they do. Something has to be done. They can't stop progress. Frankly, I think we should kill 'em all!"

An eerie feeling crept into the passenger car as all sat quiet, in contemplation of what they had just witnessed, listening to the bumpety-bump of the train as it ran down the track, gradually slowing to its normal speed.

John Meyers broke the silence. "There's more ta the story."

"What's the rest of the story?" Annie's eyes were wide with interest.

"The gov'ment hasn't handled it well."

"Whatta you mean?" Tom's brows furrowed.

"With the iron horse and more of Washington's broken treaties, Washington is now decidin' ta push the Indians further north off the Platte. Ta a smaller corner of the prairie—little game and not much water." He paused. "Indians ain't happy about it."

"Can they do that, rescind a signed treaty?" Annie frowned. "I thought things were different here in America."

"Humph! That's what gov'ment does." The cowboy grimaced. "They're not much good at keepin' promises. Just makin' 'em, pushin' problems down the road a piece for the next bunch o' politicians to jaw on."

"So, what does the government say about the Indians' dislike of the new plan to push them off the land?"

"Huh!" The cowboy laughed. "S'pose they'll be ignorin' their dislike. Or they'll just kill 'em all, now that the Civil War is behind us."

"And the settlers?" Annie's brows came together. "What happens to them?"

"Indians have prowled these plains for hundreds of years. They ain't happy 'bout the invasion by the buffalo hunters killin' off the herds for nothin' but hides. Ranchers with our fences, cattle, settlers . . . And now the iron horse and atrocities by our military. Indians have been attackin' farmers, railroad workers, trains, and cowboys all across the prairie."

"What atrocities?" Annie asked.

"Oh, there've been many. After the gov'ment issued their latest relocation order to the Indians, skirmishes erupted along the frontier.

Brigham Young, one of the few white men on good terms with the Indians, brokered a good faith summit between Fort Douglas and the Shoshoni to settle their differences, but it backfired. The US Army considers Brigham Young and the rest of his followers unsuitable for military service—too much fraternizin' with the enemy. Brigham can be a hard man, feared by some and hated by others, but he's known for keepin' his word all along the frontier."

"So, what happened with the settlement negotiations?"

"Didn't go well. The Shoshoni are proud, insolent people, reluctant ta step aside for the white man." The cowboy paused. "For three hundred years, the Shoshoni Indians defended themselves and their families against any combination of foe to protect the solitude of their mountain home. Probably no tribe west of the Continental Divide done more ta protect the balance of nature than the Shoshoni. Consider themselves the nobility of the Rocky Mountains."

"Sounds like a clash of cultures?"

"Fort Douglas met with Chiefs Washakie, Pocatello, Sanpitch, and a whole lot of Shoshoni braves. But durin' the meetin', the notorious Colonel Patrick Connor led a cavalry raid massacring four hundred Shoshoni in their Bear River winter quarters—mostly old men, women, and children. These proud Indian warriors returned from negotiations to find their families dead or dyin' in below-freezing January weather. It didn't go down well. Chief Black Eagle, who now leads some of the raiding parties, found his young wife had been gang raped, her throat cut, and his two-year-old son bludgeoned to death. His little daughter escaped by diving into the freezing river, hidin' in the bulrushes until the brave cavalry left the field of battle." Meyers was clearly disgusted. "And we call 'em savages!"

"How could men do this to other human beings?" cried Annie. "His superiors must've been appalled."

"The 'Hero of Bear River,' the newspapers called him. Brigadier

General Connor now heads up Fort Douglas." A derisive Meyers pursed his lips. "It's not only the Shoshoni fightin' back now, but the Cheyenne, the Sioux, Arapaho, Choctaw, Crete, Chickasaw, and others who've been pushed into anger. On the twelve-hundred-mile Trail of Tears, four thousand Cherokee were marched to their death, men, women, and children."

"No wonder they don't trust the white man."

"The Shoshoni's temper after Bear River is running hot, raidin' parties killin' and pillaging, especially men workin' fer the railroad, sometimes hauling off young women and children."

Annie's brows pulled together. "This is more than a clash between cultures, isn't it?"

"Folks like you movin' out west want ta make their own lives. Of course, you want your own land. The Indians are fightin' back. It's the only way they know. But in the end, they'll be decimated."

Chapter 15

⇥ • ⇤

THE LOCOMOTIVE SLAMMED ON THE brakes. Steel wheels squealed on iron track. The train jerked and shimmied, launching the passengers forward in their seats. Some hit their heads on the seat in front as the train slid to a stop to avoid slamming into the pile of rock, timber, and debris stacked high on the track.

John Meyers lunged across the aisle, almost falling to the floor as he leaped to the east-side seats to get a better look. "Oh my God! The Shoshoni have blockaded the tracks." Meyers paused to piece together what was happening. "I'm guessing they think we've got Doc Durant and the rest of the Union Pacific fellas on board. That's why they were tracking us—to see if we had cavalry protection."

"Oh no," Edie cried. "You children all come here with me."

"Tom, here, take this pistol, find a safe place to hide and be ready to use it," Meyers instructed, stern and tense. "Keep your family here on the floor. Don't confront them." Then, raising his voice so all in the car could hear, he said, "They're Shoshoni, and they're most likely lookin' fer guns and enemies—railroad and military men. Don't any of you give them reason ta do harm ta yer families. Under no circumstances be confrontational."

"Don't we fight?" Tom asked.

"There's too many of 'em to fight; you'll just get yourself and yer family killed. Benton's not far. I'm gonna ride for help." Meyers fled down the aisle toward the cattle car.

Tom tucked the pistol into his belt, turned, and stood in front of his family, who were frozen. "Get down on the floor—now!" he commanded those who were still in their seats. "Stay down, out of sight and away from the windows. Andrew, Gabriel—you and Joey stay with the women and children. I'm going up front to see what's happening." He turned to the children. "Sit on the floor and don't move, and don't make any noise." His voice was hard, giving them no choice but to obey.

"Yes, sir," they said quietly, eyes wide with fright. Some sobbed, and some had trembling hands. Some were too scared to cry but nestled under Edie, Rachel, and Annie's protective arms.

Bullets zinged past the windows, ricocheting off the roof in a frightening clatter of lead on steel siding. The window above them exploded, sending shards of glass everywhere, then another shattered, and another as Tom ran down the aisle toward the coal car behind the engine room. His heart was pounding as glass burst on both sides of the car. His breathing was fast and short. He tried to calm himself, keep a clear mind, and concentrate on the best course of action.

Tom opened the door and ran through to the next car of terrified passengers, who turned to look at him without a word, broken glass everywhere. He ran out the last door and up the ladder into the long, open coal car stationed behind the locomotive. He could hear blood-curdling shouts, a slamming metal door, and cries of terror from the engine room just below him. Howling like all of hell's condemned souls, the Indians pounded and pushed open the door.

Quickly, Tom crawled over coal piled high enough for him to peer through a shadowed opening at the raiding Indians below as they broke into the engine room. Rifle shots rang out. An Indian, blown backward out the door, landed with a thud on the dusty ground in a crumple of tangled arms and legs. Right behind him came the engineer, who cried out when he hit the ground on his back. Shoshoni lances quivered in time with the engineer's pounding heart. The young braves on horseback hooted and hollered, reveling in the frenzied moment. Their war whoops ricocheted off the engine walls and were lost in the silence of the hills. Almost all in the war party seemed in a festive mood, intent upon humiliating their victims, but one sat apart, quiet, monitoring the melee. He was older, sitting tall and regal in his simple saddle, with long, lean legs encased in fringed leather leggings up to his naked thighs. Brass beads tinkled as he moved. His head feathers and dark blue breechclout fluttered in the light breeze. His torso was bare and tightly muscled, bow and quiver strung across his chest. A rifle in its scabbard was strapped to his pony. Black rings of paint encircled his ominous dark eyes, giving him a terrifying, satanic appearance.

Tom watched as two Shoshoni braves emerged from the engine room dragging the young fireman down the steps, his face, head, and arms badly bloodied. The boy screamed as they threw him down the remaining steps and into the chaos below. Struggling to stand upright, he weaved back and forth. He was knocked right back down by the raiders, who reeled and spurred their protesting painted ponies into him. Curled into a ball, the boy vainly shielded his head and stomach from the hooves as the ponies reared up and came down on him in a cloud of dust. The rest of the Shoshoni stood by, cawing and hooting their delight.

"Someone has to do something," Tom whispered under his breath. His eyes narrowed as he watched the Indians with their painted faces, hollering and ranting. But what could he do, a lone man with a single pistol against a war party of three dozen savages, Shoshoni Indians—it would be suicide.

So engaged were the young Shoshoni braves in their fun that they didn't hear the door to the cattle car slide open or see the sleek, almost elegant black stallion with its rider in his big Stetson hat leap out. The giant horse with the glistening muscles of a warrior plunged with hooves flashing. In one fluid motion, horse and rider wheeled and galloped toward an opening in the crowd of preoccupied Indians. All in the war party were caught by surprise—except one.

The dark-eyed Indian remained calm and confident. He coolly turned to face the advancing cowboy and stallion, expertly wheeling his pony around to take advantage of the angle. He swooped down upon Meyers and the stallion with blazing speed, rising in his stirrups, drawing his long lance back. With wide-eyed determination wrenching up his face, the Indian flung his lance at the horse and rider, landing a glancing blow to the cowboy's upper torso.

John Meyers was spun off his horse. He fell to the ground, groveling in the dust, then got to his feet and woozily began to run. But the Shoshoni chief, showing no emotion, encouraged by the yapping and whooping young braves, whipped his horse back around and came right at the cowboy. Meyers swerved and stumbled to dodge him. With the grace of a skilled horseman, the calm and confident Indian drove the cowboy into the group of younger braves. They crowded around Meyers, bumping the bellies of their ponies into him. He weaved and staggered, slipped and fell, and got up again. The young braves continued to taunt him, pushing with their lances, bumping with their ponies, shouting war cries with blazing eyes and vengeful scowls. Meyers was herded and prodded along with the two men who had been pulled from the train, still weeping and pleading for mercy. And then Tom saw the conductor being dragged to join his doomed colleagues. They were corralled like field mice standing off a pack of wolves, pushed, pulled, and bumped about until they fell to the ground exhausted, disoriented, almost beyond terror.

Tom's heart was in his throat, his hands sweating, his face breaking out in a rash as he watched, helpless. "God help 'em,"

When the Indians had tired of their game, one slid off his pony and came at the conductor, taunted him by passing his knife from one hand to the other as the conductor watched it, crying out for mercy. Tiring of this game, too, the Indian drove the point of the blade deep under the conductor's ribs and yanked it upward into his heart. The stabbing was so sudden that the man gasped in painful surprise, trying to lift himself off the blade. But using both hands on the hilt now, the Indian gave a sharp twist to finish him. The young fireman watched in horror. He just stood there in shock while scalps were taken, including his own. It was the engineer's turn next. Then all three Union Pacific men were lassoed around their ankles and dragged off at full gallop by the war party. John Meyers lay sprawled faceup on the ground. His nearly naked, motionless body was bloodied and close to death. Two young braves remained behind with him.

Tom had seen enough. He scrambled down from his hiding place just as one of the Indians raised his lance high above his head. Running toward them screaming, Tom waved his pistol in the air as the Indian, using two hands, drove the lance down through John Meyers's shoulder and into the ground. Tom could hear the scrape of blade on bone, like fingernails on slate. Pinned, squirming, and screaming, Meyers's inhuman cries rang out across the silent hills, tearing at the air, searing themselves into Tom's mind forever.

Tom threatened the two young raiders with his pistol. Surprised by his sudden appearance, they stepped backward in anticipation of being shot. But for fear of the discharge alerting the departed war party, Tom did not pull the trigger. He walked toward them, the gun pointed at their heads. They put their hands up, then turned and mounted their ponies, racing off with a hoot and holler toward the rest of their companions, who had disappeared over the ridgeline.

Tom rushed to the side of the unconscious John Meyers, still staked to the ground.

And from the distance came the chugging purr of a locomotive.

⊱ • ⊰

Annie sat on the floor amid broken glass, crying children, and the rest of the horrified passengers huddled around her. Mothers sobbed with crying babes in their arms. Shocked and silent women clung to their wide-eyed men. The terrifying Indians had strewn baggage contents across the car, seeking prizes with painted faces and twisted scowls. Taking in slow, deep breaths, Annie tried to ignore the pounding of her heart. Her trembling fingers stroked the hair of a tearful Elizabeth, who lay on Annie's lap, clinging to her thighs. None of the children had witnessed the tragedy outside, but they'd heard the sounds of voices and clatter.

"I'm afraid, Aunt Annie," Elizabeth sobbed.

"It'll be all right, honey." Annie's calm voice seemed to soothe the girl.

"Is Uncle Thomas okay?" Little Tommy whimpered, his arms wrapped around Annie's neck as she held him against her.

"Yes, Tommy, I'm sure he's okay." But Annie wasn't sure at all. After their conductor had been dragged out of the car screaming, no one had dared risk getting up off the floor. It had been over an hour since Thomas had rushed off. All she knew, all any of them knew, was the fear they'd felt as the sounds of the terror outside drifted in through the broken windows. Many of the passengers had put their hands over their ears to soften their fright. Still, they had heard the men screaming and the horses' hooves pounding. But she hadn't heard her husband's voice in the commotion outside—until the end. And that had terrified her. What terrified her more was when the screaming and shouting stopped. Annie's imagination ran wild. Her lower lip quivered. She balled up her hands into fists to stop their trembling.

In front of Annie, Edie sat pale and drawn, arms wrapped around her brood of whimpering children. She wore her alarm like a shroud, snuggling in close under her husband's arm. Andrew smoothed the damp hair on his trembling wife's sweaty, ashen brow. He whispered words meant for Edie's ears only. He kissed her pale cheek, and kissed each of his children.

The doors to the passenger car opened and in stepped Tom, crazed eyes searching the passengers sitting on the floor. Annie stood. Her wondering eyes met his. With care and agility, she stepped around men and women and over children until she was in his arms. He kissed her hard, like someone drinking cool water after being desperately thirsty for days. He held her tight, rocked her. It was plain that language was inadequate at a time like this. Annie sobbed into his shoulder.

"What a welcome sight you all are," Tom murmured in a hoarse voice, as he scanned and touched each member of his family. "Are you all unhurt?"

"It was awful." Annie paused, regaining her composure. "We all huddled together on the floor while they ransacked everything."

Tom looked out at the rest of those in the car, his face drawn into a frown.

"I thought you were dead," Annie whispered into his ear. She trembled as she recalled her fear. "Oh, Thomas." Flooded with emotion, she didn't want to release her hold on him.

Tom looked into Annie's eyes, and spoke in a calm and solemn tone. "You're all safe now."

A tall, handsome cavalryman of about thirty-five stepped into the passenger car. "I am Captain Jeremiah Baptist of the US Cavalry," he explained to the passengers. "I'm here as a part of the escort for the Union Pacific executive train that has pulled up behind yours. We will be linking both trains together and proceeding on to Benton shortly. But if I may, I'd like to introduce General Ulysses Grant and General William Tecumseh Sherman, who would like to say a few words to all of you. General Grant, General Sherman." Captain Baptist stepped aside, bowed slightly, and allowed the two men to step forward.

The passengers saw a stout, middle-aged, bearded gentleman with dark brows on an iron-hard face, dressed in finely tailored banker's clothes. He stood beside a tall, impressive-looking four-star general. Both wore serious expressions.

"Good afternoon, ladies, gentlemen," said the stout gentleman with a stern look in his eyes. "I'm General Grant." With a nod and a puff on his cigar, he pointed to the striking man standing beside him. "This is General Sherman. We apologize for this tragedy you have been forced to endure. Mr. Wright has filled us in on the details of what happened here today, and I assure you we will do what we can to help Mr. Meyers, one of your fellow passengers, who has been gravely injured. With proper medical care and a little luck, he will recover from his injuries. If there is anything we can do for any of you, please let Captain Baptist know. He and his cavalry troops will be escorting both trains into Benton shortly." General Grant paused, taking another puff on his cigar. "Do you have any questions?"

Gabriel raised his hand. "Sir, may I ask, what is going to be done about the Indians?"

"Of course, it is a difficult situation, but I assure you, General Sherman will not tolerate this kind of retaliation for their grievances. Our cavalry and others will be dispatched to address these problems." Grant paused, and his steel-gray eyes looked hard into the eyes of the men and women in front of him. "But please understand, things are dangerous right now and you all must be very careful."

His statement sent a chill skittering down Annie's spine.

"We have five children and are planning to settle in the West," Andrew pointed out. "Will we be safe from these Indians?"

"We will be discussing what to do with the Indians, amongst other things, at Fort Laramie." General Grant nodded. "But make no mistake, this is truly a wild frontier."

Tom frowned. "Understand Thomas Durant, president of the Union Pacific, is a medical doctor and is here with you in his executive car." Tom paused, looking into General Grant's eyes. "Why is he not attending to John Meyers, checking in on his dead employees or the safety of his passengers?"

General Grant held Tom's gaze, expressionless, but did not respond to his query.

"Now, if you'll excuse us, General Sherman and I have things to take care of before we can be on our way to Benton." And with that, and a courtesy nod, they were gone.

Chapter 16

※ • ※

BENTON CITY, ON THE EASTERN edge of the prairie that swept westward toward the Black Hills of Wyoming, was exactly 672 miles west of Florence, Nebraska, the transcontinental's eastern point of commencement. Like most Hell on Wheels towns, Benton had extravagant dreams. Its founders were certain Benton was destined for greatness, and the Union Pacific Railroad fed into those dreams, issuing brochures extolling the virtues of this land beyond the Missouri River. Much of it they owned, thanks to the largess of a federal government anxious to populate the West with American immigrants.

With Andrew, Joey, and the rest of the family safely situated at the railway station eatery, Tom and Gabriel stood at the railing of the raised station platform overlooking Main Street. Teeming with raucous men, Benton shimmered into life as dusk settled into night.

Tom, mouth slack, was awestruck as he took in the scene. Rollicking patrons, with whisky in hand, shouted and staggered from saloon to dance hall to saloon to gambling house, all the establishments situated in giant canvas shebangs that lined the long, dusty street bathed in blazing torchlights. Each destination's gaudy signage vied for attention. Bright lanterns hanging in the open windows beckoned. All Main Street's establishments hummed to capacity with eager men of all shapes, sizes, and persuasions. Most were wide-eyed railroad gandy dancers anxious to participate in the evening's debaucheries.

Tom chuckled. "Not a tree, not a shrub, not a blade of grass." The dust was ankle deep. Everyone was filthy. It seemed to him that the whole place festered in corruption, disorder, and mayhem. The town looked like it would rot into oblivion if it didn't burn down first.

Gabriel, waving his arm at all the hubbub, offered, "I don't think I see a single man I'd trust in the company of my daughter."

"Hardly!" Tom laughed, feeling his stomach churn. "Not sure how we're gonna find a place where we won't wake up in the morning with a knife in our bellies."

"Looks like most are rented by the hour," Gabriel reasoned. "I've never seen so many drunken men in all my life."

"Looks like these are men far from home without folks to rein 'em in, and they've got plenty of janglin' coin in their jeans. Enough to get 'em into trouble, anyway."

The pair walked down the steps into the mayhem. Gabriel stopped at the first saloon, the Double Trouble. "Excuse me, sir, could you tell me where I might find accommodations for the night for ourselves and our families?"

"And maybe a shower?" Tom added.

The barkeep looked at the foreigners with confusion. "You're in the wrong place, mister," he said to Tom. "Benton's a mile from the closest water. Ten cents a pail, so there ain't much call for it when whisky's five cents a glass. We got forty-rod whisky, that's it."

"What's forty-rod whisky?" Gabriel questioned.

"Our special, villainous homemade brew, guaranteed to disable at a distance of forty rods. Like addin' nitro to these boys' eager yearnings, with not near enough women to go around."

"Sounds downright decadent." Gabriel frowned.

The barkeep chuckled. "That it is, mister!"

Tom peered around at the blurry-eyed men. "Looks like there's plenty of it." He gazed out the colored-glass windows at drunken men rushing nowhere particular. Although Tom did not understand the appeal of Main Street's clash and clatter, he knew something of the desperation of these young men. His own papa had spent many a night drinking to dull his senses and distract himself from his dim vision of a disturbing future. The destruction it wrought in his family . . . But that world was behind him now. He might not know exactly what the future had in store, but he had a wife and a plan, which provided direction, at least.

"Who are these people?" Tom wondered aloud as he looked at all the gambling tables. "The ones who take advantage of hardworking railroad men?"

"They're part of a traveling contingent of flotsam scoundrels and whores passin' through every Hell on Wheels town," the barkeep responded, wiping down the bar top. "Folks not much interested in settlin' down. There's only one thing they're good at—separatin' the workin' stiff from his money."

It seemed to Tom every one of these dives was packed with hoarse men who were mad with mirth, drink, and wildness.

Their next stop in the search for a place to stay the night was the Bucket of Blood, which was offering free drinks. At the bar, a brawny, nefarious barkeep worked with three attendants to supply a line of men standing five deep with rotgut whisky. The same questions were asked and answered. "I don't know no place like that! We offer booze, gamblin', and fightin'."

At the Dennison, a big-tent outfit from St. Louis, Tom and Gabriel were dazzled by opulence as soon as they entered. Here were elegant black-hatted, frock-coated men of leisure.

"Gentlemen of chance!" Tom observed the steely-eyed gamblers. While the men's attentions were diverted by the show, they were stripped of everything of value. And Dennison's bar had a wider selection of soul-destroying liquor.

"For a day's pay, after thirteen hours of swingin' a sledgehammer," the barkeep informed Tom and Gabriel, "one can buy a single swig of our very best."

"And what might that be?" Tom asked.

"Good Time Charley. Guaranteed to knock you on your butt, accompanied by a young lady from the house ta boot."

"Hmm." Tom repeated the same question he'd asked a half-dozen times already, "Know where I could find a place to stay the night with my family?"

"Try the North Star." The barkeep pointed down the street. "North end of town. Not much, but about all we got without the company of a whore."

⊱ • ⊰

Tom pulled open the flap of a flimsy canvas shebang and stepped inside.

"Good evening, gentlemen," the bow-tied hotel clerk chimed. "Welcome ta the North Star."

"Looking for a couple rooms," Tom said, scanning the place. Dust and filth everywhere, it could clearly use a good scrubbing. "Busy tonight?"

"Always, but you're in luck; we just had two rooms come available. I 'spect the only ones in town."

"Can I see 'em?"

"No need, one's like so"—he held out his arms—"and the other a little bigger." The clerk offered a practiced smile. "That'll be two dollars for the both of 'em."

"Pretty expensive." Tom's eyes widened as he frowned. "Let's see 'em."

Without flinching, the clerk pointed the way. "Gentlemen, please follow me."

When the wick of the larger room's lantern was lit, dozens of cockroaches ran for cover. The canvas cubicle had three straw mattresses spread out on aging sawdust, a rust-stained wash basin, a crusty pitcher of water, and one dirty towel. The smaller cubical was the same but with only two mattresses. "The necessary is outside." The clerk pointed a thumb over his shoulder.

"This is not gonna go down well with my wife." Gabriel shook his head in disgust. But he offered to retrieve their families while Tom tidied the place up as best he could. "The towels are filthy," Gabriel said.

"Our previous guests haven't seemed to mind the towels or a few bugs." The unsympathetic clerk shrugged. "Suit yerself. Welcome ta sleep in the street."

"We'll take 'em." Tom sighed.

☙ • ❧

It was late by the time the children went to sleep on the warm August night. The sultry smell of mold was stifling inside the tent. Between the biting bedbugs, sweat-soaked clothes, and the noise from town passing through the thin canvas walls, Tom couldn't sleep. So, he slipped out of the crowded tent to take a late-night stroll.

A windless, moon-filled night mantled Benton as he walked down Main Street. The roar of the evening was finally subsiding, and the night had darkened into the purr of a gorging wolverine. Scattered, spent, sobering men straggled by, retracing their steps, seeking a place to sleep off their drunken depravity. The muted yellow glare of torchlights, the candlelight in the windows, the dim, pale glow of lanterns behind canvas walls silhouetting men and muffling sounds of decadence with women of the evening—it all accentuated the blackness of the night and filled the emptying town with shadows like specters. The darkness seemed to cloak the lust, greed, and shame. It hid the flight of a fearful man; it softened the sound of brawling drunks; it deadened distant pistol shots; and it covered the broken, penniless wanderers who slinked away to lick their wounds.

Curious, Tom stepped inside the opulent Keystone Hall, the granddaddy of them all. It was another world inside—a huge, glittering, magnificent monstrosity in a coarse, decadent setting. He watched in fascination. Life inside the Keystone seemed untenable, extravagant, and hideous. One hundred feet long and forty feet wide, it had a dance floor the size of a horse corral and dozens of gambling tables filled with men. There was a bar fitted with cut-glass goblets and pitchers, and shelves crammed with bottles of liquor, all surrounded by imported mirrors and paintings of naked women of the evening. The band played to amuse and transfix the drunken patrons.

Tom watched the barkeep serve water to the young ladies and the cardsharps; to ensure they were at the top of their game, he supposed.

The gold that was not pocketed by the barkeeps went into the greedy hands of these swift and shifty-eyed gamblers or the clutching fingers of the wild women. This was a place where the faro and card tables were the workman's bench and the cardsharp and whore collaborated with surgical precision to lift every last nickel off the poor stiffs.

A good time to be had by all! Tom mused.

Around the glittering blaze of the mirrored bar stood a

drink-sodden mass of humanity shouting at each other and bursting with exaggerated laughter. All through the rest of the expansive room, knots of men stood or sat around the tables. They were intense, absorbed, listening with strained ears and watching with obsessed eyes until the moment they realized their loss and threw down their cards in disgust. Muttering curses, they pushed rolls of cash and gold toward cold, sober-faced gamblers who seemed to understand the brevity of the hour, and of life.

The dance hall was a maddening whirl of desperation, a wild fling of unleashed, hurly-burly men in a drunken spree of loneliness. The hideous, red-eyed intoxication that did not spring from drink, but from lust. The brazen, fleshy lure was raw and corrupt at this baneful hour.

❧ • ❦

When Tom returned to his tent, he looked in on Annie, feeling such a deep appreciation for her integrity, her dependability, her steadiness. He smiled at his own good luck.

She stirred. "Thomas, is everything all right?"

"Oh, yeah," he assured her with a grateful look. "What are you doing awake?"

"Well, it's time to turn over so the bedbugs can feed on the other half of me." She snickered as she got up and came to him.

"Would you like to talk for a while? Maybe go for a walk?"

"I suppose I would. We certainly aren't getting any sleep around here."

Both muffled their laughter as they stepped outside into the sultry night. "I'm told there's a trail leading to a beautiful little creek at the north end of town," Tom shared. "It's a full moon. Whatta you think?"

"Sure, let's go find it."

He took her hand, and they found the well-worn path out of town, in the opposite direction from the railroad camps. "Been walking around town watching all these unfortunates looking for happiness in all the wrong places."

"Have you?"

"There seems to be few virtuous men, or women for that matter, living in Benton on either side of the card tables." Tom sighed in derision. "But the cardsharps, whores, and shebangs aren't entirely to blame, are they? These predators prey on the bad judgment, greed, and carnal desires of desperate men, most of which spent the last five years fighting a civil war."

"Men taking advantage of men who earn their money like horses and spend it like asses!" Annie frowned. "The hotel clerk says the Union Pacific takes a cut of everything in these Hell on Wheels towns."

"Suppose it's not so different than back home."

Tom put his arm around her, his mind drifting as he looked up at the full moon in the clear night sky. "Men can be so foolish sometimes. Our lust for money, power, and sex. Our arrogant pride getting in the way of good judgment. Sometimes, we're so caught up in our own vices, we blindly open ourselves to be taken advantage of by unscrupulous characters."

"I once read a very wise statement from a scientist, who said . . ." Annie paused, trying to get it right. "There are only two things infinite: man's carnal desires and the universe. And I'm not so sure about the universe."

"Hmm!" Tom smiled. "On my stroll through town tonight, I watched wild-eyed women separate foolish young men from the last of their pay. Drinks in hand, these lonely souls sauntered after these women of the night up to their rooms to be stripped of what little dignity they had left."

"It's a pathetic commentary on the human condition."

Tom remembered a long-ago Spring Hollow evening when he'd sat by the campfire watching with fascination the zigzag dance of a female praying mantis, her antennae flailing about like wands to lure a potential mate. The male had approached in what he must have thought irresistible movements of courtship. When the foreplay was complete, they copulated. All seemed to go well until the female turned and bit his head off, leaving him to continue copulating to the rhythm of her body until his bitter end. And life went pulsing on, at the expense of one less player. "Lonely, foolish men and their unharnessed carnal desires."

"The specific circumstances may change," Annie whispered irreverently as they walked on down the path through the woods, "but the nature of men and women seems to rhyme from one place to another, one generation or culture to the next, doesn't it?"

"I know life sometimes seems overwhelming, Annie, but at least we are facing it together." Tom looked at her in admiration. "I realized tonight just how fortunate I am to have my best friend by my side."

Annie twined her arm with his as they walked.

"I suppose we all need a reminder of our blessings from time to time, don't we?" She paused to ponder her fate—what she would have lost if she had taken counsel from her fears and said no that morning at the butcher's shop.

"I suppose we do."

"As a wise man once told me, sometimes we just have to take the leap and hope to God we can fly." Annie pursed her lips, closed her eyes and remembered back to that long ago evening when Thomas had said those words to her. She knew she would never be the soulmate Lydia once was, but sometimes when she wrote Emma, she felt guilty, holding back a little because she was having the time of her life. And Emma, the beautiful thing, was stuck back in Barnsley. Annie just couldn't see how this had happened.

Tom put his arm around Annie's shoulder and gave her a comforting squeeze. "Just thankful you said yes." He paused. "It looked touch and go there for a moment."

"Are you kidding, a four-second courtship, a twenty-four-hour engagement. Most would say I was a downright wanton hussy! Couldn't wait to get you in the sack!"

"Ah, yes." He kissed her. "One of your best qualities."

She smiled to herself as she nestled her cheek into his shoulder. "Anything worth having takes a lot of practice." A warm, soothing feeling encompassed her in this most unexpected of places.

❧ • ☙

"Look, there it is." Tom had been so caught up in their conversation he really hadn't paid attention to the gradual change of scenery along the pathway. A tributary creek of mountain runoff lay before them. Only the babbling water broke the silence of the forest. Moonlight spread like searching fingers through the sweet-smelling pine to reflect off a pooling pond in a wide bend of the creek. And like diamonds, the light flashed off the shadowed surface of the water in a dazzling display of brilliance.

"I don't know about you, but I'm gonna take a long-overdue bath," Annie said as she began to deal with her buttons, ties, and hooks. Peeling off her clothing down to her essentials, she tiptoed into the water, her hands raised just above the surface.

Tom gave an anxious but exhilarated laugh. It was just the two of them on this warm summer night. "An adventuresome woman after my own heart," he called out, pulling his sweaty shirt off over his head, sliding his trousers off, and tripping out of his underwear in his rush to the pond.

Annie shot a look over her shoulder, laughing at his clumsiness. "It's cold but nice." Her mischievous eyes peeked above a sly smile. "We'll see how well those bedbugs can swim underwater."

He rushed in after her, splashing and chasing her into deeper water. "It feels good once you're in, doesn't it?"

"It does." They were both neck deep, water dripping down their faces.

Catching her arm, he pulled her close, wrapping her naked body up in his embrace. He smiled and gazed into her flashing green eyes.

Flirtatiously, he touched her nose with his fingertip, "You see, this is what I like most about you. Not too many best friends get to go skinny-dippin' together in the middle of the night."

"Are you trying to have your way with me, sir?"

"Mm-hmm." He continued looking into her eyes. "Best friends with benefits . . . I like your smile," he whispered, his lips nearly touching hers. He could feel her heart pounding against his chest.

"That's not my best feature." Her smile disappeared, sending a tingle of excitement through him.

"I remember that about you," he whispered in her ear.

Her cheeks blushed and she quieted as he kissed her neck, her ear.

As the length of their naked bodies melded together, slowly, she raised her eyes to his. Her anxious gaze filled with desire locked onto his bold, steely eyes. "I—" Her voice caught. She pulled in a deep breath that sent a warm flush through him. Now her focus entirely on him, the palms of her hands on his bare chest with a sultry invitation in her eyes, she kissed him deep and hard.

The moonlight cast the shimmering shadows of the evergreens over the calm, glassy surface of the pooling pond. Tom felt alive. Intoxicated! His senses more aware of the babble of the creek downstream, the coolness of the water, the call of the nightingale, and the sweet scent of the pine. Annie's penetrating gaze of desire drew him in further.

"We are more than best friends, you and I." He smiled dryly, sliding his hands around to her firm breasts. Her pensive face flushed, submissive. His amber eyes, glowing in the moonlight, did not release hers.

Her green eyes held him spellbound. He placed one hand on the small of her back and slowly pulled her tighter into his embrace. Tingling with desire, he breathed in deep, trying to temper the intoxication of the moment. He could feel the rising passion running through her as she pressed her soft breasts and warm body against his nakedness. Skin to skin, with all nerves firing, he no longer felt anything but the beguiling, almost chilling intensity of need. There were no more words necessary. He was sure she could hear his ragged breathing, the pounding of his heart, and sense the ardent desire pulsing through him.

He coaxed her mouth open with the soft persuasion of magical touches and anxious caresses, and she responded by wrapping her arms around his neck and her thighs around his waist. He kissed her long and hard. Passion surged, sending electricity through to his center. His breath came fast, his heart pounded, his blood rushed like a powerful incoming tide.

"Oh, Thomas." The words escaped Annie's lips in a whimper, swallowing him up in emotion.

With every nerve humming, he urgently swept her up to him. She squeezed her thighs firmly around him, pulling him further into her. Her arms tightened around his neck, and her fingers curled into the taut muscles of his strong shoulders. His breaths came fast and halting, and then stopped altogether. His whole body trembled and throbbed. His heart raced. And the mystical intensity of their joining took full control over him until . . . it was finished.

Chapter 17

≽ • ≼

Wide-eyed and panting, Elizabeth burst into the room with Abby trailing right behind.

"Uncle Thomas!" Elizabeth shouted as her eyes darted around. "There's a man—he's lying dead in the street in front of the hotel." Her hands shook as she stumbled over her words.

"Slow down, Elizabeth. Take a deep breath. Show me."

Tom and the hotel clerk followed the girls outside, where Gabriel stood staring at the dead man.

"Nope, don't know 'im." The clerk ran his hand through his hair as everyone else looked on in disbelief. "We call 'em a man for breakfast. Most mornings we find one or two sprawled out dead as a doornail lyin' in the dirt from the goin's on the night before. This 'un's been kilt with a shiv." The clerk seemed eerily cavalier about the whole affair as he turned the dead man over for further inspection. "Folks around here will strangle each other, shoot 'em, or knife 'em for a day's pay. Or ta make their next stake at the tables." He shrugged. "Or just outta spite." He puzzled over the man's chalky face, cocked his head sideways for a better look, then frowned. "It's not good for business, so's unless somebody claims 'im, we'll be draggin' 'im up ta Boot Hill and buryin' 'im with all the rest."

Tom and Annie looked at each other silently as more of the

curious gathered around to see the latest victim.

"What else a body ta do?" the clerk continued. "Exceptin' maybe put the cemetery downhill—bad town plannin', that Boot Hill." He pointed just beyond the city hall.

Tom could see Annie felt sick to her stomach. The girls stood speechless for the first time. "I think we've about had enough of Benton City," Tom said, capturing the feelings of the rest of the family. This dangerous, decadent town was no place for them to stay while they prepared for the trek farther west. "Shall we find ourselves a campsite down by the river until we can get a wagon put together and leave this place?"

"I'm with you, Tom," Gabriel confirmed.

Andrew, continuing to stare at the dead man, nodded his support.

After checking out of the North Star, Tom found a wagon train west and with Gabriel secured three wagons. While he was busy in Tradesman's Square, the rest of his traveling companions searched out a campsite along the Platte River. It quickly became clear they were not alone in this idea. They would camp along the river for the next few days while travelers gathered, the wagons were outfitted, and final preparations were made for the train of pioneers.

It seemed Tom had waited his whole life to be on his own, to shake off his indentured servant obligations and be on his way to California. No one knew what the future would bring, but he was looking forward to their own little family farm, as far away from the rest of the world as possible.

⇝ • ⇜

"Well, Annie, that's the last of it." Tom breathed a sigh of relief as he pushed a sack of dried beans forward to fit snug between the salted pork and two large sacks of flour.

"So, we're ready to go then?" she asked, hopeful.

Tom looked with satisfaction upon the weeks' worth of work. They'd secured wagons, acquired all needed supplies, organized, packed, and repacked. They were ready to leave at first light on the long trail to California.

"Everything's packed up so tight we couldn't even fit in Grand's false teeth," Joey confirmed.

"Good!" Annie threw her jacket up on the double-wide board seat.

"I see, Annie," Tom said with a deadpan smile, "you've spread out clothes, blanket, and pillows, taking the whole of the wagon seat."

"Uh-huh." She gave him her most imperious look. "I don't see there's room for either of you to fit in that seat if I'm to assure myself proper comfort." She pointed with a mischievous smile. "Looks like you'll both be walkin'."

"Move over, sweetheart!" Tom climbed up without a smile, then put his arm around her. "Trouble from the start!"

She smiled and threaded her arm in his as he reached for the reins.

"You wanna join me on a test run down to the river to water our oxen?" Tom asked.

"Sure, let's go."

With one hand holding the reins, Tom released the brake for the short drive down to the river. Pulling up at the river's edge, they slid in next to a man with a wagon stuffed to the brim and overflowing onto the seat and trailer. He had six oxen, a milk cow, two mules, beef cattle, chickens, two goats, two cats, two dogs, a wife, and a passel of children.

Tom turned to Annie. "Look at Daniel McArthur over there, our illustrious wagon master."

McArthur just stood staring at the menagerie in open disgust. With great weariness in his countenance, he commented flatly to the man, "You gonna bring yer whole farm with ya?" When the man looked at him in surprise, the wagon master added, "This ain't no picnic at the county fair we're goin' on!" Then he turned to walk away.

Annie chuckled, putting her hand over her mouth as she watched their crusty wagon master walk away still muttering to himself. "I'd find about as much satisfaction in tearing down my house, lighting it on fire, then watchin' it burn all my worldly possessions as I'm gonna find in leading this wagon train into them mountains with folks like them there in tow!'"

Daniel McArthur was a tall, rugged man in his middle thirties with steely gray eyes, powerful shoulders, and a stone-faced look most of the time. A notorious mountain man, he had a reputation for brutal honesty, great ingenuity, and dogged determination. And he was clearly impatient with the nonsense of life. He had begun putting together the wagon train in late July, and now, in mid-August, he had 411 souls signed up on the largest train of the season. Tom, Gabriel, and their families had readied themselves as best they could for the thousand-mile trek over the Rocky Mountains, through three rivers, before reaching Virginia City, bordering California's Sierra Nevada mountains. "But as always," Mr. McArthur had advised, "there will invariably be things ya've missed, or ya'll have to leave on the way."

McArthur would prove to be a man of enormous energy, a driving force to be reckoned with. He would keep their wagon train disciplined, orderly, and moving in the right direction for the next four weeks through the dusty heat of long, often windy days and chilly nights. They would cross buffalo-filled plains, forge raging rivers, and climb over mountains through inclement weather and filled with Indians before they arrived at their destination.

⤳ • ⤦

Their wagon train had been on the trail a week when they were confronted with their first major obstacle. A freak summer storm had melted the heaviest winter snowpack in a decade, turning the normally tranquil Platte into a deep, quarter-mile-wide, fast-moving river. The rushing water carried dangerous submerged debris with logs big enough to stove in a wagon or knock an animal off its feet.

The wagon train scouts moved up and down the riverbank looking for a suitable place to ford.

"There doesn't seem to be an easy place to cross for five miles in either direction," said the scout, Rowdy Battersby, who rode beside Tom. They were just ahead of the train on the low bluffs along the easterly water's edge of the Platte. Rowdy was tall, lean, and an experienced frontiersman. He sat in the saddle like he had been born there.

Daniel McArthur was coming their way on horseback, dragging a cloud of dust behind him. Rowdy raised his arm to pause the train of wagons.

"This spot looks as good as any," McArthur said loud enough for most to hear. "It's the same all up and down the river—wide but relatively shallow, fast-moving and muddy. Maybe a little overhead, except for near the center section. We can either cross here or wait a week for the waters ta recede and hope there ain't no more rain comin'?"

It took only a minute of debate before the decision was made not to wait. McArthur proposed partially unloading the first few wagons to lighten the load for the crossing and ferrying those belongings over on the specially designed flat-bottom boat. After unloading some of its contents onto the boat, Tom positioned his wagon first in line to cross.

McArthur knew that with the river bottom deep in mud, the oxen might get stuck and panic if they stopped for even a moment while crossing. Extra measures would need to be taken. Fortunately, logs from previous crossings had been left behind along the shoreline, and McArthur had the tools and experience to work them into place.

Tom and McArthur got to work, and together they lashed large logs on either side of the wagon box to help float the wagon and buoy the oxen up out of the mud in the heavy current of the deeper water.

Once the logs were secured to the lightened wagon, Tom brought it to the river's edge. But the rapids spooked the oxen. They wouldn't go any farther. Tom sat on the lazy board, which extended out over the river. That way, he could work both the reins and brake together.

He took a deep breath. "Do you think you can do this, Annie?"

"I can do it."

"Okay then." He traded places with Annie, handed her the reins, and climbed down from the wagon. He stood on the opposite side of his team of oxen in waist-deep water. "You ready?"

"I am."

An admiring Tom smiled up at her, grabbed the bridles, and gently coaxed the oxen into the swift-flowing river while Joey pushed the wagon from behind. For a few dangerous moments, the fractious oxen joggled the wagon, causing it to slip and slide down the muddy bank as Annie held on precariously to the end of the lazy board. Tom continued to calmly whisper into the oxen's ears, quieting them down until the big beasts found their footing and proceeded uneasily into the river. As they sank deeper into the water, the floating logs did their job to help buoy up the wagon and make it easier on the oxen. Slowly, the oxen pulled the floating wagon into the deeper, swifter current. Then, without warning, the log secured to the downstream side of the wagon box behind Annie pulled loose from its moorings. The unbalanced wagon tilted in the swirling water, twisting and turning in the flow of the river. It drifted farther downstream into the heaviest current at the middle of the river. Panicked, the oxen wheezed and jerked their heads, trying to keep their noses above the waterline.

"What do I do, Thomas?" There was panic in Annie's voice as she held the reins tight in one hand and hovered over the brake with the other.

"Pull 'em in," Tom yelled over the rush of the roiling water. "Then wrap 'em around the brake." But he was distracted, consumed by his effort to hold back the powerful beasts who jerked, kicked, and swung their heads, eyes wide and blazing, as they fought to find traction on the muddy bottom. The oxen's jostling of the wagon broke off the loose log just as the wheels violently careened off a submerged tree stump. The wagon swung around, panicking the oxen further, and they tugged with all their might in the opposite direction. The heavy wagon rocked and rolled. Annie was thrown off the lazy board headlong into the flooding river.

&. · ⋖

Her heart raced as she plunged into the icy cold water. She tried to call out but her breath caught, and the flooding river dragged her beneath the surface.

Her chest tightened in the cold fist of understanding. Mouth filled with grit, sinuses clogged with muddy water, blind in the murky rush, she lunged toward the loose safety line, frantically kicking with all her might. Her wet, heavy clothing held her back as she broke the surface of the swirling water and gulped for air before being pulled back under.

Rolling and tumbling in the churning rapids, she was hysterical for help. But there was none. Her lungs burned. Her heavy arms slashed at the raging water to stay afloat. Hitting hard on a submerged tree stump, pain shot through her and she sucked more flooding water into her lungs. Despite her heroic efforts to lunge toward the light at the surface, the rapids dragged her ever deeper.

Exhausted, helpless, Annie tried to cough her lungs clear and shout. Her chest was on fire. Her heavy tangle of clothing had wrapped around her, tightening its grip on her arms, her legs. She felt like a moth struggling to extricate herself from a cocoon. Her eyes were wide in panic, every muscle strained to its breaking point, until she was too tired to fight anymore. Panicking, she gulped more water than air, her heart racing to keep up with the lack of oxygen to her brain. She was drowning, drawing ever closer to catalepsy. She clenched, gasped, and in a burst of brilliant white light, she convulsed into semiconsciousness. A benevolent darkness. With her heart continuing to pump blood to her brain, for a time she would still be cognizant of what was going on around her. She felt her body continue to roll and tumble along the bottom, bouncing listless off boulders and tree stumps, drifting helpless downriver. In her thoughts she called out, *Mama I'm scared.* Vaguely aware of her impending death, her mind began scrolling rapidly through the catalog of meaningful memories—*Thomas, my babies, Emma.*

⤇ • ⤆

Annie awoke convulsing, coughing, and sputtering up water and vomit through cold lips and chattering teeth. She was lying in the mud along the side of the river, water lapping at her side, spent, unable to hold a rational thought in her head. She felt the slight breeze against her skin and saw the most beautiful clouds she had ever seen floating in a stark-blue sunlit sky. She drew in one deep, precious breath of air after another. Beside her, coughing up vomit himself, was . . . Gabriel?

⤇ • ⤆

Tom sat staring into the fire. He poked at the embers to encourage the flames. Everyone but he and Gabriel, who sat across the fire from him, had gone to bed.

Tom was shaken by the near tragedy that morning. He had been of no help at all. The vision of her rescuer lying beside Annie, nearly drowned himself, his chest heaving, throwing up his breakfast—Tom had grappled with all that long day. Again, with a shudder, the implications rolled over in his mind. Gabriel had nearly drowned himself to save Annie. The crackle and sputter of the fire was all that broke the silence.

"I fear I misjudged you, Gabriel."

"I'm sorry?" Gabriel looked up in surprise. "How have you misjudged me?"

"I've held you responsible for the worst of your aristocratic heritage, resented you," Tom whispered. "I see now I've been blinded by my own prejudice."

"Ah, that." Gabriel leaned back against the tree, his poker in hand. "I think I kind of understand, Tom."

"Do you? I'm not sure I do. I'm pretty confused right now."

"Are you?"

"You came close to losing your life to save my wife this morning. I've wondered what must have gone through your mind to leap into that cold, flooding river. Why would you risk everything, your life—your own precious life with your family? I've struggled all day to understand." Tom paused, looking up from the crackling fire. "I've been all wrong about you Gabriel . . . Haven't I? And now that I see it, I'm bit ashamed!"

"I know how you feel about an aristocracy who used you, abused your family, caused the death of your cousins, your Grand. And I know about Lydia and the match factory."

"You do?"

"I understand, and I'm so very, very sorry, Tom, but I'm not him. I'm not my father."

"I was wrong about you from the start, wasn't I? Blind to your efforts to disprove my estimation of you." Tom paused, straining to get it right. "How do I make amends?"

"Let me tell you something, Tom." Gabriel fell quiet for a long moment. "For a long time, Rachel and I have wanted to get away from the destructive influence of my father and his single-minded lust for money and power." Gabriel poked at the scarlet embers in the fire. "Your family has taught us how people should live together in a family. Rachel and I have watched Annie, Edie, the children, and even you, Tom. Your family has been an inspiration to us. We will never see family the same. We've changed because of the influence of all of you. You've disproved our long-inherited prejudices, with love, giving kindness, respect, and the long-suffering consideration you show each other."

"I was so enmeshed in my own distorted view of the world I didn't recognize the influence my charming wife's kill-'em-with-kindness approach to life was having on you." Tom scrunched his face into a frown. "She can be disarming, winning the admiration of us unwitting reprobates around her. I'm sorry, Gabriel."

"I jumped in to save Annie." Gabriel smiled. "I wouldn't have done it for you."

Tom returned the smile from across the campfire.

"You're right, Tom," Gabriel continued. "My father is a stingy, heartless, and sometimes cruel miser. And I'm afraid he's not that uncommon among the aristocratic class, sharing little of his money with those who work for him. You may not believe it, but in many ways, it was hard as an only child growing up in his household."

"It may have been hard to live with that very wealthy miser," Tom said with a chuckle, "but he'll make a great ancestor to his beautiful granddaughter."

Chapter 18

❧ • ❧

THE PALE BLUE SKY WAS fading at the edges as the sun began its long rise in the east. Annie and Edie had decided there was still time to sneak down to the creek, to do the wash and bathe in the cool, shaded waters privately before beginning late Sunday breakfast preparations. So, baskets in arms, they hiked down the mountain and waded through the dense thicket to the creek.

"Martha would tan our hides if she could see us now." Annie smiled at Edie as she piled her clothes on a large rock at the water's edge. "Only the second time we've done laundry since leaving Liverpool two months ago."

"Yeah!" Edie rolled her eyes, laughing.

Annie picked up Tom's filthy shirt. It looked like it had been dyed with the same gray-brown mud that covered her bare toes as she burrowed them beneath the cool running water. She dunked the shirt and laid it out on a rounded slab of granite, and with a bar of soap in her right hand and a scrub brush in her left, she got to work. "At least it gives us a chance to talk. How is Elizabeth doing? She and Abby seem to spend every moment together."

Suddenly, the shrill whinny of a war pony permeated the air. Both women froze. Their smiles gone, they turned and stood at attention. Hands still clutching soap and wet clothing, dresses tied up to their knees, they stared like spooked deer. Annie's green eyes flashed upon a half-dozen Indians ambling toward them on restless ponies. The brightly colored feathers on their shields and ponies riffled in the light breeze, and their long breechclouts fluttered with each step, giving them a carnival air.

Straight black hair framed faces that were young and chiseled under gaudy red paint that slashed from cheeks to chin. Each young brave wore a bow and quiver of arrows strung across their tanned, muscular chest. Their long, naked thighs were encased in fringed deerskin chaps, and beads jangled with each step of their mustang ponies.

Foreboding swelled in Annie's stomach and spread to her chest. She heard her heart pounding and felt it in her throat, her palms sweating. The very air seemed filled with fear.

"Oh Lord," whispered Edie.

Without further warning, a guttural war cry and a surge of ponies engulfed them. Howling like all of hell's condemned souls, the riders wheeled apart, spurring their rearing, protesting ponies around the shrieking women. The ground under their feet was vibrating from the thunder of hooves. Edie screamed and sobbed in horror. The pounding drowned out her screams as she tried to flee, the stacks of unwashed clothing flying everywhere. But Annie turned and stood her ground, hands on her hips and elbows out, mouth set fiercely. "Don't touch us!" she yelled.

The Indians cawed and hooted. The unearthly cries rang out across the silent hills, tearing at the air. Dust rose in billows, blinding the women as two Indians came galloping up to them, ponies and riders as one, so close together their stirrups touched. With graceful precision, they pulled apart at the last moment as each swept one of the women off the ground.

Annie's wrist was in the grip of a tall, lithe Indian brave with black rings around his eyes and a startling satanic leer. He flung her face first across the front of the galloping pony. Excruciating pain shot through her body. She clung for dear life to the pony's shoulder, screaming in terror, vomiting her lunch, and wetting herself. The man's powerful arm held her against his pumping thighs, which glistened with sweat and oil and smelled of smoke, tallow, and leather.

The Indians hooted, hollered, and cantered off on their mustang ponies thigh deep in waving grasses and sunflower stalks. Annie and Edie disappeared over the mountain, beyond the edge of rescue.

※ · ※

Tom had headed into the forest before daybreak to check the snares he'd placed the night before. It had become his habit to take his bow and a sheaf of arrows out each evening before dinner to track game and set his traps for rabbits and squirrels or an occasional raccoon. His twitch-up snares were designed to catch and pull the prey up off the ground, out of the reach of predators. And since the deer came out at dusk to feed, Tom would even bring back venison for dinner sometimes. His forest hunts had become so successful that the family invited others from the wagon train to share and trade in their bounty around the campfire on some nights.

On this particular morning, Tom brought back two rabbits. "Where's Annie?" he asked as Rachel and the girls gathered to prepare breakfast.

"She and Mam left just after you to wash clothes and bathe down at the creek," Elizabeth replied. "They promised to be back in time to help with breakfast." Her brows drew together in concern. "No one has seen them since."

"It's not like her to leave you girls with all the little ones, and shorthanded for breakfast too," Tom said.

"We're fine, Tom," Rachel interjected. "Annie deserves a break. She's still recovering. These past few days have been difficult on her."

"How's Gabriel doing?"

"He seems fine."

"Fair enough. Annie's been unusually quiet since the accident. It's not like her." Tom frowned, his forehead creased. "Still, I'm concerned. I'm gonna go find 'em."

"I'll bet they're sitting on a rock along the creek, talking it all out. They've just lost track of time."

"Probably."

"Indians! Indians!" The call came in shrill, anxious voices.

Horsemen raced down the line of wagons. Panic escalated as the word spread. Like lightning, fear struck the entire train before the wagon master had even the chance to advise caution. The word *Indians* alone had a chilling effect; it spawned images of bloodthirsty savages. It gripped hearts and riveted minds shut to rational thought.

Tom had no time to digest what was happening. His anxious eyes swept back and forth, scanning the horizon looking for any sign of Indians. *Where are they coming from?* Trying not to panic, he was more determined than ever to leave the family to fend for themselves and rush off to find his wife and sister. *Where could Annie and Edie be?*

Tom ran to collect his rifle. He cocked his pistols, calling out to Andrew and Joey, ordering those around them to circle the wagons.

In the chaos, women were screaming at their children to run and hide inside their wagons. Practiced teamsters prepared to squeeze the train of wagons tighter together, and drovers moved to corral the herd of grazing cattle within the protective circle, trying to calm the animals while they themselves grew more frantic with fear.

"Be calm!" shouted Rowdy as he galloped down the line doing

his level best to stem the panic. "Take care! Gather close in the circle of wagons. Be prepared to defend yourself. Be cautious and prepared, but for heaven's sake don't overreact and escalate hostilities. The Shoshoni have placed a blockade over the trail. They're armed and there's too many to start a fight. Keep your rifles hidden and your pistols close but out of sight."

Rowdy reached Tom's wagon just as Tom had saddled up a borrowed horse to begin his search. The tall, slender cowboy reined up and pulled in close to Tom and his gathered family. "Mr. Wright, Mr. McArthur wants you to join him immediately," insisted Rowdy calmly.

"Not possible, Rowdy," Tom said, dismissive. "Annie and Edie have gone missing. They left for the stream over an hour ago and we haven't seen them since. I've got to go find 'em."

"I understand, Mr. Wright. Mr. McArthur is speaking with the Indians at the blockade about them right now."

"What?" Tom's heart jumped into his throat. "Talking about Annie and Edie?"

"I think it best you come with me!" Rowdy urged.

"Oh my God. I'm coming too," Andrew chimed in.

Rowdy paused with concern in his eyes. "Okay then. Both of you, but now."

Tom slid his Winchester into its scabbard, got into the saddle, and prepared to follow Rowdy. Andrew did the same, and the three rode to where Daniel McArthur and Jake Wyatt, a wiry, leather-faced, seasoned scout in his early thirties, were talking to the large band of Indian braves.

After two weeks of nothing but mud and prairie, cool summer nights and rugged frontier, the sight greeting Tom as he rounded the circled train of wagons sent a chill down his spine. A contingent of fearsome-looking Indians had gathered. The heaviness of the warm summer afternoon, filled with buzzing insects, increased the anxiety a hundredfold. The Shoshoni's brutality had been a topic of morbid curiosity to most on the train, but it was a sight Tom dreaded ever seeing again.

Seasoned Shoshoni braves sat on horseback like graven images, with one hand on their hip and their other holding a rifle. Each stared at Tom and his approaching companions with expressionless painted faces and fierce eyes.

Tom could hear Daniel McArthur and Jake Wyatt talking to these hardened, hostile braves, insisting on a meeting with their chief to secure passage and the release of hostages.

Tom edged forward, sidling up to Rowdy. "What hostages?"

McArthur overheard Tom's question and turned his horse around to approach. "Tom, Andrew, the Indians have Annie and Edie, and I invited you here because I knew you would remain calm in this moment of crisis, which is, of course, very important right now. We are sitting on a powder keg here with a tribe of three hundred to five hundred Indians. Their village is just out of sight along the river. I don't want any outbursts—do you understand?"

"They have our wives?" Andrew asked in a panic.

McArthur nodded. "Afraid so."

Tom's heart sank. "Well, how do we get them back?" He asked this in a calm voice, though inside his stomach was churning, his heart pounding, his mouth dry. He was holding tight to the saddle horn to stop his hands from shaking.

"Hold on there, Tom. There is no *we* here. Neither of you are going anywhere. These are dangerous Indians, and I can't risk the entire wagon train on the chance you might incite a disaster for all of us."

Tom's perspiring face reddened; he could feel a rash coming. He wiped his sweaty hands on his leather chaps.

"This is my wife, Mr. McArthur," Andrew interjected, fear written across his face. "She's the mother of my five children. It's Tom's sister and his wife too. I insist we go with you into that village and bring them back."

"Listen, I am not going to sit here arguing with you in front of these very dangerous and skittish braves." McArthur glared at Andrew with cold, hard steel in his eyes. There was a long moment of tense silence. "I'll tell you what I'll do. Tom can come, provided he doesn't say a word and wipes that terrified expression off his face. Andrew, you go back to your five children and wait. They're going to need you if anything goes wrong, or God forbid something happens to us. There will be no argument—that's it or nothing. Understood?"

"Understood," Tom answered in a stern voice for the two of them. Turning to Andrew, he said, "We'll do everything we can to bring her back, Andrew. See to the children. They can't afford to lose both parents."

Andrew returned Tom's concerned frown. He started to object, but then he nodded, solemn and accepting.

The tension was palpable as Tom rode close behind Daniel McArthur and Jake Wyatt, trailing the Indian braves into the village as clouds quickly moved in and a light rain began to fall. Hidden among a grove of aspen mixed with cottonwood and evergreens, the village was strung out along a tributary creek to the Platte River. Tom could feel a thousand eyes following him as they passed through the village outskirts and into the borders of scattered tepees and curious murmurs. Plumes of smoke rose from openings at the tops of these impressive tepees. Hastily constructed trellises cut from cottonwood shaded robust, busy work areas strewn with splintered wood, axes, and other tools. The foreign sights, the arresting sounds of children and yapping dogs, and smells of venison and buffalo hanging from trees, the smoke-filled air drifting from the campfires—all of it assaulted Tom's senses.

Most of the braves along the winding pathway were painted for war, holding rifles and other implements at the ready. The closer the travelers got to the village center, the higher the tension rose. The young Shoshoni boys crowded in close, pushing and shoving and bumping the horses. They yelped, bared their teeth, and stared into Tom's face, intent upon testing their mettle against these intruders.

A young brave burst out of a crowd of older warriors and recklessly raced toward Tom on horseback, giving a blood-curdling yell. At the last moment, he turned away, daring Tom and the others to react. Tom thought his heart might explode from his chest as he sat in the saddle stone-faced, continuing to stare straight ahead. He knew he must appear unafraid and avoid taking the bait that could lead to conflict. Then another brave came, and another, bumping Tom's skittish horse, causing Tom to jump in the saddle.

Dizzying visions of disaster swirled about in his mind. He reminded himself there were those depending on his steadfastness. He pulled in the high mountain air through his nostrils and steeled his courage. He stared straight ahead into the surreal atmosphere of shadowed, smoke-filled chaos, not allowing his anxious eyes to dart left or right at the jarring sounds, erratic movements, and intimidating shoves.

Through it all, Daniel McArthur seemed calm and collected, slowly walking his horse through the crowd of Indians toward the great fire pit at the center of the village surrounded by intricately decorated giant wigwams made of painted strips of aspen bark on a framework of cottonwood saplings. Passing through well over two hundred Indian braves and boys, he did not react to the turmoil around him or do anything to make the restless afraid. No sudden moves, no reaching for his rifle as he pierced and parted the undulating throng of Indians.

Near the center of the village, Tom saw blood-drained human scalps hanging from a long horizontal pole. The grizzly sight sent a chill skittering down his spine.

"Maybe Sioux or Lakota, their mortal enemy," Jake whispered, "or maybe—"

"The raid on our railroad train!" Tom interrupted in a strained, dry-throated whisper, wondering which one belonged to the conductor.

"Maybe?"

Tom felt sick, afraid he might expose the fear he knew these Shoshoni youth hoped to see. Then he spotted a tall, menacing Indian straddling the pathway in the distance. The giant of a man stood defiant, motionless, expressionless in heart-stopping grandeur. All in the village, including the braves on horseback, showed deference by staying back. Tom and his two intruding companions were left to continue on alone. They were unmolested for the remaining thirty yards. Even the dogs stopped barking. There was a clap of thunder, and all at once a warm summer cloudburst exploded with enormous rain drops.

McArthur, Jake, and Tom came to a halt. They dismounted, soaked through. Without hesitation, McArthur handed his reins to Jake. Moving with deliberate confidence, McArthur walked the remaining distance through the pounding rain to the steely-eyed Indian. Jake followed, with Tom right behind, his sloshing boots feeling like they were filled with lead. His hands were clenched into fists to stop their shaking. He hoped Daniel McArthur knew what he was doing.

McArthur focused only on the Indian before him, lifting his hands from his sides, away from his two pistols in low-slung holsters strapped around his waist, one hanging on either hip. Slowly, he approached the stone-faced Indian, whose dignity seemed unaffected by the drenching rain. Just as quickly as it had begun, the downpour stopped, and the sun broke through the passing clouds.

The intimidating Shoshoni's dark, intelligent eyes flickered. Well over six feet in height, surely weighing more than 230 pounds, he was a sight unlike any Tom had ever seen. His powerful shoulders tapered down to a narrow, taut waistline. His sleeveless, open deerskin shirt stretched tight across his sharply defined chest and tucked into a belted waistband of etched and pigmented buffalo hide. His smooth skin shone like copper in the sunlight, scarcely concealing the rippling muscle of his arms and chiseled stomach. He had a leather loincloth and fringed deerskin leggings on his long, powerful legs, and he wore soft-soled moccasins.

Two seasoned braves had moved in to stand on either side of him, their rain-dripped faces painted red with heavy black around their eyes. It made them look fierce, but they were clearly subservient to this much taller, more powerfully built chieftain. His face was an exception to the braves', unmarked except for a single diagonal red and white stripe high on each cheekbone. His jet-black hair was parted in the middle, and his smooth, chiseled face was framed with two tight braids that cascaded down his shoulders and chest. At the back of his head, a single eagle feather stood tied to a multicolored beaded headband.

"Hello." McArthur nodded, stopping well short of the awe-inspiring Indian and raising his right hand still higher in the universal sign of peace.

There was an almost imperceptible nod, a simple flicker of acknowledgment in his piercing eyes.

"Do you speak English?" McArthur asked.

"I do."

McArthur turned slowly, gesturing with his arm toward the wagon train circled in the distance. "I am Daniel McArthur, wagon master. We come in peace. We are your friends, your brothers."

The Indian's dark eyes glanced at the train, then looked back at McArthur. His searing gaze and commanding presence sent a chill through Tom. The Indian carried no weapon of any kind, but his iron will, his clear intelligence, and his strong, sinewy arms, circled by copper bands, demanded deference.

After what seemed to Tom an eternity, the man spoke. "I am Chief Black Eagle." With a wide sweep of his arm, he pointed toward the horizon. "You cross our land."

Tom's eyes widened. His heart pounded. This was the Indian whose wife and child had been slaughtered by Colonel Connor and the US Cavalry.

"Yes," McArthur answered, seeming calm.

"You must pay."

"Your English is good," McArthur said, clearly trying to engage Chief Black Eagle in conversation. "Where did you learn it?"

"This is none of your concern," Black Eagle responded without guile. "You are entering the Shoshoni Nation. Your cattle feed on our grass. Your wagons trample down the feed for our horses. You destroy our streams, hunt our buffalo, deer, and elk. You must pay to pass through our lands."

McArthur nodded soberly. "I understand, but we have little to pay with. We are poor travelers just passing through. We can give you what we have, but it is not much." He stopped speaking, but the stoic Indian said nothing more, waiting for some further offer that could justify their passage.

McArthur went on. "What is it you want?"

"We want your guns, ammunition, your horses."

"Can't give 'em ta you," a cautious McArthur answered. "Need 'em for protection, survival of our families, but we'll give ya what we can." Then in a plea for reconciliation, McArthur added, "I'm called by Brigham Young ta help your people, ta share with you what we can. We are committed to being your brothers."

In his first visible reaction, Black Eagle lifted an eyebrow slightly; his eyes flashed. He looked directly into McArthur's eyes, as if continuing his silent examination of his character. The silence lingered until it was painful. To his credit, Daniel McArthur did not flinch nor turn away; he returned the gaze with the confidence of a man who was telling the truth. Black Eagle looked next to Jake, then into Tom's eyes. Tom did his best to remain composed, expressionless despite his pounding heart, the perspiration on his brow, and his clenched fists.

Without another word, Black Eagle turned and walked back to the great tepee, where three elderly Indians were grouped together with four deferential, terrifying braves by their sides. So focused had Tom been on the giant of a man that he hadn't noticed the three elder chieftains now facing Black Eagle.

The eldest of the three chiefs, maybe sixty, was clearly the most respected, Tom thought. He had powerful features and a regal presence, standing over six feet tall and surely weighing in at more than 250 pounds of solid muscle. His hair, which hung to his waist, was streaked heavy with gray. His eyes were intelligent and cautious.

"Guessing that's Washakie," McArthur whispered to his companions. "He's got a relationship with Brigham Young. Hope it's still a friendly one."

Tom's stomach churned watching these Indians decide their fate.

"Other's Pocatello." McArthur paused. "Like all Indian chiefs, they say Pocatello means coldblooded killer. God only knows what it really means, but in his case I wouldn't be surprised." McArthur paused again. "Youngest is Sanpitch."

"Oh my God," Tom whispered. How could he have not noticed Sanpitch before? The terrifying, dark satanic eyes. The sullen, defiant expression. The Indian who had so coldly knocked John Meyers off his black stallion. Tom began to perspire even more profusely. Scorched into his memory was the image of the lance being driven down hard into John Meyers's shoulder, the metallic scrape of blade on bone, and the inhuman cries of pain tearing at the air. Tom could still smell the sweat and blood, see the crystal-clear image of John Meyers squirming in anguish.

As the four Indians conferred, all seemed deferential to Chief Washakie. Tom tried to follow Washakie's mood and expressions, but it was impossible. Black Eagle spoke quickly in soft, almost musical tones. The three elders listened gravely to his comments, consulted for a moment, and then Chief Washakie turned and said a few words to Black Eagle. The three nodded, and Black Eagle turned to walk back to McArthur.

Black Eagle stood silent, once again looking into McArthur's eyes long and hard, then Jake's, then Tom's. Tom stood still as a scarecrow, his heart near bursting. It was as though Black Eagle's eyes were penetrating his mind to discern the truth.

"You are a follower of the great white teacher Brigham Young?"

"I am," McArthur answered. "As are many others in these wagons who will be settling by the Great Salt Lake."

"I learned my English from Brigham Young's missionaries as a boy."

Surprised, Tom took in an involuntary sharp breath.

"I know of your history," Black Eagle continued, speaking slowly and methodically. His sharp features softened as he looked off into the distance. "Not so different than our people, driven from our homes, and, like the dew on the morning facing the summer sun, our women and children hewn down by the ugly white man without honor after being promised peace as long as the waters flow and the grass shall grow. Just like they kill the antelope and the buffalo for no reason, leaving them to molder upon the land and return to the earth."

"I understand."

Black Eagle looked into McArthur's eyes. "Brigham Young has spoken truth to us. His people learn our language, respect our customs. They have built bridges, ferries, and cut river crossings, allowing our people to use them to hunt game as promised. Planted crops for travelers and our people in times of famine, dug wells for times of drought."

With a wide sweep of his arm, Black Eagle pointed toward the hills and the plains. "You may cross our lands and enjoy their bounty as our brothers!"

Then, turning toward the large tent behind him, he nodded to the two braves standing guard at its entrance. They entered the tent and emerged with Annie and Edie, bound and gagged, hands and feet shackled with leather straps. Their feverish eyes, blazing in fear, darted from Tom to Black Eagle. Both were escorted over to stand by the giant Indian. Tears of confusion trickled down their faces.

"You may take back your women." Black Eagle nodded to a brave who then removed the women's gags and shackles. Both flung their arms around Tom's neck and hugged him tight, sobbing and heaving, too afraid to look back at the Indians who had held them captive.

"We were sore afraid," Annie cried in a whisper, her burning tears coming harder now. Her hands shaking.

"You're safe with us now."

McArthur turned to the Indian leaders, doffed his hat, then turned to Tom and Jake. "They say we're free ta go. Discussion is over. No need for any of us ta say more and risk a change of heart," McArthur whispered.

Chief Washakie stepped forward and spoke in near-perfect English. "Travel in peace through our lands and consider yourselves friends of our nation for as long as the waters flow and the grass shall grow." Then he smiled at Annie and Edith, who were too terrified to look up into the eyes of this giant of a man.

Tom nodded his appreciation, one arm around his wife and the other his sister, who both held tight to him. He felt as though the weight of the world had been lifted off his shoulders, but he tried hard not to let his emotions reach the surface.

As he passed Washakie, McArthur acknowledged the chief's welcoming offer with another tip of his hat. They mounted their horses, Annie behind Tom and Edie behind Jake, and headed back toward the wagon train. Both Annie and Edie were deathly quiet except for halting sobs and shivers of emotion. Annie, sitting behind Tom, held him so tight he could hardly breathe.

Chapter 19

❧ • ❧

"Don't be fooled into thinking these are simpleminded Indians," McArthur warned. "Washakie, as the chief of twenty thousand Shoshoni, speaks English, but also French, Spanish, Cheyenne, Sioux, and several other Indian dialects. He is cunning, fierce, and greatly feared by the US Cavalry, as are the other three chiefs that stood with him."

As they rode back to the wagon train, Tom asked McArthur, "Had you heard of Chief Black Eagle before today?"

"I recognize the name," shared McArthur. "The Bear River massacre."

"We've heard the story."

"A tragedy." McArthur sniffed.

"No wonder they don't trust white men," said Tom.

"If these Indians' offer of trust is abused, broken, or they are provoked in any way, we can expect them to be hostile and very dangerous. They have chosen to be gracious, and we must not betray that trust." McArthur turned to Jake Wyatt with a stern expression. "Mr. Wyatt, go down the line and tell all to drive slow, smile, and try to be friendly as the wagon train passes by the line of Indians in the morning. They have offered their friendship and respect; we must do the same in return."

"Yes, sir!"

"And under no circumstances should anyone pick up a gun or appear to be a threat to any Indian, or there will be hell ta pay—if someone does it and is not killed by the Indians, then, by God, I will personally shoot him myself," McArthur added.

⊱ • ⊰

That night, after the children had been put to bed, Daniel McArthur stopped by the campfire to see how Annie and Edie were faring after their ordeal.

"Still a bit shaken, but it helps to talk about it," Annie said. "Thanks to you, Mr. McArthur, I think we'll be fine." She frowned up at him. He smiled. "It was terrifying for a few hours, but with the benefit of being able to look back, they treated us well enough, I suppose. The heartrending fear was mostly in my mind." She paused. "I'm just relieved it turned out the way it did."

"Good!" McArthur touched her arm with compassion.

"What did Black Eagle mean," Tom asked, "when he spoke of the abuse to your people being the same as to theirs?"

Daniel McArthur's brooding gray eyes squinted, reflecting the dancing flames of the fire for a long, uncomfortable moment.

"In Missouri, they shoot Mormons."

"What?" Annie, eyes wide with confusion, put a hand over her mouth. She was still fragile, and his words had a chilling effect on her. "I don't understand?"

"Some years ago, a congregation from this generally feared religion moved west from upstate New York ta settle on the Missouri frontier. There were so many of 'em, the population exploded, threatening to change the politics of all of Missouri. The mostly poor white folks living in this southern border state were filled with prejudices. The church's religious sympathies for the Indians and abolitionist tenets didn't sit well with these existing residents. As Thomas Jefferson had predicted decades earlier, they were part of a mass migration that upset Southern politics and rung the antislavery fire bell. Southern Missouri became a flashpoint for rebellion. A lightning strike that ignited the powerful emotions surrounding slavery, bursting into a firestorm that burned everything and everyone in its path, ultimately ending in a ragin' civil war."

"It must have been bewildering for these people to move into a state where negros were enslaved," Annie said, emotion close to the surface, revisiting her helpless terror after being unjustly carried off and held captive by the Indians. "How awful to be pulled into the center of it all."

"When the church began takin' in Indians, free negros, and mulattos as members, the good citizens of Missouri were incensed. Negros were to be enslaved and Indians kilt, not proselytized to."

"The practice of slavery must have been soul destroying for all involved," Tom interjected.

"Missouri, angered at having their way of life upended, descended on the Mormons. They attacked their homes, destroyed their farms, businesses, abused their families, intent upon driving 'em outta the state. The Mormons fought back, and Missouri Governor Lilburn Boggs issued an extermination order on all Mormons." McArthur paused, his voice cracking. "Most would not recant their faith. Some were murdered; countless men, women, and children fled further west at the point of a gun, many more dying on the long march in the dead of winter." His distant eyes still reflected the dancing glow of the fire. He said nothing for a long moment, checking his emotions. "Not so different than the Indians' Trail of Tears."

"How could they do that to their neighbors?" Annie felt the deep sense of violation, the anger these well-meaning people must have experienced being so miserably mistreated in their own country. Annie hesitated for a moment. "The way you tell it," she whispered, horror churning in her stomach, "sounds like you have some personal history in it?" Her brows furrowed as she looked up at Daniel MacArthur, who stared into the crackling fire. Her hands sweating and her breathing shallow, Annie clenched her fists.

"I was seven when the state militia rode into Haun's Mill in a thunder, givin' no quarter and takin' no prisoners the day after the extermination order was signed into law. Was hidden in the hay bin, Ma's hand over my eyes, when they murdered my pa. He was unarmed. In his last moment of life, he fell over top of my brother Sandy . . . to protect him. In my nightmares, I can still hear the scrape of boots on the dirt floor as they dragged my dead pa off Sandy. The click of the hammer being pulled back on the shotgun. Deputy Reynolds's words—'Nits make lice.'" McArthur's voice caught. He wiped a hand slowly across his eyes. "The sound of the cannon blast inside the barn when they shot my ten-year-old brother point-blank in the forehead."

"Oh, dear God!" Edie turned from the fire and shut her eyes tight.

"Ma's other hand went tight over my mouth. The tears were running down my cheeks."

"Oh Daniel, I am so sorry." Annie wiped a tear from her eye. "I can't . . ."

"Killed seventeen of us that day. We escaped ta Caldwell County, where a month later Ma delivered my little sister. Three months later we were driven from our shared home in the dead of night after my ma was raped and I was abused. We were without any protection against the cold winter winds, snow, or marauders all along the hundred-mile march east ta a patch of desolate marshland on the

Illinois frontier. There were hundreds of us." McArthur stared into the fire, pain written across his face.

Annie couldn't speak. No one could. Her eyes were riveted on Daniel McArthur, her mind trying to fathom man's sometimes unconscionable inhumanity to man. The feeling of injustice, helplessness after being so terribly wronged.

"I still remember Ma's last words ta me as she pulled our handcart across the frozen Mississippi. In the bitter cold, I'd wrapped my little sister and myself in gunnysacks. My hands and bare feet were nearly frozen as we both lay clinging to each other in that cart. 'Is she dead yet?' Ma asked. I'll never forget that desolate look in her eyes. I was so cold I could hardly speak. 'Sis is stiff,' I told her. Ma turned away with a heaving sob and just kept pullin' that cart across the snow-covered ice. That night, on the banks of the frozen Mississippi, Ma died, too, leaving me an orphan."

Daniel McArthur and all others around the fire sat quiet for a long time. "I was raised by the McArthur family. We settled in along the river and called it Nauvoo. It was a mosquito-infested marshland. In less than six years, Nauvoo rose from a Mississippi swamp ta near the size of Chicago, filled mostly with bruised and battered Mormon families. Then our leaders were assassinated by another Missouri mob, and like the Indians, we were driven more than a thousand miles west into these mountains. God bless 'em, they wouldn't back down from their religion."

"I'm so very, very sorry," Edie whispered. "How could people be so cruel?"

"It's impossible for a boy ta suffer a thunderclap like that and still believe in a merciful God. I ain't never been back ta church since, and when I was old enough ta leave home, I became a mountain man."

"I see!" Annie whispered.

"Where was the Constitution, the Bill of Rights in all this?"

Tom asked. "I thought America was all about preserving the rights of men, including freedom of religion."

"States' rights happened." A cynical smile slipped across McArthur's face. "Incited by salacious documents sent ta a pro-slavery, anti-Indian, racist governor. And counterfeit reporting in the Missouri newspapers, not so unlike what's bein' done with the Indians right now. Politicians and angry hotheads do as they please on the frontier when it comes ta the rights of men." McArthur paused. "Our Constitution is a beautiful thing, nothin' like it anywhere in the world, but it's got a few soft spots. Folks in Washington said there was nothin' they could do—Missouri's problem, they said. A young Abraham Lincoln running for congressman was just a few miles away in Springfield, Illinois, speakin' about fixin' those soft spots in the Constitution when Ma froze ta death crossin' the Mississippi. Twenty years later, President Lincoln was workin' his way through fillin' the holes when they shot him dead."

≽ • ≼

Dearest Emma,

When I left England, I envisioned an America that does not entirely square with what I have found. Oh, it is indeed a magnificent land of promise, where for most, opportunity abounds. But what I had not anticipated in this vast land of liberty is that not all people would be given an equal opportunity. Maybe I was just naïve, but there is still prejudice here for some folks who are different. And today I thought I was about to lose my life in an Indian attack because of it. I have never felt so isolated. I have never been so terrified.

This is a land of righteousness and the preservation of the sanctity of individual rights. It is a land that offers the right to pursue happiness, unless you're a negro, a native Indian, or of the wrong religious faith. These contradictions of justice, sometimes sanctioned by government and enforced at the point of a gun, have been a surprise to me. I now better understand Jefferson's lament: "I tremble for my country when I reflect that God is just." The United States is in some ways a contradiction of ideals, principles, power, and morality. Still, Emma, this is the greatest country on earth, a bastion of liberty for most, free speech, the freedom to be left alone, and the land to spread your wings. But sometimes, too, it is freedom to make mistakes. Sometimes big ones. But here you also have the freedom to learn from those mistakes, and that makes Americans unfit to be a slave to a ruling class. I must agree with George Washington: "God help us if we ever allow our new country's burgeoning freedoms to be crushed by a ruling class, or an overbearing government, like every other country before us has."

Forever yours,
Annie

⇁ • ⇽

The next morning, the wagon train packed up camp to head west. Annie walked with Thomas just behind Abby and Elizabeth, one hand holding on to the wagon being driven by Joey. The wagons moved forward in a steady, unyielding procession. There was an uneasy separateness in the air. Remembering the hostage crisis of the day before, fear flashed through Annie's mind as they approached the Indian village. When she saw the Indians lined up along the trail, a shudder skittered down her spine. Her knees felt weak. It seemed the entire Shoshoni village stood watching the wagon train pass by. No one spoke—not Indian, not white man. Each watched the other with guarded interest.

The pioneers were weary, sober faced, yet spellbound by the intriguing foreignness of the American Indian. The passing mothers held their children close, and the beguiled children stared at the Indian children from the safety of their mothers' arms. Fathers kept their rifles out of sight in the sideboard, but cocked, ready and close. The men tried their best to appear as strong, protective patriarchs, forcing strained smiles, nodding mechanically at frequent, preordained intervals. Annie just wanted to get past these Indians who'd left her feeling violated, distrustful, hurt, and angry. She moved closer to Tom and took him by the arm, bringing her hand up to wipe the smell of fear from her nostrils, and to swallow down the heavy taste of guilt.

The Indian women stood behind their children, looking more reserved than the men behind them. The women were dressed in soft two-piece deerskin skirts belted at the waist and wide buffalo-hide tops fastened at the shoulder with curious antler-bone clips. They wore knee-length leggings fastened at the knees with buffalo leather and adorned with elaborate designs made of porcupine quills and beads. Their feet were shod in decorative moccasins. Some let their soft and silky jet-black hair flow in the wind, while others wore theirs in braids down their backs. Annie noticed that in their shyness, the women did not look directly at the curious members of the wagon train. Instead, they preferred stolen glances.

The stoic braves, both on foot and on horseback, wore cotton shirts with breastplates of colorful beaded designs or intricate quillwork much less elaborate than what the chiefs wore. All had weapons by their sides. Many had raised scars disrupting otherwise smooth copper skin, browned by years in the sun. The men were lean, hard, with flat stomachs, strong arms, and unreadable faces like carved stone, neither speaking nor acknowledging the passing train.

But it was the Indian children who broke the spell of Annie's uneasiness, softening her heart. Unlike the adults, they seemed to have no guile, no reservations. They stood enthralled, as though they were lined up along a holiday parade route. Their enormous eyes shined black, like marbles set in inquisitive faces. They chattered to each other like chipmunks. The little girls covered their faces with cupped hands, spying and whispering through spread fingers. Their excitement at this adventure erupted in peals of nervous laughter, sometimes causing them to bend over in uncontrollable giggling. These charming Indian children, wearing simple deerskin clothing, often without moccasins, rose tentative hands to wave shyly at Edie's four little ones peering curious through their wagon's canvas openings. In turn, Edie's brood waved back at the long line of Indian children, giggling and laughing themselves.

For reasons not readily apparent, the Indian children went wide-eyed and silent when Abby, hand in hand with Elizabeth, approached. The Indian women gaped at her as well. They pointed, whispering urgent messages, reaching up to pull at their own hair.

With a tentative smile, Annie leaned down to tell the two girls why the Indians were intrigued. "I think it's your bright red hair that's causing all the fuss, Abigail."

Abby reached up and touched her hair, and the children's mouths fell open. They giggled, self-conscious, and some of their mothers did, too, staring from behind spread fingers. Some blushed at being caught. A few shyly turned away, only to sneak another look when they thought no one was watching.

"I think you're right, Aunt Annie," Elizabeth chimed in.

"I'll bet they've never even seen red hair before," Annie whispered. "Look at them, they're riveted."

"Can you believe it, Abby?" Elizabeth giggled in nervous excitement.

The train approached where Chief Black Eagle had stationed his family along the trail. Next to the powerful warrior chief stood the most beautiful young Indian woman Annie had seen. Her complexion was flawless; her silken jet-black hair, adorned with intricate beadwork, shone in the late-afternoon sun, cascading to her waist like a dark, glistening waterfall. Her right arm interlaced through Black Eagle's left. The chief held their small son, who was wearing nothing but what the Lord had blessed him with at birth. Clinging tight to his father's neck, the little boy snuck a curious peek under his papa's chin. His deep brown eyes flashed through his shyness as he pointed at Abby's red hair.

Standing in front of the two regal Indians was a stunning young girl. Although maybe only a year younger than Abby, the striking child was clearly transfixed. She leaned back into her mother for protection, but she couldn't take her eyes off the red hair. Annie could see her saying something to her mother, who nodded in response, her own eyes never leaving Abby.

When Abby returned the child's gaze, the Indian girl's copper cheeks reddened. She looked down, but only for a moment. Annie could see Abby and the girl lock eyes, and a contagious, acknowledging smile spread wide across both faces. Abby waved at the girl. And with a bright and ardent smile, her eyes sparkling, the girl shyly lifted her hand and waved back.

Annie smiled. The entire interaction didn't go unnoticed by Black Eagle, though his stoic expression remained unchanged. The mighty warrior handed his son to the boy's mother. Black Eagle stepped carefully forward through the Indian children lining the path of the wagon train and approached Abigail and Annie.

The tension went up a notch. Annie straightway pulled up closer to Thomas, intertwining both arms around his. Tom came to attention and cautiously moved closer behind the girls. The wagon train slowed to a halt.

All eyes were now focused on the tall, powerful, and intimidating Black Eagle, who stepped up to Annie, whispering his request. In turn, she looked toward Rachel, who nodded. Black Eagle went down on one knee to speak to Abigail face-to-face. Gently, he touched her red hair, and with an almost imperceptible smile, he said, "My daughter says your hair is like fire."

Abby, seeming not at all afraid, was quick to respond. "And your daughter's hair is the most beautiful silky black I have ever seen." Then boldly she asked, "Do you think I could talk to her?"

The response from this petite pioneer girl so surprised Black Eagle that for a moment his stern countenance faltered, revealing a warm, infectious smile. He glanced up at Tom and Annie, his bright eyes beaming approval.

"What is your name?" he asked Abby.

"Abigail," she replied confidently. "What is your daughter's name?"

Black Eagle turned, calling his daughter and her striking mother over. As they made their way to stand beside him, he whispered, "My daughter's name is Shantea."

"Shantea—such a beautiful name!"

He bowed his head slightly and then looked at her again. "You, too, have a beautiful name, little one." With a simple smile, he looked up at his apprehensive wife and daughter.

Abby and Shantea stood smiling at each other. Unshackled by prejudice of age or culture, they shared a unwritten language only children understand.

Abigail's cheeks tuned apple red. Her eyes sparkled like precious emerald gems, widening with inspiration. "I need to get something out of the wagon!" She clattered off in a flurry of excitement, her animated hands motioning toward the back of the wagon as she began rummaging through the disheveled pile of her belongings.

Both Indians and pioneers alike watched curiously. Annie, cautiously intrigued, craned her neck to see what Abby intended. Other children farther away stood up on their wagon seats. The tension seemed to disappear from the air and Annie's heart as the humanity of this interaction touched her.

Then a wide smile spread across Abby's face. "I found it!" she shouted, holding up her favorite red-haired rag doll in triumph.

Abby looked toward her mam for confirmation. Rachel nodded her permission.

With her characteristic vivacious smile, Abby slowly approached the young Indian girl, her outstretched hands offering her precious gift of friendship. The offering seemed to transcend their vast differences.

Shantea's mother smiled in appreciation. Gently, she pushed her shy daughter toward Abby while smiling at Rachel. Two mothers from different worlds, sharing a commonality of all peoples, from all cultures: love of children.

"This is for you, Shantea." Abby handed the little Indian girl her favorite doll.

Blushing, Shantea shyly took the doll in her arms. She touched and caressed her red hair, tracing the yarn strands with her finger. Then she flashed an appreciative smile at Abby before looking up at Black Eagle.

He smiled at his daughter. "Thank you," he mouthed to her.

Shantea turned back to Abby and offered an enthusiastic "Thank you! Thank you! Thank you!" Her timid countenance gave way to a fervent smile of friendship.

All the other little Indian children followed suit, smiling and repeating the words "Thank you! Thank you! Thank you!" They giggled in delight, clustering around Shantea to see and feel the gift.

Black Eagle glanced toward Annie, nodded, and without words, an understanding passed between them. "One little girl alone cannot change the world," he said, "but she can cast a stone across the water and make many ripples."

Relief flooded the faces of pioneers and Indians alike. Both groups had witnessed the wonder of this simple shared act, this moment between children who were unspoiled by the prejudices of the world that come with age. It was a gift of the heart that soothed Annie's soul. *We are very different peoples,* she thought, *but in some ways, we have more in common than not.* This kindled a hope for mutual respect between these cultures, respect that she thought might lead to better understanding and strengthen the budding friendship that had begun on an isolated Wyoming mountain trail. Bridges had been built, possibilities for generations to come. For all their differences, these cultures shared a common core: love of children and family.

Chapter 20

❖ • ❖

SUMMER HAD FINALLY REACHED THE Grand Tetons, which were cloaked in white from the heaviest snowfall in a decade. Ten months of layered snowpack held firm to the igneous rock, but with the warmth of the sun, it had begun to thaw. Melting continued in earnest when gusty showers from a westerly summer rain slipped unnoticed over the magnificent craggy peaks. Driven by fierce mountain winds, the rain turned into steady gray sheets, cutting the midday light into an early evening.

As evening fell into night, the rain came harder, roaring and swishing torrents of runoff cascading down the mountainside, ripping up roots of the hawthorn bush and scattered twisted pine, spilling into tributary creeks that wound their way down into the Wind River Canyon and the meandering Green River. The flooding waters joined the Big Sandy, and the two great, swollen rivers merged and snaked through the canyon and into the spreading valley below.

All through the stormy night, and the days and nights that followed, violent lightning ripped open the sky. Unrepentant, raging waters flooded the storm-ravaged valley, delivering more destruction and debris than in a hundred years. The churning undermined the ancient evergreens, willows, and cottonwoods, bending them in muddy water.

When the wagon train pulled up on the plateau overlooking the Green, the families were met with a worrisome sight: The fury of the summer storm had made Wyoming's Green River impossible to cross. Tom could see full-sized trees barreling along in the rushing water. Long sections of riverbank had been breached, flooding the surrounding plains.

The company of worn travelers were soaked to the bone. Streams of water ran from Tom's hat to his shoulders. The edges of his coat dripped and his shoes squished as he jumped down off the wagons into the ankle-deep mud to assess the situation with their wagon master.

"Ain't much most of the year, but come late summer it can sweep you away, and this summer is a sight to behold, twelve- to fifteen-feet-deep rushing water coming down the river," McArthur said. "This rain has eliminated any chance of a ferry crossing for the time bein'."

"What do we do?" Tom asked, squinting through the downpour.

"We wait."

"Can't we try to launch the ferry?" asked Annie.

"You put a ferry in that, and before you reach the other shore, you'll wind up back in Laramie, if you're lucky enough not to be drowned first." Lewis Robson, the ferryboat operator, hooted like a barn owl. "Just be thankful it ain't ten feet of winter snow."

So, they waited while the earth whispered under the beat of the rain. In the evening, the families huddled together under the canvas wagon cover listening to the splattering overhead. It worked at the canvas until it found entry, sending streams down into the wagons, soaking bedding, food, and everything else. Both the Wright and Stone families huddled together and waited in wet clothes for seven interminable days until the rain stopped, but the runoff from the great Teton mountains would continue raging through the steep canyons and into the valley for many more days to come. Late-starting parties caught up to them and joined the wait. The only consolation Tom found was that the horse-drawn rigs that had blithely passed McArthur's train in the preceding weeks were fretting at the river's edge, same as everyone else.

Each morning McArthur went down and inspected the river with Mr. Robson, and each afternoon they studied the skies and discussed possibilities. The decision each evening was always the same: The river was too high.

"With a bit o' luck, a little sunshine will come ta soothe 'er down," a dejected Mr. Robson proffered.

Camping on the few islands of high ground in the flooded plain left little for the travelers to do. For more than a week, the train prepared equipment, reorganized wagons, searched for game, and made ready the ferryboat, waiting for the day when Mr. Robson would deem the river passable. Finally, the weather cleared and the flooding river began to drop. All were anxious when Daniel McArthur and Lewis Robson once again met to discuss their options.

Then came the news. "Today showed real promise," McArthur announced. "Tomorrow, we cross!"

≻ • ≺

Tom and Annie were understandably wary of the upcoming crossing, and Tom took a moment to discuss it with Mr. Robson.

"We've replaced the parts for the guy rope and pulleys needed to traverse the river," Mr. Robson reminded him. "And with the improvements to the raft, we should easily be able ta transport two wagons, a couple large families, and three yokes of oxen at a time."

"How does it work?" asked Tom, concerned but fascinated by the engineering.

"We've set the guy rope taut, well fixed ta the abutment rock on either bank of the river," Mr. Robson explained. "There'll be some heavy tension passin' through those pulleys, but with the rudder on the ferry set proper, we'll use that fast-movin' current ta pull us across, slick as ya please."

"Quite ingenious."

❧ • ❦

The next morning, McArthur, his scouts, and the teamsters were the first to take the ferryboat over with a few horses and cattle. Everyone watching from both shorelines cheered as Mr. Robson and his first cargo reached the far bank without mishap. It would take several trips over two days for all to cross.

This time, Joey, Tom, and Annie were prepared. They had been careful to organize their wagon for the crossing, with safety tie-downs, long trailing ropes in case they got separated from the wagon, and strategies for every possible emergency. There would not be a repeat of their mistakes on the Platte River crossing.

Both Tom and Andrew's wagons were among the first to satisfy Mr. Robson's ten-point checklist and receive clearance to cross together on the same ferry load. So, Abby sent Elizabeth off with a hug and her best good luck wishes.

Tom edged the wagon slowly and steadily down the riverbank. The chaise bounced and jostled its way over the steep, heavily eroded slope to the river's edge, stopping just short of the waiting ferryboat, and then Mr. Robson guided it onto the ferry. Joey walked beside the oxen to calm them. Tom was in the rear, and Annie moved inside the wagon, securing their belongings. Her hands were shaking, and she took in deep gulps of air, trying her best to calm her nerves. She had gone over every step, checked and rechecked the safety precautions a dozen times. Still, she was nervous. Her near disaster crossing the Platte was lodged firm in her mind.

Once loaded onto the raft, the animals calmed, and the safety checks were rechecked. Mr. Robson and his teamsters pushed off to cross the five-hundred-foot-wide river. A tense, solemn quiet filled the air. Only the sound of the rushing river passing under the ferryboat broke the silence. Annie never made a sound and never took her eyes off the fast-moving water beneath them. She kept a white-knuckle grip on the wagon seat, her whole body rigid. Gradually the river deepened. Annie took deep, controlled breaths, gripping tighter. They approached the center of the river, the swifter current passing beneath the raft, lapping up the edges, as they moved ever closer to the shallower shoals. Finally, they touched softly on the western shore.

Annie let out a whoop for all to hear.

With much scrambling and snorting, the oxen found their footing, sloshing laboriously up the muddy slope, dragging the wagon behind. The travelers shared collective gallows laughter, replacing the tension with exuberant joy in their hearts. Smiles spread from ear to ear.

"They made it!" Abby let out her new two-finger whistle. "They made it look easy!" She waved ecstatically to Elizabeth, who waved back with energetic jumping jacks.

"We did it!" shouted Annie, relieved to step onto the west bank. "I've never been so happy to be on land in my life." She grinned at Thomas. "I don't think I took a single breath the whole way!"

"Why, I couldn't tell you were nervous at all, Annie," Tom chided. "I was thinking I might suggest to Lewis that you go back and assist the next load of wagons."

She pushed him aside. "You liar. You know I was shakin' in my boots! I ain't goin' back nowhere! My river crossin' days are over!"

"My chores are done, Mam, our wagon's cleaned up, reorganized, oxen brushed down, the animals set to graze, and still Abby has not crossed the river," Elizabeth complained as the shadows of dusk began to fill the cloudy sky.

"Be patient, young lady," Edie said to her daughter as she and Annie finished up dinner. "Remember, patience is a virtue."

Elizabeth rolled her eyes as she sat down on the picnic blanket strategically placed high on a grassy knoll overlooking the river. She was intently keeping her eyes on the other side, watching for Abby and her family's ferry crossing.

Edie gave her daughter a questioning look and shook her head. "I'm sure Abby will be here soon." She turned to Annie. "These two girls have become joined at the hip."

"Mam, can Abby and I have the day off tomorrow to go exploring?" Elizabeth looked at Edie with pleading eyes. "Please, Mam. My chores are done, and I've scouted out some really great places for adventure."

"Let me speak to Rachel. Remember, you have brothers and sisters, but I think we can probably work something out."

Elizabeth sat, legs crossed, elbows on her knees, watching events across the river unfold. "It's gonna be dark soon," she muttered.

Annie sat down beside her. "She'll be here soon enough."

"I hope so." Elizabeth put her chin in her hands.

Both watched Gabriel readying the fractious oxen on the far distant shore.

≻ • ≺

"Sorry, folks," Daniel McArthur called out to the rest of those waiting in line to cross. "Gabriel and his family will be the last wagon to cross this evening!"

Annie found it fascinating she could hear his voice clear across the river on this quiet, windless evening. She continued listening. "We'd like to get as many o' yer animals as we can on the west bank ta feed on the fresh grass," Mr. Robson said. "We can't swim 'em in this current, so line 'em up and we'll take as many as we can on this last raft."

"Poor Gabriel." Annie frowned as she sat next to Elizabeth, watching him struggle to get his oxen to do as he wished. "It's been a long day for all of them, one problem after another. But we'll have a nice dinner ready for them. A little pampering will make it all better."

"Of course, Aunt Annie. You're always right."

"You're so sweet."

Like so many nights before, both families were looking forward to sharing dinner, a little music by the fire, and good conversation before bedding down.

With Gabriel in the front, Rachel on the wagon seat, Abigail inside the wagon, and one of the teamsters at the rear, they started toward the ferry. Bumping and jostling their way down the slope, the oxen were pushed and pulled to the water's edge.

To make more room for cattle and extra oxen, only Mr. Robson planned to accompany this last ferry on the final crossing of the day. "Okay, Gabriel, load 'er on," he called out.

Gabriel took hold of the bridle and in a calm, steady voice, coaxed the oxen onto the raft, guiding them as close to the upstream edge as possible. At the sight of the swift-flowing river, the oxen grew more fractious. Their eyes darted from side to side as they stepped onto the sloshing raft. When they were on, Rachel pulled tight on the brake to keep the wagon from rolling. Abby was laying her body over all their worldly possessions to hold them in place inside the wagon.

"They're awful close to the edge." Annie shuddered. She could see the raft tilting to the weighted side and water splashing onto the deck.

The yoke of oxen was cut loose from the wagon for safety, then pulled tight to the wagon seat, making more room on the raft for livestock. One by one, the teamsters squeezed oxen and cattle onboard, filling the floating transport until it had sunk nearly flush with the water's surface. Then, the heavily loaded raft was pushed off with a swoosh, settling even lower into the rushing river. Mr. Robson tugged hard on the guy rope. The swirling current dragged the lumbering ferry steadily across. There was an eerie quiet as the sun began to set in the west. Annie felt uneasy in the stillness of the evening. She could hear only the sound of water, snorts, huffing and puffing of the oxen as the raft made its way toward the deep center of the river.

The setting sun reflected off the underside of the cloud cover in a blaze of color that turned the surface of the river dark orange and red, obscuring shadowed sandbars, submerged tree limbs, and other obstacles. The crush of animals stood shoulder to shoulder, their eyes darting. Feeling a restless shiver, Annie watched Gabriel and Mr. Robson speak in soothing tones close to the animals' ears. They gave the beasts gentle touches to calm their fears as the river lapped up against the wagon wheels on the upstream edge of the raft.

Rachel cast nervous glances toward her husband, then at Mr. Robson, who was manning the rudder. But Robson, clearly tired, seemed calm and unconcerned after a long day of successful trips. He smiled back. Still, Annie was left with nagging worry. "No fooling around, just get them over here." Annie couldn't help but remember something Martha had once told her, "Sometimes, there is nothing quite as vulnerable as entrenched success." Annie's hands began to sweat. She wiped them on her skirt.

It began with a single yoke of oxen shifting their weight, bumping their neighbors. The skittish neighbors reacted, pulling away with a start, and in turn they bumped hard against a two-ton ox on the opposite side, who bumped his neighbor even harder. Startled, the ox began to panic, trying to turn around in the confined space. Even at this distance, Annie could see the blazing eyes and jerky movements indicating panic in both man and animal. Horns swinging and hooves stamping, one ox pushed and bumped his way from the claustrophobic center toward the upstream edge of the ferryboat. Gabriel and Mr. Robson rushed to quiet the animals just as Rachel, eyes wide with terror, stepped out onto the precarious lazy board to pull back on the brake and shorten the reins. But it was too late. The moment had been lost. There were too many animals on the move now.

With the oxen's excitement, the cattle spooked, too, mooing and stamping their hooves, eyes round with fear, pushing and shoving. They followed the oxen toward the upstream edge of the ferry just as the raft reached the heaviest currents at the center of the river. The sudden uneven distribution of weight sank the upstream edge below the oncoming current. The water flooded over the deck of the hapless raft at more than a hundred cubic feet per second, sweeping away everything in its path. Men and beasts plunged into the river, flailing and slashing at the fast-moving water. Annie watched in horror—the chaos, the panic, the snorting beasts with horns swinging and eyes bulging as they tumbled over each other in the sweep of the raging rapids. The shore was still nearly three hundred feet away in either direction.

The upstream edge of the now rudderless raft had submerged well below the surface of the river and could not hold back the furious rush of water. The hydraulic force snapped the guy rope, which shot through the air like a bullwhip in a crack of thunder. In a violent recoil, the raft heaved back to right itself, catapulting Rachel from her perch on the extended lazy board like a slingshot hurling a stone far out into the river. And right behind her came the covered wagon, landing upside down in the river, swirling in circles with Abby trapped inside as the water rushed in.

The currents sucked the wagon deeper into the river, collapsing the cover in the churning water. The saturated ropes, clothing, bedding, and canvas-covered wagon trapped Abby in a claustrophobic tangle of all their worldly possessions.

Annie thought she heard Abby scream, but the icy cold water quickly silenced all sounds from inside the wagon cab.

Annie, racked with fear, vomited what remained of her lunch. Her own experience taught her that Abby must be struggling with every fiber of her adrenaline-driven muscle to free herself. In a panic, desperately trying to draw breath from the dwindling pocket of life-saving air. But her struggle would only further entangle her. Abby's lungs would be burning, her heart racing to keep up with the lack of oxygen to her brain.

Elizabeth stared in horror, screaming as the surreal scene played out before her, blind to all else around her she raced to the edge of the river.

No longer tethered to the guy rope, no longer weighted with passengers, the raft had been swept swiftly downstream, past the sinking wagon, past man and beast fighting for survival.

In the chaos of the darkening evening, Annie saw Gabriel amid the thrashing animals. In a single-minded focus he grasped both horns of a giant ox frantic to get to shore and dragged himself high up on the animal, above the writhing fray. Eyes wide and gasping for air, Gabriel searched frantically up and down the river for his wife and daughter. All the while the current was carrying him farther downstream, away from the nearly submerged wagon.

"Rachel! Abigail!" Gabriel desperately called. "Rachel! Abigail!"

Annie and Elizabeth, following along water's edge, were now even with Gabriel, both ignoring brush and brambles tearing into their skin.

"Abby is in the wagon!" Elizabeth screamed.

Pushing his way through the wild-eyed beasts, Gabriel fought the swift current to swim upstream toward the capsized wagon.

Transfixed by the unfolding nightmare, Annie watched Gabriel struggle to lift his heavy, jacketed arms out of the water. Flailing and slapping the surface with each stroke and nearly drowning himself, he began pulling at the wet clothes, trying to remove them, with little success. At long last he reached the semi-submerged wagon. He clung to it, clearly exhausted, panting hard, searching the surface of the raging river for a glimpse of his wife.

Annie, scrambling through brambles, slipping, sliding, and falling into the mud, kept pace with the slowly drifting wagon. "Rachel is downstream!" she yelled out. "Can you see her? She's over there." Her arm frantically waving in the air, she pointed and cried.

Then he saw her, in the far distance downstream, in the midst of the fastest-moving current of the flooding river. She was alone, turning over and over in the rapids, her long, encumbering skirts wrapped around her in a suffocating cocoon that dragged her under the rapids again and again. Even from the shore Annie could see she was drowning.

"Rachel!" Gabriel called out in a desperate voice. "Rachel!"

Annie watched in horror as Rachel, with seemingly superhuman strength, called out with what seemed the last of her reserves. "Abigail . . . trapped . . . wagon." She sputtered, trying to pass on the most important message of her life. "Save my baby! Please . . . Oh Gabriel, save my baby!" She begged in an anguish with beseeching eyes that Annie would forever remember in her worst nightmares.

"Help!" Gabriel called out, over and over again, pleading for someone to come to their aid. His raspy voice cracking, delirious, haunted with piercing fear. But despite the mountain of will, there was no one capable of helping this desperate family in the cold, raging river.

"What am I to do?" Gabriel's cry echoed across the surface of the river as darkness closed in on the moonless night, leaving only the ambient light of a sun that had already set. "Don't make me choose between the two I love most in all the world."

His contorted face showed the exhaustion, the defeat as he called his final words to his wife: "I love you, Rachel." But Rachel was beyond listening now. No longer fighting, she tumbled over and over in the downstream current.

Annie buckled to her knees in the muddy water, her voice gone. Her hands, arms, legs, and face were scratched and bleeding. Deranged with heartache, she was nearly blinded by her streaming tears.

Gabriel took in a deep breath and dove beneath the surface of the dark water in search of his precious daughter. Moments passed, seeming like a lifetime. Annie and all others on shore held their breath, helpless, waiting for Gabriel to resurface. It seemed he was under forever, but when he finally came up for air, he was empty handed and clearly spent.

Now, Annie could only hear the tormented cries from a delirious Elizabeth standing beside her: "God, help her. She hates the dark."

Annie put her scratched and bloodied hands over her open mouth to stop the silent scream that rang in her head louder than all hell's pandemonium.

Men on both sides of the river searched all night. Abigail's body was the first to be found, two miles downstream in a rocky cove. Annie had been so sick with the news that it was all she could do to make herself walk the distance to the washed-up wagon.

From somewhere deep inside her came a sound high and sharp. Her eyes fell upon the once beautiful young girl's bent and broken body lying quiet among the scattered belongings and debris. The air seemed still, but the river rushed past Abby, who was caught in the tangle of the wagon's wreckage. Eddies pushed Abigail's lifeless body to and fro. The sparkle in her crystal-clear green eyes, windows into an intelligent mind, was gone. She stared dull and lifeless into the cloudy skies overhead. Her rosy cheeks, sprinkled with freckles, were now chalky gray. Her flaming-red hair, now coated in the silty browns of the river bottom, waved listlessly in the current. The vibrant girl was no more, her larger-than-life presence extinguished.

Tenderly, Elizabeth knelt to her knees in the water to hug her dear friend one last time. Her long braid falling across Abby's shoulder, Elizabeth pulled her up and rocked back and forth with Abby in her arms. Annie found herself imagining when Abby awoke, she would tell her how tender Elizabeth had been. How much she loved her. But then maybe it was she herself who was asleep. Nothing seemed real, everything out of place.

Both Rachel and Gabriel's bodies were found two days later, miles downriver.

Chapter 21

❖ • ❖

THERE HAD BEEN GRAVES TO dig, burials to prepare for, and sermons to give. Then a broken-down wagon on the flint-hard mountain trails, worn-out shoes and hooves, and split iron tread on the spoked wheels of the wagon in the most tempestuous weather so far. Rain, wind, and a furious squall cresting over the Tetons made it even more difficult for Annie to contain the turmoil in her heart. The storm blew for days, but she scarcely felt its chill as the broken wagon limped and clamored down the trail through the rugged Wyoming territory.

For over a week, Annie and Thomas had not spoken of the tragedy or their fruitless search for meaning in it. The fragility of life. The unfairness!

It had affected Annie in ways she had not expected. But she could not speak of it, despite Thomas's encouragement to do so. In the confusion, she tried to sort out her feelings, her fears. She could not make sense of the hurt that tore at her heart. With the death of Rachel, a light in Annie seemed to have gone out—that spirit of life. She feared once it was lost, she might never get it back. And worst of all was knowing she might have to go through this struggle all alone again.

After putting the rest of the family to bed, Annie crossed the campsite to where Thomas sat alone by the fire. This was the first clear night since the tragedy, and the glow of stars strung by the thousands shone like sapphires all across the night sky to the distant line of the Tetons. She considered the empty place on the log next to her husband, then sat down across the fire, putting her hands out to warm them. The gilded flame danced through the smoldering glow of embers, warming the cool night air on this high mountain summer evening.

Only the sound of crackling logs broke the silence. Tom, lost in his own thoughts, didn't seem to notice her. He sat solemn, prodding the aromatic logs from one side of the fire to the other in a halfhearted effort at keeping the flames alive. Their carefully laid plans for the future had been left in shambles. When Gabriel died, Mr. Stone shelved his plans for the Comstock Mining Company. Of course, there were the pressing matters of daily survival. The family had eaten the last of their food supplies. The money was gone, and they had no idea where they'd earn more now that everything had changed. And they were not at all prepared for the coming winter. Moreover, Tom seemed to be left without a plan, no idea where to go or how to get there. It was as if he had been suspended in midair, not quite sure of anything anymore, not even himself. Annie knew he was caught up in the worry about what to do. But she couldn't think about that now.

She stared transfixed into the fire. The hole in her heart had been magnified through the lens of tragedy. There was no Emma to talk to, and now that Rachel was in the ground and their lives in such turmoil, she felt panicked.

"Annie, will you at least talk to me about it?"

Thomas's question startled her back into the moment. She looked up from the fire to see his eyes upon her. "Aw, I think I'm coming down with a cold. All the bad weather and . . . sleeping on the cold ground." They had been letting Elizabeth sleep in their wagon, while they slept under it, trying to stay out of the rain without making it too inviting for diamondback rattlers looking for a warm place to spend the night. "It's taken its toll."

"It's more than that, Annie. It's been a week. Can't you talk to me about this?"

Annie froze in the flicker of the firelight between them. She had kept her secrets hidden, preserved in amber, trapped beyond reach. She felt too much hurt to continue to pretend there was nothing wrong. A wedge had been driven between she and her husband, but she was afraid to share her fears. The ache had sat hard after Rachel's death, like a festering knot deep in the pit of her stomach, as if Satan himself had taken command over her heart. Despite her efforts to push it aside, the image of Thomas standing in front of Lydia's grave had been resurrected. Maybe an irrational fear, brought on by the tragedy. Nevertheless, the vision was seared deep, and now it hung over her like a pall. She had always known Lydia would be her husband's treasured soulmate, but that knowledge did not make it any less painful on her heart. Even in death Lydia held him captive, and her too. "I'm so sorry, Thomas, but no, I can't. Not about this."

Tom poked the burning logs hard, causing sparks to fly, and Annie jumped, putting her hands on either side of the log she sat on to steady herself.

"You can be exasperating, Annie," he whispered into the fire. "At the very least . . ."

"I know, Thomas," she responded to the frustration in his voice. "I'm hurting. We all are, but this has made me go places in my heart that I thought I'd sealed off. Now I find it difficult to . . ." Annie intended to forestall a plunge into the subject she feared bringing to the surface. "I wrote to Emma about it, for I know no other soul as dear as my sister."

As soon as she said it, Annie felt a pang of regret for the hurt she saw in Thomas's eyes.

"Except for me, Annie? Except for your husband! Was it not so before all this happened?"

"In many things, yes, Thomas, but in this thing, I cannot tell you how I feel." She supposed if she didn't love him so much, she could talk openly! With Emma an ocean away, Rachel had become the port of refuge for her innermost fears, but now she, too, was gone. The loss of her child and her friend, the ghost of Lydia—it was all too traumatizing to speak of to Thomas. Annie was alone, without a confidant.

"Do you not think I want to be told of your concerns, Annie?"

"Oh, I am sure you want the best for me in all things. You have always had my interests at heart and try to be considerate. But . . . It's difficult to explain what's in my heart right now."

"Try me!" He came around the fire and sat beside her, put a gentle hand over hers. "Please, Annie, it's been a week and you've hardly said a word."

Annie's hands began to sweat, her lip quivered. She wanted to confide in him. To lean on him. To have him hold her. She wanted him to love her above all else in the world. Maybe she was selfish in that way, but still she wanted him—all of him. Maybe her fears of addressing the subject were irrational, but at this moment she could not risk hearing the resentful tenor of his voice, seeing the confirming flash in his eyes. There seemed a distance between them, and she was terrified to cross it. She didn't think she could bear the confirmation of being second place in his heart. Not now. It would be too hard. She was too fragile and the price too high. "I'm sorry, Thomas, but I can't." Wiping at her eyes, she stood. Feeling guilty, she turned and walked away into the night without another word.

PART II

September 1868

Chapter 22

☙ • ❧

TOM SAT IN THE SADDLE atop Old Brea, ambling along the Echo Canyon ridgeline, overlooking a geologic architecture as unique as any in the world. The pale, cold sun was rising behind them, revealing the stark, rugged beauty of the high mountain plateaus. Jagged hillside banks ran deep in red and orange. Scattered cottonwoods were already losing their leaves with the promise of an early winter and one of the heaviest snowfalls in a decade.

Tom pulled up alongside Mr. Ritter. Taking in the reins on Old Brea, he cast his eyes down Echo Canyon, a natural pathway through the mountains where buffalo, Indians, explorers, the Pony Express, Mormon pioneers, California gold miners, and the stagecoach had traveled for centuries. Now, it marked the route the transcontinental railway would follow. He marveled at the sight. In the far distance, thousands of men and animals scurried about, shouts and equipment breaking the sacred solitude of the mountains. The slow, peaceful evolution of eons was being shattered and reshaped by the imagination and handiwork of man. Vegetation was stripped, and the rocky geology dismantled, ripped, and carved to make way for progress. The Union Pacific was building a railroad for the Millennial Marvel, which would echo through this canyon, belching smoke and carrying people and goods of all kinds, tying the Eastern gentry to the Wild West. It would be three thousand miles long, from New York to San Francisco, when finished.

"Wow." Tom wiped the sweat from his brow. "This is incredible, John."

"I told ya it was a sight to behold."

"Whadda ya think?" Tom asked as Joey, Annie, Andrew, and Edie pulled the wagons up alongside.

"I guess it's time you got started breakin' some rock," Joey offered.

John Ritter's expression hardened. "As I told you at Fort Bridger, all I can promise is sixteen-hour days of hard work, swingin' a sledgehammer and carryin' iron rails."

The muscles in Tom's jaw twitched. "At least it'll put food on the table." He looked up at the clear blue sky. "I suppose we'd best appreciate the good weather, shouldn't we?"

"Yeah," John cut in. "It'll be gettin' a whole lot colder in these mountains over the days ta come."

"I'm sure you're right, but it feels great to arrive someplace we can plan to stay for a while," Andrew added, looking out at the mountains.

"And you have a wagon to sleep under," said John Ritter. "Most of these poor buggers got nothin'."

It'd been agreed that as soon as they got a little money, Edie and the children would continue on to Park City, sell the oxen and their wagon, and find a place to live, leaving the remaining wagon for Annie and the men.

All sat quiet, looking in awe at the thousands of men hurrying about over the hillsides. It was the hustle and bustle of thriving industry, men and their machines cutting grades down steep terrain and carving roadways as smooth as silk, drilling holes in rock to fill with black powder to reconfigure the rocky geology of millennia.

The canyon was being transformed before their very eyes, readied for the dozens of crosstie sleeper and creeper crews to lay parallel ribbons of iron rail.

⁂

"This is the fellow I was speaking to you about, Mr. Young." John Ritter introduced Tom. "He's been breaking rock and carrying rail for me the past two weeks."

Tom was busy helping Annie with dinner. He wiped his hands on his trousers. "Mr. Young." He nodded at his family. "My brothers, Joey and Andrew, and my wife Annie."

Joseph Young shook Tom's hand. "Mr. Wright." He nodded to Joey, Andrew, and Annie. "Mrs. Wright. It's a pleasure."

"Mr. Young, with Sharp & Young," John pointed out, "has the contract with General Grenville Dodge, the director of operations for the Union Pacific, to build the Echo Canyon line, including the four tunnels."

"Of course." Tom nodded.

"From what Mr. Ritter here tells me," Mr. Young began, "your work experience, technical knowledge, and leadership abilities with the men . . . Well, we just might have something to talk about, Mr. Wright."

"Would you like to sit down by the fire?" Tom asked.

"I apologize for interrupting your dinner." Joseph Young tipped his hat to Annie. "But if I could just borrow your husband a few minutes, I'd sure appreciate it."

"Absolutely."

Joseph Young shared a studied smile as he followed Tom and John to the crackling campfire, which was bringing a bit of warmth to the cool fall evening.

"I'm not sure what Mr. Ritter has told you, but we've got a construction schedule that some say is impossible to meet." Mr. Young paused to let his comment sink in. "I understand you know a little about cutting tunnels?"

"I spent most of my life blastin' jagged arteries and diggin' airless capillaries through veins of coal a thousand feet below ground."

"He was the explosives and technical director for the Silkstone and Elsecar Coalowners Company, the largest coal mining operation in the United Kingdom," Joey interjected from afar. "He handled the most difficult technical and logistics problems for all their mines."

"Well, thank you, Joey." Mr. Young nodded thoughtfully. "Impressive!" Turning back to Tom, he asked, "Have you seen much of our operation here?" He gave an appraising look. "We have four tunnels to excavate. Castle Rock #2, just above Echo Canyon, will be the longest tunnel on the entire line. At 775 feet when it's finished, one of the longest in the world."

"I've had a chance to look around a bit over the last week between swings of my sledge."

Mr. Young smiled. "We'll probably need three, four hundred men for those tunnels alone." He looked into Tom's eyes, and Tom held his gaze with cool confidence. "Mr. Ritter tells me the men you're working with all seem to respect and admire your abilities. Some even fear you, which can be a good thing in a leader of men."

"Big project." Tom blew out a breath through pursed lips. "Suppose it goes with the territory. Mr. Ritter has been kind enough to share some of the details on the tunnels."

"Well, did he tell you we need all the help we can get to meet the nearly impossible schedule? That over the past month I have already paraded a dozen possible candidates to run the tunnel operation before General Dodge."

"He did!"

"Why do you think you're the man who can master this little project, Mr. Wright?"

Without dropping his penetrating gaze, Tom lifted one corner of his mouth in a half smile. "Nothing little about it. You have a lot of hardworking men—very impressive."

Mr. Young smiled back. "Why do I get the feeling you have a caveat coming?"

Tom chuckled. "No intention of bein' critical, Mr. Young. Of course, my family appreciates the work. But as with all operations, there might be a thing or two could be improved."

"Such as?" Mr. Young was clearly doing his best to discern the character of the man sitting before him. "I would appreciate your candor."

"Fair enough. I might suggest a change or two in your blasting operation. Cutting tunnels through rock is a far different proposition than setting grade to place rails. It can be complicated, expensive, and very dangerous in a confined tunnel, but if each segment of the work is broken down to its component parts . . ." Tom paused to make sure his audience was following. "Well, it's not so complicated. It's all about the process, procedures, managing men and logistics properly."

"Go on. And please be specific, if you will?"

"Don't mean to be impertinent, but yes, there are a number of changes I might suggest." Tom nodded toward John, whom he had already had this conversation with. "The geology going through the Castle Rock mountain changes, the type of rock changes from limestone to harder conglomerates. And in tunnels three and four, it's a much harder dark blue quartzite. It would be more effective to use a five-hole slant pattern in setting off explosives. Quartzite and the granites especially require a much different blasting pattern than the limestone and sandstones you've been working with, and even in the conglomerates, the geologic character changes dramatically. A reconfiguration would save time and money. Dark blue quartzite is a metamorphic rock, and has much different geotechnical properties, with an angle of inclination—"

"Okay, Mr. Wright, okay," Mr. Young interrupted. "You lost me at metamorphic. It sounds like you have some thoughts that might be better shared with someone more knowledgeable on the engineering details." His eyes brightened; he was clearly impressed with Tom's understanding of the work. "Would you be willing to join us in a meeting tomorrow morning with General Dodge? He is a brilliant engineer, very particular and detailed. President Grant says General Dodge's strategic planning was the reason the North won the war."

"That'd be fine."

"Well, good then. How about six a.m. sharp. There might be something to talk to you about other than swinging a sledgehammer."

"Look forward to it."

"I'll be frank with you, Tom. General Dodge and I have been looking for someone to run the tunnel operation for some time. It is a very difficult and dangerous job, where the lives of many men depend on good judgment and disciplined leadership, not to mention the fortunes of my company and those of the Union Pacific's in their race to the finish line." Joseph Young paused. "But I wouldn't be forthcoming if I didn't tell you we've gone through a lot of good men trying to find the right fit. Some with far more education and better credentials than yours. Pedigrees, if you will. Even if I like you, I've found that matters little to the general. He'll be making the decision."

Tom arrived at Castle Rock at the crack of dawn. "Good morning, Mr. Young."

"Thank you for coming, Mr. Wright. I'd like to introduce you to our manager of construction, Captain Peter O'Leary, whom, if this works out, you'll be working with." Peter O'Leary was a giant of a man in his mid-forties with strong arms, broad shoulders, and a powerful back from decades of hard labor in the Chicago stockyards. Some said he could wrestle a bull to the ground and tie him up by himself. He had a broad forehead and a large mustache extending below his chin. He'd had no formal education, but he'd been a captain in the Union army, where he fought under General Grenville Dodge during the entirety of the Civil War. Honest to a fault, some said he'd come through that great war with reverence for the general, and he would follow Dodge's orders to the minutest detail.

"We look forward ta havin' ya joinin' us, Mr. Wright." O'Leary nodded in Tom's direction. "If'n the general's of a mind."

"My pleasure, Captain."

"Right! Got a whole lot of work ahead of us. Shoulda started these tunnels weeks ago," O'Leary said.

"If you two gentlemen don't mind, let's hike up to the ridgeline platform and meet General Dodge." Mr. Young squinted up the hill.

"Yes, sir," said O'Leary. "You lead the way."

The three men trudged up the pathway, Mr. Young stopping to catch his breath at a flat overlook near the ridgeline. "Take a look down there, Tom," he said, pointing at the work in progress below Castle Rock's peaks. It was clear why they called it Echo Canyon. The picks, shovels, and machines clinked and clattered, the sounds reverberating up the rock walls.

"I've never been in a war," Tom exclaimed in awe, "but this looks like a mighty army on the march."

"The UP's got plenty o' men just off the battlefield." Captain O'Leary spit a chaw of tobacco on the ground. "Damnedest thing I ever seen, North and South alike, workin' side by side. Mostly crackers from the sticks, but we got all kinds. Micks, kikes, chinks, and papists too. We even got coloreds—sometimes it gives me the willies. O' course, we got no red savages 'cause everybody knows they're a mean, shiftless bunch and ya gotta keep an eye on 'em fer stealin'. We got Mormons too," he whispered in Tom's ear, glancing over to Joseph Young, "and plenty of 'em. I ain't got no quarrel with Mormons. And now we got one from Eggland who might just be runnin' the whole damn show? Maybe?" O'Leary spit out another slug with a derisive laugh. "Sometimes there's a little friction around here, but it ain't nothin' we cain't handle after the war!"

Mr. Young offered a thoughtful smile to Tom before turning to O'Leary. "Thank you for that colorful description, Captain."

Tom looked at Peter O'Leary with tight lips and furrowed brows. He'd heard this was a fair man to work for, a man who worked hard, long hours, but it was clear he had no sympathy for those different from himself, especially the black man or the Indian. Tom knew there was an appalling sedition that dwelled at the center of prejudice, but reluctantly, he found himself giving O'Leary a noncommittal nod. He needed the money, and this job paid a lot of it.

"Yup, I was a sergeant fighting under General Dodge at Gettysburg, and it looked a lot like this here, only a whole lot more killin'. By the end of the three-day battle, General Dodge had promoted me from corporal ta captain." O'Leary paused in solemn memory. "Thousands of men workin' and livin' in them camps down there. All a part of a well-oiled machine. We're in a war, all right—with the Central Pacific in a race ta the finish line."

"Impressive!" Tom offered.

"General Dodge's expectin' a lot from us, crackers, coloreds, and Johnny rebs alike." O'Leary's eyes flashed. "Ya ready for it, son?"

⊱ • ⊰

"Thomas Wright, meet General Grenville Dodge."

General Dodge nodded, his cobalt eyes narrowing on Tom for a long moment. Both men were similar ages, heights, and temperaments, calm and possessing thoughtful intelligence. The celebrated general was the son of a congressman and a graduate from MIT, and he'd gone on to become a top engineer in the country, a New York investment banker, a millionaire businessman, and at thirty-one, the youngest general in the Civil War. General Ulysses S. Grant had once credited Dodge's strategic planning as the reason the Northern army won the war, and when Grant became president, he insisted Dodge was the only man to head up the Union Pacific's operations if the UP wanted any help from the government.

"Pleasure to meet you, General." Tom returned his gaze with equal intensity.

"Likewise, Mr. Wright."

"You have a very impressive operation here," Tom offered. He pressed his lips tight in determination.

"Mr. Young seems to think you might be the right man to head it up. At least this most important tunnel construction."

"Suppose you'll let me know about that, General."

General Dodge smiled, clearly intrigued by the man standing before him. "Gentlemen, would you mind if Mr. Wright and I excused ourselves for a bit while we take a walk?" And with that, he put a hand on Tom's shoulder and led him away from the rest of the men.

"Of course, I'm sure you've been told of the importance of these four tunnels." The general shook his head, frowning in concern.

"I know if the tunnels are not done before the line is finished at Promontory Point, the UP will not receive any credit or land grants along that hundred and ten miles of track," Tom confirmed.

"Exactly. A disaster." The general was clearly pleased at Tom's keen perception of the problem he would face. "You've seen the plans, our very aggressive schedule. Can you do it?" He looked into Tom's eyes. "Maybe shave some time off?"

"I can share a few tricks that will speed up the work!" Tom was clear and decisive, returning Dodge's penetrating gaze. "It's about breaking down the process into its smallest parts, honing, finely tuning each separate task, compartmentalizing, simplifying, then safely executing with precision. Efficiency will improve, and speed will follow." Tom paused, waiting for General Dodge to catch up. "Of course, we'd pursue construction of all four tunnels simultaneously from both ends of each tunnel to meet in the middle."

"Both directions? Hmm! You would need extremely precise surveying to do that."

"I don't need to tell you, General, it can be done with the new surveying transits we use in England. I saw them in use in New York as well."

"Hmm." General Dodge considered the thought. "You're right, of course. But it would also require careful cooperation between the different crews and precise implementation."

"And maybe a little extra financial encouragement might be in order to put together an elite team of three, maybe four hundred men, General?"

"Maybe?" General Dodge smiled at Tom's ingenuity and brash confidence.

Reaching the top of Castle Rock, they had a bird's-eye view to witness the wonder of nature being subdued by the imagination of man to build what some were calling the eighth wonder of the world.

"There is nothing like it anywhere else on earth." General Dodge looked out over the canyon with the cold, hard eye of experience. "I like these Mormon boys—dignified, respectful teetotalers to the man, who work as hard as any man on the line. Look at that grading. Nowhere else do we have better finish work, their timber bridges are good, ties and rails are as good as anywhere along the line without the damnable problems of the Hell on Wheels crowd." General Dodge spat a wad of tobacco at the ground and peered down at the workers. "Some speak better English than I do, and they eat real food without any of those godforsaken proclivities of the Chinese! We'll need as many of these damn Mormons as you can get, Mr. Wright."

"Agreed, General. I've had a couple weeks to work beside them swingin' a sledge, and they would be a good fit for these tunnels."

General Dodge chuckled. "How was that? Breakin' rock with a sledgehammer?"

"Humbling. It gave me a greater respect for these men."

"Hopefully not too humbling."

Tom answered numerous questions about engineering, construction techniques, procedures, and operational strategies he might use if he were to manage the building of these four tunneling projects. General Dodge used his considerable experience judging fighting men to discern Tom's potential to turn hundreds of rugged, hard, difficult men into a disciplined construction force for this complex, time-sensitive project. Tom liked this man and couldn't help but be excited discussing the problems to be unraveled and the innovative solutions to be implemented.

After four hours of touring the site together, it was evident Tom Wright was the man for this important, difficult, and exacting work of engineering, blasting, excavating, timbering, and managing.

"You know, General, if we have any chance of making this schedule, we'll need to be running two or three shifts of crews, using the whole twenty-four-hour day." Tom held the general's gaze.

Grenville Dodge paused to look Tom Wright square in his eyes. Then he reached out to shake the hand of the new director of tunnel construction. Tom would be building all four tunnels for the Union Pacific Railroad. It was one of the most complicated tunnel projects ever built anywhere in the world.

"I'm looking forward to doing business with you, Mr. Wright." General Dodge patted Tom on the back. "Now listen, Captain O'Leary is a good man. He would do anything I asked him, but he is in over his head with this complicated and demanding engineering work. And Joseph Young, well, he's a businessman. I'll make arrangements with the two of them to have you reporting directly to me on a regular basis."

"You're offering me the job, General?"

"Let me speak to Mr. Young about it. It's his construction company, after all." General Dodge looked at Tom with a twinkle in his eye. Both knew it was Dodge making the decisions, regardless. "I'll tell O'Leary to get together with you and pick out three or four hundred of the best men to work on those tunnels."

"Fair enough, General!"

"I'll want you to put together your schedule, budget, workload needs, and the equipment you'll need. I'll give you two days to get it to me. Time's a wasting. I'll be here from time to time to go over any special problems. You up for the task, Mr. Wright?"

Tom was about to play a major role in a project like nothing else ever before contemplated in the world. "I am, General!" He smiled, then muttered almost to himself, "Only in America." He was in awe of the difference he found in this freewheeling country, where a man's ability to produce held sway. It was such a change from the paternalism of his homeland, where the aristocratic class were given all positions of leadership, regardless of ability, and together with the government made all decisions.

"What's that, Mr. Wright?"

"Oh, nothing!" Tom smiled at the general. "By the way, in England, they've started using a new material for making track rails. Much harder, more durable, and more elastic than iron. They smelt two pounds of iron ore, two pounds of coal, half pound of limestone, mix in a dash of magnesium to make a pound of Bessemer steel. I saw it used in New York City for their new overhead rails. Came from a plant opened a couple years ago in Pennsylvania. 'Spect many of the miracles of this country's expanding future will flow from steel . . . Gonna make someone very rich. UP should be using steel rails for tunnels and bridges, not iron."

"Hmm, I'll look into it." Dodge smiled. "Quite a step up from breakin' rock with a sledge."

"Yup!" Tom made the short walk to camp that evening alone. He was leaving his old life behind, excited by the prospect of picking up his new one. He had stepped into the river that takes you forward, with all that had gone before preparing him for just this moment.

He remembered his mam's words many years ago. Martha had often told him, "If you prepare yourself to make a worthy footprint of an honorable life well lived, the opportunity to seize the moment will come."

He shook his head. "Good on you, Mam."

Chapter 23

≻ · ≺

Later that night, Joseph Young rode up to the family campsite. "Well, Mr. Wright," he began with a smile as he pulled up on the reins and swung down from his horse. "Captain O'Leary and I just finished speaking with General Dodge. Congratulations, you're now a railroad man."

"Thank you, sir." Tom was standing at the campfire with a fire iron in his hand. He looked at Annie's smiling face, raised his brows, then turned to Joey and Andrew, whose eyes were alight with pride. His heart pounded; he couldn't stop the rise of emotion in his chest or the smile from spreading wide across his own face. He had been preparing for this moment all his life—since before his first day in the coal mine on his seventh birthday. Today he was being judged solely on the merits of the man he had become. This was American capitalism at its best.

"I've always wanted to be a railroad man's wife." Annie giggled. "It may have been worth marryin' you after all."

There were elated chuckles all around.

"Meet me at the trailer tomorrow morning with Captain O'Leary and we can go over all the details. We're woefully behind schedule, but I really think you're the man to get us back on that schedule, Tom."

"Like to join us for dinner, Mr. Young?" Annie asked as she glanced at Tom for confirmation.

"Surprising what Annie can do with a rabbit caught in one of our traps and a bit of sage from the mountainside." Tom smiled.

Mr. Young hesitated. "I don't want to barge in, Annie."

"If this slim fare is acceptable," Annie said, "we'd love to have you."

"I'm sure your cooking is much better than mine." Mr. Young nodded in appreciation. "Especially with all your practice on those smelly gandy dancers you're feeding down at the canteen."

Tom offered a prime cut of rabbit to his guest.

"We can talk about the job tomorrow morning," Mr. Young stipulated, "but if there is something else any of you would like to ask me? Please, feel free. You, too, Annie, I owe you that much after your offer of this fine meal." He nodded to Tom's two brothers as well.

"Thanks!" Tom responded. "Mind my asking how Sharp & Young got a contract with Union Pacific to build part of the transcontinental?"

"You must be aware Brigham Young is my father. He started me on planning the alignment of the line several years ago with a young engineer, Mr. Theodore Judah."

"Who's Theodore Judah?"

"Teddy Judah and his wife Anna spent the better part of a decade traveling between California, New York, and Washington, DC, arguing the merits of a transcontinental line on their crusade to win funding. The whole idea of building three thousand miles of railway across the entire continent, over mountains, through rivers and vast Indian-infested plains was ludicrous, unthinkable to most Americans at the time. It wasn't long before the country celebrated Lewis and Clark as national heroes for completing the nearly impossible trek in over a year. Teddy Judah was drummed out of state legislatures, and still every year like clockwork, he presented his case before the US Congress. They called him Crazy Judah." Mr. Young picked up the poker and stoked the fire between them. It popped and crackled in the cool night air as his words sank in. "But Teddy persevered, 'To bring the country together from sea to shining sea,' as he put it."

"Only in America," Tom mused.

"Teddy, living out his fantasy with Anna always close behind, met with anyone who would listen, including my father. Brigham was a big supporter, and he arranged for me to work together with Teddy on a route through the Intermountain West. I spent most of a spring and summer helping Judah with his alignment surveys while Anna painted wonderful pictures of the mountainous terrain for what became their Washington, DC, railway museum."

"Sounds like a wonderful adventure for the both of them." Annie smiled at Tom.

"It wasn't until Judah found the key to success that the project took off."

"So, what was the key?" Tom couldn't hide his enthusiasm for technology.

"A young Illinois railroad lawyer, Abraham Lincoln, saw what Judah saw in his meticulous surveys and well-crafted plans. Then he became president, and that made all the difference."

"I can see how that might help." Andrew narrowed his eyes, looking impressed.

"One thing led to another, and the rest is history."

"The newspapers say your father doesn't want the railroad," Annie interjected. "They say the arrival of the good citizens from the East will wipe out his empire."

"Newsmen are in the business of selling newspapers." Joseph Young smiled. "Brigham was the first cash investor in the Union Pacific."

"How did he . . . and Sharp & Young get involved in the construction?" Tom asked.

"Brigham learned everything he could, then just waited."

"Waited?"

"Doc Durant, the notorious president of Crédit Mobilier and the Union Pacific Railroad, sent a long telegram this past May to Brigham. It was designed to convince him of his patriotic duty to help the UP. It said Brigham's help would be looked upon favorably by the government and good citizens of the East. In short, if the UP had any hope of not embarrassing themselves in the race with the Central Pacific, they desperately needed good working men out West, and plenty of them. It didn't take a genius to see Brigham could solve the UP's problem; he was the only one with access to thousands of men."

"Sounds like that was the opening he'd been waiting for?" Andrew smiled.

Mr. Young paused for a long moment. "It was a very difficult time for all of us in the Salt Lake Valley. We're primarily a farming community with little to trade, few to trade with, and almost no cash. We were in a terrible drought, and for the second summer in a row, hordes of locusts darkened the skies over the valley, devouring everything in sight—every crop, every bush, and every blade of grass. The entire territory was left with no grain, corn, or feed for the stock. No crop for man or beast. Our economy had collapsed into depression. There were families, and still are, all over the valley starving." His eyes looked far away as he continued. "When the first locust arrived, the chickens on our farm were as happy as pigs in mud, running around in a frenzy chasing the bonanza landing all around them. But soon they too had enough, like every other man or beast. Stuffed to the point they could hardly walk, they crawled into the houses and barns and hid out in the wagons for a little peace and quiet from the swarm. In the end, the valley looked like devastation after a war. Even the Great Salt Lake was blanketed in dead locusts. Farmers resorted to feeding dried locusts to the livestock." He paused. "That's when Brigham received Doc Durant's telegram request."

"Desperate, hungry, nowhere to turn." Tom remembered the starving coal miner families. Children suffering malnutrition, begging on the village streets. "You needed the work."

"In Brigham's mind it was divine providence. He simply wired back 'YES!'"

"No negotiation?" Tom asked.

"Oh, that would come later. My father is a sly old fox. He had the unscrupulous Doc Durant salivating to do business with him, and Durant sent his New York City attorneys, Mr. Reed and Mr. Seymore, to close the deal. Two weeks later, both left Salt Lake City shaken, but with a contract for five thousand of Deseret's finest. They told Durant, 'He clamped his mouth shut like a steel trap until we agreed to his terms.'" Joseph Young smiled.

"Sounds like folks in this Wild West territory picked the right man for the job." Annie coughed, wiping her sleeve across her runny nose. Her cold had been hanging on for weeks.

"He cut deals with both the Union Pacific and the Central Pacific, then sent telegrams. 'Let's get crackin' gentlemen, you're burnin' daylight!'" Mr. Young laughed. "I'm sorry, I've been prattling on. It's getting late and we have a big day tomorrow, Tom." With that, he stood. "See ya in the morning. We've got big plans for you." He smiled at Annie. "Thank you for the wonderful meal."

Chapter 24

⊱ · ⊰

OVER THE FIRST WEEK AS director of tunnel construction, Tom spent little time in camp with Annie and his brothers. He'd been working long hours planning, preparing truss and tunnel design details and specifications, surveying tunnel alignments, putting together crews, setting up procedures for building these four technically complex tunnels. They were now ready to start blasting.

"You remember Andrew and Joey are on errand in Wasatch?" he reminded Annie after returning to camp late that night.

"And we'll be eating alone." She coughed. She'd been looking forward to spending a little time alone with her husband, but she could see as usual he had something else on his mind.

"Right," Tom confirmed. "I know it's been especially hard on you working long days down at the canteen feeding those ignorant gandy dancer construction workers, then having to cook and clean for us too."

"Someone needs to keep you healthy."

"How's that croupy cough of yours? Sounds worse."

She knew he was looking at the dark circles under her eyes and her chalky complexion. Lately she'd been so very tired. She just couldn't seem to get over her cold, and her back hurt from coughing.

"I'm fine." She shrugged. "I'm feeling better, really." The candle-wax plaster proved no help, and now her stomach was busy practicing somersaults.

"I'm concerned, Annie. Artist—you know, the black farmer on my blasting crew who grew up around here? He tells me we're expecting a brutal winter." Tom paused with honest worry in his eyes, then proceeded, cautious. "Andrew received a letter from Edie today."

"Oh, how's Edie liking Parley's Park City?" Annie gave Tom a suspicious glance.

"She thinks it's great!" He looked hard at Annie while he sharpened the kitchen knife on the whetstone. "She wishes she had an adult to talk to—an occasional reprieve from the children."

Annie glanced up at him. "What are you saying, Thomas?"

"She would love to have you to come stay with her and the children."

Annie winced and looked back down at the hash she was stirring, jabbing at it hard with her wooden spoon. "Yeah, well, that ain't gonna happen." She paused. "This is why they're not here for dinner, isn't it. You wrote Edie?" Anger began to rise in her.

"You've cut me, Annie!" Tom tried to make light of it.

Annie hammered down the wooden spoon hard on the stove and took the pot of hash off the fire. Without looking up from her dinner preparation, she curled her lips down, irritated. "Sorry, I only meant to scratch your eyes out."

"Ah, Annie," he pleaded. "You can't spend the winter here. You'll end up with pneumonia. You have to look after yourself. We've got a brutal winter coming."

"Well, come with me to Park City then."

"There's no work in Park City or anywhere else in this entire territory. You heard Joseph Young: all the crops have been devastated by drought and locusts for two years straight. But for the railroad, the economy would be in deep depression."

"Don't you see? I don't want to be apart from you, Thomas."

"Annie, I've just been offered the opportunity to run the entire tunnel-building operation, including one of the largest tunnels in the world, under one of the most talented engineers in America, on one of the grandest projects ever conceived by man. And it's not because of my aristocratic heritage, the university I studied at, or how much money my family is worth. It's because of who I am as a man. All I have done for a lifetime has prepared me to seize this moment, to do what I was born to do."

"But you're risking your life."

"I risked my life every day in the coal mine for a pittance, just so I could buy enough overpriced food from Lord Fitzwilliam's company store to keep my family from starving. I had little choice but to do His Lordship's bidding." Tom paused, taking in a deep breath, remembering those awful days when he was still a boy but his family's sole breadwinner. "Sure, blasting tunnels through the middle of a rocky mountain is risky. I'll be working sixteen-hour days, seven days a week, but this is a risk of my own choosing, and they're offering me more money than I've ever seen in my life. Why? Because I have the skills to build those tunnels better than anyone else. Annie, this is why people from all over the world sacrifice everything to come here, and by summer, we will have enough money to buy that land."

"Hmm." She bit her lip. Her heart was pounding. She was losing the argument. "You and your damn land."

"Look, I'll be fine." He pulled in a deep, frustrated breath. "I have Andrew, and Joey says he'll do the cooking."

"What good are they?" Annie guffawed. She was anxious! Fidgety! Her heart was in her throat as she fought a losing battle. "Between the two of them, they can't boil tea." She rolled her eyes as she dished out the hash, slamming the spoon to each plate. "And Joey, I've seen his cooking. What he does to food most people can only do by digesting it."

"Mr. Young has decided that because the men are only getting a small portion of their pay until the Union Pacific government bond money comes in, he's going to expand the food services program." Tom recognized that stubborn look in Annie's eye and knew she wasn't having any of it. But he was tired and exasperated, so he went on with his explanation. "To ensure every man has at least one good meal in his stomach every day, an afternoon lunch is to be provided, on the company."

"That's not enough!"

"Damn it, Annie, you're going to Park City to spend the winter with Edie."

She slammed down her wooden spoon in the pot and glared at him with an unsettling, impenetrable frown designed to disable even the most confident husband. "I don't think so!"

It had been a long day and Tom was in no mood for further debate. With one last try to coax her into seeing the way it was going to be, he took a deep breath and reached out to softly touch her shoulder. She jerked away.

"Look, it's gonna be a cold, brutal winter. You'd be sleeping under an open wagon on frozen ground, in the icy wind." He gave her his best hardened look. "It's not gonna happen."

A pall had fallen over the bond between them. It had been festering since the death of Rachel and her family. And finally, Annie was letting loose. "Your project? Your land? Your plans?" She was seething now. "It's all about you, isn't it, what you want, your hopes, your dreams? You're the center of our universe—the sun. And I'm like a spinning planet, just orbiting around you!" Her eyes were wide and blazing. "What about me, Thomas? What about what your wife wants? Don't you see I want to be with you, for better or worse? I don't just want to be your partner. I want to be loved and cherished by you. I want to be a family, struggling together as families do. And I don't want to go to Park City!"

Tom's eyes narrowed, and his mouth set in a tight line. "Well, we all have to learn to do things we don't want to."

"Hmm!" Bitter, she recoiled at his insinuation. "Like accepting your husband only married you for a traveling companion, because you're a hard worker, a funny conversationalist. In a practical arrangement he can set aside when it pleases him." She took a deep breath, her heart pounding. "Like accepting his heart will always belong to another."

"Don't go there, Annie."

"I've always known it would be my cross to bear. I just didn't know it would be so hard. You've taken possession of my heart, Thomas Wright, my very soul. You have the advantage on me and there is nothing I can do about it." She stopped to take control of her emotions. She knew if she opened this well inside her, she might never get it closed again. "Oh, don't get me wrong, you have always been the perfect gentleman, but I know she is your one true love and will always have your heart. But somehow, somehow . . ."

"Somehow, you wished I loved you more?" He paused. "Honestly, Annie?"

"Do you deny it, then?" With clenched fists and hurt in her eyes, Annie went on. "Losing Rachel, my desperately needed confidant after Nannie died, brought it into focus. I never saw it coming. Or at least I tried to avoid looking at it." She ran on, trying to control herself enough to get it all out. She turned away, refusing to let him to see the tears welling up in her eyes. "But with this terrible tragedy, bringing me so close to the harsh reality that life . . ." she paused, careful to organize her thoughts. "Rachel's death not only made me see the fragility of life; it made me face the reality that there will never really be enough room in your heart for me because it is filled to the brim with Lydia."

"It's not like that, Annie. When I decided to come to this country, I knew there was no one else I would rather go with than you, my cherished best friend." Tom paused, seeing the distress in her eyes. "I'm so sorry you feel this way, Annie, but don't you see—"

"I don't want your pity, Thomas," she interrupted. "I'm not sure I want to be your best friend. I want your love. I want you to honor and cherish me above all else as your wife! Not just bed me. They say pity is akin to love, but it's not for me, and I don't see how any woman wants her man's pity, no more than a man wants his woman's."

"Pity is the last thing anyone—"

"What happened to you in Spring Hollow after Lydia died to make you want me? Did you pity me when you came to me after those long months of isolation?"

"No, it wasn't like that, I—"

"It seems to me you did. Was ours not just a contract of convenience to you?"

He looked at her with a blank stare.

Annie wiped at the infuriating moisture in her eyes. "After our Henry died, I stopped by the cemetery and saw you at Lydia's gravesite clearly confiding in her." Annie remembered how she'd suffered the loss of her son in silence, not wanting to burden her husband with her grief while he was recovering from his awful accident. The anguish. The weariness of heart that shackled her limbs with chains of despair. She'd been grieving their son, needing her husband all those many months. Enduring the distance, the silence, coping with her pain all alone. She'd felt demeaned as she watched him standing in the cemetery speaking with Lydia. Strangers to each other, no comfort of marital trust and commitment—she had felt her heart split in two. "To come face-to-face with it. All those months I had suffered the loss of our son alone. It was too much. It forced me to see I was a wife who failed to inspire the fidelity of my husband's heart. That vision has torn at me. With all that life throws in our path, I find it difficult—no, impossible—to grapple with Lydia's ghost too. Don't we have enough without this coming between us?"

"Yes, Annie, we have enough, but—"

"I've tried to stop the hurt, but no matter how hard I try . . . You never told me of your frequent visits to the cemetery to speak to her there." Annie paused, her hands trembling. She made them into fists and took a deep breath, holding back the tears. "Then after Nannie's death and a tragedy like Rachel and her family . . . Being in second place in your heart, or worse—Thomas, I know I must, but honestly, I am having a hard time learning to bear it."

"I never told you at the time about my visits to the cemetery because I didn't trust myself to find the words—"

"That you find it difficult to live without her?" Annie interrupted. "I get it, she was beautiful, vivacious, charming. She was all the things I am not and never will be." Annie looked at her husband with wounded eyes, but she was determined to steel her courage. "I am not that starry-eyed young girl any longer. My heart is like a stone, heavy and burdensome. There's an ache deep inside me that may never be soothed. We seem to be strangers to one another, you living in the past, five thousand miles away with Lydia's ghost, and me here in the present making you dinner, washing your clothes, and . . ." She looked hard into his eyes, teeth clenched. "I'm flesh and blood. I may have entirely lost my heart, but not my self-respect. I'm certainly not perfect, but this is all there is to me. Maybe it's not enough. I'm afraid I need more than you can give, and it scares the hell out of me!" Her voiced pitched bitterly. "I don't want to be a stranger to my husband." Her frowning lips tightened, her brows raised to the lines in her forehead. "No woman wants her husband to consider another woman more desirable." How much must she be asked to trade to defeat the lonesomeness in her heart?

"So, this is what you think of me?" Tom was reeling, having been unable to defend himself. In frustration, he lashed out. "Oh, and you're so right, Annie, Lydia was a woman like no other. I only had eyes for her and loved her beyond what I had ever imagined possible. There is a part of me that will always think of her with strong emotion, but there is nothing I can do to change that. Is that a crime? If it is, then I'm guilty. Don't you think I would change it if I could?" Tom stepped toward her in his hurt, pausing long enough to let his anger cool. "Do you think I can pick and choose this battle within my soul? Her death came at me unannounced, against my will, and I have struggled to put my loss in its rightful place—praying that time and distance would heal the wound in my heart. I know in my mind I must do so, but in my heart . . ." Tom stumbled over his words, earnestly pursuing absolution for his sin in Annie's eyes. His passion raging, he drew his face near to hers.

She saw the hurt in his deep brown eyes flecked with flashing green. They searched her face for what seemed an eternity. But she did not break her gaze, shy from his fury. Her hands began to sweat. Her stomach churned. "I don't think you understand."

"Oh, I understand." He nodded curtly, his jaw set, trying hard to retain his dignity. "Forgive me, Annie," he added in a calm, cold voice, "but I had no idea you thought so disdainfully of me."

Annie, gone quiet, could hardly breathe. She was already feeling regret.

"I must leave you now." Tom seemed to have regained his composure, sounding icy calm, but his intense eyes revealed otherwise.

"I've promised to meet Mr. Young in Wasatch this evening. I'll be staying the night with Andrew and Joey. I've made arrangements for you to leave first thing in the morning on the supply wagon to Park City." With a slight frown, he gritted his teeth, bowing slightly. "Please excuse me." And with that he turned away and was gone into the night.

Annie looked on after him, not quite sure just what she had done.

Chapter 25

❖ • ❖

Tom began physical construction on the four tunnels with his handpicked blasting and demolition crews, followed by grading and truss crews in an efficient sequential process schedule. Little time was wasted as each team rotated from one tunnel to the next. He stressed the importance of seamless coordination between surveyors and the various specialized crews and fostered a competitive spirit. Each day as work progressed, the precision, execution, and safety all improved.

"The key to our success," Tom told his crew foremen and superintendents, "is to set in place a finely tuned process. Each man, each crew, each team becoming meticulously proficient in every aspect of their work, with a working knowledge of the responsibilities of the rest of the team. Every crew must hone their skills until they're perfect in every detail."

To drive home his point, Tom singled out Artist Able, a tall, powerfully built black man with intelligent eyes. His family had been slaves until they ran away and joined the Mormons in Missouri. When the war started, Artist joined the Northern army to fight his former masters, and now he lived with his wife and family in the Utah Territory. "Artist learns fast and pays meticulous attention to detail," Tom told the crew. "You're a foreman now, Artist. You must ensure your crew's spoke in the wheel of this team is working perfectly. No time wasted. No safety sacrificed." He looked around at all the men, who were focusing on his every word. "I've been given a free hand to choose the best men here, and you're it, gentlemen. Now this is a competition between crews—who are the best of the best? You do your part well, your crew will win that competition and we'll all be more successful for it. And I promise you those bonuses. Good luck and Godspeed!"

Tom managed more than three hundred men working on the tunnels both night and day: crews for surveying, engineering, blasting, grading, and building trusswork, tunnel supports, and line work of every kind on all four tunnels simultaneously. Working around the clock—by torchlight at night—in the kind of cold that ached in the lungs, froze eyelashes, and burned fingertips and toes. Each man worked twelve hours on and had twelve hours off. Sleepless energy was consumed by the tedious drilling of cores, and kegs of black powder blasting jagged arteries through solid rock. The spaces were so confined it sounded like heavy artillery shells ripping the tunnel rock to smithereens on both the fore and aft tunnel cuts. Masses of rock were loaded by men and steam shovel onto trams carted down track to canyon fills.

The road up Weber Canyon was crowded with teams hauling up ties, rails, spikes, and equipment. Crews jumped from one tunnel to the next, never stopping, perfecting their craft and deftly coordinating their efforts. There was a pride in the competition between crews, which improved the quality of the work and the speed at which it was accomplished.

To the casual observer, they would appear as a mighty army of men, equipment, and tented campsites fighting a war. It was difficult, tedious, meticulous work, both night and day. There was nothing else like it in all the world.

Most nights, after his sixteen-hour workday and a bite to eat, Tom climbed into his wagon bed so exhausted he fell asleep as soon as his head hit the pillow. But there were some nights when his mind was full of thoughts and he couldn't sleep.

One night, in the midst of a snowstorm, he lay awake buried under a pile of blankets, his mind wandering. Lost in thought, he hadn't noticed the storm retreating until the clouds parted and the brightness of a full moon shone through the open end of the wagon.

Propping himself up on a sack of flour, buried under his pile of blankets, he looked outside into the cold quiet of the night. The shimmering glow of moonlight flung recollections of Spring Hollow across the freshly fallen snow in a kaleidoscope of color. There was neither footprint nor sign of life. The solemn, sacred beauty of the pristine, snow-covered mountain was breathtaking, a lonely grandeur he'd first glimpsed in Spring Hollow. A smile stretched across his face when he recalled of his Spring Hollow roommate, Mrs. Shrew. She had helped pull him through that long, cold winter when he almost let nature take its harsh course with him. She was his only companion. Their one-sided conversations had made it possible to keep his sanity on those endless lonely nights.

"Maybe she didn't do such a good job of it after all," he whispered.

Tom remembered the day when the sun had no longer been willing to stand by and submit to the bitter cold and darkness of winter. It had elbowed its way in on that first crisp spring morning. Mrs. Shrew had gotten herself pregnant several weeks earlier. And on that morning, he watched as this doting mam cared for her six little shrewlet pups with big brown eyes and voracious appetites. He had a front-row seat to witness his ever-busy roommate venture from their shared home for her first family outing in the harsh, cruel world. She lined up her fluffy little balls of fur, each caravanning one behind the other, each holding on to the tail of the one in front. With Mam leading the way, her whiskers swinging for direction, they traipsed down to the pooling pond in the roly-poly shrew family express. As always, they were in search of food. Tom couldn't help but feel a tug at his heart as he remembered this first shrew family field trip.

When the little family reached the water's edge, Tom watched Mrs. Shrew leave her clan onshore while she slowly ventured into the water. With her little legs churning, in chase of a dragonfly, she miraculously began to skip across the surface of the pond. But in a twist of fate, a great trout surfaced and Mrs. Shrew's life was cut short. The predator had become the meal, and life changed on the spot for this little family of shrews. It was a heartbreaking incident, but there was no evil in it. No right or wrong, no moral turpitude or code of nature broken, no judgment made. It was but one of the shades of light and shadow in which the natural world is cast. The Almighty's schoolroom of natural selection provided Tom quite an education. The shrew had lived a short, fast, and furious life and died hard, and now, so would her little ones. For all who lived in the meadow were intertwined in the natural rhythm of life and death.

Life is fleeting. It can bring such struggle! It can be so beautiful and yet unforgiving at the same time! He saw it in the woodland glen every day, a front-row witness to the reality of nature's way. The vignettes were sometimes beautiful, sometimes touching, sometimes harsh, cruel, and halting to the heart.

Nature had nurtured, tutored, and transformed him when nothing else seemed to be able to. The living waters of the pooling pond and estuary brought forth life and took it away too. All God's creatures had a role to play in this intricate balance, including man and beast, he thought. Large and small, beautiful and grotesque, we live, we give birth to another generation who sometimes pass away before we even have the opportunity to share our love with them, before we can raise a family. The shrew lives by instinct, like the salmon who swims upstream to bear its young and die, like the roe deer who goes south to bear its young in the spring. They all live by instinct.

But man is different than the animals, he thought. *God's greatest creation. We live by reason, not instinct.*

Tom smiled. *Man can learn to manipulate and transform his environment.* He may not have fully understood the implications when he was young, but he did now. And mankind was not meant to walk the earth alone, but yoked with another in love.

Tom wiped at his runny nose. "Thought I'd grown so smart, so sensible, so wise when I asked my treasured friend to marry me. But what did I know, really?"

In his rational mind, Tom had thought there were a dozen practical reasons why they were compatible, why they would be an asset to each other's lives, why they would make good traveling companions, best friends forever. But love is not practical. Unlike the shrew or the rest of his fellow inhabitants in the glen, who lived by predictable instinct, men and women are not predictable, they are oftentimes irrational.

"We laugh together. We cry together. We grow together . . . hearts change." Tom pondered the thoughts. "I didn't see it sneak up on me, but I see it clearly now. We fall in love. Oh, Annie, I'm so sorry. I suppose you knew all along we were always meant for each other. And now I know it too. I really do love you!"

※ • ※

With his back facing the door of the clapboard construction trailer, Tom was leaning over his desk studying the next day's work schedule when Joseph Young and an angry General Dodge walked in. They'd clearly been arguing.

The door slammed behind them. "Listen, Mr. Young. You've got to pick up the pace on those tunnels," Dodge barked. "If you don't, we'll never complete them before the rest of the UP crews reach Promontory Point. They're a hundred miles down track already."

"Tom and his crews are doing everything they can, working twenty-four-hour days in what has become very hard rock." Both men glanced at Tom standing at his worktable with Peter O'Leary going over plans for the day.

"Which is more than I can say for the UP paying their bills," Mr. Young angrily added.

General Dodge fumed, his blazing eyes drilling in on Joseph Young. "If those tunnels are not done before we meet the Central Pacific's line coming from the west, it will be an absolute disaster for the Union Pacific. We'll get no US bond money for that hundred and ten miles of track, nor any of the contracted land and coal fields surrounding it, costing millions. Without those coal fields, we have no fuel to run our trains unless we buy it from our competitor. What price do you think the Central Pacific will charge us?" General Dodge glanced at Tom, who was now looking up from his worktable. "More importantly, there will be no money to pay these men if we lose this race."

"General, we've tried everything to speed up construction." Mr. Young stood tall and wearily set his jaw. "This nearly impenetrable rock we've gotten into has slowed progress to a crawl."

"Wallowing in the detail of why it can't be done begs the question." General Dodge sneered. "If you don't step it up, we won't meet our schedule, and Sharp & Young won't get paid. It's just that simple."

Joseph Young stared at the general, finally realizing the full implications of not meeting the tunnel construction schedule.

"Nitroglycerin!" Tom interjected himself into the argument. The two men turned to look at him. "The only alternative is to use nitroglycerin," he said calmly.

"Are you crazy, Tom?" Joseph Young blurted out. "Are you aware of what happened to the Chinese workers when the Central Pacific tried that unstable, incredibly dangerous explosive?"

"They lost well over a hundred men before abandoning it."

"Probably more. They weren't too particular about counting up Chinese deaths. Using nitroglycerin to tunnel through the Sierra Nevada granite was an absolute disaster!" Agitated, Joseph Young was about to lecture Tom further when General Dodge raised his hand to stop him.

"Let the man explain himself." He nodded. "Tom?"

"I've studied it a bit," Tom proceeded coolly. "Invented just across the English channel in France, nitroglycerin was what we considered using in the Yorkshire coal mines. In the end, we decided it was too dangerous." He paused, judiciously choosing his words. "Mr. Young accurately points out the extreme instability and unpredictable nature of the explosive. But without question, it's the only possible answer to this dark blue metamorphic quartzite. And the geology suggests we'll be in it for several hundred feet more before we're done. Nitro is probably eight times more powerful than black powder—"

"And a hundred times more dangerous," Joseph Young interrupted. "The CP gave up for a reason."

"Exactly! Too hot and it explodes. Too cold and it explodes. Dropped or shaken and it explodes, but the CP didn't have my men." Tom paused, locking eyes with General Dodge.

All three stood staring at each other.

"I know most of these men in your crews," Mr. Young said, aghast. "I've personally known most of their families since I was a boy. I'd be the one who would have to tell their mothers, their fathers, wives, and children it was my decision. I was the one who caused their death."

"Go on, Tom. Let's hear the whole of it," Dodge encouraged. "Tell us how you're gonna get those tunnels completed in time to avoid this financial disaster."

"I'll need a few days to study it further, explain the risk to the men, plan out a strategy. If a plan can be put into place and you can promise to give me what I need . . ." He looked into General Grenville Dodge's eyes. "It just might be possible!"

"You've got three days." Dodge saw the recalcitrant look in Tom's eyes. "What?"

"I'll let you know, when I know." Tom held the general's expressionless gaze.

General Dodge studied the brash young man who stood before him, clearly perturbed by Tom's arrogance. "Are you a courageous man, Mr. Wright?"

Tom did not respond. Joseph Young and Captain O'Leary stood quiet, their mouths agape, looking back and forth between the two men.

"Make it happen, Mr. Wright." General Dodge had issued his final benediction on the matter.

"Let you know, General." Tom's matching iron will shone from his dark eyes.

Dodge smiled. "A fearful man must die a thousand times before his death, but . . . the courageous man, confident in his abilities, tastes of death but once." He gave Tom a quizzical look.

All but Tom appeared confused. "I believe that was Shakespeare, wasn't it, General? These are proud men. They will want to win this race, but we need to make sure it's safe and they're gonna get paid for it. Any agreement will need to include catching up on back pay. Extra hazard pay with a promised bonus if we meet the schedule would go a long way to help convince the men. We all have families to feed."

General Dodge narrowed his piercing eyes, put his hands on his hips, and smiled. "I believe you're right, Mr. Wright. It was Shakespeare. And you'll deserve all of it, if you make that intractable schedule." He raised his brows and nodded. "Tom, Mr. Young, Captain O'Leary. Please have that plan and schedule for me in three days." Then he turned to leave.

"Yes sir, General." Joseph Young nodded.

"What play was that, Mr. Wright?" General Dodge asked, his hand on the doorknob.

"I believe it was *Julius Caesar*."

"Ah yes." The general tipped his hat. "Gentlemen." And with that, he was gone.

Peter O'Leary stared at Tom. He had learned Tom was creative, brilliant, precise, and would be intrigued by the challenge. If it was possible, he would come up with a workable plan, and his men would follow his lead. They'd walk barefoot over broken glass if he asked them to. But if he said no, he knew these men would never do it without him. For they trusted him like no general he'd ever served under, not even General Grenville Dodge. Either way, Tom Wright would be the final arbiter in this decision.

※ · ※

Three days later, Tom met with Joseph Young and Peter O'Leary to discuss the matter of using nitroglycerin.

"Whaddya think, Mr. Wright?" Joseph asked.

"Spoke to the men. No one said no."

"General Dodge has promised twenty percent hazard pay, and if you complete the four tunnels by the end of April, the UP will double that as a bonus."

"Considering the UP's payment history, I'm sure you can appreciate we'll need that in writing from both the Union Pacific and Sharp & Young."

Mr. Young blanched. "Okay."

"The men know the race is on and wanna win. It's the American way, isn't it?"

"I suppose it is."

"These are good men." Tom handed the list of demands to Mr. Young. "This is a list of what I'll need, including required security precautions, equipment, and contract provisions. We're going to need blasting caps from England and a lot of diatomaceous earth." Tom still didn't have all the answers to using this dangerous explosive in the tunnels, but with a little time to put it all together, he thought it could be done.

"I don't know what all that stuff is, but seems fair enough. We can go over the final details on General Dodge's return tomorrow."

"I'll need my past wages paid," Tom added. "I haven't been paid in four months. For some of the men it's almost a year."

"The UP is waiting on the government bond money," said Mr. Young. "But you have my word and Brigham's. And I'm sure General Dodge will confirm. One way or another, you'll get paid."

"It'll be done on schedule," Tom confirmed.

"I wish you the best of luck. I don't see how you can do it, but please keep those men safe."

Tom cleared his throat. "One last thing. This plan includes three sets of setting and blasting crews to work around the clock, eight hours per day for each crew and no longer. No twelve-hour days. I want the men handling nitroglycerin to be fresh. I want them sharp. Another three sets of crews for handwork and another three for rock removal after blasting. Here is the list of men I've selected for those crews. I want them working for me and no one else. I'd appreciate your confirmation of my choices." Tom breathed deep and handed the list to O'Leary and a copy to Mr. Young. "It will take about 320 men."

"I don't think that will be a problem. Will it, Captain?"

O'Leary ran his finger down the list, commenting without looking up. "These are mostly Brigham Young's imported Welsh miners."

"They're the best."

"That they are," O'Leary responded, "but wait, ya got Artist Able headin' up the explosives crews."

"Nerves of steel. Best foreman on any of my crews," Tom said as a matter of fact.

"But he's a black man!" Peter O'Leary exclaimed with a look of disbelief.

There was a tense silence. "He is," Tom said.

"He's a negro," O'Leary pressed. "You can't have a man like that handlin' nitro, riskin' the lives of all those men."

"Like what?" Tom squinted his hard eyes at O'Leary. "Artist Able has the hands of a surgeon. The steadiest I've ever seen. He's calm and cautious on a nerve-jangling job." Tom locked eyes with Captain O'Leary. "I thought men in this country were judged on their skills, the content of their character, not the color of their skin. Didn't this country just lose nearly a million men fighting a war over that? Didn't Artist Able risk his life in that war himself, as a demolition expert for General Grenville Dodge?"

"It just don't seem right."

The corners of Tom's lips pulled down, hard and tight. "Had a bit of a bad experience myself with prejudice, Captain. Didn't much care for it." He straightened up to his full height and clamped his mouth shut, making his position clear. "Artist is my man. I'm not budging on it."

Joseph Young looked at both men. "I don't doubt Tom's

comments about Artist. I've known Artist and his family since I was a boy. His father Elijah is a leader in our church, and Artist's a good man, extremely intelligent, and calm under pressure. He just happens to be black, just like you happen to be Irish, Mr. O'Leary."

A chastised Peter O'Leary sat quiet.

"You got it, Mr. Wright," Joseph Young promised. "All of it."

Chapter 26

⇾ • ⇽

THE SCREEN DOOR SLAMMED AS Edie, going through the mail, walked into the house to catch Annie and Elizabeth playing cards in the kitchen. "Annie, I've a letter here from Thomas."

"Oh, a letter from Thomas." Elizabeth flashed a knowing smile. "It's your chance to avoid getting thrashed by me once again."

Ignoring Elizabeth's comment, Annie snatched up the letter, her hands already beginning to sweat. Licking her dry lips, she left the table to find a quiet corner to read in peace.

⇾ • ⇽

My Dearest Annie,

They tell me these December snows are the heaviest in a dozen years. The frozen ground is covered with twenty feet of it. Yet Castle Rock is still humming with men and machines, working day and night by torchlight. And although I haven't had much time to myself, I've thought a lot about our last evening together. It was hard on both of us. I've considered all you shared that evening. And now better understand why it had to be said.

I've been negligent in expressing my feelings to you. A fool really. I apologize for that. To be honest, I hadn't anticipated falling so hard for you. It caught me off guard! I'm in love with you, Annie. Really in love with you. And now I find I miss you more than I had imagined possible.

When you got pregnant with Henry, I at long last fully recognized the importance of family, how desperately I wanted one and your role in my happiness. I had no idea of the powerful emotions I would feel for my son and you in turn, until I held both of you in my arms. We were a family. I never expected the flood of emotion would run so deep. Love took total control over every thought, every fiber of my body. Henry was flesh of our flesh, bone of our bone, and when we lost him, I was absolutely shattered. Confused, devastated, and conflicted, I wanted to crawl in the ground and lie next his coffin, but I couldn't. I knew how his loss crushed you and was afraid to tell you it had devastated me as well. I thought I had to be strong for you. I certainly didn't feel strong. I'm so sorry! I know now I didn't handle things right.

After we buried our Henry in the ground, I made a commitment to keep fresh flowers on his grave. I stopped by the cemetery most every week. Not to talk to Lydia, but to tell my son how much I missed him. As for my visit to Lydia's grave on the day we left for America, I was there to offer my final farewell. Letting her know you and I would be starting our new life together in America as I had promised her I would. And praying that time and distance would heal the wound of her loss in my soul.

You're right, I was drawn to you because of our profound and precious friendship that seemed to transcend age, experience, and even romance. You're a force to be reckoned with.

Irrepressible! Indispensable! Irreplaceable! But what began as a marriage of practicality with a strong, passionate woman, grounded in trust, respect, and admiration, has blossomed into a deep and abiding love. You have transformed me, made me a better man, given me a new sense of purpose to my life.

I am so sorry Annie! Can you forgive a foolish husband for not seeing, for not hearing and for not saying what should been shouted from the rooftops—I love you deeply. I would give my life for you.

I miss you, Annie, and despite the heavy snows and incredibly demanding work schedule, I promise you this, I will leave these cold nights in the mountains for the warmth of you in my arms on Christmas.

We have a lot of living ahead of us.

Your loving husband,
Thomas

☙ • ❧

Annie leaned against the windowpane, took in a deep, ragged breath, and placed her hand over her mouth. She wiped at her runny nose, folded the precious letter, and put it back into its envelope. His supplication had melted the edges of her hurt and left a desperate need to mend what had been broken. She would never have imagined she could love this man more, but what she felt now in the deepest reaches of her soul defied imagination. Tears streamed down her cheeks. She longed to have him put his arms around her and never let her go. But out of pride, she was determined to not respond to his letter. She would wait to see what Christmas brought.

☙ • ❧

The darkness had long since fallen when Tom and his brothers finished cleaning up after dinner. They sat down in front of the fire. It was Tom's first chance to relax at the end of a long day. He was tired when Joseph Young pulled up in his buggy, stepped down, and sat on the log next to Tom.

Tom absently poked at the logs in the fire. "What can I do for you, Mr. Young?" he asked without looking up.

"Tom." Joseph Young nodded to Andrew and Joey across the fire. "I just received a telegram from General Dodge. He has been talking with Crédit Mobilier about back pay."

"Hmm!" It had been almost two weeks, and all other contract items had been approved and materials were on their way. But still there had been no resolution of the payment due from the Union Pacific. Tom pushed the burning logs around with his poker. "And . . . what promise does Doc Durant have for us this time?"

"Durant has promised right after Christmas. Apparently, Crédit Mobilier expects bond money from the government very soon and it's to be used for that purpose."

"Damn it, this is not what we agreed. I suppose you expect me to tell all these men and my family no money for Christmas?"

"We have the general's word. Your written contract is signed. You'll get your money after Christmas. That's the best I can do, Tom."

Tom poked hard at the coals, gritting his teeth while he considered this latest development. "I have no choice but to suggest to these men that we pull back from our agreement to use nitroglycerin until the back pay issue is resolved." Tom gave Joseph Young a look of conviction. "Frankly, I wouldn't discourage them from pulling off the job altogether if they don't receive their back pay right after Christmas. I know I will."

"We'll get you paid up."

Tom blew out a breath, frustrated at having to push the issue.

He had given his word to more than three hundred men who hadn't been paid enough to keep their families from death's door after two years of drought and failed crops in the Salt Lake Valley. Some of them had been waiting almost a year. "I'm going to Park City to see Annie for Christmas. Joey and Andrew are coming with me. I can't speak for the rest of the men, but my family will insist on our back pay when we return." Tom nodded at Joey and Andrew.

"Fair enough!" Mr. Young paused. "Look, this may not be the time, but I've been wanting to ask . . . your plate has been so full . . ."

"And it would be a lot fuller if that damn Doc Durant would pay his bills."

Mr. Young went silent until Tom looked up at him. "It's probably a coincidence, but when I heard you hailed from an area around the famous Wentworth-Woodhouse mansion in Yorkshire, England, I wondered if you'd known a fellow by the name of George Wright?"

"George Wright?" Tom snapped to attention. He fixed his gaze on Joseph Young. "What do you know about George Wright?"

"He was a journalist around here a few years back. Late twenties. Credited his mom with making him into a writer instead of a coal miner." Joseph Young squeezed his brows together and frowned in concentration. "I liked him. My father liked him. I've often wondered what happened to him."

Tom's throat tightened. His intense eyes focused on Joseph Young. "I know him."

"You do? A passionate young man. Interested in everything."

Tom glanced over to a somber, wide-eyed Joey, then to Andrew. Both were sitting quiet by the fire, intently following the conversation. "George is our brother."

"Is that so? What's he doing now?"

"We don't know. Lost contact with him." A restlessness coursed through Tom's veins. "Been looking for him since we arrived in this country. What do you know about George?"

"If you're asking if I know where he is, I have no idea. As I mentioned, about five years ago I spent the summer working with Teddy Judah on the alignment of the railway through this Intermountain territory. George spent quite a bit of time with us, intent upon writing a book about Judah and his dream of a transcontinental. The two of them had hit it off when they first met back East—George and Teddy Judah, I mean."

"He never mentioned Teddy Judah." Tom looked to Joey for confirmation. "How?"

"George was inquisitive, fascinated with Teddy and Anna's transcontinental plan." Mr. Young took on a serious expression. "As I understand it, George met Teddy at the Tremont House, in Chicago. Both were there to interview the first Republican running for president, Abraham Lincoln."

"Wait, George met Abraham Lincoln?" Joey's eyes went wide, and he placed his hands atop his head as he looked at Tom. "How could he not mention that?"

"Really!" Tom frowned.

"I don't have any idea why George wouldn't mention it. Except . . . He was one of the few journalists I've ever met not full of himself. George was fascinated by Lincoln and his Republican ideas to abolish slavery, bring the North and the South together with the war, and the East and West with the railroad. George wrote an article in the *Tribune* about it, 'Bringing the American Dream to a Continent,' a brilliant piece." Joseph Young paused, looking at Tom, who stared back in disbelief.

"He spoke about Lincoln in his letters, but nothing about—"

"That story was the impetus for George's book he always seemed to be working on," Joseph Young interrupted. "Arguing in support of the founding principles of this country, even the very unpopular ones—freedom for the slave, fairness to the Indian, the push for the Bill of Rights, not just in the US Constitution, but required in every state."

"We knew nothing about any of it," Joey interjected.

"The four of us, including Judah's wife Anna, all young idealists, would talk for hours about the future of America, President Lincoln, and the Civil War raging back East. Teddy's dream, of course, was to tie the country together as President Jefferson had first envisioned. Mine was to overcome the country's fear of my faith. And Anna's was for women to someday be fully valued, get the right to vote, and be respected for their contributions to this great country. George . . . Well, George wanted it all, and was passionate about his role in it. We saw Lincoln as the great uniter. A visionary, born at the right place and time. We imagined him changing the world."

Tom stared into the embers of the fire, his eyes wide in disbelief. "George often wrote us letters about the war, Lincoln, America's ideals, saying it was the best hope for all mankind around the world. His letters were the lure that brought us here."

"I suppose I'm not entirely surprised." A soft smile stretched across Joseph Young's face. "George was one of the few truly unpretentious men I've ever known—driven, but without the sin of pride. The ideal American who always wanted to do the right thing, not for accolades, but because he thought he owed it to the country he loved so much. He reveled in the kind of sacrifices our founding fathers made without financial reward of any kind or expectation of power after their selfless service. He loved that George Washington passed on the offer to be king to go home, work on his farm, and raise a family. That Thomas Jefferson almost went bankrupt while he served his country. Adams, Madison, Lincoln, all of them inspired him to—"

"George often wrote about their unpretentious sacrifice," Tom interrupted. "Severe physical and financial hardship, service to God and country. Maybe he felt unworthy to revel in his accomplishments in their shadow. A better man than me." Tom's heart was still pounding at the revelation. He thought of his mam's admonitions to her children. How many times had he heard Martha say it takes determination and a whole lot of courage, a dash of faith, hope, and charity, to keep evil at bay and preserve our God-given rights. Oh, how he missed her.

Mr. Young smiled. "That sounds so like George. Besides, things were happening so fast during that war. Things a lot more pressing, more important than railways and books on the American story."

"Not sure we'd have understood if he did share it," Tom said. "I see things so differently now. Putting power in the hands of the individual citizen is not as easy as it sounds. Such far-reaching implications of individual responsibility."

"After Leland Stanford was elected the first Republican California governor, halting plans for California's succession to the Confederate states, President Lincoln signed the transcontinental railroad into life." Joseph Young spoke in fascination, his eyes alight as he recalled that heady time as young idealists. "Teddy, Anna, and I celebrated Congress's approval, and George wrote a newspaper article about it. Not long after, Lincoln gave his Gettysburg Address, consecrating that hallowed ground of sacrifice by fifty thousand Americans lost in the battle for freedom for all those who had been denied it."

"Incredible!" Joey leaned back, staring across the dying embers in astonishment.

"George said in one of his letters," Tom recalled, "Lincoln had refined the art of telling people to go to hell in such a way that they often seemed to ask for directions."

Joseph Young laughed. "That sounds like George." He took on a nostalgic look. "Lincoln's accomplishments were remarkable."

"What happened to Judah?" Tom asked.

"He gained the support of Congress with construction planned to start when the war ended. But Teddy Judah died."

"Oh no!" Andrew's brows came together in a frown.

"He never saw a single rail of track laid."

"How?" Tom asked.

"I'm not sure exactly. I lost track of George, Teddy, and Anna after we finished mapping the alignment through these mountains. They all left here together for Sacramento. The war was in full swing and the country in chaos."

Chapter 27

⇾ • ⇽

After a two-day sleigh ride, Tom and Andrew arrived in Park City late in the afternoon of Christmas Eve. Edie and her family were ecstatic to see them. But after a welcome home kiss, a bite of food, and the loan of snow shoes, Edie ushered her brother back out into the bad weather with detailed instructions for the long trek up the mountainside to a cabin where, she promised, Annie would be waiting.

The fading glow of dusk cast a muted blaze of scarlet on the underside of swirling storm clouds as Tom started up the mountain. Jagged flashes of lightning ripped through the clouds to light up the sky, chased by cracks of thunder. The storm had arrived with a vengeance, and snow was beginning to fall in earnest. Pulling farther into his collar against the cold, Tom could almost taste his rising anxiety. His lips were numb. His mouth dry. He clenched and unclenched his fists, wiping his sweaty palm across his mouth. Drawing in a deep breath to steel his nerves, he trudged on through the now blinding snow flurry, finally cresting the cold, windy ridgeline.

Across a wide snow-covered meadow, he spotted the light from a lonely cabin nestled into a forest of evergreens and quaking aspen. Smoke lifted from the chimney only to be sliced off by the wind and carried across the snow-covered meadow overlooking the scattered lights of Park City well below.

Tom felt an uneasiness as he trudged toward the cabin. A tension rising in his chest. He hadn't heard from Annie since their last night together in Echo Canyon, nor had she responded to his letters. A lot had changed for him. He'd missed her far more than he'd imagined he would, thinking of little else as he lay in bed at night sorting out his feelings. Tom took in a deep ragged breath. His shoulders slumped and he exhaled through pursed lips. She'd become a part of him now. The better part. He had been a fool not to recognize sooner how deep his love had grown. Now he only hoped it wasn't too late.

≽ • ≼

With the light of a crackling fire in the hearth, Annie stood in her long white linen nightgown, looking out the large plate glass window over the snow-covered meadow. Park City, well below, glistened white in a flash of lightning. For more than two hours, her wide, luminous eyes had been filled with worry as she stared out the window, searching the horizon in the oncoming storm. Now with darkness settling in and the snow falling heavy, she could see little. Absently, she wrung her hands. "Oh, Thomas, I need you with me tonight."

Over the past two months, she had read her husband's letters more times than she was willing to admit. It had taken all the courage she could muster not to give in to her emotions, not to write him back spilling out all her hopes, dreams, and desires. All that seemed foolish now. She feared for him in this blinding storm. What had she been thinking? Every night she lay in bed wishing he were with her. Her mind often drifted into private imaginings in long restless nights of untethered dreams, lost in the warm glow of a multitude of beguiling desires, touches, and anxious caresses. She wiped her moist hands down her nightgown, drew in a shaky breath, nervously biting her lower lip. Lightning flashed across the tumultuous sky, and she saw the shadow of a man. Her eyes straining, she struggled to follow his shadow coming across the snow-covered meadow in long, determined strides.

Her hands shaking, Annie's heart leapt into her throat at the click of the door handle. She drew in a deep, ragged breath, brushed her nightgown smooth, then turned her head to look back over her shoulder as Thomas pushed open the door. The sight of him sent her heart beating unevenly, his penetrating gaze holding her frozen. His rich, wavy, unkempt hair hung over straight dark brows and deep-brown eyes with flecks of green reflecting the firelight. The striking lines of his ruddy face, reminding her of chiseled stone, were covered in a three-day growth of beard. Heat flowed through her entire body as she stood speechless.

Embarrassed by the rush of emotions, she tried to turn away but couldn't pull her eyes off him. Despite her effort to feel otherwise, she was fixated, breathless, undone.

"Hello, Annie," he whispered, wide eyed, a tentative smile easing across his face.

She smiled back, bashful. "Hello!"

He seemed anxious, flustered, not quite sure what to say. "What a wonderful place to spend Christmas Eve." Clearly nervous, he looked about the cabin. Filled almost to the brim with a large bed, there was barely enough room for a tiny washroom, kitchen nook, and the large window next to the crackling fire where Annie stood. "I love my sister, nieces, and nephews, but . . ."

Annie watched him without uttering a word as he pulled off his coat and cap. Then, locking his eyes onto hers, he smiled that broad, inviting smile of his. And though she didn't want it to, it vexed her. She imagined he could read the helpless desire in her sparkling eyes. Overcome, her knees felt weak. Demurely, she turned away to look out at the storm.

She could feel his presence as he came to her, his breath on the back of her neck. She thought she could hear his beating heart as she focused intently on his reflection in the window. "You didn't write back," he whispered.

"I didn't."

"I'm so sorry, Annie." His words lingered in the silence. "I was blind, foolish. Everyone could see it but me." She felt the heat rise, her pulse quicken. Tenderly, he put his strong, gentle hand on her shoulder. "Please forgive me?" Her chest rose and fell with his touch. His hand dropped from her shoulder, trailing slowly down her arm to her elbow, drawing her up in an ache of desire. Then he leaned in and kissed her softly on the nape of her neck, grazing his rough cheek against hers and sending a disarming tremor through her.

Annie closed her eyes, willing the paralyzing anxiety to drain from her body.

"Did you mean what you wrote?" she whispered, her lower lip quivering.

"I did, more than I ever imagined possible. I never knew how much until you forced me to think about losing you. Being apart these past weeks has made me see the impossibility of living without you. You are a part of me now—the better part." He paused. "Can you forgive me?"

"I don't know?" She smiled softly to herself, brows raised. "I love my grudges."

She leaned back against him, feeling his warmth, the pounding of his heart. "How do you propose making it up to me?" she whispered in a sultry voice.

He let out the long breath he had been holding and wrapped his arms around her. At last. She wasn't really sure now why she had been so afraid, for when he took her in his arms, everything seemed all right. She turned her head ever so slightly, his ragged breath on her cheek, his gentle kisses to her neck, her ears, sending a tingle of electricity down the length of her spine to her very toes.

She dropped her chin to her shoulder. "I've missed you." Her voice cracked, the stinging pleasure of tears coming to her eyes.

When she turned to face him, his smile faded. She looked down at her hands on his strong chest. Slowly, she lifted her eyes to gaze with intensity into the depths of his. Then she rose on her toes and kissed him. "I can't bear to think of you leaving me ever again," she said in a husky voice.

"So don't. Think only of our night together." Tom reached down to gently wipe the tear from her cheek.

She smiled wistfully. "My tears of happiness. Maybe the morrow will never come."

"Hmm."

"I've worried about you working so hard up there in those dangerous mountains. The thought of losing you sends a shudder through me . . . Maybe it's an irrational fear, but then maybe I've become an irrational creature."

"Hardly." He smiled. "You'll never be an irrational creature, my love. The work is hard and the days and nights long. I've grown ragged from digging tunnels. My body suffering under the brutality of it."

The firelight from the crackling hearth lit up his warm-brown eyes. They were filled with passion. Annie slid her hands up his strong chest, across his shoulders, and back down again, wrapping her arms around the narrowness of his waist, taking in the faint scent of his masculinity. "On that point, sir, I would beg to differ. I see some definite benefits from the hard work."

Holding her close, he gazed earnestly into her eyes. "Please forgive me for not seeing, for not hearing." He kissed her softly, then again, and again, the sweet taste of rising passion in each kiss.

Lightning ripped across the sky, reflecting the light in his eyes. The thunder cracked.

"That storm is growing angry outside." She paused a long moment. "I can't bear to think of another storm rising up between us."

"Then we must take care to avoid the thunder." Tenderly, he swept his hand across her cheek and ran his fingers through her hair.

She wondered how many of life's blessings most miss waiting to see the rainbow without recognizing we should be thankful for the storm. "I suppose we may both have some things to learn about each other. But in other things . . ." She offered her best seductive smile.

"Hmm!" He pulled back with a faint smile of understanding at the corners of his lips. "I love that inviting smile, and of course the meaning behind it."

He leaned in and whispered in her ear, "And I love this nightgown too."

She could feel the tingling from his breath on her skin, the hot touch of his lips on her neck, her ear. "Do you?" she whispered back in a sultry voice.

He covered her breasts with his hands and looked into her eyes. "It would look even better draped over that chair."

Her face flushed pink. "Are you having carnal thoughts, sir?" She struggled to keep her voice steady, "I have more to offer you than my linen nightgown." She paused to let him drink in the thought. "It's always been my intention to astonish you, sir!" Her heart quickened in anticipation of what this night might bring.

"Does this mean we are no longer strangers?" he asked in a husky voice.

"Well, if we are," she whispered, "then we are strangers who know every inch of each other's skin!"

He lifted his hand purposefully, hushing any further conversation with the almost imperceptible touch of his fingertip to her lips. She leaned into him, wrapped her arms around his neck, and kissed him in earnest. Feeling the passion rising in him brought a welcoming tremble to her lips. He pulled the full length of her body tight up against his and wrapped her legs around his waist, then leaned her against the cabin wall. There was little doubt now that the treaty had been ratified on both sides. Both looked forward to the peacemaking that lay ahead.

With snow falling furiously outside, they were warmed by the burning embers of the hearth and the fire of passion within. She craved his touch, his kisses, his caresses. She yearned for him body and soul.

In a kiss deep enough to drown out any lingering thought of discontent between them, he whispered against her ear, "I want you." With pure iron will in his voice, "I want every inch of you!"

His words settled into her very center, and there they caught fire. "Oh, my husband." She melted into his arms, inhaling his scent, reveling in the electricity of his touch, the taste of his kisses.

His fingers ran through the softness of her hair. She was undone by the indulgent touch of his hands on her face, her neck, her shoulders, and down her body and the sweetness of his lips brushing her breasts. There was nothing else in all the world she could think about but her husband's consoling body, the touch of his hands on her and the relinquishing desire that ran through her. He claimed her mouth in a kiss that drew from her a sigh as mystifying as the wind in the trees on a fall afternoon.

Impatiently, he released his grip on her trembling body. She slid down him to stand on weak knees. Between long, sweet-tasting kisses and inviting caresses, buttons, ties, and hooks were dealt with and clothing pulled free. He helped rid her of the interfering nightgown, leaving her body to glow pale in the firelight. Then he took her in his arms, and in one powerful, fluid motion, swept her off her feet, softly laying her on the sprawling bed of fresh linen.

Stretched out on the comforter amongst a jumble of pillows, her dark, rich hair cascaded over her shoulders. She took in a deep ragged breath and released it, and just lay there watching him intently with a little frown of concentration as he finished undressing. Ignoring the sound of the crackling fire and the storm outside, she focused only on him. He raised his strong arms high to pull his shirt off over his head. Her breath caught as she reveled in the rippling movement of his muscular body, marveling at the beauty of his masculine form. He leaned down over her. Her body was hard from work in the fields and an impoverished diet. He smiled that beguiling smile of his and soaked her up with his eyes but did not speak a word. She felt her heart skip a beat, her pulse flicker, the air move in and out through her lungs. Enthralled, she reached up to softly trace the hard curves of his chest, his arms, his shoulders. She let out a long breath, her finger pausing its journey over his skin as she gazed up at him in the blush of firelight. She smiled in wonder. "You are so beautiful!"

She could see it in his eyes, feel it in the tenseness of his consoling body, but still she urged him by her touch to say it.

He leaned down and whispered against her ear, "I love you! I want you and plan to take every inch of you." So many emotions flooded through her. She pushed all else aside to concentrate fully, completely, on the task at hand.

Her blood leapt at the softness of his skin as he gathered her up against him and claimed her mouth with his, soft, supple, and inviting.

She was with her man. She knew most lived their lives in search of moments like this, never finding them. She reveled in the feel of her skin against his. For a moment, they just held each other, warm with desire in each other's arms. Then, slow and gentle, came the ardent caresses and sweet taste of kisses, one upon another. The craving for his exploration. His whispers in her ear and his soft touches along her neck and shoulder, over her welcoming breasts, her waist and thighs. Slow and patient, he moved along the length of her willing body, sparked with electricity to her very center. She pulled in deep a breath of unbounded passion as they lay intertwined as one, the tension easing for only a moment before it began to build anew. As he scattered soft, electric kisses along her tender neck, over the soft swell of her breasts, down her outstretched body, only the sound of her breathing and the crackle of the fire broke the silence. She rose to him with a desperate ache to be soothed.

For an instant she locked on to his gaze in the firelight. Then the emotion overcame her. She passed her arms under his. And in a primitive, visceral movement, she drew him down on her. First came gentle, small movements that drew from her a sigh of surrender. Then, as his muscles tensed, came the throbbing desire that urgently needed fulfilling. His body tensed with purpose even as hers softened, drawing him in. She gasped; her fingers curled hard around his taut shoulders.

"Oh, please. Please don't stop!" Her whole body ached in desperate desire, a deep, yearning need for that great hollowness to be filled completely. She took in the intoxicating smell of their closeness and knew he must hear the pounding of her heart, feel the panting of her breath, taste the sweetness of her mouth on his, and see the unmistakable need reflected in her eyes. A great wave of overwhelming desire swept through her as she felt the power of life surging through him, shaking her to her very core.

Sweeping her arms back over her head in total surrender, she pressed her hands against the headboard and arched her trembling body into him. The intensity of her passion reached parts of her she never even knew existed. His cheek trembled, and he let out a sound of surrender that brought her to the edge of unbound lucidity.

The unreserved intimacy, the ultimate symbol of total union, flowed into her not only physically but emotionally and spiritually. It was the complete merging of man and woman, not only their bodies, but their hearts, minds, and souls. All came in a rushing tide that rose, receded, then rose again higher.

"Please?" she whimpered. The rising tide swelled and flooded higher than ever before, wave after rolling wave of the waters of life rushing over her until nothing, nothing in all the world, could stop it. Rushing all the way in, in one final surge of life-giving force, all their hopes, all their dreams, all their todays, and all their tomorrows came in a total giving to each other, as ordained by their maker.

When it was finished, he held her in the warm safety of his arms, their exhausted bodies intertwined, skin to skin. She snuggled her head into the crook of his neck, and in the quiet of the night, without words, happy in spent emotion, she lay quiet in sanctified bliss within his arms.

As emotions ebbed, she tenderly touched her fingers to the scars on the back of his hands. Sweetly, she pressed her lips to them, then to the scars on his forehead. These were the scars of remembrance—Silkstone, Hoyle Mill, the loss of their little ones, the shadows of discontent. She kissed away any lingering feelings of those terrible times in their lives.

Completely drained of strength, but smiling, Annie was filled with nothing but peaceful thoughts, her head buried in Thomas's shoulder as he slept, as they lay together in front of the dim light of the dying embers. Not wanting to be drawn away from him, even in sleep, she fought to stay awake. But as the glow of firelight faded into darkness, she, too, lost her battle with sleep and drifted contented toward the blessings of deep and restful slumber in his arms.

≽ • ≼

Inevitably, night turns into day. As they lay interlaced in the shared warmth of their bed, protected against the bitter cold outside, Tom and Annie heard the winter wren sing its song of sunrise. The faint light of day broke softly through the windowpane, bringing with it an untethered awakening.

Annie turned away in the nest of blankets and pillows, pulled the warm covers up tight under her chin, snuggled in closer, and closed her eyes against the morning.

"Annie," whispered Thomas into her ear as the wren's song drifted in. "It's time!"

"No, my love. It's only the nightingale in the moonlight," Annie countered with a hopeful heart.

"I only wish it so."

"You must tell me it's not the harsh light of dawn. The rising sun of a new day that has no pang of conscience for our separation, that would dare to take you from me. I couldn't bear it. So, it cannot be."

But the sun had begun to rise in the east, to shed its unforgiving light on the newly fallen snow.

She wanted to draw the curtain of ignorance against the outside world. "I forbid it." But now, the half-light of the rising sun touched softly on the frosted windowpane, shattering into a rainbow of a thousand colors. Reluctant, she was drawn to bitter resignation. Her battle with her heart was lost. Quietly, she accepted the verdict. She slipped out of bed while Tom lit a fire in the hearth. Without further words they went about the business of preparing for him to go. Tom sat at the tiny kitchen table. Annie leaned over his shoulder and put his breakfast before him. "This is all I have to offer you for your travels, my husband." Then she whispered in his ear, "Aside from the memory of last night!"

The corners of his mouth turned up in recognition of a Christmas well spent. He touched her arm and whispered in her ear, "The best days in a man's life are the day he's born and the day he realizes he is with the woman who is the completion of him." He paused. "We'll never be broken again, Annie. And you can lean on that without concern."

Pulling him to her, she kissed him.

"You're an irreplaceable part of me now."

"Oh, Thomas." Annie sighed. "It was never about a practical arrangement for me, compatible pragmatism or any of that stuff. I was not at all of the sensible mind you sometimes attribute to me. There was not a rational thought in my head! You bewitched me from the moment we met. I was entirely at your mercy from the start, with no choice but to say yes when you asked me to marry."

"I have a Christmas present for you!"

She smiled with a chuckle, curiously searching the corners of the room flooded with the crisp light of morning. "A Christmas present—where? You already gave me my present."

"No! That was a 'consummation of understanding.'" He grinned. "This is intended as a reminder that we will never again become strangers." Tom opened his outstretched palm, revealing the most beautiful sparkle of cardinal-red stone set in a polished silver setting.

Annie's eyes teared up at the sight of the rare beauty and—more importantly—its meaning. "It's beautiful!" The tears were coming again.

"I took you away from your home without engagement or honeymoon. Then gave you nothing but work, nothing but my absence." In a soft and serious voice, he added, "You deserve this. You deserve better, frankly, and I promise you better things to come."

"Better than last night. I can't imagine it."

He smiled. "We found a bit of red emerald in the middle of the mountain. Apparently, it's very rare." He quieted to watch the dancing sparkle in her eyes. "Can I put it next to your wedding ring? Next to our circle of promise." With a nod of consent, he carefully slid the ring on her middle finger. "Merry Christmas."

"Oh, Thomas." She stood up on her toes and kissed him.

Without smiling, he looked into her eyes, "Don't fear the flooding waters. We'll face the storms together." He paused, showing her the matching talisman pendant around his neck. "Made with the rest of the emerald. I'm keepin' it on to my grave."

She held his gaze, "That better be after me. I don't think I could live through it." Annie wiped at the tears on her cheeks. "I'm so sorry, Thomas. I should have spoken to you earlier, but I was sore afraid of what I might hear. I didn't think I could bear it."

He stood quiet for a long moment. "I thought I had all the answers. A self-centered fool, I suppose, who sees only what he wants to see. I'm sorry." He reached out and grabbed her hand. "But you have me now. I'm all yours to do with as you will." He looked at her, love evident in the crinkle of his eyes.

"Don't be sorry—just love me."

❧ • ❦

The storm over, the soft glow of the morning sun crested over the mountaintops, crept through the trees, and settled quiet on the crisp whiteness of the newly fallen snow. Tom gave Annie a long, sweet kiss as they hugged each other one final time in the stillness of the fresh mountain air on the windless morning. Each felt comfort in the power of their interdependent love.

"It's so hard to let you go, my husband." She looked up into his eyes. "It hardly seems fair that you must leave this morning," she said in a husky voice. "Tell me again why the work is so important that it draws you away from me."

"There's little choice in the matter. They've held back our pay. I'll send it as soon as I get it—enough to keep us going. And, I hope, by summer enough to put a substantial down payment on a piece of land—one step closer to our goal."

"And your life there," she interrupted, not wanting to hear any further reasons why he must leave her, "is it so much better than here with me, in this grand bed beside a warm fire?"

He smiled. She loved that crinkle around his eyes. "Giant snowdrifts, black ice, and the Castle Rock chilblains." He frowned. "Bad food and smelly men!" Tom was arguing more with himself than her, knowing the company and thousands of men in the Salt Lake Valley a hundred miles away from his tunnels depended upon him. He paused to kiss her again. "What could be better than sixteen-hour workdays in that desolate, windblown canyon, knowing one mistake can blow us to smithereens?" Tom paused, letting his words sink in. "I'll miss you, but soon we'll be together for good."

"How long will it be?"

"We're expecting about five months more." He looked apologetically into her eyes.

"Hmm." As much as she wanted him to stay, she knew he must go. He had prepared his whole life to do what no man before him had ever done, and she knew it was not only a source of income unmatched anywhere, but a confirmation that his life's work was well spent.

"You're the best of me, Annie. I'll be back as soon as I can."

Annie frowned. She pulled her brows together, then raised them. "I'll miss you," she whispered.

Tom set his jaw. "I'll miss you more. But remember this, hard times don't last. You and I . . . our love . . . and someday our own family and our own land to raise them as only we see fit. That's what will last." He held her in his arms one more time. Kissed her. Then, pulling away, he smiled at her for a long moment—that intoxicating smile of his. "Think of all the people who wish all their lives for what we have now."

"And most never will have it." She frowned. "What a tragedy."

He smiled down at her again. "Until then, my love!" And with one last kiss goodbye, he turned and walked away.

Annie smoothed out her breakfast apron, gazing after him until he disappeared over the horizon.

"It's gonna be hard without you here with me," she whispered solemnly on the beautiful, bittersweet morning. "I need you to come home to me." Their Christmas had been too short, but it was one to remember. She traced the red emerald ring on her finger. This was soon to become a habit, a constant reminder of his love for her.

All alone in the quiet landscape of freshly fallen snow, she pulled her coat tightly around her. Wistfully, she turned and walked back with crunching footsteps into the quaint little mountainside cabin, where she would spend the remainder of her Christmas Day reading by the fire.

Annie bundled herself in the down comforter and sat alone with her thoughts in front of the dying fire, drinking English tea. It brought a warmth to her veins that reminded her of summer. In a wonder of all wonders, by some unexplained revelation, she knew deep in her very soul that the purposeful melding of their bodies on this Christmas Eve had conceived another life inside her. It was the ultimate unity of purpose with their maker, tying them together through creation of a unique human soul, one never before witnessed by the world, one that would never again be duplicated in all the ages of human existence, nor in the eternities beyond.

Staring at the fire, she remembered Martha's letter left atop the mantel. "To be opened on Christmas morning" was inscribed on the envelope. She had been anxiously waiting for weeks to open it. She smiled in anticipation, put her tea aside, and picked up the letter. A warmth at the memory of her mother-in-law flooded over her. Bundled in a warm blanket, she curled up in front of the crackling fire, quietly opening the letter only to find another envelope inside marked with the words "To: Mrs. Thomas Wright. For her eyes only."

Annie's brows rose, then scrunched together, a puzzled little frown sweeping across her face. Delicate lettering on a yellowed envelope. It wasn't Martha's handwriting. Slowly and carefully, she opened the sealed envelope. With her trembling fingers, she pulled out a letter, unfolded it, and began to read. Her hand flew to her mouth.

≽ • ≼

To the woman my husband loves,

If you are reading this letter, then it must surely be true— Thomas loves you deeply!

I am leaving this letter with Martha for safekeeping with very strict instructions. I have learned to love and trust Martha, for she knows him well! She has been a great strength to me, as I'm sure she will be to you.

I wanted to write you this letter to let you know one very important thing: I am so very, very glad he found you!

I'm watching him while he sleeps in the chair at my bedside. He is exhausted, worried, and although he is trying his best for me, I know he is devastated. He looks so sad, so discouraged, so despondent. It breaks my heart. As I look at him asleep beside me, it is my fondest hope to see him happy again.

I know it won't be long for me now. And then he'll be alone. Despite losing him, I am grateful for so many things from the time Thomas and I have had together. But now, as I lay here contemplating my death, he is my biggest worry. Accepting my passing has been so difficult for him, but I have been absolutely insistent he must go on without me. He must make the most of this priceless gift of life.

I wish, somehow, I could meet you. For I am leaving in your hands the most precious thing in all the world to me. I am passing on to you my love for my husband. I can only hope you feel the same about him as I did. Outside of him, you are the most important person in the world to me now. All my hopes, all my dreams, all my desires for him are left in your hands. I am sure they are capable hands, for he would not have chosen you if they weren't. Take care of him. Make him laugh. Hold him when he struggles. Stand by him in his times of trial. He is just a simple man of simple needs, but with tremendous potential locked within. I leave that for you to unlock.

My thoughts of you give me hope right now, at the lowest ebb in my life—a hope that Thomas will again experience what it feels like to be young and in love. I hope that you and he will have the children and family we never did.

My one last hope is that somehow, I will be a positive force in your life to encourage you on in the trying times that life will inevitably bring. I pray that your thoughts of me and my hopes for you will be a welcome gift, a help to strengthen your love for him and the family we never had, but pray you surely will.

God bless you and preserve you. Please accept my thanks, my blessing, my best wishes, my gratitude. Godspeed and a happy life for the both of you! Thank you for making it possible for my hopes and dreams for his future to come true. With all my love, best wishes, and support,

Lydia Kaye Wright

⇾ • ⇽

Annie folded the letter, sank back in the large feather chair in front of the fire, and wiped at her eyes with a smile. She sat watching the glowing embers dance in the hearth. "You must have been a remarkable woman." At her most desperate moment, when all was lost, Lydia had not thought of herself, but Thomas. "Could I have done that? I think not! God bless you, Lydia."

Chapter 28

※ · ※

ANNIE SAT ATOP OLD DIXIE, plodding along the trail through the Wasatch pass overlooking the Salt Lake Valley. The afternoon sun gleamed off the many sprawling buildings below rising out of the ground on a checkerboard of perfectly square blocks of streets spreading out from the city center. Salt Lake City had been laid out by Brigham Young two decades earlier when he led the first wagon train of pioneers into the valley, and construction had never stopped, even in years of drought and famine.

"Could you please tell me where I might find Brigham Young?" Annie asked a well-dressed gentleman walking down Second Street.

"The Lion House, just down State Street, a block east of the Temple," he answered in a cheerful voice.

"The Temple?"

He pointed easterly. "That two-hundred-twenty-foot-high building under construction."

"There seems to be a lot of construction around here," Annie commented.

"Well, that's why we call it Deseret. You're in beehive country," the gentleman smiled. "Not even drought and locusts can entirely stop progress here."

"Thank you, sir." Annie plodded on. Tying ole Dixie to a hitching post across the street from the impressive three-story Lion House, she stood in awe for a long moment, admiring the grandeur of the beautifully carved balustrades and exquisite detail of the façade. She wondered what she could have been thinking coming all this way on a two-day ride in the hope of speaking to Brigham Young, the governor of the territory and charismatic religious leader. Her stomach churned, and she felt like she was going to be sick. But then she had felt like that a lot recently—she was pregnant. And she had no intention of burdening Thomas with that worry after the loss of their first two babes. At least for now, she thought, she would bear it on her own. Annie shored up her courage, took a deep breath, climbed the six steps, and knocked on the front door.

An elegantly dressed, very attractive middle-aged lady with kind, intelligent eyes answered.

"Good afternoon. How may I help you, miss?"

"Afternoon, ma'am." Annie patted her belly and smiled back. "I'm Mrs. Thomas Wright. I was hoping I might speak with Brigham Young." Even as she said the words, they sounded ridiculous. Why would the governor, living in this magnificent home, be willing to take the time to see her?

"Is he expecting you?"

"No, ma'am. But I've traveled a long way to see him."

The polite, well-dressed woman looked sympathetically at Annie. Without any further questions, she invited her in. "You can call me Eliza—Mrs. Snow, if you prefer," she said. "Please have a seat in the parlor, Mrs. Wright. I'll see what I can do."

"Thank you, ma'am. I mean . . . Eliza." Her voice caught in her throat.

Eliza smiled and nodded.

Annie stepped inside onto a lush blend of the finest quality carpet. Her eyes adjusting to the shadowed entry saw her reflection in the largest mirror she'd ever seen. She ran her chapped, scraped, and calloused hands through her hair, then tried straightening her tattered, ill-fitting clothes. Turning away in defeat, she scanned what she thought must be the most beautiful parlor west of New York City, her eyes stopping on a finely polished mahogany grand piano. She had never before seen anything like it, nor the glass panels in the ceiling-high bay window and exquisite brocade curtains that framed it. She sat nervously on the edge of the satin-covered window seat, waiting and watching people rush along the bustling city streets below.

It was only a few minutes before the dignified Eliza returned with her comforting smile. "Mrs. Wright, Brigham will see you now. Please, follow me."

Eliza led Annie up a half flight of stairs and down a long corridor, where she opened the door to a magnificent office. "You may go in, Mrs. Wright," she nodded, with a slight smile of encouragement.

As Annie walked through the door, she was greeted by a tall, handsome, powerfully built man. He stood up from behind his enormous rolltop desk and walked toward her with an outstretched hand and an arresting smile.

"Nice to meet you, Mrs. Wright." Brigham Young, a big man at over six feet tall and two hundred pounds, was in his early sixties, yet he still appeared youthful with an expressive face and the strong shoulders of the carpenter he once was. Born and bred in Canada, he nevertheless had a Westerner's restlessness. "Please take a seat." He pointed to the chair in front of his desk.

"Pleased to meet you, sir. I am sorry to interrupt your day."

"It's just Brigham, young lady," he boomed in his larger-than-life voice. He was a man electrified by his faith, his politics, and zeal for the western expansion of America. He had a reputation for unmatched tenacity to get things done that set him apart from other men. Annie imagined him as the kind of man who swept into a room working the crowd, his charisma alone causing people to trail him like pilot fish. But the surprise of the man was his understated, kindly manner. There was something intangible, an air about him, that she imagined made people believe the world was bound to bend to his wishes.

Annie stammered a reply, "Yes, sir, Brigham sir."

Brigham Young grinned with a boyish chuckle.

"What can I do for you, Mrs. Wright?"

Annie began. "My husband Thomas Wright and I just recently arrived from South Yorkshire, England. Thomas and his brothers Joey and Andrew are working on the railroad in the Castle Rock area of Echo Canyon."

"I have spent some time in Yorkshire myself," Brigham responded as he continued to size up the character of the woman who sat before him. "What part of the county are you from?"

"We're from the Woodhouse area, sir—Mr. Young . . . Brigham."

"That's coal mining country, isn't it?" He paused in thought. "What kind of work did your husband do there, Mrs. Wright?"

"He's been a miner since he was a wee one working the slag heap. He can do just about anything in the trade. One of the finest technicians the coal mining industry has ever produced. He ran the design, logistics, and explosives operations for the Wentworth Company of Mines before we left England, and he is currently managing the tunnel construction crews for the Union Pacific's Castle Rock tunnels."

"Hmm." Brigham sat smiling. "He wouldn't happen to be the tunnel construction manager my son Joseph speaks so highly of, would he?"

"I can't imagine it would be anyone but my Thomas!"

"Thomas Wright," Brigham drawled, searching the card catalog of his memory. "I hear tell George Wright was his brother."

"You knew George?"

"I was acquainted with an article or two of his in the *Denver Post*," Brigham offered with a telling smile.

"Really?"

"I usually only read the advertisements in that newspaper. That's about as close to the truth as they ever get when writing about our community, Indians, or negros. Some say truth is a valuable commodity, maybe that's why most journalists economize on it." He smiled. "Trample on it, rather than trade in it."

"I see."

Brigham sighed. "George Wright was one of the few I ever met who gave a damn about the truth of the matter."

"I'll tell my husband you said so."

"Do that, Mrs. Wright! I understand your husband's doing quite a job for the line. Those Castle Rock tunnels are a difficult proposition. Joseph calls your husband a student of invention. I hear he's started using some pretty serious explosives."

"And I'm not happy about it," Annie said testily. She had found out about the use of nitroglycerin not from her husband but from Edie, who'd heard it from Andrew. She could only suppose Thomas knew it would terrify her, which of course it did.

"Well, I suppose I can understand that," Brigham interjected.

She cleared her throat. "Brigham . . . I understand the Homestead Act of 1862 allows that we might be able to acquire a grant of land in this territory with permission of the acting governor. So, I'm here to get your blessing."

Brigham's eyes twinkled. "What land did you have in mind, Mrs. Wright?"

"Just east of Park City, up the mouth of Narrows Canyon,"

Annie shared with an earnest smile. "I would like to acquire a parcel of land along Chalk Creek."

"That's mighty beautiful country. Some of the best in these mountains." Brigham paused, drew his brows together, and pushed his lower lip up in a thoughtful frown.

Annie waited patiently. From the moment Annie had seen this land, she'd been seduced by the very thought of owning a piece of it. Stunning like nothing else on earth, it was land that could inspire, enrich, and anchor a family. She envisioned her family flourishing there. Kneel in the dirt, tend it, and watch the seeds they'd planted sprout, push up from the earth and turn green. It could mark their new beginning, be a promise for the future. She was so taken by this land that she could imagine some archeologist finding their bones there a thousand years from now.

Brigham studied her for a long moment. "You know, madam, women in this country can't own land. And what would an intelligent, educated woman like yourself want with land in those rugged mountains?"

Annie was caught off guard by his comment. "I'm surprised at you, sir! Holding educated women in such small regard. I'd heard you were one of the few leaders in this country for giving women the right to vote. Why not own land?"

"Fair enough, madam. Your point is well taken. There are more than a few things in this country that deserve rethinking." Brigham looked back at her for another long moment, clearly impressed with her tenacity and candor. "Do you always speak your mind?"

"I try to be honest to who I am."

Brigham stood and began pacing. "There is coal in those mountains. We have started exploratory borings in search of a site for a coal mine not too far from Narrows Canyon." Brigham put his finger to his lips in thoughtful repose. "A quality coal mining operation in that part of the Wasatch Mountains looks promising. The Salt Lake Valley is in short supply of coal, you know?"

"You should hire my Thomas. You'd be lucky to have him!"

Brigham pursed his lips. "I like you, Mrs. Wright. I'm gonna remember that. We'll do our best to keep him safe while blasting the hell outta that mountain!"

"I'd appreciate that."

"I bet you would. You've done your homework. I'm guessing you'd make a mighty fine salesman!"

Pushing the flattery aside, Annie forced a smile.

Brigham studied Annie's face for a moment. "Times have been hard for folks around here the past couple years. I'm afraid quality land like that is in high demand. It was never intended for these government folks to give it out in land grants."

"Hmm." Annie felt her heart sink. "I'm sorry to hear that . . . Brigham!"

"It was great to meet you." He smiled, then shook her hand. "I dare say, Mr. Wright is a lucky man."

"Thank you for meeting with me." Annie turned to go.

"By the way, before you leave town, Mrs. Wright, please see Mrs. Snow. She has something your husband has been looking for."

"Thomas?" She looked at him, confused.

Brigham smiled. "Let's just say I have my fingers in a lot of pies."

Annie nodded, trying not to let her disappointment show.

Brigham escorted Annie to the door of his office. "Thank you for stopping by, madam." Brigham opened the door for her, adding, "That's a wild and brutal part of the country. It's no place for a woman of breeding, but I'm guessing you might just be a match for the challenge."

"I'll take that as a compliment!"

"It was meant to be. I'm sure you'll do just fine. And if your husband is anything like you, have him come see me after he finishes building that railroad."

⇝ • ⇜

Dearest Thomas,

I am horrified to find out from someone else my husband has decided to use this new, terrifyingly dangerous explosive to build his damn tunnels. I'm upset about it, but I suppose I have to keep my temper, because God only knows neither you nor anybody else wants it.

I suppose any fool can criticize, condemn and complain—most do! So, as much as it turns my stomach to be complicit in this folly, I have enclosed copies of "Patent Studies for Stabilizing Nitroglycerin," Alfred Nobel, 1865; and "Central Pacific Railroad Engineers Journal Report, Lessons Learned Using Nitroglycerin in the Sierra Nevada Mountains," Mr. James Strobridge. I'm sure you're wondering how I came across these professional engineering journals—let's just say I've got friends in high places who are interested in your success. I don't understand a word of either, but I'm hoping you can learn enough to bring my husband back home to me in one piece, including all the toes and fingers I sent him away with to that God-forsaken mountain. If you kill yourself, I will never forgive you.

I desperately miss you and probably won't sleep a wink til you come home to me safe and sound.

Love,
Annie

Chapter 29

≽ • ≼

AFTER TOM WAS ASSURED PREPARATIONS were complete for their nitroglycerin venture, details checked and rechecked, he gathered his nearly four hundred handpicked men together.

"With the procedure in place," Tom began, "it's now just a matter of execution. Very careful and precise execution! There's no room for error here. This is dangerous work we are engaged in. I've chosen you because you're the best, and you will be compensated for it. Carelessness, negligence, or complacency will not be tolerated. Mistakes or errors in judgment will almost certainly mean a death warrant for some if not all of us." Tom looked at his men with a cold, hard stare of conviction. "If you are responsible for any error, you will be replaced, and any hazard pay and bonuses revoked. Are we all clear on that?"

"Yes, sir, Mr. Wright," the men echoed.

≽ • ≼

With over three hundred men carefully accounted for, all but Tom and Artist Able were stationed behind protective barriers constructed well outside the blast zone. Using a special carrier Tom himself had designed, he transported into the tunnel the first four cylinders of nitroglycerin mixed with Dr. Nobel's stabilizing diatomaceous earth. The shadowy space gave way to deeper darkness as they walked toward the location of the detonation corings. Tom felt a bit claustrophobic carrying the most dangerous and temperamental explosives the world had ever known. The quiet of the tunnel turned his thoughts to his Grand. He imagined how Grand must have felt, blinded by the darkness in the heavy air after that mine explosion, knowing the afterdamp would kill him, and he would be buried under a thousand feet of rock and earth for all eternity. A chill shuddered down Tom's spine.

Tom and Artist carefully slid the four cylinders into their redesigned cores in the dark-blue quartzite. They attached detonation caps, connected them to the three hundred feet of wire leading out of the tunnel, then with the fastening junctions to the ignition plunger stationed behind the protective barricades.

When all had been readied, connections checked and rechecked, safety measures checked and rechecked, Artist and Tom joined the others behind the safety barricades.

Tom's stomach churned. He clenched and unclenched his fists, remembering the hundred men killed during the Central Pacific's attempts to use nitroglycerin.

"Think we're ready," Tom alerted Peter O'Leary with a nod.

"Right then, Mr. Wright."

"Mr. Young, would you like the honor?" Tom offered.

"Is it safe?"

"Soon find out." Tom, with a sly smile, led a very nervous Joseph Young to the ignition plunger. "I just hope Dr. Nobel knew what he was talking about."

"Huh?"

"Here, put these ear plugs in."

All stood silent in the quiet innocence of the pristine morning, hands held over ears, breathing fast, hearts pounding, anxiously awaiting the countdown for what seemed an eternity. Joseph Young, with his heart in his throat and the fear of God in his heart, listened intently while Tom went through the detonation checklist one last time and then began the first countdown to detonate nitroglycerin since the disastrous attempt in the Sierra Nevada mountains. "Five, four, three, two, one, ignition ready. Fire it up, Mr. Young."

When the circuit closed to send a charge of electricity three hundred feet down tunnel, the most powerful explosive the world had ever known was igniting.

The confined blast from deep within the tunnel chamber shook the earth like the thunder of Armageddon, ripping through the seemingly impenetrable bedrock like a raging bull crashing through a sapling gate. The world around them shook, pitched, and was torn asunder. It seemed everything but the evaporated quartzite at the point of detonation had been turned into projectiles of rock, splintered wood, and ash, to rocket out of the tunnel like military ordnance shot from a cannon to pummel the heavy-timbered safety barricades. Then came the percussion wave convulsing through all in its path. Nails shrieked, connections sighed, the ground rumbled. And despite being stationed behind the protective barricades, the shockwave lifted both Tom and Joseph Young right off their feet. But the barricades held.

The blast caused the old mountain to heave, groan, and reverberate from basement bedrock to summit. It rang in thunderous waves resounding off the Echo Canyon walls, until finally only the dust and smoke was left to settle on men, barricades, and machinery alike.

With eyes wide, teeth clenched, and hands clapped over ringing ears, every man within miles reveled in the cruel whip this crack of doom had rendered on the tenor of nature's innocence that first morning. With his insides still churning, Tom was sure no man on earth had ever seen anything like it before.

When the dust had settled and only the metallic taste of the smoking explosive remained, there was a long moment of numb, humbled silence before the first sound of man was uttered. It began with nervous laughter, then clapping, ending in a concert of thousands of roaring men, astonished at what they had just witnessed. This explosion had begun a new era, one in which the wonder of nature was conquered by the imagination of man.

Dazed, Joseph Young turned to Tom. "Wow! That was humbling!"

Tom felt numb, his mouth dry, his hands shaking, his insides still moving. His lips curled down in awe of the demolition power he'd just witnessed. "Think we might wanna use a little less nitro next time."

Chapter 30

> · <

Tom and his men were as good as their word. Day after day, week after week, and month after month, these men methodically, meticulously, and expeditiously went about the work of blasting four tunnels through solid rock. For four months, this great army of men and machines showed due respect to the nitroglycerin beast, and together they plowed through the mountains, on their way to finishing the historic tunnels in record time, well ahead of schedule. There was not a single casualty; the only injuries were a few scrapes and bruises obtained by men scrambling to hide behind the protective barriers as one of man's greatest inventions dismantled the geology formed by nature over millions of years. This accomplishment demonstrating man's incomparable ingenuity was unprecedented.

> · <

"General Dodge, Mr. Young," Tom began. "Appreciate you meeting with us to discuss late pay for completion of these tunnels."

"Tom!" Dodge nodded.

Tom's hard eyes gleamed, indignant in the evening firelight. "You happy with our work, General?"

Dodge nodded. "Absolutely!"

"Quality is good?"

"The best!"

"The work was completed on time?"

"In fact, three of the four tunnels should be finished ahead of schedule, and it looks like all four will have track laid by the end of April, as I understand it." He paused. "I really didn't think it possible."

Tom paused. "The UP will receive the government bonds and promised land all the way to Promontory Point?"

General Dodge's eyes squinted, considering his next comment. "Look, I'll just say it, you've exceeded all expectations. I think what your crews have accomplished is just short of miraculous."

Tom nodded, appreciative, holding General Dodge's gaze. "Then why the hell haven't we been paid as agreed in our signed contract?" Tom did not drop his eyes. "My family hasn't received a dime since Christmas. That's almost five months. And many of these men"—he glanced at his superintendents—"who, as you say, 'exceeded all expectations' haven't been paid for a year on the promise they would not only be paid in full but receive hazard pay and bonuses when the government bond money came through. Some have families who are starving." Tom stood like an iron pillar, eyes cold and threatening, then sternly added, "We deserve better, General."

"There's no excuse, no acceptable answer for not being paid all these many months," General Dodge, clearly disturbed by the dishonesty, apologized. "You have more than fulfilled your part of the bargain. Durant, Crédit Mobilier . . . and I . . . have not met our payment obligations to you or Sharp & Young."

Tom looked him in the eye. "So, what do we do about it, General? We didn't bargain with the board, Doc Durant, or those other fellows. It was you, sir, and Mr. Young here, who gave your personal guarantees. It's your honor and integrity at stake. By your own words, we've satisfied our part of the bargain, and you, sir, have not!" Tom paused. "More than three hundred men put their lives on the line. Are we to be left looking like fools because we trusted you?"

"Wait a minute, Tom," Joseph Young fired back. "The general and I have been doing everything in our power to get you paid, and—"

General Dodge held up a hand to stop him. "Tom's right. You and I both made commitments to these men and have not kept our part of the bargain. We owe the money. It must be paid." He frowned, his brows pulled together in frustration. "I have personally followed up with Washington, and I will be traveling to New York City to meet with Durant and Crédit Mobilier next week." He looked directly into Tom's eyes. "That's not meant as an excuse. You do deserve full payment. Unfortunately, once again I'm obliged to ask for your patience."

"I fear, General, if the Union Pacific doesn't fulfill their obligations here, there'll be more than a little civil disobedience."

"Is that a threat, Mr. Wright?"

Tom's hard amber eyes were ablaze with quiet anger. "Men can become mighty vindictive when their wives and children are left to starve." He held Grenville Dodge's gaze with unrepentant resolve. "How difficult it must be for you to hear that the responsibility for these starving families falls on your shoulders, General. . . But how important it is for you to remember it."

· ·

My dearest Thomas,

I pray this letter finds you well. It seems so long since I lost sight of you passing over that mountain. It has brought a peace to me to know you are out there each day working hard on our behalf.

Things have been difficult here with all the families whose husbands and older boys are off working on the railroad. The failed crops of the past years have only made things worse. There is very little work in Parley's Park City and no men to do it. Please understand, we are more fortunate than most and I don't want to add to your already heavy burdens, but the children are without shoes, their clothes are ragged, and food is scarce. So many families are far worse off than us here. Edie and I do what we can to help, thanks to the money you sent after Christmas, our carefully cultivated garden, and what little work we are able to find. Some of the fatherless families have six or more little mouths to feed. Often three or four families to a house down in the tight living quarters of the Park City shambles. With a basket on my arm, I deliver vegetables from our garden or bread from the bit of scavenged flour to the worst of them. But we can't do much, for we have limited resources. Of late, I've begun to see more and more children who are starving—distended bellies, sunken eyes, and other of the telltale signs. There are homeless families, too, in some cases suffering untold hardships in these formidable mountains. I'm sure Mr. Smithson would evict many more of these families, including us, if he thought there was a chance at another tenant who could pay the rent. But all here are struggling, some barely holding on, hoping, praying the money from the railroad work will be coming soon.

I miss you, our conversations, the touch of your hand. I miss your strong, confident, comforting smile when I am frightened. I miss Christmas Eve. I find you have vexed me, sir. You have stolen possession of my soul. I suppose without you even knowing of your theft.

I find it difficult to revel in this beautiful country without you here to share it. I can't help myself. I am in mourning for

*what I do not have. For your skin on my skin, our union . . .
But they tell me after every storm there comes a rainbow!
I am desperately looking for that rainbow, my husband!*

*Forever yours,
Annie*

⁂

Tom folded the letter and slid it into his pocket. He missed her. He'd promised to wait out the rest of the week until Dodge had his meetings, but no longer. "I've 'bout had enough of this place, Annie," he whispered, staring into the fire, ready to pack it all in, go home to his wife, and retreat to some isolated place in the mountains. "One way or the other, it's over tonight."

His anger was simmering in his gut when he heard the sound of the horse and buggy approaching.

"Woo boy!" Joseph Young pulled up on the reins, stepped out of the buggy, and walked toward him. "Tom," he said with a nod.

"Mr. Young." Tom stiffly returned the nod, getting right to the point. "Do you have our pay?" Tom could see in Joseph Young's eyes that he didn't. He poked hard at the flickering embers. "No, didn't think so."

"I'd like a word if I might?" Joseph Young said.

Tom shook his head wearily. "Pretty talked out." He looked back down at the fire, poking at the coals.

Joseph Young cleared his throat. "Look, Tom. We're all together in this thing and—"

"Save it. We're not all together in this thing." Anger flashed in Tom's eyes. "Don't look like you've missed many meals, and that's a pretty fine buggy you have there." He paused. "I hear down in the valley, the workers from the East received most of their pay. We the poor stepkids? Out of sight, out of mind up here in these mountains."

Mr. Young stared at Tom. "Look, Tom, you've been honest and forthright with us. It's only because your crews met the brutal completion schedule the UP can take credit for those hundred and ten miles of track down into the Salt Lake Valley, get all those government bonds, land transfers, and Ogden's coal fields. You're a very talented young man. I knew it the first day I met you—"

"Please, don't pander. It's demeaning. I haven't received a penny for my work since Christmas. Some of these men are more than a year in arrears. Platitudes are insulting."

Joseph Young sat quiet for a long moment. "I want to be perfectly candid with you, Tom."

"Really?" Tom responded grudgingly.

"General Dodge has gone all the way to New York City on your behalf. He got quite riled up with Doc Durant and Crédit Mobilier over this issue. Rumor is ol' Doc argued no one would give a damn if a bunch of Mormons, Indian sympathizers, and a few black men weren't paid. Dodge went through the roof calling them scoundrels, your men being the best workers on the entire line and the like. He demanded the despicable Durant use the government bond money to pay your men immediately, including bonuses."

"So, where is it?"

"They fired General Dodge!"

"Really! So much for the great General Grenville Dodge?"

"If he could, that celebrated Civil War general would've left corpses of Durant and those slimy New York City Ames brothers on the boardroom floor. But the war's over. We're civilized now, with government officials on the take redefining corporate decency."

"Suppose that means no help from the government either?" He

sneered. "Brigham Young's entreaties to these disingenuous bureaucrats have ended in frustration."

Hearing the unvarnished truth was like tearing the scab off Tom's simmering anger. "Risked our lives on written promises from you, Brigham Young, Grenville Dodge, and that damn Durant and his railroad company. "S'pose a contract is only as good as the men who sign it."

Joseph Young winced. "Doc Durant called General Dodge a black eye on all he'd accomplished with this great feat to build the eighth wonder of the world, and they're—"

Tom interrupted again. "Save it! Bottom line is we ain't gettin' paid—right?"

"Betting on Durant ever paying poor immigrants, disenfranchised war veterans, blacks, and Mormons for their work . . ." Joseph Young had more than a little irritation in his voice. "That bet would have very long odds in the Hell on Wheels casinos. They're not payin' unless forced!"

"Frankly, Mr. Young, I don't give a damn about Grenville Dodge's impatience, your problems, Brigham Young, or shifty Doc Durant's eighth wonder of the world. My family will survive." Tom's flaring eyes looked directly into Joseph Young's. "But what do I tell the men who have wives and children starving? Who continued working on my promise? Damn you for putting me in this position."

"The Union Pacific and Washington, DC, have garnered more than a little mistrust around this part of the country," an indignant Joseph Young remarked, ignoring Tom's outburst for the moment. "Durant is basking in the limelight, collecting his millions and the accolades from an adoring public for a job well done." A sneer washed across his face. "And Washington politicians? They're all mouth and no trousers."

Tom was sick to his stomach. Shameless, greedy men stood to

become some of the wealthiest in the country, with enough money to pay ten times their debts to those who risked their lives to make it happen. Still, Tom wondered why he was being told all this. It left him with an uneasy feeling. "So, what is Brigham suggesting?" Tom looked askance at Joseph Young.

"He suggests if you want to get paid, it will take some proactive convincing."

"Proactive convincing?" Tom looked Mr. Young in the eye again. "What does that mean? This is your responsibility."

"Not sure you're aware, but ol' Doc has been given the honor of driving in the golden spike at the completion ceremony planned in a little over a week." Joseph Young was clearly choosing his words judiciously, allowing time for their meaning to be understood. "I hear they're planning on connecting a telegraph wire to the spike and one to the hammer. Most of the free world will be listening in with planned celebrations when the spike is driven in and the two lines connect, telegraphing completion to the whole world."

"Frankly, Mr. Young, I have more pressing concerns right now."

"Brigham gave me Doc's train schedule. Where he's gonna be and exactly when. His stops along the way. Everything an interested party might want to know."

"Interested in what?"

"Doc, being the guest of honor and all. Of course, it's imperative he arrive on time for the ceremony," Mr. Young said. "It wouldn't do to have the guest of honor miss the party when the whole world is watching, only to find out the now filthy rich robber baron skipped out on his debt to the men who actually built his eighth wonder of the world."

"Who gave your father this information?"

"Didn't say, but says he's now included General Grenville Dodge in his prayers."

"Hmm. And what does Brigham suggest be done with this information?"

"Didn't say." Joseph Young's face pulled into a duplicitous frown. He took a turn with the poker, fiddling with it and pushing the logs to the far side of the fire. "You've gained quite a reputation for being creative, capable, a man of principle. I'm guessing he thinks you'll want to do the right thing by your men."

Tom looked up to glare with hard, cold eyes into Joseph Young's eyes, pondering the not-so-subtle message being delivered. "A man would have to be a fool to dare do something like that," Tom said, indignant, his eyes flickering with anger.

"You might be right there, Tom. That would be very dangerous. Some might say downright reckless, like playing with hair-trigger explosives in a tunnel." Joseph pulled the logs back to the near side of the fire with the poker. "I understand Doc's special executive car will be protected by a single Pinkerton security guard. Probably be celebrating, 'cause the Ames boys back in New York City just received a pile of bond money to keep them enjoying the extravagant lifestyle they've grown accustomed to."

Tom frowned. "Hmm!" He gritted his teeth.

"Word is ol' Doc and Crédit Mobilier double-crossed the government."

"What?" Tom's jaw clamped tight. "Not surprised." He shook his head in disgust.

"Some say millions were stolen from the taxpayers."

"And yet Durant hasn't paid the men who risked their lives to build his road to fame and fortune."

"It looks like several million went to senators and influential government officials to grease the skids, turn a blind eye to Doc's shenanigans." He paused to let the revelation sink in.

"So, he bribed the wolves charged with guarding the henhouse,"

Tom said. "What does all this have to do with me?" He looked into Mr. Young's eyes, waiting for him to come out with it. He could feel the hairs on the back of his neck raise, the wheels in his head turning, mulling over the suggestion of suicide. Anyone foolish enough to hijack the president of the Union Pacific Railroad would be crazy, certain to get himself killed. "How do you know all this?"

"Brigham has irons in a lot of fires." Joseph Young put down the poker and slapped his hands on his knees. "Well, gotta get back, Tom." He stepped over to his buggy and retrieved a large envelope from the saddle bags. "I don't know if you're aware, but Brigham thinks very highly of you and what your men have accomplished. He's sent you a little something." He handed Tom the envelope. "Do with it as you see fit."

Tom stood up and took the envelope.

Joseph Young tipped his hat. "Mr. Wright, it's been a real pleasure working with you. I've never met anyone quite like you before. Your planning, meticulous attention to detail—quite remarkable." There was clear admiration in his voice. "Ya know, General Dodge said to me he thought it impossible to meet that tunnel schedule. But you did it with time to spare, and not a single casualty. Never seen anything like it."

For a long moment, Tom stood watching Joseph Young ride off into the distance. Trying to unravel the full meaning of the conversation, he sat back down on the stump in front of the fire. His stomach churned with the possibilities. And despite his efforts to set aside the impossible musing of an overactive imagination, he couldn't.

Carefully, he opened the envelope. Inside, he found all the money owed him, including his bonus. Clipped to the money was Anna Judah's address and a round trip train ticket to Greenfield, Massachusetts, leaving first thing in the morning. Also inside was Doc Durant's detailed schedule and a new identity card. Tom squinted, pondering the information about the Weber bridge and Piedmont Station.

Finally, there was a note.

Apparently, George was with Anna and Teddy in Panama. Anna knows the details of what happened to your brother. I sent her a letter. I've enclosed this ticket for the first train out in the morning to Greenfield, Massachusetts. Take a few days, go see Anna Judah. I'm sure with a little time to think things through, you'll make the right decision on what to do. You're a good man, Tom. God bless you and best of luck to you!

Tom's heart rumbled in his chest. His throat caught. His palms began to sweat. He knew he should take the money and run. Look out for himself and his family. After all, these other men's problems were not his. *Take care of your own*, he thought. *I don't owe these men anything. Do I?* His face was perspiring. His stomach churning, his mouth dry. *To hell with everyone else.* Tom resolved to learn the lesson of capitalism from these railroad men. *Look at Durant, using others to live his life in luxury.*

His memory of the slaver ship flooded into his mind. He pushed back on the inconvenient truth. It was made magnificent because good men had not the courage to do the right thing.

Tom poked angrily at the fire. He watched the sparks fly. The guilt bore down on him. His hands were shaking.

"Damn it!" he cried aloud. "No! That's not right!" His face wrenched in frustration. "Damn you, Brigham. Damn you!"

He paused, staring into the fire. "This is not about Brigham Young," he said quietly. "It's about me. I'm a witness to my own weakness, to my own wretchedness." Tom's own words rang in his ears. "That slaver was only possible because good men stood by and did nothing to stop it."

He stared at Doc's schedule, Mr. Young's note, the tickets, the envelope full of cash, more than enough for expenses to . . . He poked hard at the fire again, chewing over the conversation. He hated Brigham Young, Joseph Young, General Dodge, but most of all he hated the deceitful Doc Durant. Something had to be done. "But what if someone gets hurt, gets killed? Then am I a murderer? Or worse, I'm the one dead!"

It tore at his insides to think Doc Durant could get away with it, while he stood by, locked in the prison of his own fears.

For Tom, it was a long night laying on his bedroll by the fire, struggling with his conscience. "I'm afraid!" His voice cracked, as he stared into a million stars strung out like diamonds across the blackness of the night sky. "I'm scared!"

*　•　*

My dearest Annie,

My work here is finished, but I must leave this night for Boston. I cannot give you the particulars, except to say I intend to find out once and for all what has happened to my brother George, and what comes next for us.

Oh, how I envy this sheet of paper which will soon be in your hands, pressed to your breasts, perhaps even to your lips. We are parted by distance, but you live in my heart and I miss you more than I had ever imagined possible. Day by day, time and my love for you have rendered my past life to feel more and more like a foreign country.

I will come home to you, holding you in my arms as soon as humanly possible.

I miss you. I love you, and remind you to never doubt that I will love you to my dying day.

Your husband forever,
Thomas

Chapter 31

❖ • ❖

TOM WALKED THE DISTANCE FROM the train station through the city of Greenfield, Massachusetts. Anna and Theodore Judah's quaint country home had been in the family since before the Declaration of Independence was penned. It was constructed when Greenfield was a colonial stronghold near the birthplace of America. Anna, who had inherited it from her parents, lived there alone now.

Tom was nervous as he approached the front door. Initially intoxicated by being on the threshold of discovery after all the years of wondering what had happened to George, he now felt awkward, anxious. He stepped up to the door, his palms sweating, his heart quickening at the thought of meeting the wife of the man who conceived the greatest technological achievement of the nineteenth century—and also had the key to his brother's disappearance.

He took a deep breath, shook his hands loose by his sides, practiced his introduction, and tried to regain his composure. He knocked three times and took a step back, drew in another deep breath, coughed out his nervousness, and stood waiting.

The door opened, and there she stood. For all her accomplishments, he had not expected the driving force behind such an important figure in American history to be an ageless, diminutive woman. She was unassuming in her bearing, and still after all these years, appeared young, beautiful, and elegant in her own way.

"May I help you?" Anna Judah said in a clear, intelligent voice, a questioning look in her eyes.

For a moment he stood without a word, steeling his courage. "I'm Tom Wright."

"Oh my!" Her hand came to her mouth as she stared at him. "Of course you are." There was an expression on her face he could not read. It wasn't disapproval, or horror from seeing a man of inferior birth, nor any of the sentiments he might have expected. She simply stared at him fixedly, a peculiar, stunned look across her pale face.

The moments stretched out; a self-conscious Tom fumbled to push a cloud of unruly hair from his brow, awkwardly trying to find a place for his hands.

"I can see him in you. Your eyes. And you have his voice," she sputtered out, looking at Tom intently. She was clearly quite undone. "After all these years . . . the wonder, the searching . . . and now here you are."

"Excuse me, Mrs. Judah?" Tom questioned, feeling increasingly anxious as she stood staring at him.

"I'm thrilled to see you," she answered, ignoring his surprise, an excitement filling her face. "Joseph Young told me you might come. Please come in, Tom." She stepped aside, opening the door wide to invite him into her fastidiously appointed parlor adorned with tasteful artifacts collected from the travels with her husband. The glowing embers in the hearth filled the room with warmth. "Please, make yourself comfortable while I make us some tea." Anna disappeared into the kitchen.

There were dozens of her paintings on the walls: mountain passes, snow-covered ridgelines, lakes, mountain streams, expansive plains, and high mountain meadows with rivers meandering through them.

"I'm so glad you're here," Anna called out from the kitchen as she went about making tea. Tom strolled the museum of paintings, artfully displayed maps, and artifacts from all over America.

Shortly, she returned carrying two teacups filled with hot cinnamon tea, politely served on Victorian saucers with petite ornate silver spoons. The sugar and cream were in silver containers. She set them down on a beautiful carved stone coffee table, then sat back and looked at him again. "I can't get over it, after all these years."

"These paintings are wonderful," Tom said, not quite knowing what else to say.

"Thank you! Teddy did his railroad surveys, I painted, and George wrote all about it. We trekked together through the San Joaquin Valley, the Sierra Nevadas, the Wasatch, the Rocky Mountains, the Tetons of Wyoming, and the plains of Nebraska."

Mrs. Judah looked at Tom, seeming to ponder the man she saw before her. "I'm sorry for staring, Tom, but you look so much like your brother it is uncanny. It's left me a bit frazzled. George was a wonderful man, a godsend to Teddy and me." She paused to drink her tea. "He saved my life—did you know that?" Anna ran on, not able to take her eyes off him. "And he tried his best to save my husband's as well. I was devastated all over again when we lost your brother."

Tom's heart leapt into this throat. His fingers shook, forcing him to put down his cup of tea, and his face went pale. He had just received confirmation his brother was dead. He supposed he'd always known it, but to hear that his long search was over had a sobering effect. There was a long pause as both sat in silence.

"Oh, Tom, I'm so sorry. I thought you knew. When I got Joseph's letter . . . I thought . . . I'm so sorry to have to be the one to tell you."

Tom sat silent. He picked up a spoon to stir his tea while he tried to make sense of this stunning validation. He was surprised at how the official confirmation tore at him with such finality. "Mr. Young intimated as much, but he suggested I speak directly with you. And of course, we hadn't heard from George in years."

She looked undeterred into Tom's eyes, then in a soft, concerned voice, she said, "I had hoped you would come see me. Both Teddy and I enjoyed a closeness with your brother that touched my heart." She looked at Tom with sympathetic eyes. "He was like a brother to me at the end. Though sick himself with yellow fever, it was your brother who alone pulled me off the brink of a nervous breakdown while we both fought the losing battle to save my husband's life. It was only after he had stood by me and Teddy in those final heart-wrenching days as we traveled home from Panama that he, too, collapsed with yellow fever. I had thought he was feeling better. But then he relapsed and I lost him too. It was all so very tragic. It's still difficult for me to speak of, even after all these years."

"Forgive me. I'm sorry for your loss. I hear Teddy was a wonderful man," Tom said feebly. He could say nothing more. His melancholy heart was still trying to absorb the finality of it. His long search had come to an end. But at least he, Martha, and the rest of his family had closure.

"I tried for years to track down your family," Anna added tenderly.

"We were fearful of this end after George's letters stopped," Tom responded, his mind still lost in a fog. "It was my mam's parting wish to find out what happened to her son. I'm not sure why, but we knew nothing of you or your husband."

The silence dragged on, neither quite knowing what to say further, until Anna plunged in. "George was tireless in his journalistic pursuit of truth and the rights of man." She paused. "Arguing in support of the founding principles of this country, even when they were unpopular.

He championed my husband's dream to build a railroad across the country when most thought Teddy a fool." She began to sound nervous. "Then when Lincoln came to his rescue, and greedy, powerful men tried to take away his dream, your brother was there." Her eyes were no longer on Tom, but on the past. "George was an idealist."

"Mr. Young told me George met Teddy in an interview with Abraham Lincoln." Tom stared at the fire in the hearth in confusion. "We had no idea he was—"

"Your brother was an enormous fan. We all were. Lincoln was an unusual man who sacrificed everything for human rights. Never was there a man so hated, despised, ridiculed, or acquainted with grief. Yet he gave his wholehearted might, mind, and life to help fulfill our American covenant with Almighty God," Anna proffered. "George had hoped to write a book about it—he didn't get that chance. At the last, with shaking hands, he wrote a long parting letter to you and the rest of his family explaining everything."

"Never got it."

"No," Anna admitted, "I was so distraught myself, I didn't realize I had no way of forwarding it to you until too late. Sadly, I had no idea where to send it." She shrugged and raised her brows in embarrassment. "So, it was by divine providence I received Joseph's letter. I cried reading it. I had every intention of tracking you down, but my letters came back postmarked 'return to sender.' Now here you are in my living room. It seems surreal, a reminder of those heady days traveling together with my Teddy and George, when we were all young, idealistic, driven."

"Here I am." He really didn't know what to say.

"Do you know what a heavy burden of guilt you've lifted off my shoulders, knowing I can finally deliver George's last letter?"

"We had no idea . . .," Tom repeated, astonished, but too overwhelmed in the moment to add more.

"Joseph shared as much." Anna paused, watching Tom stare into the fire.

She handed him the bent, smudged, thick, and yellowed envelope. "This is the letter George wanted me to send to your family."

Tom took the envelope, looked at it solemnly, then tucked it into his pocket. "Are you planning to go to Promontory Point for the ceremony . . . in celebration of your husband's remarkable achievement?" he asked, changing the subject.

"I wasn't invited, but God bless you for asking." Anna smiled politely. "Joseph tells me Brigham wasn't invited either."

"I can imagine, considering it's the Union Pacific putting on the event. Doc wouldn't want to share the limelight!"

"No matter, I'd have refused myself to everyone on that day anyway." Anna paused, looking at the fire. "As it happens, it's also our twentieth wedding anniversary. I'll be spending the day here, in solitary confinement with the spirit of my brave husband, my paintings, and his letters, unseen and unheard by the world."

"God bless you both! I won't be there either."

"Joseph told me a bit about that." There was a clairvoyant look in her eye.

"He and his father have an uncanny way of placing heavy burdens on my conscience."

Anna smiled, the words unspoken but understood.

"They were always good to us," she allowed. "Brigham and Joseph, two of the few who caught Teddy's vision right from the start and treated us with respect."

"Hmm." He'd been no fan of Brigham Young. Tom suspected he was just being played like a pawn in his master game of intrigue. But maybe Brigham Young had only opened a window to his soul.

"You know it was Brigham who introduced George to many of the men, including leaders of the Cheyenne, Ute, and Shoshoni tribes."

"Really?" Tom pondered the thought. "Do you know if George ever met Chief Washakie of the Shoshoni?"

"He did. Right after the massacre at Bear River. Pocatello too."

"Did he!" Tom frowned at the ironic coincidence.

"I can tell you this, there were a lot of those pious folks who hated Brigham and who were dishonest, inhospitable, and despicable to us." Anna Judah paused in recollection. "People who have no vision themselves can oft times be so cruel."

"Only a very few men see into the future with clarity," Tom said. "I suppose you learned a lot about dishonest men over those years."

"Huh! True enough." She sat in quiet. "There are few things worse than standing by watching a brilliant, honest man put his very best on display for all the world to see, only to be laughed at and vilified by ignorant journalists and the foolish, self-important ne'er-do-wells." She frowned. "Especially one you love. I learned men like Doc Durant, Crocker, and Hopkins cared for little more than their own unfettered greed and were willing to destroy the real visionaries to that end."

"There must be a special place in hell for men who ridicule, abuse, and take advantage of the truly gifted for their own selfish purposes," Tom offered. "Like gophers who object to mountain peaks, or lemmings who complain about crowds."

"After reading Joseph's letter about your work on the tunnels, I knew I'd like you."

"You stood alone," Tom said. "Defied public opinion and slanderous criticism to pursue a dream. The Millennial Marvel doesn't seem so crazy to the world, now."

"Surprising, the lengths some went to mock us."

"Despite the obstacles . . . it's people like you who make things happen in America, isn't it?" Tom hesitated. He looked at Anna Judah, lost in the memory of her late husband. Like all great men and women who stand before God in full sunlight with the conviction of their visionary dreams, their dreams had been declared sacrilege by the unimaginative self-righteous in order to publicly demonstrate their own virtue. How difficult it must be for genius to cast their pearls into the muck and mire of humanity, where a whole concert of lesser souls sing out their arrogant indignation, deriding them for seeing the future as it could be rather than accepting that things will never change. How difficult it must have been for her to see her brilliant husband ridiculed. "Most just talk, but never actually make things happen." Anna watched Tom. "You remind me of your brother. He was a ponderer too. He saw through all the deceitful power brokers. Men like Doc Durant, who would manipulate and bribe dishonest senators and government officials for their own financial gain at the expense of the creators, the builders."

Tom looked at her in surprise.

"Oh yes, I know about Doc Durant." She frowned. "It's a shame a greedy shyster can sully this most monumental accomplishment by men like you and my husband."

"Nowhere else but in America could this engineering, social, and political feat have been possible."

"You're right, of course." She paused. "This country's principles can be cumbersome, sometimes even messy." She looked into his eyes. "But never give in to 'em, Tom."

"It's a beautiful thing to aspire to!" Tom was coming to realize that freedom was the flame that lit the torch of human ingenuity, creativity, progress, and happiness too, making anything possible. But if every good man did not stand strong, that flame could easily be blown out.

"Indeed!" She looked at Tom for a long moment. "It's unfortunate that sometimes great men have to be sacrificed to make things right."

Government by the people, for the people could be a difficult and unwieldy monster. There was always a price to pay for the benefits, Tom supposed. Always unscrupulous men, who for money and power would try to impose their will on the creators, on those who don't just talk but make things happen. With his elbows on his knees, his hands folded, he looked into the crackling fire and considered his own dilemma.

"Your brother was entirely taken in by Abraham Lincoln's vision of America, who believed our country was divinely inspired and set aside for greatness by God. And because of that, Lincoln argued, America could not be destroyed from abroad or by any military or outside force. 'If destruction be our lot,' he said, 'we must ourselves be its author,' because we allowed evil men to destroy us from within—'death by suicide.' George, like Lincoln, felt strongly all of us in this country must do our part to stand up for the right, no matter the cost."

Tom talked with Anna Judah late into the evening. "Thank you for everything."

"You're surely welcome." She looked into Tom's eyes, long and hard. "I'm convinced Joseph was right about you." She paused. "What will you do, Tom?"

Tom's own words rang in his ears: *That slaver was only possible because good men stood by and did nothing to stop it.* He took in a deep breath to steel his resolve. This was not about the Youngs or their game of intrigue. It was about Tom himself. His knees were weak; his hands shaking; his breathing short. He could feel his pulse pounding at his temples. This was about finding the courage to stand up to the despicable robber baron who would steal the dreams of struggling American families. And despite the thorns and thistles of doubt, Tom would not let fear hold him hostage. He knew what he must do. In answer to Anna's question, he stood, reached into his pocket, and pulled out Doc Durant's executive train schedule.

"God bless you, Tom! And may He watch over you."

Chapter 32

~ • ~

ANNIE HAD FANTASIZED A DOZEN times about her husband's return. Every day she thought of him, and especially at night. "Sometimes I imagine him walking up the road to our little Park City bungalow," she shared with Edie one evening as spring edged into summer.

"I know my brother, and I'm sure he wishes he were here with you."

"I imagine him opening the front door. Dropping his knapsack at the sight of me and sweeping me up off my feet into his strong arms."

"Hmm." Edie smiled at her sister-in-law's enthusiasm.

"If he knew how much I missed him." Annie paused in thought. "It's embarrassing—don't you dare tell him—but I reread his letters over every night."

Annie frowned as she looked in the full-length mirror at her protruding belly. "I was no beauty when he left me here, but there's no tellin' what he's gonna think of me now." She chuckled. "He might just turn tail and run right back to that rock pile!"

"Oh, nonsense! He's gonna be so excited to see you, and thrilled you're havin a bairn." Edie laughed. "If I know Thomas, he'll be treating you like a queen."

"This mirror must be designed to make everything look bigger than it actually is. I can't be this big, can I, Edie? I look like the Pumpkin Queen at the county fair!"

Edie giggled, trying to stop the tears of laughter from coming.

Annie, who could outstare an owl, continued to ponder her reflection in the mirror. "I just keep telling myself Thomas says I'm beautiful." A mischievous smile crept across her face. "I think we may need to get him glasses."

Edie tried to stop her escaping laughter. "Oh Annie, you're looking at the reflection all wrong." She knew her best friend often talked more when she was scared. "My advice? Break the mirror. You're a beautiful woman, with a heart of gold."

"Yeah, and look where that got me." Annie giggled, turning sideways. "A walking illustration of my love's adoration."

Edie, now holding her shaking tummy, was rolling on the bearskin rug, out of control with laughter. "Stop it, Annie, please," she gasped. "I can't breathe!"

"I'm thinking sweeping me off my feet may a bit optimistic." Annie frowned. "Maybe an entirely unrealistic proposition? Maybe he could just push me in a wheelbarrow?"

Edie lay on the rug looking up at her sister-in-law. "I can't imagine being crammed into this tiny place chasing my five wild ones around without you to make me laugh when I should be crying. You know they all adore you. Who wouldn't. Remind me to thank my brother for this blessing!"

Annie thought about what Martha had said on the dock as they left for America. "Please help Edie with my grandchildren. She's not as strong as you." It had been a joy, Annie thought as she lowered herself into the chair. "We'd better stop our giggling. We'll wake 'em up." She leaned back and placed a hand on her belly. She felt a kick, which brought a shy smile. She looked down at Edie for acknowledgment, and Edie smiled. "Despite it all, some things about being with child are downright wonderous." She sighed. "Aren't they?"

"They are," Edie said.

Annie pulled in a deep breath. "I tried to put on my best face for everyone around me after Henry died. Everyone thought I was so strong." She remembered how sometimes her emotions got the best of her and she couldn't hold back the tears. "But I'm not." Annie wiped at her eyes. "Oh, Thomas, how I miss you."

A somber expression crept over her as she stood again facing the mirror. She stared transfixed at her reflection, recalling the devastating loss of her children. "Everyone told us we were brave when we lost our two little ones. But I wasn't brave. I was terrified. I wasn't hurt. I was demolished! I was . . . I guess we both were holding our breath just to survive another day. I wasn't sure if it would bring us closer or tear us apart." She paused again, trying to control her emotions, staring into the mirror. "I never once felt brave. Losing a child does something unexplainable to your brain. Losing two, I went insane. Poor Thomas!" She wiped at her eyes with a soft smile.

Edie was quiet, adopting Annie's somber mood, not wanting to interrupt her. She was a witness to the spiritual wonder of a mother and her baby in the womb. Edie looked on, wiping at her eyes, thinking of her five precious children.

"Thomas sounded desperate when I last heard from him. I made it worse by writing that letter telling him of our troubles. I'm sore afraid for him, Edie. I hope he doesn't do anything foolish. We'll still survive if they don't pay him." Annie wiped at her runny nose with the back of her hand. "Oh, Edie!"

Edie wiped at her own eyes.

"You know, Edie, Thomas doesn't even know I'm with child." Annie went on, "Maybe I should have told him, but I didn't want to burden him needlessly, put him through that fear again. Was I wrong, Edie? Should I have told him? He appears so strong on the outside. He tries so hard to control his beautiful mind, to keep it from running away with him. Oh Edie, it has to be all okay this time!" Annie laid her hand on the swelling contours of her body. "Please, God, I so need my baby to be healthy!" She again wiped at the moisture in her eyes. "I'm such a mess!"

In her own world now, Annie continued to look at her reflection in the mirror. "I know you're just waiting to come join us. I know you will bring us even closer together. A family in this new land—the first of a generation born American." She looked in awe at her reflection, the miracle of this life inside her. She was hopeful. She was heartened. She was scared to death. "Please, Father in Heaven, give me a healthy baby this time. We've suffered enough."

Edie felt the tears burning on her cheeks. She thought of her precious children. What would she do if she lost even one? Feeling the guilty observer, not wanting to interrupt her, Edie left Annie alone to her thoughts. She quietly slipped away into the bedroom to look in on her own babies, sleeping peacefully in their beds. "You are the best of me." She acknowledged the five blessings of her good fortune lying so innocently asleep.

PART III

May 1869

Chapter 33

❖ • ❖

As darkness settled in, Tom watched the steady stream of men plodding across the pasture and into the farmer's barn. He saw the nervous tension in their eyes, the disenchantment. Their darting glances across the fallow fields, their slouching gait. They had worked hard, taken life-threatening risks, and now because of the disgraceful greed of a few despicable men, they and their families had fallen on hard times.

By dark, the barn was full with thirty men having special talents for the task at hand. They had been secretly handpicked by Captain Peter O'Leary. Most had fought in the great war under General Grenville Dodge and had trusted him with their lives. These were hardened veterans. Mostly single. Fighting men capable of awful things. They talked among themselves, whispered, and waited. They knew they were going to be asked to break the law, risk prison, or worse.

Tom wondered just how this moment had come to pass. How things had deteriorated to the point of violence. It was not an accident of poverty; these were not the kind of men who would stand before their benefactor to beg for their just due.

This is how it must have been behind barricaded ramparts on the field of battle, Tom thought. Hearts pounding as the the fighting raged all around them. A devastation of spirit torn by self-centered greed. In some ways this injustice by fellow Americans was more vicious, more dangerous to the freedom of every American than any explosive in the arsenals of Fort Sumter.

Grand's voice rang out in his head, "Ya gotta stand up to the bully, Tommy. We all have fears. Courage is the fear you ignore. It's the choice you make when you're afraid that matters most." Tom blew out the breath he'd been holding. *God, give me strength to fight this evil for these men or someday it'll be me and my family left to stand alone.*

He stepped up onto a large crate. Waiting in silence, he looked onto the familiar faces of these loyal, hardworking men who had fulfilled their part of a very dangerous bargain yet were left uncompensated for their part in it by a few greedy men who thought they'd be easy prey. Some had been driven into this territory because of their religious beliefs. Some were immigrants. Some were outcasts, casualties of prejudice. They were Irish, negros, Mormons, Chinese, and even an Indian scout. Tom had come to care about these hard men and the rest of the over three hundred unpaid workers not invited on this night. They had trusted him in all things, including completing what others had called an impossible task. Tom glanced at Peter O'Leary with a smile of recognition, nodding his appreciation. He had come a long way.

All stood quiet, their eyes filled with hope fixed upon him, trusting he would make things right. Tom was fortified by the resolve he saw in their faces, the anger in the tightness of their jaws. A testament to why good men everywhere must stand together, support each other. God forgive him if he got them killed. He took in a deep breath. "My family gave up everything to sail halfway around the world for a chance at a better life," Tom began with conviction. "We are a nation of immigrants. Immigrants who came here because this is the only country on earth where men are free to determine their own destiny." He was breathing hard. The heat of passion coursing through his veins. "This is a country where other principled men have given their lives to secure God-given rights for you and for me."

He paused to let his words sink in, looking into the eyes of these hard, determined men. "Sometimes, it takes courage. It takes action to protect those rights—risking all to fight injustice in pursuit of our hopes and dreams. My grandfather used to tell me that courage is the rarest of all virtues. It doesn't come from the strength of our backs. It comes from personal conviction, the invincible will to put aside fears and stand up for what's right."

Tom's hands were shaking. His voice rose in chilling resolve. "Your ragged clothes, beaten and battered bodies, sunbaked faces are badges of courage—badges of honor." Tom squinted, locking his gaze onto the eyes of each man. "Look what you have accomplished! But for you, none of this great achievement that has captured the fascination of the entire world would have been possible. By the strength of your will, you have shown who you are, the best of the best at what you do." His voice rose with conviction. "Not because of who your parents were. Not because of where you come from, the color of your skin, your faith, or how much money you have. But because of who you bloody well are. And don't you ever forget it."

"We fought a war fer these rights, lost our brothers in arms," one man called out in anger. "Worked sunup till sundown seven days a week fer that pay." He raised his fist. "We're Americans, by God. 'Tain't right what they done, leavin' my wife and little ones ta starve."

"You've earned every penny, Daniel."

A rumble of support rolled through the crowd of men.

Tom took in a deep breath. "It takes men of courage to stand up to powerful, greedy robber barons who bribe senators and cheat our families for their own self-interests. But then, this country was founded by such men of courage. Many of them died for it, including your brothers in a civil war. You know firsthand, far better than I, of the sacrifices required to extend and keep our God-given rights for all citizens of this country. We must stand up shoulder to shoulder against tyranny if we are to preserve those rights for ourselves and our brothers in this fight. If not now, then when? If not here, then where? If not us, then who will stand up for what is rightfully ours? It must be settled by force, if necessary; taken from the powerful men of industry who've lied, cheated, paid off government officials, and stole from our families." He paused. "Mark Twain may have said it best: 'It's never the wrong time to do the right thing.' This great American experiment will end when good men cower before the powerful on bended knee. We may have forgotten that for a time, but now it's time we must stand up for our own dreams!"

Tom took in a deep breath of resolve. "It seems clear, despite our legal rights, no one is going to stand up for justice against these robber barons . . . unless it's us."

"I say it's time we go get what's owed!" Peter O'Leary called out, cold and determined.

"It's time!" The crowd of men shouted in unison. "It's time!"

"Well, gentlemen, that's why you're here tonight. It's time to make things right. We may all hang together, but at least we'll stand for the right as free men of conviction."

⇝ • ⇜

On the morning of May 6, 1869, under dark clouds and light rain from a summer storm, Dr. Thomas Durant and Union Pacific's bookish finance director John Duff approached Piedmont station, Wyoming, headed west after leaving New York City two days earlier.

Traveling in a single-car executive train, they were on their way to the transcontinental line completion ceremonies scheduled for two days later at Promontory Point, Utah. Comfortably ensconced in the luxurious train car, sitting in gold-leaf chairs, Doc Durant and Mr. Duff eagerly discussed their future plans to spend the millions they'd receive from their completed railroad. Their sole Pinkerton security guard sleepily stared out the window at the monotonous countryside. Suddenly, their morning turned from dreams of opulence to nightmarish terror. Rifle shots rang out. Bullets zinged past the gold brocade curtains, ricocheting off the metal roof in a frightening clatter of lead on steel. Doc Durant ducked below the windows while John Duff sprawled on the floor, pulled his chair down over himself, and began crying in terror.

With brakes squealing, the train slid and jerked to a stop in front of piled-up crossties on the tracks. Sounds of angry men clamoring outside rushed the executive car. Within seconds, three brutish men and another twenty standing behind them blasted through the doors into the executive car's secured chamber. They stormed in with rifles pointed and angry demands directed at the two distinguished passengers and single Pinkerton security guard.

"Down on the floor—now!" one of the gruff, hard-muscled hijackers demanded.

Doc Durant and his lone Pinkerton escort, who'd already dropped his gun, joined Duff on the floor.

"Don't hurt us," begged Duff. "Please, oh please, dear God, don't let them hurt us."

"Keep yer faces kissin' that floor," a burly hijacker bellowed. "Move and I'll shoot yer ass!"

Outside, behind the mob of hijackers, a masked Tom Wright, in a slouch hat and colorful Mexican serape, sat astride his bay horse in the falling rain. "Okay, boys, move in, uncouple Doc's car from the engine."

Duff, Durant, and the Pinkerton guard were hauled to the balcony platform at the front of their executive car and forced to face the crowd of angry men chanting, "Make 'em pay." Some of the hijackers uncoupled the executive car from the engine.

Tom looked up at the engineer and the coal fireman, who had their hands raised, standing between two surly hijackers. "Pass down your weapons, gentlemen." One of the hijackers passed the men's rifles to Tom. He stared at the engineer and fireman. "That all of them?"

"Yes, sir."

"Apologize for the delay. We'll have you on your way momentarily."

"You fellas are in a lotta trouble," offered the engineer. "General Dodge is at Promontory Point. He'll skin ya alive."

"General Dodge!" Tom responded with a sarcastic edge and a knowing smile. God bless President Grant for insisting Durant rehire General Dodge after that unpleasant debacle in New York. "Please give the general our kindest regards."

"Huh?" Tom turned his stern, cold eyes to Doc Durant, who was holding tight to the railing of the ornate executive car. "Doctor, Mr. Duffy, they'll be remaining with us."

"What the hell is going on here? Do you know who I am?" blustered a panicked Doc Durant.

The engineer and fireman turned to stare at the petulant Doc Durant as Tom ambled his horse toward the executive car. Tom had always envisioned this master manipulator who bribed senators and cheated his own partners, seemingly devoid of any moral conscience, as a giant of a man, with a strong chin, bold features, and rich dark hair graying at the temples. But what he saw in front of him was a frail man who looked like a just-hatched bird. His clothing was of the finest wool and silk blend, and it fit like it was made for his unusual shape—concave chest, narrow shoulders, long, thin neck, and a wide forehead descending to a pointy chin. His graying hair, parted in the middle, was pasted to his skull with an expensive tonic. He had a long, thin beak of a nose with flaring nostrils, and his ears jutted out from a face covered by a scraggly beard. His dark, shifty, intelligent eyes squinted against the sun, and he was clearly trying to look as fearless as he could make himself out to be. But his manipulative charisma didn't work on these no-nonsense men who'd faced death in a civil war. It was difficult for Tom to imagine this was indeed the heartless master of deception who had defrauded these hardworking men and their families.

"Don't you worry about ol' Doc," Tom advised the engineer in a voice as rich and bitter as burnt sugar—just loud enough for Durant to hear. "We'll take good care of him. If he does his duty, we might just let him go. If not . . . Well, either way, he'll get what he deserves!"

Under increasingly dark clouds and drizzling rain, Tom pulled up his horse at the railing and stared belligerently with cold, dark eyes at the reprehensible Durant. Durant squirmed; he wiped his sweaty hands across his profusely perspiring brow despite the falling rain.

"Yes. We know who you are, Doc," Tom said clearly. "You're the man who owes us a lot of money."

Durant was drained of color. Silenced by Tom's words and intimidating stare, he now wiped at his face with his handkerchief. His other hand was holding tight to the railing to stop his shaking. John Duff stood well behind him, a sniveling mess of frazzled nerves.

"It's all very simple, Doc," Tom began. He drew closer to Durant, his escort of two dozen gunmen surrounding him. "Your stay with us can be a short and pleasant respite, or if you can't arrange to pay us our wages now, it can be handled more violently. Trust me, after five years of war, most of these men are good at that kinda business." He squinted as he paused to let the message sink in. "We've all learned separating our pay from your greedy hands can be quite painful!" The sadistic edge in Tom's warning seemed all the more dangerous in his cold, commanding voice.

To emphasize the point, one squinty-eyed masked man pulled out a very long and menacing bowie knife; another cocked his sawed-off shotgun. And the jumpy men behind Tom began to laugh derisively as Durant's frightened eyes widened, dancing from man to man. Clearly in need of support, he grabbed the railing tighter, both hands shaking now.

"These fine gentlemen here, and quite a few others waiting for our return, have worked mighty hard to make you rich," Tom went on. "In fact, as I understand it, because of their efforts and the greed of some in government, you stand to make a whole lot more money than expected." Tom's men muttered their discontent while Durant stood silent, his pale, perspiring face almost gray. "Unfortunately for you, payment for our efforts to make you a very rich man is sorely overdue. We hope you and Mr. Duff here haven't treated your financiers with the same disrespect you've shown these men, or I'm afraid it's going to end badly for you both. Could be a very bad day indeed . . . You might not be attending the same ceremony you were hoping for."

While the angry mob shouted out their contemptuous eagerness for retribution, Tom paused yet again. His icy cold eyes locked on Durant, who squirmed and dragged the back of his hand across dry lips. "I'm thinking a nice dirge could bring some smiles back to the faces of these boys standing behind me," Tom concluded.

"Gentlemen, gentlemen, please," Doc Durant began in slimy oration, a forced smile like cold grease floating over his fluid voice. "I am in full sympathy with your demands, but of course I don't have that kind of money here. I promise you as soon as we finish up with this business at Promontory Point, payment of your back wages will be the first thing I do when I get back to New York. You have my word on it. We will get all of you men paid in full, including the bonuses due."

"Your word?" Tom snarled, staring at Durant. "I'm afraid, Doc, that your word has lost all credibility, if it ever had any to begin with. It just won't do. Your reputation precedes you like scum on slack water." He stared Durant down. "I think we'd rather be paid now. Luckily, we have the telegraph station right here for your convenience, with an operator standing by."

Durant stood silent, perspiring, his hands trembling.

"You will send a telegraph to Mr. Oliver Ames and Mr. Dillon at Crédit Mobilier," Tom advised. "You will explain to these gentlemen your predicament. How both your lives hang in the balance." Tom let the tension build for a moment. "Hopefully, you're convincing. Or, how do they say it in this part of the country? You're buzzard bait." He laughed, volatility in his voice, his blazing eyes narrow and menacing. "Of course, you will remain our guests until our money arrives, or until your partners decide you're not worth the expense. And frankly, who could blame 'em." Tom's eyes showed disgust. "Either way . . . These men behind me will get something they want badly!"

"I can assure you, gentlemen, that I have every intention of paying you fellas your just due," the unscrupulous exploiter of good men pandered. "Just give me some time."

"Wonderful! We'll give you time—just not much of it. You ain't leavin' here standing unless we receive our money in a timely fashion. Otherwise, you and your companions will be leavin' in a pine box and your mistresses left to spend all that railroad money."

The wily Doc Durant paused while he gathered his wits. "How much were you thinking?"

"The fellas you see here are just the tip of the iceberg, Doc. We figure, with back pay and bonuses owed... about a half-million dollars."

"This is outrageous," Durant blustered, wiping the sweat from his brow. "I don't have access to that kind of money."

"Sure you do, Doc! Pay your debts out of the millions of bond money you intended to bribe those senators and government officials with! Pay up, and with a little luck, you'll be on your way shortly to drive that golden spike into the heart of an adoring public. Free to collect accolades for our monumental achievement. And there will be no need for us to pursue this nasty business any further."

Doc Durant's wide, fearful eyes darted around the blazing eyes peering out from behind masked faces of the two-dozen angry hijackers.

"Ever been to a hangin', Doc?" Tom stared into Durant's eyes. "If you squirm, death comes torturously slow." Tom paused again, then growled, "Horrific to watch. Now get your scrawny ass down here and over to our telegraph office. Move!"

The masked man next to Tom cocked his twelve-gauge shotgun and pointed it at Durant's legs. "Give me the word and I'll make a mess o' this here lyin' city slicker."

"We'll let the folks in New York know the telegraph line going west is out," Tom said. "We'll be intercepting all telegraph transmissions here at the Piedmont Station coming east or west. If you or Crédit Mobilier need to share any messages with General Dodge, Fort Douglas, Fort Laramie, Fort Bridger, or others, we can do that for you." Tom's eyes were dark, menacing beads. "Just know this... Doc, you and Mr. Duff will be dead men by the time any rescuers get to you. You might be dead men anyway if this takes too long. So, I suggest you get on with it right smartly."

Doc Durant jumped into action. He headed down the stairs, nervously sidestepping Tom's horse without looking up, and scurried along behind his escort to the telegraph station.

Tom turned back to the train engineer and fireman. "You're free to be on your way, gentlemen." And with that, the crew climbed back aboard and headed down track to Evanston, Wyoming.

With the engine passing out of sight, the executive car was pulled by hand cart onto the roundhouse turn table, cranked on a rotating arc into position, then pulled into the repair garage. The door was closed behind it, and the turntable was returned to its original position, leaving the executive train car completely out of sight to any passersby.

≻ • ≺

"Mister, I'm receiving a message from Evanston," the telegraph operator informed Tom. "What do you want me to do with it?"

"Read it to me."

The operator began to read aloud for all to hear. "Dear Brother Mark, stop—"

"What?" Doc Durant burst out. "That telegraph operator's your brother?"

The operator turned to him with a frown. "In this part of the country, we're all brothers and sisters."

"So, it's just a religious thing?"

The operator laughed. "Actually, in this case, he is my brother. One of eleven, but it wouldn't make any difference if he weren't. Everyone around here despises you, Doc, for what you done to our brothers and sisters. I don't know who this man is holding you, and I don't wanna know, but you ain't got any friends in these parts. Not for a hundred miles in any direction."

"That's enough sparring," Tom interrupted. "Read the rest of it."

"Yes, sir." The operator picked up the telegram. "There is a train engineer here with his long johns all in a twist, stop. He wants to get a message to Fort Bridger, stop. To send out a rescue party for Doc Durant at Piedmont Station, stop. The engineer is standing by awaiting an answer, stop." The operator looked up at Tom, with the question in his eyes.

Tom stood at the operator's shoulder. "Tell him: Message received and understood. Will deliver to the proper authorities. Fort Bridger rescue party on their way shortly. Engineer is advised to proceed on to Devil's Gate."

There was desperation in Doc Durant's eyes as he sat listening.

The operator sent the message, then turning to Tom, said, "Fort Bridger is seventeen miles southeast of here. Ain't no telegraph, but I'll be seein' the Bridger folks at church on Sunday. I can tell 'em then if you like, mister."

Doc Durant looked at the operator, aghast. "That's four days from now."

"Right, Doc," Tom interjected. "And by then you'll be dead. Unless the money arrives in time to save your sorry ass." Durant dropped his elbows on his knees. He put his face in his shaking hands. "Judging from these telegrams, Doc, someone could get the impression your partners might just prefer less partners to split their ill-gotten gains with."

"There's another message coming in from General Dodge, mister."

"Read it."

"To be forwarded to Oliver Ames at Crédit Mobilier, stop. You've wasted enough time, Oliver, stop. You owe the money, stop. Wire the $500,000 to Omaha Bank before they kill that son of a bitch, stop. The entire world is watching you greedy buffoons, stop."

"Send it on with this addition," Tom instructed: "Send the money in small denominations to Devil's Gate. You got two days or he's a dead man and all the world will know why.'"

"Devil's Gate, that's probably a hundred miles west of here!" Doc Durant said.

"Right!" Tom looked at him without expression. "Add this to the message: Two engines only, no cars, no rescuers, or your partners are dead men."

⇾ • ⇽

When the money arrived, the engines were put inside the roundhouse garage alongside the executive car and another carload of political cronies that turned up, also on their way to the celebration.

Tom pulled Captain O'Leary aside. "Listen, Peter, after we've gone, lock up Durant with all these other fellows in their celebrity car, then close those garage doors."

"Got it!"

Tom smiled to himself as he laid out the rest of the plan. "I noticed that fat-ass engineer who just arrived is almost as big as you. You think you could change into his UP uniform, and when the troop train does eventually come along, maybe wave them on to Devil's Gate?"

Peter O'Leary smiled. "I can do that."

"See you in Rockport." Tom patted big Peter O'Leary on the shoulder. "Make sure Durant is watching us when we leave."

"You got it."

Tom looked him in the eye. "Thank you, Peter. If not for you and your special relationships, this whole thing would never have been possible."

"'Twas the right thing ta do. We all knew it, includin' the general. Ya done good, Tom."

Tom strode on over to where the rest of the hijackers had corralled Durant and company. "Well Doc, looks like the fear of public perception saved your ass." Tom tipped his hat as he climbed onto his horse. "Until next time." He smiled. "Been a real pleasure. I'm sure the men, while disappointed at missin' your hangin', are right grateful for your contribution to their families." Tom's eyes flashed. "If you don't mind, Doc, we'll be takin' our leave." Pointing to Captain O'Leary and the men with him, he added, "These fine gentlemen will take good care of you. And Doc . . . Give my best to General Dodge and the US Cavalry. I'm hopin' to deprive them of the satisfaction of stretchin' my neck."

"I'll be there for your hanging."

"Maybe so, but then death smiles on us all, doesn't it? Best a man can do is to smile right back with a clear conscience. How's that workin' out for you, Doc?" Tom paused, staring down at Durant with a surly look. "This I do know," he said with an icy stare. "There'll be a lot less jangle in your pockets."

Then they were gone, heading south under a cloudburst of heavy rain. And when out of sight, Tom and his gang of thieves turned west toward Rockport.

≻ • ≺

The rescue attempt by the Fort Douglas cavalry failed when they reached a disabled Devil's Gate Bridge over the Weber River, flash flooding making it impossible to cross on horseback. The arrant rescuers were forced to abandon their mission and return to Fort Douglas, delivering their message of defeat.

The next day, a message finally reached Fort Bridger. A company of army troops set off on a second attempt to rescue Durant, Duff, and their company. Even with Fort Bridger's late start, it seemed inevitable that Tom's luck had run out. But, if the delayed rescue wasn't problem enough, more bad luck came when the troop train was waved on west by Piedmont Station employees to Devil's Gate, nearly a hundred miles down track.

After three days of failed rescue attempts, Tom and the rest of the hijackers were well on their way to Rockport with a wagonload of gold, silver, and bank notes in small denominations. Finally, Fort Laramie's cavalry arrived at the site of the hijacking to set Doc Durant free and on his way to the Promontory Point completion ceremony, two days late. The skies had cleared on the hot, dry summer afternoon when forty mounted cavalry troops unloaded down steep freight car ramps to begin tracking down the hijackers.

In a rush of pounding hooves, their horses thundered across the low swell of prairie. Moving fast along a wavering dark line of the Castle Rock cliffs, a cloud of dust stretched out almost a half mile behind the fast-moving cavalry as they headed south along red rock canyon walls. Tom and his hijackers, loaded down with their payment, rendezvoused at Rockport with Artist Able's demolition crew coming from the Devil's Gate Bridge over the Weber River and Captain O'Leary's crew from the Piedmont switching station. Seemingly, it had been a brilliant strategy. And thanks to bad weather, it had paid off, giving these hijackers and their accomplices time to prepare and organize over three hundred separate bundles of cash.

Chapter 34

✦ • ✦

Andrew had intended to finish packing, meet up with Joey, and head home to Park City when Tom returned from his meeting with Joseph Young. Those plans changed when a message arrived from his brother-in-law. Tom hadn't said why, only that it was absolutely imperative they gather together all the tunnel construction crews in Rockport in exactly one week's time. Andrew had wished Tom would have left more explanation, but there was none, except that it was absolutely necessary to keep it strictly secret from anyone but these men.

Most of the men were still in Echo Canyon finishing up laying the steel rail through the tunnels. But a few had to be tracked down, some all the way into the Salt Lake Valley, more than a hundred miles down the line from Castle Rock.

As they visited the homes of these men, whose families for the most part had come to this rugged country with nothing but the will to survive and a hope for a better future for their children, Andrew found it particularly distressing to see the conditions under which most lived. Hunger. Desperation. Heartrending poverty. Field after field of crops chewed by grasshoppers to below ground. Fifty acres of this devastated land could not support a single cow. It was only

May and summer had already arrived. By July, the hot sun would blast away what was left, turning it into nothing but cracked earth and dust. Dust that would cover everything. Andrew could already taste it in his mouth, feel it down the back of his shirt. He found it difficult to breathe in the dusty dryness. These mothers and their children had valiantly fought to survive through freezing winters, sunbaked summers, two years of drought and locusts while their men worked the railroad. These families had done everything with tenacity, courage, and self-reliance, asking for nothing from anyone but an honest wage and the opportunity to hack out a life in the wilderness.

"They're an inspiration," Andrew shared with Joey. "I have no doubt, given the chance and treated fairly, most will become stronger from the challenges." No cracked earth, no burning wind, frozen winters, or locust attacks were a match for the indominable spirit of these American women and their men. "I only wish there was something we could do to help them with their fight."

When they reached Artist Able's home, they found a clapboard building made from scrap lumber, a thatched roof, and wet and dirty blankets spread around on a dirt floor. Andrew winced when he met Artist's wife Mary, a proud woman who told them her husband was away looking for work. It was clear she had been pretty once, with a long, slender body, umber skin, and wavy dark hair that hung over large, intelligent eyes circled in pain. She invited them in as her three little children huddled around her in front of the smoky fire, warming a half-filled pot of watery muskrat stew. There were smoke, grease, and charcoal stains on her hands and face. Her worn, faded, and ragged dress was stained beyond recognition up to her knees. Her children clung to her, hiding behind her skirts from the two white men. The little waifs wore tattered clothing and had shoeless feet. But even in these deplorable conditions, Mary Able held herself with a certain solemn dignity Andrew couldn't help but admire.

Feeling guilty, Andrew reached in his knapsack and pulled out what little food he had. "Would you like this bread roll?"

Mary gratefully took it. "Thank you, sir." She broke it into thirds, giving one to each of her three children.

After leaving the shack, Andrew remarked to Joey, "Did you notice she gave the entirety of that bread to her little ones? It reminded me of your mam—Martha was that kind of mother who would sacrifice everything for her children."

※ · ※

Andrew and Joey arrived in the north Salt Lake Valley on May 10 to meet with the last of the workers to be notified of the Rockport meeting, with only a day left before their scheduled rendezvous. To their pleasant surprise, they arrived in time to witness the delayed railroad completion ceremony, previously scheduled two days earlier.

After watching the meagerly attended driving of the golden spike ceremony at Promontory Point, they followed the crowd into Salt Lake City, where tens of thousands from every part of the country had gathered in celebration. Standing shoulder to shoulder with more than eight thousand to hear John Taylor speak on the "Millennial Marvel," they slowly edged their way into the enormous fifty-foot-high domed Tabernacle. As they moved toward the front of the crowded Tabernacle, they chatted about the unusual circumstances of the morning's events.

"Ol' Doc looked pretty pathetic, didn't he?" Joey snickered. "So feeble and haggard. He could hardly lift the sledge off the ground, let alone drive in that railroad spike." Joey paused, his brows scrunched together in thought. "Why do you really think he was two days late to his own party?"

"I don't believe that story about the Weber River flood." Andrew's brows rose in a ladder of creases up his forehead, his face in a skeptical smile. "And what was Brigham Young's telegram about?"

"Yeah," Joey muttered with a smile. "'*Sorry you missed it Doc. The party was great!*'" He paused. "Curious. Like a joke only they were privy too."

"That must be John Taylor standing at the podium."

"Looks like it."

Mr. Taylor stood silent for several minutes as the nearly eight thousand filed in, took their seats or settled in the packed aisles before beginning to speak in the enormous Tabernacle. All grew eerily quiet and then he began.

"As a boy living in England, I rode on the first train ever made in all the world, thirty-six miles between Manchester and Liverpool. I remember that day in 1830 as if it was yesterday."

"1830," Joey muttered. "Tommy was born in 1830. Our little shanty was just down the road from those tracks. Sometimes our paths cross, and we don't even know it."

"The idea of conveying thoughts from one continent to another, instantly, would have been considered black magic in my village," Taylor continued. "And now, here I'm celebrating the completion of a railroad that has linked together the entire North American continent, a moment shared almost instantaneously around the world by a telegraph line running alongside the tracks. Both impossible miracles just five years ago. My words are being transported all the way to England, where members of my family now listen to me, literally as I speak. This absolutely spellbinding accomplishment, perhaps the greatest technological achievement in this millennium, has catapulted our country a hundred years into the future and put our quiet mountains front and center on the world stage." Mr. Taylor paused while the audience drank in his statements.

"The shock wave over the past two days has set off parades in Chicago, New York, London, Paris, San Francisco, Berlin, Amsterdam, and a whole lot of other places around the world. It is a heady time. *The Boston Globe*'s front-page article read, 'The Central Pacific Railroad charging fast from the west collided with the Union Pacific from the east in a cataclysmic change to America's race into the future . . . It has shrunk the world, and now the vast wildlands of middle America are open for business. What once took a year, risking life and limb, and costing a fortune, now takes an inexpensive six days.'

"Two days ago, all across the nation bells pealed. Even the venerable Liberty Bell in Philadelphia was rung. Two hundred and twenty cannons in San Francisco alone. A hundred in Washington, DC. Countless bells rang and cannons fired all over the modern world. More than during the entire battle of Gettysburg. Everywhere fire whistles. Singing and prayers in churches. Chicago had the biggest parade of the century with ten thousand people participating."

Joey couldn't help but think of his mam. Maybe she was listening in Liverpool.

"Waving grasslands along the railway stretch out a thousand miles, unobstructed, in all directions with untold future possibilities. Thousands will regularly travel into these Rocky Mountains. Brigham wrote an editorial yesterday where he said, 'Life in this isolated valley of the Lord will be accessible to all, for them to judge for themselves who we are.'

"Ours is a country of dreamers, and their dreams, like this one, often come true. Our children's children will see the day when enormous wealth, created by a flurry of progress along this line, will stretch from New York all the way to San Francisco," Taylor prophesied, clearly intoxicated by his own imagination. "Railroads branching out in every direction. Businesses, farms, even universities. Millions of people could live out there and still be lost in the immensity of the land.

"They say there has been nothing like this celebration of change in our country's future since the end of the Civil War . . . But this time, it was without any of the killing."

※ • ※

It was after dark when Andrew and Joey arrived at the Rockport meetinghouse. A community high in the mountains of Utah, Rockport was completely surrounded by an eight-foot-high, two-foot-thick rock wall constructed after a two-day siege by Black Hawk Indians two years earlier in which many of its residents had been killed. It was designed to discourage intruders. Not just Indians but federal troops as well after Johnson's army had invaded several towns in the Utah Territory years earlier, further alienating the local residents from the government and the outside world. Sentries had been stationed at the entrance and exits gates, along Main Street, and inside and outside of the meetinghouse. Nervous, holding rifles at the ready, some men wore masks, their eyes darting this way and that, carefully identifying each man as he entered through the town's front gate and came down the street and into the building. Although Andrew knew these sentries, they seemed to have no interest in talking. Clearly, they wanted to be done with their business quickly and get the hell out of there.

When Joey and Andrew entered the meetinghouse, there were already nearly three hundred men standing in disorganized groups, speaking in hushed tones. Andrew, with Joey right behind him, did his best to squeeze in close to the stage, where men were packed in like sardines.

Everyone seemed to be keeping an eye on Tom, who was huddled on stage with Peter O'Leary and Artist Able beside the undisclosed bounty piled high on a line of tables that stretched across the stage, conspicuously hidden by a canvas covering. Tom seemed solemn but calm as a summer breeze.

It wasn't but a few minutes later as the few remaining men filed in that Mr. O'Leary stepped to the podium. He stood silent until a hush fell over the crowd of men.

"Gentlemen, we've come here tonight bearin' gifts." He glanced toward the covered table. "Obtained by corruption, aided and abetted by one of the finest men I've ever met." Peter O'Leary smiled at Tom, then stepped aside allowing Tom to replace him at the podium as a rumble passed through the crowd.

With all eyes focused on him, Tom, standing stern and deliberate, nodded toward Artist Able and Peter O'Leary, who lifted the canvas covering from the line of tables to reveal hundreds of bundled packets containing gold and silver coin and paper notes.

"Your back pay, gentlemen." Tom paused as a gasp rolled through the crowd of men. Andrew, like all else in the congregation, pulled in a quick breath of disbelief, eyes wide, mouth gaping, speechless, in awe of what lay before him. "Not all of it," Tom added, "but enough to put a big dent in what's owed."

For a long moment, there was not another sound in the meetinghouse. It seemed no one knew what to say, what to do, what to think. Then came a flurry of voices of confusion from all directions.

Both fear and elation rose in Andrew's chest. So unprepared was he for this announcement, he couldn't quite comprehend what was happening. He turned to Joey, his eyes wide, stomach churning. "What has he done?"

"This is why he wasn't at the ceremonies yesterday." Joey's face had gone pale. "This is why all the secrecy."

Tom's eyes shone with a fierce, quiet power. And when he held up his hand to silence the crowd of men, all in the room obeyed. Then he took in a deep breath.

"America is more than a country. It is an idea. It is a vision to men like you and I all around the world—a nation of laws to protect our individual rights. Laws laid down for the people, by the people to ensure justice for all men—you, and me . . . But sometimes even in this great country, everyday citizens like us must step up to the brink of fear to ensure justice is served."

The crowd of men stood silent, mouths agape, not daring to interrupt Tom as he looked on in solemn, grave repose. "There is a great invisible strength when men who are in the right stand together with conviction. I've learned it's one of the things that makes this country great. I've been a witness to that strength in these worthy men who stand with me here tonight." Tom glanced at Peter O'Leary, Artist Able, and the other men who had been with him in their effort to right this wrong. "These men have been an inspiration to me."

An acknowledgment of appreciation due rolled through the crowd.

"Now if you'd like to join us and become complicit in our indiscretions, please queue up to receive your packet of back pay from Captain O'Leary or Mr. Able. The coin and bank notes have been packaged in substantially equal packets—one for each man."

Andrew's eyes were wide in astonishment.

Questions began to come in a flurry from the crowd.

"Gentlemen, please." Tom raised both hands. It seemed his strength of will alone quieted down the men. "There is neither time to explain nor is it in your best interests to know the details of how we acquired your back pay. Suffice it to say, no lives were lost nor men hurt. Except possibly the pain of separation from their ill-gotten gains." Gallows laughter erupted through the audience of men still standing in astonishment.

With a deadpan face, Tom added, "And a bit of well-deserved

humiliation." This brought another rumble of laughter, helping to calm Andrew's churning stomach.

He looked up at his brother-in-law on the stage. "You've done it," he whispered. "I don't know how the hell you made this happen. But by God, you've done it!" As much as he admired the calculating ingenuity of his brother-in-law, Andrew was scared for him. He looked around at all the questioning faces, recalling the deplorable living conditions some of these men and their families had been forced to bear.

Some men wept at the burden now removed from their shoulders. Others just stood silent with shock on their faces. And still others were giddy with excitement. But all would never forget what Tom and his brave partners in this crime had done for them and their families. He didn't need to do it, but he did, clearly at great risk to himself and a few brave men.

The posted sentries were anxious, jittery, looking over their shoulders, not at all entertained by Tom's commentary. It made Andrew even more afraid. Since arriving, he'd observed how these men had been strategically positioned in the shadows. They seemed agitated, clearly wanting this to be over, to get out of there.

"Needless to say," Tom continued, "our financial benefactors are not at all happy about your good fortune. Please pick up your packet and go home. We are all at risk with the law. If you take the money, you are as well."

As each man passed by the table, he was handed more money than he had ever seen at one time in his life.

"It is extremely important," Tom explained, "to tell no one where or how you received this money. Our lives and yours depend on it. Give no details at all. If asked, answer only that you're appreciative of the Union Pacific Railroad's payment of their obligation."

Again, there was a rumble of uncomfortable laughter.

"Thank you. And God bless you," said one man after another as they collected their packet of back pay. It was money they certainly deserved, desperately needed but never expected. Money that resurrected their dreams. And they knew Tom had provided it at great personal risk. Through it all Tom seemed to remain calm, although Andrew was certain that inside he must have been feeling a hurricane of emotions.

With business complete, Tom turned to the sentry by the door. "Smitty, bring up the horses." Then turning back to all who'd gathered there, he said, "Gentlemen, I hope all remains well with you and your families. Be safe, and have a good life!" He gave a quick smile. And for the first time, his nervousness was visible to Andrew. "You must forgive our lack of hospitality, but we must go now before the US Cavalry arrives and upsets us all. We will do our best to draw them away, but it is imperative you collect your things and leave here as quickly as possible. Do not write or speak of this meeting to your wives, family, or anyone. Stay off the streets, take the back trails, disappear into the night, and don't stop to talk to anyone. Your lives and ours depend on it. As for myself and those with me, we will be doing our best to disappear and avoid a hanging. Now, gentlemen, you must leave as fast as your feet will carry you."

The tension in the air made it difficult to breathe. Andrew inhaled and exhaled deeply. He made a special effort to focus on Tom. The din of the crowd and the chaos around him faded. He could feel his heartbeat in his throat, the pulse of blood running through his veins. He wiped the sweat from his brow with cold, clammy hands. Even after witnessing the whole affair, he wasn't sure it had really happened. Every man there moved forward in silent reverence. Then, spontaneously, the entire auditorium erupted in applause.

Tom would have none of it. He just waved off the standing ovation, and with the last packet of money, he stepped down from the stage and walked away,, the crowd parting to allow him to pass. The clapping, hooting, and howling continued.

As Tom left the meetinghouse, he handed Andrew the last packet with a scribbled note. "This is for Annie," he said. "The cavalry is right behind us. If they catch us, there'll be hell to pay. Go, quickly! Now!"

Andrew and Tom exchanged a tense glance. Tom took a deep breath and gave Andrew and Joey a hug. He whispered in Andrew's ear, "Tell her I love her and regret I can't tell you anything more. If I am found out, the first place they'll look for me is home, and Annie's not a good liar."

"Let me come with you?" Joey begged.

Tom stood to his full height and looked at both of them with hard amber eyes. "Sorry, I can't tell you where I'm going, and you can't follow. Take care of her, little brother."

⊱ · ⊰

A cold rush of wind blew through the front door as Andrew stepped into the Park City cottage on the late afternoon of his return. He was greeted by Edie's warm, welcoming arms. Both were quickly overrun by a rush of children caught up in the excitement of their papa's return. Hugs were exchanged, openhearted kisses given, and tears of relief shed amid the joy of his long-awaited homecoming.

Annie looked on, silent. Feeling the intruding observer, she quietly awaited news of her husband, wringing her hands. Why wasn't he there? His last letter, though mysterious, had said he would be. With her heart lodged firmly in her throat, she waited impatiently to speak to her brother-in-law alone.

Seeing the concern in Annie's eyes, Edie began shooing her children outside. "Now, you children go and play while Papa speaks to Aunt Annie for a moment. Go on now!"

"Oh, Papa!" the children shouted, grabbing his hands, pulling at him. "Can't you come play with us, Papa?"

"All in good time, my lovelies." Andrew smiled as he shushed them, their requests clearly tugging at his heartstrings. "All in good time, but right now Aunt Annie and I need some private time."

Edie herded her children out of the parlor, then stepped into the kitchen to prepare tea, cheese, and crackers for the three of them, leaving Andrew alone for a moment with Annie.

"You're with child, Annie?" Andrew stared at her. "I didn't know."

"Never mind that." She was too anxious to talk about anything but Thomas's whereabouts. Afraid, desperate now, her hands shook as she saw the concern in his eyes. Her breath came faster. "Where is he?" There was an awful feeling deep down inside her churning stomach.

Andrew sighed. "I can't tell you much, Annie. We don't know the whole of it." He mopped the sweat from his brow and stared nervously at Annie's swollen belly. "I'll tell you what I know, but you better sit down."

"Please, Andrew! I don't want to sit down." She stamped her foot to discourage any further delaying tactics.

"I don't know much. Honestly, I don't," Andrew began with a frown. His eyes were wide and earnest. She could tell he was dreading this chore, knowing it had to be done with the greatest of care. "He may not be coming home anytime soon."

"What do you mean?" She slammed her fists to her sides in frustration. "What are you talking about?"

"He wouldn't tell us." Andrew took in a deep breath. "But he promised to return to you as soon as it was possible."

Annie's brow furrowed. "And when might that be?" She felt lonely, numb with distress, guilty for not being ashamed of making Andrew face the brunt of her anger. She took to her habit of spinning her red emerald ring around her finger.

Andrew resumed his halting explanation. "Tom has purposely kept us all in the dark. He said we're better off not knowing. The less we know, the less likely we'll be caught in a web of deceit, forced to lie about his whereabouts."

A high color rose in Annie's cheeks. Her heart was pounding. "Better off—for who? I'm not better off." She took a deep breath to push back the nausea driving her churning stomach into her throat. She bit her lip trying to let him speak. Woozy on her feet, she grabbed the back of the chair to steady herself. Andrew quickly came to her aid, helping her into the large stuffed chair.

She slid down and plopped onto the soft cushions. She brought her shaking hands to her temples to rub away her rising headache. "Tell me what you know about this thing. All of it. Please, Andrew. I can't bear it." Feeling lightheaded, and finding it difficult to breathe, she leaned back to relieve the pressure of her stomach. She inhaled and exhaled deeply, trying to gain control of her body.

Andrew sighed. "Tom asked—no, demanded—Joey and I gather all his men together and meet at Rockport. Annie, there were more than three hundred of us there to take care of business."

She bit her lip as he got through the whole of it—the secrecy, the hundreds of thousands of dollars, the shock of the men. She listened intent to all of it until he got to the US Cavalry.

"Cavalry?" Annie burst out. She stood up, but feeling dizzy, she immediately fell back into the wing chair. She took another deep breath to even out her panic and push down her rising heartburn. With her hands on her head, she rocked backward, opened her eyes wide, then put her badly shaking hands over her unborn child, as she listened to the rest. "The cavalry? What has he done? Oh my God, what has he done?"

"I'm sorry, Annie."

"Oh, Andrew." She was so upset it was difficult to speak. "Couldn't you stop him?"

"Stop him? Is that ever possible when Tom puts his mind to something? Besides, Joey and I knew nothing of it. Still don't, really!"

Annie sat frozen in fear, wringing her hands. The ring finger on her clammy hand had been rubbed raw from nervous spinning of her ring round and round. "Go on, Andrew," she encouraged, looking up at him.

"After finishing his business, he turned and left. There wasn't time—"

"Oh, Andrew!" she interrupted in a gasp, putting her hand over her mouth. "I'm scared."

"As he left with the others . . ." Andrew paused for a long moment, until Annie, in trembling silence, nodded him on. "He gave me a message for you. 'No matter what happens,' he said, 'I will return to you as soon as humanly possible. But till then it's best we have no contact, no letters, no conversations, no information on my whereabouts—for your safety's sake.'"

Annie sat silent with her hand over her mouth. "How could he?"

Andrew retrieved the note and envelope filled with the desperately needed cash from his knapsack. He handed it to her. "He risked his life for that money, then gave it all away to those he thought needed it more. He kept nothing more for himself. Who does that?" He paused. "Everyone in that room was filled with awe," he whispered. "He'd given them back their lives."

Annie was quiet, her anxious eyes wide as she sat back, took in a deep breath, and opened the letter.

⇾ • ⇽

Dearest Annie,

Please forgive me. I have made a decision that may change the course of our lives without asking you. I'm writing you before I do this thing and maybe you'll know more of the outcome by the time you have a chance to read it. My love for you is unbounded. And yet my obligation to those who have put their entire trust in me blows over me like a strong wind and I feel I must do this thing come what may. The risks I am taking are great, but I am convinced it is where my duty lies. And I know if you were in my position, you would do the same. And I love you all the more for it.

Please forgive me my many faults, the pains I have caused you, my sometimes foolish notions about our life together. Never forget how much I love you. God willing, we will still live a long, happy, and beautiful life together. I will do all in my power to come back to you—that I promise! But if I don't, do not mourn me. For we shall meet again. And know that my last breath will be to whisper your name. I shall always be with you on your brightest days, or darkest nights. Always! Always! Always! And when the soft breeze touches your cheek, it shall be my breath, my spirit passing by.

I love you. I always will!
Thomas

⇝ • ⇜

"Oh, Andrew!" She sat up and hung her head down, spinning her emerald ring for all it was worth. Heart pounding, struggling to breathe, then dizzy with fear, she leaned back again to catch her breath, pushing her clammy, shaking hands over her swollen belly. "I don't care about any of them or the money. I want my husband."

The acrid taste from her churning stomach rose into her throat. Like a locomotive with failed brakes, awful thoughts rushed through her mind.

"Alone with his enemies all around," she said softly. She was entirely undone with worry. Her horrid imaginings caused her heart to pound so fast she could hardly hold a rational thought in her head.

She stared out the window in a daze. A red pool of waving grasses on the low meadows in the distance shimmered under dark, fast-moving clouds as dusk settled in. Her mind torn with dread, she whispered, "He wasn't right, you know."

"Wasn't right?" Andrew timidly questioned. He was hesitant now, not wanting to agitate her further. "Who wasn't right?"

"When Mr. Ritter drove me from Echo Canyon to be with Edie in Park City, he told me I would get along fine without Thomas."

"I told him, 'I'll never forgive that clumsy fool if he blows himself up!' I said it to hide my desperate fear of losing him, the panic churning in the pit of my stomach."

Annie didn't speak for a long minute as she continued to look out the window.

"I pray he is all right in this awful thing, because I can't get along without him. I can't live without him! I won't live without him!"

Chapter 35

☙ • ☙

CLOAKED IN FRINGED DEERSKIN SHIRT and leggings, soft-soled moccasins, and beaded breastplate of furs with feathers flying in the wind, Black Eagle ran hard in pursuit of his prey. He scrambled up the heavily forested hillside and down again, weaving in and out of the evergreens, spreading cottonwood, and densely packed aspen. In brisk strides, at one with the forest, he laced his way through the piled rock and remnants of the beaver dam to leap the meandering creek in a single bound. Then running fast through the shadows of blue-gray mist under the gathering of dark storm clouds, he cut off his prey by traversing along the ledge of the waterfall.

In the fading afternoon light that spread like searching fingers through the sweet-smelling pine, Black Eagle froze in his tracks. Crouching silent behind a rock outcropping. His heart pounded, and sweat poured down his copper-colored face and beaded on his chiseled arms. Calming his heavy breathing, he loaded an arrow on the bowstring and put it to his shoulder. He waited for the great buck to move from behind the protective stand of quaking aspen, the loose feathers on his breechclout fluttering in the breeze.

The powerful, majestic animal stepped out of the trees. He turned to face his pursuer. Head up, ears cocked, and dark, luminous eyes alert.

"We honor your courage, your strength, your sacrifice. But I'm sorry, my brother, you are needed at our campfire this day to feed our families." Black Eagle locked eyes with the great white-tailed buck standing regal across the narrow draw. Taking deadly aim, he drew back on the taut bowstring. He let his breath drain out and the arrow fly. But the great buck had been alerted by the thundering sound of intruders in the forest and bolted into the safety of the dense stands of aspen.

As the rain began to fall heavy, Black Eagle saw, in the far distance, the line of cavalry coming up the mountainside.

≻ • ≺

Tom and his men, worn down and tired after weeks on the run just ahead of their pursuers, sat shivering in the cold rain. They huddled in front of a fire burning bright orange under a canvas fly. Their wet clothes, bedding, and shoes were laid out on the hot rocks to dry.

After leaving Rockport, Tom had decided he and his partners in crime must split up if they were to survive with the cavalry close behind. Joining with Peter O'Leary and two others in their small party of criminals, they had abandoned their borrowed saddle horses and melted into the high mountains of the Wasatch on foot, avoiding use of their rifles at all costs.

Tom would rely on his skills with the bow and snare, skills he had learned as a boy. A smile eased across his face as he thought back to Grand in the forbidden forest. Those skills had kept food on the table in his family's desperate time after Grand had been killed in the mine. The warm days of June in the Wasatch had melted the snow, and game was plentiful. Still the cold nights in these high mountains took their toll. What Tom had learned in his former life had so far kept them alive and ahead of their pursuers.

"We've got to move on in the morning, Peter." Tom sighed. He was exhausted. The cavalry never seemed to let up. So Tom never stayed long in one place and dared not risk sending out a message to family or friends. As the weeks rolled on, Tom had more and more difficulty sleeping. He was skittish, paranoid, seeing shadowed men behind every tree in night shadows. He'd become a little less observant, a little less vigilant, a little more careless. On this night, hidden deep in the forest in a dense thicket of trees, he huddled with his men under the canvas fly in front of the fire. Only a faint sliver of light escaped into the cold rainy night. But it was enough.

Cold and shivering in the wind, watching rainwater dripping off the canvas covering and dampening the fire, Tom pulled the remaining half loaf of stale bread from his knapsack. He broke off a piece and gave the rest to Peter. "Not much left, but you're welcome to it."

"Thank ya, Tom." Peter, too, broke off a piece and passed the rest around. "Thank ya fer all of it!" A smile of admiration eased across Peter O'Leary's face.

Tom's ears perked up at the whinny of a horse obscured by the pelting rain and buffeting wind. His heart leapt into his throat. Then came the sound of thundering hooves of the cavalry's horses barreling up the mountainside in the darkness. But it was too late. The cavalry burst into the encampment, catching the cold, desperate men unprepared. For a moment Tom considered standing to fight. But quickly, his mind cleared and he realized it would be foolish to do anything but run from these wild-eyed cavalrymen turning this way and that in their saddles, hurrying blind into their camp, waving their rifles, sending the hijackers scurrying for their lives.

Under the cover of night and heavy rain, Tom and his men scattered in different directions, each running for his life. Tom sped through the woods, frantic to find a place to hide. He weaved, reckless and wild, through the dense forest, quickly losing sight of his men. Racing down the craggy deer trails in the pouring rain, jumping over great boulders, sliding down slopes, his only hope of surviving was to stay deep under cover in the dense forest on this stormy night. Veering across the flank of a hill, his heart pounding, he angled downhill, sliding, slipping, and falling through the trees. The cavalrymen seemed to have lost him in the tangle of the thicket, the darkness, the fog, and the rain. He crouched behind a wall of stacked rock alongside an Indian trail, panting, lifting his shoulders in a struggle to catch his breath.

Hunkered down in the wet, heavy foliage, his chest heaved like a trapped animal's. He was camouflaged under a canopy of cottonwood, choked dense with aspen. He held still and quiet, sweating, only partially dressed. He was soaked and splattered in mud. The rain continued to pound down on him. Muddy water flooded over his feet. Eyes wide and darting, trying to blink away the rain, he sat listening, all his senses on high alert. He clenched his cold fingers into fists to stop their shaking.

Tom dared not move. He tried to control his heavy breathing. The sticky, wet mud had splattered across his face, covering his hands, in his hair, leaving a gritty taste in his mouth. The rich, musty smell of earthen humus filled his nostrils. Had he lost them?

Then, pandemonium broke all around him, the hammer of noisy men, the clink of steel gun barrels, the clomping hooves of horses sloshing through the mud just yards away on the other side of the rock wall where he knelt in hiding. Men were shouting. Tom could see their faces obscured by branches, the dull glint of rifles drawn. Rain was pelting the captain's hat, and his horse was turning in the mud as the man yelled out orders.

"You men, divide up, scour this ground. I want every inch searched. I want these hijackers."

Tom crouched down farther into the cold, wet mud, listening intently to the cavalrymen moving through the dark shadows of trees, breaking branches. Despite the rain, Tom's mouth was dry; he was thirsty, his breathing ragged. He thought they might hear his heart pounding as the wide-eyed horsemen ambled and skittered past him, one by one. Then came more shouting, a rustling in the trees. Men were coming at him fast, tearing limbs off as they spurred their horses through the bushes and trees along the other side of his rock wall.

One of the cavalrymen stopped, peering through the trees. The others continued their search through the forest in the dark night. Horse and rider were directly above where Tom crouched in the mud behind the wall. Tom turned to stone, not even daring to breathe. Puffs of breath came from the horse's muzzle. Tom could see the whites of the young cavalryman's wild, darting eyes. He could smell the wet steam of perspiration and fear coming off both horse and rider. Then the cavalryman turned in his saddle and drew up his Spencer carbine. Tom's eyes followed the glistening steel of the rifle's hostile barrel as it pointed at Peter O'Leary just yards away. Cornered in the trees at point-blank range, O'Leary was wide-eyed, breathing heavily, fear spreading across his pale face.

The cavalryman squeezed down on the trigger. There was no time but now. Without thinking, Tom lunged from his hiding place, grabbed the rifle barrel, and pulled down hard, just as the crack of the shot rang out. Tree limbs snapped, and there was a thud on the muddy bank. The cavalryman let go of his Spencer, and Tom, still holding on, slammed down hard and rolled in the mud with the rifle.

It all happened in the blink of an eye while Peter O'Leary disappeared into the forest. The mare spun in a tight circle with her ears pinned to her head, bucking off her rider like a three-year-old breaking into saddle, then bounded off into the trees.

Tom grabbed up the carbine out of the mud and pointed the cold, muddy barrel at the cavalryman. He had lost his hat, and he stood staring at Tom. He was only a boy. It looked as though his first shave was still ahead of him. There was a moment of stillness when boy and man, standing ten feet apart, locked eyes on each other.

"Don't want to kill you, boy." Tom nodded, poking the muddy Spencer at the boy, who had his hand on his pistol. The boy's frantic blue eyes were empty, darting, skittish. "Let go of the pistol in its holster nice and slow. Put your hands up."

"You'll kill me anyway if I do." A steamy mist rose off the body of the panicky boy. "I ain't doin' it."

"Damn it, boy, I'm lookin' for a way not to kill you," Tom cautioned in a calm, steady voice, rain pounding their words into the mud.

Nothing of the boy moved but his hand, and it flashed quicker than Tom could see as he drew his pistol firing. The pistol shot rang out with a loud crack, drawing the attention of all in the forest. The bullet hit Tom in the shoulder, spun him around, and dropped him and the rifle into the mud. The kick on the big pistol caused it to leap out of the boy's hand like it was trying to get away. From the ground, Tom picked up the carbine and pulled the trigger as the boy scrambled up and dove for the pistol, but the Spencer was jammed with mud. He threw the rifle at the boy, who jumped out of the way and was again scrambling for the pistol. Tom leaped over the wall, howling curses at his luck. Running fast through the sloshing mud, he ducked low behind the wall.

The boy almost fell as he got to his feet. He rushed to the wall with his pistol held high in both hands, and he fired again at Tom, who was running scared in a zigzag pattern like a flushed deer. The shot went wild, snapping tree limbs by Tom's head.

"I found one, Captain!" the boy screamed out as he ran after Tom.

"Shoot him!" the captain yelled in the ensuing mayhem, shouting encouragement for a death sentence. "Shoot the son of a bitch!"

Another shot rang out, and there was another thud. Heart pounding in his throat, Tom couldn't breathe. He was slipping and sliding in wet mud, adrenaline rushing through his body as he ran reckless, as fast as his aching legs would carry him. With all he had left in him, Tom raced just ahead of his hell on earth. Seconds were centuries, tens of seconds ages. Then Tom saw it, an opening between two staggered rock walls where bullets couldn't reach him. He swung wide to make the turn at full speed into the safety of the opening just as he stepped into a rabbit hole, badly twisting his ankle. His body flew forward into the air, slamming into the rock wall. A fourth bullet went wild, ricocheted off the wall and into a tree next to him with a thud, limbs snapping. He lifted his head woozily, the ferocity of pain in his head, shoulder, and ankle shooting through him. There was blood everywhere.

"I got 'im, Captain."

Tom tried to scramble up, staggering clumsily, falling toward the safety of the opening. Another shot pierced the night. A searing blaze of hot lead passed through his back. The impact of the bullet spun him around, tree limbs snapping as he slapped down into the muddy water in a crumpled heap behind the wall. He let out a death scream of anguished pain, retching, clutching his chest. Another shot rang out, catching him in his side. Stabbing pain ripped up his torso, squeezing his chest in a vice. Icy cold. His body went rigid, seized in violent tremors. Unable to control his muscles, he shuddered and shook. He couldn't breathe. Then he went limp, sprawled out unconscious, half buried in the mud. Lying motionless, his arms and legs in a tangle, he oozed warm, sticky blood into the mud. In the swirl of disjointed thoughts came flashing, cracking white light. His world was falling away like chalk, dusting his tangled body while he looked on from above. He saw his crumpled body lying in muddy water running red with his blood.

So, this is it. This is how I'm gonna die—out here on this cold mountain, all alone, buried in the mud in this godforsaken place! Tom's mind wandered. The rain was pounding. The cold wind blew. "I'm so sorry, Annie!" His time had run out. He wanted to sleep. He'd given his last full measure of sacrifice. Then all his earthly cares were gone.

※ · ※

The boy's hand was around Tom's neck, pulling at the shiny pendant. "He's dead, Captain!" the boy screamed out through pounding rain.

"Leave him," growled the captain. "Come on up outta that muddy mess, Private! Let's get the hell outta here. The damn rain and mud's makin' it impossible to do any more tonight. We'll pick up the trail on the rest of 'em in the mornin'. They can't go far."

For three long days it rained without letting up.

※ · ※

My Dearest Thomas,

I pray this letter winds its way along the darkened paths you must be following. I pray it finds you wherever you are. I think of you every minute of every day and especially in the night when my imagination wanders. I often awake in a fright, my heart pounding, my hands trembling, my breath caught.

It's been seven months and for three of them I haven't heard a word from you. Not a single sign of life. And yet I am certain you're still out there, somewhere. I fear I cannot endure the present much longer without you in it. I miss our conversations, your touch, your strong, comforting smile when I'm frightened.

Often, I find myself tracing my emerald ring, remembering who gave it to me and why it is next to the never-ending circle of my wedding band. Remembering that you have the other half of this precious stone to remind you that without you there is a hollow place in my heart that will never be filled.

Where are you, my love. I have not heard from you for so long. I fear for you. I just can't help it! We can't help it, for I am with your child!

Please come home to us!

Forever yours,
Annie

Chapter 36

≽ • ≼

"We appreciate you meeting with us, Mr. Young." Andrew shook Joseph's hand.

"Of course, Tom was a good man."

"Was?" Joey questioned, anxious. "Is there something you can tell us?"

"I received Annie's letter a couple of weeks ago. She asked for my help."

"Of course she did. Annie has been frantic, sending letters everywhere. I suppose we all are." Andrew took in a shaky breath.

"I understand." Mr. Young nodded. "We've been tracking down every lead. We received sketchy information from several different sources, but piecing it all together paints a pretty compelling story. It's not good, I'm afraid."

"Oh no!" Joey gasped.

"We've spoken to most all his men and are still going through the list, but—"

"But? It doesn't sound like you know for sure Tom was—"

"There is not much that happens in this part of the country that Brigham doesn't hear about, including inside Fort Bridger and Fort Laramie. It seems the captain who tracked down the hijackers described the man they shot and killed. It matched Tom to a tee." Joseph Young paused for a long moment before handing Joey a small pendant on a silver chain. "I received this yesterday. They took it off the dead man. It's Tom's—isn't it?"

Joey stared down at the red emerald pendant. "It's his!"

"I'm so sorry. Probably the hardest message I've ever had to deliver, Joey."

"Tom never took it off, not even to bathe, work in the tunnels."

"I really am sorry."

"Oh my God." Joey took the pendant in his fist and held it to his forehead. He tried to catch his breath. He felt dizzy. With his world spinning, his knees began to buckle.

Andrew, who'd stood thunderstruck by the news, reached out to steady him.

"How can we tell Annie . . . in her condition?"

☞ • ☜

In late spring of 1869, even before the railroad had been completed, scores of Chinese workers, laid off from the Central Pacific, began flooding into Parley's Park City on rumors silver had been discovered and mining operations were sure to follow. The Chinese poured into this sleepy village inhabited mostly by struggling, destitute Union Pacific Railroad families. Many of these resident families were fatherless, their men still working the UP's line through Castle Rock. The Chinese pitched their canvas shebangs at the center of town—homes, special dietary establishments, saloons, opium dens, and brothels. All squeezed in together along densely compacted Main Street.

Right from the beginning there had been tension between the locals and their new neighbors. It was a problem that seemed to follow the Chinese wherever they went across the West. Prejudice ran hot against this divergent culture. An outraged public called for a halt to further Chinese immigration on American soil, in the hope most would go back home. But America was the land of opportunity, even for persecuted Chinese.

On a hot summer afternoon, a gang of Irish ex-Union Pacific Railroad workers entered one of the Chinese saloons hankering for a fight. It wasn't long before an argument ensued over the ten miles of track Central Pacific's Chinese had laid in a single day to win a running bet with the UP on their race to Promontory Point months before. Tempers flared, threats were made, and before long a kerosene lantern was thrown against the bar, igniting the canvas shebang. The saloon went up in flames. They quickly spread from one shebang to another until most of downtown was afire. Canvas shebangs and dry, unpainted clapboard shanties were engulfed. The fires pooled and strutted, flowing from structure to structure then on to the forest of highly flammable pine and aspen. Within minutes all of Park City erupted in shooting flames, smoke chasing ash high into the sky. The appetite for oxygen was such that leaves, branches, and trees were sucked into the flames and disappeared in an instant. Swirling wind spread the raging fire, rushing through the forest at terrifying speed. It jumped from pine to aspen to spruce to fir, consuming everything in its path. And there was no way to stop it.

⋆ • ⋆

On a warm, windy summer day, in a surprising burst of energy, Annie worked feverishly in the garden. At just over eight months pregnant, she tired easily. Still, after a long day in the fields and chores at home were done, she spent hours each evening in her vegetable garden intent upon making sure there would be food enough to get through the winter, especially with the baby coming. Leaning the hoe against her shoulder, she placed her hands on her hips, stood up straight, arched her back, and decided in the rising heat of the day to leave the rest of her gardening for tomorrow. She rolled her neck and shoulders around. She wiped the sweat from her brow and placed a hand on her belly. Her enormous belly was not all that had grown. Everything seemed to grow with this child inside her, especially her exhaustion.

"There is nothing bigger in all the world than a mother's heart," Edie had told her, and literally it was true. Her heart had grown larger, with more heartbeats now, rapidly pumping blood for two. In truth, from the moment Annie began carrying this new life, nothing about her heart would ever be the same; it had become a refuge of inexhaustible love. And she hoped it would be the soothing destination where her children could always find peace and comfort.

Annie looked out over the forest separating their cabin from Park City below. An early spring had melted the heavy snows, bringing forth dense vegetation of all kinds, and the warmth of the summer sun had turned much of it into dry kindling. A light wind bent the brown grasses in rhythmic, indolent waves across the meadow, and the edge of the forest wall was just behind.

She looked out over the meadow, the pine and thick clusters of quaking aspens beyond. The air seemed heavy. Her brows scrunched together against the smoldering orange sun risen high in the sky just as a rabbit ran right through her garden.

"Where are you going, little bunny?" Then a doe and her fawn broke from the forest running right at her. So unusual for them not to keep their distance. It brought an uneasiness. Annie tented her hand over her eyes, trying to see through the haze drifting above the forest. Her breath caught. Her face flushed, eyes ablaze. It was smoke. She dropped her hoe and ran into the house, her heart pounding.

"Edie, gather up the children," Annie called out, "there's a fire coming."

Startled by a noise at the door behind her, Annie spun around, her heart pounding. A large Indian filled the entire doorway. "What do you want?"

"You must go to river."

"What?" Annie, Edie, and now Elizabeth stood frozen, wide-eyed, staring at the tall, powerfully built Shoshoni.

"You must leave. Fire coming. To widest part of river. Stay until fire passes." Then he was gone as quickly as he'd appeared.

As the women frantically gathered the children and stuffed their most important things in a knapsack, hot ash and cinders began drifting down from the sky. Heat was rising. The fire was coming fast.

"The town's on fire, Edie. Burning fast through the forest." Annie tried her best to remain calm, clearheaded. "We have to go down to the river now—hurry, children!" Annie began directing traffic.

"What's happening?" Elizabeth gasped, frozen.

"It's a fire, honey," Annie said in a calm, decisive voice. She tried to wrench Elizabeth out of her shock. "Grab what you can. Help your mam with the little ones. We need to go right now."

"Oh, where's Andrew?" Edie exclaimed in panic.

"We need to go now, Edie," Annie demanded. "The men are in Salt Lake. It's up to us and we must go now!" Eyes flashing, Annie grabbed the hand of three-year-old Tommy and headed toward the door as Edie, Elizabeth, and the rest of the children followed right behind in blind obedience. Outside, heavy smoke and ash were blowing in the hot wind, making it difficult to see. "Stay close, children!" Annie didn't stop, but she called out warnings to those they passed: "Follow us down to the river."

Men, women, and children, the old and the young, emptied from their houses carrying what they could down the smoky pathways, running scared to the river. Mothers carried babes in arms, dragging toddlers and pulling older children behind, heedless of obstruction, charging through anything in their path.

White man and Indian alike crowded along the riverbank. Some were already wading into the frigid water. Clouds of smoke and bright flashes of flame leaped among the evergreens. Sap popped. Timbers snapped. Quaking aspen fluttered wildly in the hot winds of fire. Heat sucked the humidity from the air.

Children cried and whimpered, and faces contorted to stare up with frightened eyes at flames rising high into the sky. The heat bored into them. Annie's lungs burned. She coughed. Her heart pounded in her throat. Trying to hold down her emotions in the rising heat, she drew in shallow, shuddering breaths through tight lips. She brushed at the descending tendrils of smoke as they drifted down from above, carried on the wings of the hot breeze.

Sweat blurred Annie's vision, running down her face, her neck, and between her breasts in itchy streams as she ran with her family along the riverbank to the widest part of the river. There was not a word spoken. She waded in ankle deep. The rushing water was mercilessly cold. "Come Elizabeth, Edie, children . . . Follow me."

She picked up her crying nephew. Tommy was refusing to enter the icy river, for even the hottest day could not warm water imprisoned over the frozen winter. She shuffled gingerly along the cobbled stone bottom with Tommy in her arms, tears rolling down his cheeks. The cold water soaked through her shoes and numbed her feet and legs as she edged deeper into the current.

It was getting harder to breathe. The wind was fierce now, blowing hot, smoky air and dropping gray ash from their burning homes and trees onto everyone who'd crowded into the river. It whipped the smoke and beat the flames into a dance. The fire reached out with golden arms and voracious hunger, gorging on everything in its path. Brush was gone in lightning flashes; dense forest and aging cabins along the river burst into flames.

"Edie, Elizabeth, you're going to be all right," Annie called out as they followed her deeper into the river. She looked from river to fire to the little ones in their arms. "Oh Thomas, where are you?" she muttered.

Edie and her crying children followed Annie's every move, too shocked to do anything else. Annie rocked little Tommy in her arms, trying to calm his terrified screams. The roar of the fire drove her ever deeper into the fast-flowing river with Elizabeth and Edie and the other children right behind.

"Look!" shouted Annie, pointing to a mountain lion standing on the cliff high above a bend in the river. With the fire lapping right behind him, the lion, ears pulled back, plunged into the river with a splash. The hot wind carried the smell of his scorched fur. The wild things that had hesitated at the edge of the river hesitated no more. Moose, deer, elk, bear, wolves, and bobcats crowded into the river with all the rest. The smoke thickened, and the only sky to be seen was dense with ash, blocking out the smoldering sun. Annie waded still farther into the rushing water. The swifter current made it difficult to keep her footing, her balance. She braced herself and dipped under the water to cool little Tommy's hot face and her own.

The flames shot up along the river's edge like a dragon's ragged fringe. Its brightness shone through the heavy smoke that burned her throat and suffocated her lungs, causing her, Tommy, and the rest of her family to cough hard. She closed her irritated eyes against the heat and smoke and brightness, feeling like sand was caught under her lids. She encouraged Tommy to do the same. The hot ash falling from the sky singed her eyelashes. The heat blistered her face and cracked open her skin until she thought she could take it no more.

The child in her arms screamed unceasingly. Annie waited until he pulled in a deep breath, then clamped her hand over his mouth and nose. She plunged below the surface of the water to bring relief to them both. When she broke the surface, gasping for breath, the little boy cried and sputtered all the more. But he was alive. Again and again, Annie repeated the dunking, holding her breath each time until she could hold it no longer, and she emerged each time thankful to hear his cries.

Darkness began to fall. At a narrow neck in the river, she watched as the fire leaped in a bridge of flame from shore to shore, the orange light spookily lighting up everyone in the water. The rising heat chasing ash high into the night sky.

※ • ※

It seemed like they had been in the water forever. All had gone eerily silent, leaving only the hypnotic, translucent flames, the crackle of burning wood, the awful smell of smoke, and the taste of ash. Finally the smoke began to clear in the night sky. Annie's body and mind were too numb to feel the cold of the river filled with ash and debris.

Annie didn't know when it stopped hurting to swallow, when their faces no longer needed cooling in the water, when the river of fire ceased flowing over them. The smoke and fire were dull and silvery now, the brightness gone. She was too tired to think about it more. Her mind drifted. Her thoughts wandering back to an early spring morning at the butcher's shop. She'd been preparing the shop for the day's work as the sun peeked over the Yorkshire hills. Thomas seemed to appear out of nowhere. She had not seen him for over a year while he'd hid away in Spring Hollow. His rugged face was tan. His eyes filled with hope, and he held out a bouquet of primrose. Her wildly beating heart leapt into her throat as she stood mute, her work dress tied behind her knees, the mop handle leaning against her shoulder. Her brows rose in confusion, she pushed the errant strands of hair behind her ear and wiped her hands down her apron in the hope of making a difference. And when he asked her to go with him to America, it had taken just long enough for the mop to drop to the floor, the errant strands of hair to slip from behind her ear, and her heart to stop beating before she whispered her answer, "Yes! When do you want me?"

Without warning, Annie and her now quiet charge, shivering in her arms, were being lifted from the river.

"Thomas?" she mumbled in delirium. "Thomas?"

"It's Joey, Annie," he answered, as he dragged both their listless bodies to shore. "I have you now. Everything will be all right."

Chapter 37

⇝ • ⇜

Annie awoke feeling warm under blankets on an unfamiliar bed.

"Here, take this, love." Edie held her hand under the back of Annie's head, helping her to sip the warm herb tea. "It'll give you strength. You've had a rough couple of nights. It's your body healing itself and keeping your baby safe."

"My baby?" Annie looked around the room. "Where am I?"

"These kind folks are letting us share their cabin for a few days until we can find a new place. Thankfully we have the money from—"

Annie interrupted, still in sleep-drawn confusion. "Where's our house?"

"It's gone, honey. But thanks to you, we're all safe and sound. Others weren't so lucky."

"Thomas?"

"He's not here, honey, but we're with you," Edie whispered as she held Annie's hand. Annie fell back and drifted off to sleep again.

⇝ • ⇜

Restless, Annie felt a stirring deep within as she lay in an unsettling half sleep. There was no denying the fear she held in her heart for her husband and for the impending birth of her baby. This suffocating fear had an iron grip on her. She missed Thomas's comforting touch to soothe her anxiety.

"Where are you, Thomas?" she muttered, tossing and turning in her sleep. "Why aren't you here?" She felt his absence in her bones and the panic in her heart as she rocked herself in sleep.

"Please," she begged. Her eyes squeezed shut in the darkness. She knew Andrew and Joey were searching for her husband. "Oh, please bring him home to me."

With a longing ache, her wandering mind drifted back to Christmas Eve. She felt his hands on her, the luxuriant stirring deep inside. He'd left her with the certainty that he loved her. She longed for the calm steadiness of his protection. Her heart beat with the desperate desire for a family of their own. Somehow, she had seemed to know even then this sweet babe had been conceived in her womb, with the hope of their very souls being tied to one another in a family.

"Are you getting anxious, too, my little one?" she mumbled in her sleep. "Stay with me, my son. Don't leave me too." She twisted and turned in her bed. She could not bear to lose yet another of her babes now. She spread her hands protectively over her belly, anxiously awaiting his arrival. This baby was a part of her now, and more than ever, she longed to hold him in her arms.

"I will face this with grit and courage, my little one. Your papa will be so proud."

Again, she drifted into sleep.

❧ • ☙

It was the wee hours of the morning; the embers in the hearth had burned out. The night was cold. She wished for the heat of the day to return. Her back ached terribly. But a slow rhythm within her body brought a foggy notion that her babe was not willing to wait.

Her eyes snapped open. Her heart beat furiously in her chest when the first real pain hit. With all the courage she could muster, she willed her heartbeat to return to its proper pace, trying to control her fast, heavy breathing, her emotions. But the predawn light brought with it the knowledge that her baby's arrival was imminent. And with that revelation, her water broke.

"Edie," she called out fearfully, trying to control her panic. "He's coming!"

Edie had been sleeping in the same room to keep an eye on her. It took only a heartbeat for her be at Annie's side. Neither was prepared for this birth, coming a month early, but Edie remained calm, a veteran of five births of her own and having assisted in many others. With precision and efficiency, she woke Elizabeth and sent her running for the midwife. Then she helped Annie wriggle out of her cumbersome nightdress, soaked in sweat and birth fluids. Edie prepared a basin of hot water and sat bedside speaking in soothing tones, holding a cool, comforting cloth on Annie's hot, profusely perspiring forehead.

The wrenching pain hit Annie hard, gnawing at her very core. The biting backache of an encircling python left her panting in a whimper. She lost her hold on time, focusing on nothing but the pain. The steady pattering of rain outside dampened her moaning call into the first light of daybreak.

Then another contraction came. This time even harder. But there was something wrong. Edie did her best to calm Annie's fractious nerves as the miracle of birth began in earnest.

Annie convulsed in pain and gritted her teeth to keep from crying out and waking the rest of the children. Edie sat beside her, stroking her head with a damp cloth.

"Go ahead and scream when the pain comes."

"It's . . . comin'," she cried out between pants. "I can't . . ." It came in a surge of insurmountable throbbing Annie had never felt before.

"Oh . . . Edie! Edie! Oh . . . Please help me!" Annie screamed. "Something's wrong!"

Edie knew that every woman had a sixth sense about these things, and she, too, became fearful. She ignored her children, who looked in on Annie and their mam with frightened eyes.

Elizabeth came rushing in. "The midwife's not there, Mama," she said in a panic. "What else can I do?"

Edie knelt beside Annie, stroking her wet hair through the pain. "Please get another pan of hot water and another sponge," Edie answered calmly. "And the scissors too. And please get the children out of here."

Feeling Annie's belly, it didn't take Edie long before she could see the baby had not yet turned.

"Annie, your baby is breech. He must be turned before he enters the birth canal," Edie instructed in a calm but firm voice, for both knew the baby and Annie could die if he was not turned properly. "No matter how hard it is, you must hold back on your contractions. You must not push, no matter how much you want to. Understand?"

Edie placed her hands together high up on Annie's belly and leaned in with all her might, pushing on the baby, forcing him to her will.

The next contraction came in a rush. Annie screamed, "It's—nooo!"

"Hold it, Annie. You must not push," Edie demanded in a voice strong and clear, trying her best to harness her own fears. "You can do this, Annie. I know you can, honey."

This time it will be different, Annie told herself as she began again to pant. *I must hold back. I must!* She felt a roar of anger running through her and cried out, "I will do what I must! Please, God . . . Help me . . ."

The contractions came hard now. An involuntary muscle spasm pulsed through her whole body.

"Hold it, honey! Don't!" Edie, with all her strength, pushed harder now.

Slowly, the baby began to turn. It was a long and arduous effort. Again, Edie pushed as hard as she could on Annie's belly. The baby had come around a long way but still not enough. "You're doing great, honey. We're almost there."

"I'm . . . too . . . I can't hold it back."

Edie saw the fear in her sister-in-law's eyes, and she only hoped Annie's body could take care of the rest of the turn. "You can do it. I know you can. Okay, that's it, honey! Push . . . Push now!" Her voice was loud and clear over Annie's cries.

"I can't . . . lose . . . him . . . Don't let me . . . lose him . . ."

"I know, honey," Edie answered. Babies died under the best of circumstances, and Annie had already lost two of them.

"Push!" Edie encouraged. "It will be all right."

The pain increased in wave after wave of cramping agony that left Annie gasping for breath. On and on it went, into the harrowing morning that turned sticky with the returning heat and intermittent rain. The long day faded into the dark, choking hours of another eternal night of exhaustion. The rain was torn away by wind; the summer lightning lit the night sky overhead. Still, Annie could not deliver the babe through the raw loins of her spreading birth canal. Blood was everywhere as Edie continued her ritual by Annie's side.

"If I die, Edie, you have to promise me—"

"Nonsense, Annie. Don't talk like that," Edith interrupted her.

Annie screamed imprecations at God, at Edie, her husband, anyone who might hear, until the python relaxed its grip and slid off the bloody bed, leaving Annie spiraling down into unconsciousness in a plum-colored mist of deathly exhaustion.

Chapter 38

❥ • ❦

After the longest, most harrowing near-death delivery God would allow, Annie awoke to the sweetest joy she could have ever imagined. She held in her arms a strong, hungry, beautiful baby boy, wrapped comfortably in a warm swaddling blanket. He lay there yawning in the precious way only contented, healthy newborn babies do. He was born on a Wednesday, which would now and forevermore be Annie's favorite day of the week.

Filled with indescribable emotions, Annie couldn't keep the tears from welling up in her eyes. In her opinion, he was the most beautiful baby ever born of woman. There was a euphoria about her she could not describe. Joy? Happiness? No, there was no word for it in the English language. Nothing could adequately describe what motherhood meant to her as she held him in her arms. She rocked him, offering the soft sweetness of a mother's melody to her precious little boy.

"Whether we hold you in our arms for only a few hours, a few days, or God willing the rest of our lives," Annie whispered, remembering those babes she had loved and lost, "we hold you in our hearts forever. You are what God gave mothers time on earth for." She looked onto his beautiful rosy complexion. "I can't wait to share this priceless gift with your papa!"

Edie said nothing. Her brows pulled together, a tight line of anguish on her lips as she sat at Annie's bedside, looking on at the touching scene of mother and child.

"He is strong and healthy, isn't he?" Annie looked up for confirmation in Edie's eyes. "With eyes and ears and five fingers on each hand, and five toes on his little feet. And that precious little nose that fits so perfectly on his adorable little face. A face with no story yet written."

"Yes, Annie. He's a beautiful baby." Edie was happy she could honestly confirm the heartfelt questions of her beloved sister. "Think of it! Your voice is the first he will ever hear. Your image the first to be imprinted on his mind and heart."

"I suppose that's right, isn't it! I pray that image is a force for good." Annie sighed. She would love him! Nourish him! Make him strong to face the trials of life and prosper in their new land. "Thomas will be so proud of his handsome boy! Thrilled!" Annie turned to look at Edie. "Don't you think?"

Edie sat quiet, revealing nothing but a solemn sigh. She put her hand on Annie's shoulder to ease the desperate concern sparked by her own somber eyes. "He is a handsome boy." She looked softly on the baby. "Sometimes I wonder how far away from heaven we really are. As I look at you, your babe in arms, I think maybe on this morning heaven is right here." She wiped at the moisture in her eyes, not wanting this moment to end, postponing the finality of Thomas's loss.

Annie tried to fully appreciate what she owed to the Almighty for this treasured gift. She, better than most, understood the miracle of it, the mantle of responsibility that had been placed squarely on her shoulders. The unbound exhilaration at the prospect of their lives together as a family was overflowing.

"Finally, a family," Annie whispered for his and God's ears only. "Your papa will be so proud when he comes home to us."

Edie pondered this angelic picture of mother and child. *Motherhood, shared by women for millennia, is more than the difficult task of bearing children, although it surely is that. It is the essence, the best of who we are as women. It can define our very identity. It can be the cure for the disease of our own self-centeredness, the antidote to strong, stubborn pride, and the balm for the soul-crushing heartache of loss that Annie will surely bear.*

Edie had been so afraid of Annie finding out the devastating news of her husband that she'd refused to allow Andrew or Joey in her room. It had been almost two days since the baby was born when Andrew convinced his wife the inevitable could be delayed no longer.

"Annie, love." Edie entered her room. "I have a couple visitors for you, if you don't mind?"

"Sure, who is it?" Annie, still weak from the ordeal, was sitting in her robe in front of the mirror brushing her hair. When she saw a solemn Andrew standing behind Edie in the reflection, a shiver skittered down her spine.

Edie swept in. "Here, let me take the baby while you talk." She left Annie still staring at the reflection, which now showed Joey's anxious, pale face as well.

Annie stood and turned toward them, her chin up high, her heart pounding, her palms beginning to sweat. She looked at them quizzically. Her brows pulled together, her breath caught in her throat. "Where's Thomas?" she whispered.

Andrew nervously burst out with the news. "I'm so sorry, Annie, he's been killed!"

The words hit Annie like an eclipse of the sun. She wanted to look away, to swallow the surreal moment, but couldn't. Breathless from the impact of the harsh and sudden news, she said nothing. Then seized with violent tremors, she began to buckle at the knees. Joey swooped in and with strong arms helped her sit on the side of the bed. His touch felt hot and clammy against her cold skin.

"No, Joey." She pushed him away with a sweep of her arm, her chin still held high. "I won't be comforted for something that isn't so."

Andrew rambled on, wringing his hands, sharing Joseph Young's condolences. "All will deeply miss him—that's what Mr. Young said. He said Tom was a good man, courageous, generous, and loyal to the end. Thomas thought of everyone but himself. We'll not see the likes of—"

"Stop it, Andrew!" She groaned, gritting her teeth and raising her flat hand to him. She had heard enough.

Andrew fell silent, then apologetically held out the red emerald pendant.

Dizzy, she stared at its luster in his hand. Shakily, she grasped the pendant from him and crumpled to the floor. Knees folded under her, hands on her lap, she held the precious pendant. With tremendous concentration she forced herself to breathe. She didn't hear Joey's kind, caring words or feel their hugs of sympathy. She was left with only the bitter taste of heartbreak, not willing to contemplate going on without the love of her life. When Andrew tried to explain more of what he knew of Thomas's death, she refused to hear it, to accept the finality of this declaration. She would not accept her baby being left fatherless.

Sitting up against the edge of the bed, eyes cold, staring at her two brothers-in-law, she spit out her words with a frown. "I don't believe it, and I'll hear no more of it. Now, leave my room. Both of you, this instant!"

Nervously, hats in hand, both backed out as she'd bid.

That night, the thunder growled. The rain clouted the windowpane. And Annie crawled into bed alone. Despite her conscious pleas to turn away from the restless thoughts, it was impossible. To defeat the loneliness, she imagined Thomas there with her. While her fate sat watching, Annie held her husband in her heart and sobbed herself to sleep.

It was the middle of the night when she awoke in half sleep, restless, unsettled, breathing heavily. She tossed and turned. Her yearning mind drifted into private imaginings, wandering untethered into fitful dreams. Lost in the warm glow of a multitude of beguiling desires, touches, and anxious caresses, she struggled through the dark night of thunder. It was heartrending, debilitating, her own private hell. Then abruptly, she sat up in bed sobbing, gasping for air. Her nightgown soaked in sweat, she struggled to draw in a ragged breath. It wasn't enough. Panicked, she felt as if she was suffocating in the dark, dank room. She clawed at her covers to pull them away. Panting, desperately trying to inhale the stale, stifling air.

"I can't breathe," she sobbed.

"I'm here, honey." Edie held her in her arms as Annie drew in a breath of lifesaving air. The panic began to subside. As Annie pulled in one breath then another, reality began to resume its rightful place in her mind. She swept her wet, tangled hair from her face, pulled back from Edie, and lay back, staring up at the ceiling in the shadowed darkness.

Lightning flashed and the thunder cracked as the storm raged on outside.

"He cannot be gone from me forever." She breathed in heavily, trying to calm her frazzled nerves. *I'm afraid. I'm so alone. I don't know what to do. But I know I can't give up on him. Not now. Not ever.* She wiped at her eyes and finally drifted off into unsettled sleep, the pain of longing gripping her chest in the same relentless dream, ending unwillingly in an illicit awakening. She sobbed and pushed away the harsh reality, unwilling to accept she may never see him again, never hear his voice, smell the scent of him, taste his sweet kisses, or feel his skin against hers.

"No!" She clenched her teeth and pursed her lips, resolved. "I will not give up on you!"

Chapter 39

☙ • ❧

As the sun rose in the east on a late summer morning, Annie stood rocking her nearly month-old babe in her arms. Still not yet fully recovered from her long, difficult delivery, she had passed through the weeks that followed in an excruciating daze. With no home to return to, and only the possessions they'd carried from the fire and the money from Thomas, the family had found a place to live up in the Narrows, a few miles east of Park City, on the border of Wyoming territory. She knew her family thought her a delusional soul, rejecting their efforts to console her or to make her see reason. She refused to listen to "I'm so sorry" from either family or friends. For she was not near as courageous as some had supposed. She suspected that to confirm the finality of her husband's fate would destroy her.

On this morning, Annie had gotten up very early and wrapped her baby tightly to her breasts in his papoose so only his inquisitive eyes peered out from the bundle. Concentrating intensely on his mam, his sparkling eyes brought warmth to her soul. Annie smiled at him. For a moment she thought of her Henry and Nannie. She had three children now and knew in her heart she always would. Annie smoothed and caressed the red emerald ring as she did every morning, remembering its meaning.

She had made a long list of things to do around the house that morning but wished she could find someone else to do them. Looking out the window, she watched the sun as it peeked over the mountains. For no particular reason, she pushed open the front door with its disagreeable squealing hinges, and in her bare feet, she stepped out into the awakening day as the first rays of sunshine broke through the trees to warm her back.

Pausing to revel in nature, she drew in a deep breath of crisp mountain air. She could almost taste the freshness of autumn, acknowledging the summer days had begun their slide into fall. The sounds of the mockingbird, the thresh, and the distant chugging purr of a passing train filled her ears. A blaze of autumn color covering the mountainsides brought a faint smile. The orange, red, and yellow leaves fluttered up the Narrows, cascading in an almost indiscernible breeze, carrying with them the sweet, intoxicating smell of the purple aspen daisies that surrounded their little cottage.

There was no shadow of dust from soot-filled coal mines, no rotting flesh from the butcher's, not even the hustle, bustle, and clatter of shops opening for the morning rush of patrons. There was only the peace of nature in these majestic mountains.

Taking care to avoid the sharp edges of the stones, she felt the urge to continue. She stepped gingerly along the pathway toward the cottage gate. The moss between the flat stones felt like velvet on the bottoms of her bare feet. Driven by some unrecognizable force, Annie continued down the path, beyond the squeaky iron gate of the yard, and out along the lane canopied in bright yellow cottonwoods. The cracked and broken stone scraped at her tender feet, yet still she was compelled to walk on.

In the far distance, she saw two men riding in a wagon as they came around the mountain bend in the road. A single horse plodded slowly, pulling the small wagon up the roadway. Recognizing something familiar in the one who held the reins, she cupped her hand over her brow to shade her eyes against the morning sun. She focused on the familiar face. When the wide smile of Joseph Young came clear, she raised her arm to wave. She didn't recognize the man sitting beside him when he lifted his head; his bearded face was the color of dusty shale. He was drawn, fragile, and thin. He had long, shaggy hair sweeping across his eyes, like blazes of black coal in clouds of ash. Without expression he stared blankly into the distance, as still and quiet as a blue heron watching the water, frozen in time and patience. Then his eyes turned toward hers, widened, and locked with a flicker of acknowledgment as her waving hand drifted down.

In the years to come, she would ask herself what had drawn her outside on that cool, early fall morning at exactly that moment, but deep in her soul, she knew. And whenever she smelled the sweet purple aspen daisies, the memory would flood into her mind, her heart would warm, and a smile would sweep across her face.

Annie's pulse quickened. Her heart leaped into her throat. Her hand flew to her mouth, attempting to hold in the rising emotion. But it was hopeless. Her rosy cheeks broke into a welcoming smile, her green eyes danced, and tearful emotion rushed to the surface as she began to run.

※ • ※

They say absence makes the heart grow fonder. That was certainly the case with Tom Wright. All had seemed lost on that fateful night when he'd been struck down by the cavalryman's bullets. Cold and shivering, he felt his gut had been turned inside out. His dry mouth was filled with the metallic taste of blood—he lay dying in the mud and he knew it. He could hear only the sound of the whistling wind through the trees and the pounding of rain where he lay silent, near death, drifting in and out of consciousness. As his soul headed into the unknown, he had thought of little else but Annie. It had surprised him, though now he wondered why. She had calmed his tortured soul with her kindness, her ever-present humor, her sweet smile and undying love. His love for her had blossomed, extending deep and powerful roots into his heart.

When all had seemed lost, his guardian angel, in the form of another caring soul, had come for him in the storm. Leaning down to where Tom lay deathly still, blood mixing in a stream of water, Black Eagle had slid his powerful arms under Tom's limp body. This giant of a man, with superhuman strength, had appeared out of nowhere. He'd lifted Tom up out of the mud.

"Hold on." Determined to get this barely alive white man back to his village, Black Eagle had trudged in fits and starts along the deer trail and up the craggy mountainside all through that rainy night. The wind had howled through the trees like dead souls denied paradise. Black Eagle's legs, arms, and back ached terribly, but still he made the fifteen miles through the torrential weather to his isolated Shoshoni village before the sun rose, sending its rays through the angry clouds.

Hidden deep in the mountain forest, cut off from the outside world, the women of the village had all pitched in to help their medicine man nurture Tom back to the living. Using native remedies perfected over generations of living in this rugged country, they seemed to have a single-minded mission to help this fugitive from the white man's justice survive his life-threatening wounds. For weeks he struggled, delirious and near death. His survival was a miraculous accomplishment by these purveyors of mercy in the forest.

Tom hadn't heard a word from the outside world, and no Indian in camp seemed to know what had happened to his wife and family after the fire. It was not until Joseph Young rode into the village one afternoon with Annie's letter in hand that Tom found out where they had gone.

Joseph Young had come with news. "The storm has passed as fortunes poured into the pockets of Doc Durant and the Union Pacific Railroad. And just this past week, Doc Durant, the Ames brothers, and Crédit Mobilier were indicted for conspiracy to defraud the US government, bribing both senators and bureaucrats along the way."

"How did that happen?" Tom had asked.

"Brigham has his fingers in a lot of pies." Joseph had smiled.

"Oh my gosh."

"There is no more interest in pursuing those who only took what was rightfully theirs. It's time for you to go home, Tom."

Tom had thanked Chief Black Eagle and those who for almost two months had fought to bring him back to life. Friendships had been formed that would last a lifetime. Although Tom was in no condition to travel, he wanted to go home. And no amount of effort to convince him otherwise was going to make any difference. He cut short his long road to recovery. And aching in every part of his body, he coughed and limped his way onto a borrowed wagon, and Joseph Young drove him all the way up the Narrows to find his family.

※ · ※

"Thomas!" Annie shouted, her brows pulled up, her hands quivering, her voice cracking. The intoxication of seeing her husband quickened her bare feet, numbed them to the rough roadway. She ran with reckless abandon, tears streaming, arms waving, frantically calling out his name.

A wide smile slowly spread across Thomas's face as he registered the sound of his wife's voice, the sight of her running toward him.

Holding his ribs, gritting his teeth, he stood up in pain. Fixedly he watched her run, babe in arms, skirts flying, seemingly heedless of the road and all else around her. His voice broke with emotion as he called out her name. And despite Mr. Young's protest, Tom ignored the pain, climbed down from the wagon, and with his crutch under his arm, hobbled toward her.

She ran into his open arms, nearly knocking him to the ground. Both hearts pounding. He tried to speak, but she smothered his face with kisses. Taking in the familiar smell and taste of her, he held her tight, pressing his body against hers. He reveled in the miracle of her presence and the tears of joy coursing down her cheeks.

Out of breath, Tom looked into her eyes. "Can you forgive a fool for leaving you alone?" He paused, offering a wan smile. "I missed you more than I ever imagined possible."

"Maybe?" The warm glow of her rosy cheeks gave way to a bright and ardent smile, and the sparkle in her crystal green eyes lit up her face. "I knew you were alive. I knew it. I knew it deep in my soul. I knew you would come home to me. I knew it, even when they told me it couldn't be so!" Her overflowing tears were lost in the fabric of his shirt. She was laughing and crying, smiling in happiness.

"I missed you so!" he cried, the pent-up emotion released. He kissed her, then kissed her again. "Oh, Annie!"

It took Tom more than a few moments to break the single-minded, spellbound attraction to his wife, but finally his attention shifted to the little one. "You're too much, Annie Dale Wright, keeping this secret from me. Joseph Young had to tell me." He smiled, wiping a tear from his eye. "Show me my son."

Grinning still, Annie pulled the papoose around and lifted the corner of the little blanket so Thomas might see the healthy, cooing, wonderous face of his beautiful baby boy.

"So, who do we have here, my love?" With intense eyes, Tom looked into his son's.

"He's my present to you . . . Papa."

"Oh, and what a present he is!" Tom's eyes brightened, and he reached down and tickled his little son under his chin to bring a smile. "How did your Mam keep you a secret all this time? All those months. What a beautiful homecoming present you are!" Tom looked into Annie's smiling face. "A healthy little devil. A downright brute."

"Yup, that's how we do it out here in the mountain west. He's made me a believer in love at first sight," Annie said softly, with a crack of emotion in her voice. "I thought you wouldn't mind if we called him Georgie."

"Mind?" Tom's eyes crinkled at the corners as his smile spread wider across his face. "Hello, Georgie," he answered, looking deep into Georgie's eyes, wiping yet another tear from his own. "Leave it to your mam to pick the perfect name for our little man." He looked again at Annie. "He's so healthy. All five fingers on both hands. So perfect, learning to touch and feel, and I suppose they will get him in his share of mischief. Where on these little knees will the scars from sliding down hills be? Tom tickled him under his chin to bring a smile. I've got big plans for you, Georgie."

Annie looked into Tom's smiling face, seeing his eyes dancing with his son's. She had to blink to make sure it wasn't a dream. Tom put his arm around her, leaning on her just a bit as they began the walk back to the cottage together, Tom discreetly wrenching in pain, Joseph trailing with his wagon.

Noticing the concern in Annie's eyes, Tom smiled. "I'm a bit buggered up, but I'll mend. It's good to be home."

"We're looking forward to pampering you, aren't we, Georgie?"

"He is a beautiful baby, isn't he?" Annie looked up at Thomas for affirmation. "Tell me he's beautiful."

Tom gazed into her eyes, wondering why he had been so blind. "You're beautiful! I don't believe there is anyone like you!" He felt a disabling surge of love course through him. "You've made me a proud family man."

Annie's heart was lodged in her throat. "I'd like to show you a little something after you've rested up, if you have the time?"

"I've all the time in the world for you. From now on I'm all yours—feel free to show away."

"Fair enough. It's a date, then!"

He gave her a mischievous smile. "I'm starving. And I wouldn't mind a little food for breakfast either." His eyes crinkled playfully.

"All in good time, my husband." She giggled, with a sly smile of her own.

"How are we gonna find a little time to ourselves with a house full of family?"

"Thanks to your tarnished reputation, I've become socially connected. I think I just might be able to arrange a private cabin dinner. And a little dessert too—but you best rest up first." She smiled coyly. "I look forward to showing you some of my secret places!"

Chapter 40

※ · ※

After breakfast Tom slept in until almost suppertime of the following day, exhausted from his injuries and the long wagon ride. With the afternoon sun dropping on the horizon of the Wasatch Mountains, Tom and Annie took a short stroll up the canyon path with Georgie wrapped in his papoose.

Annie weaved her arm with Tom's, holding on tight as he leaned on her slightly. "You feel good enough to do this?"

"Sure! I need to get out into the fresh air."

"Andrew told me what you did to deliver the back pay to all those men."

"Yeah, I wouldn't blame you for chastising me, risking my life and yours only to give away all that money."

"I'm proud of what you did." Annie frowned. "Except the part about risking your life and scaring the hell out of me." She grew solemn. "I . . ." She turned away and wiped at her runny nose.

Tom smiled softly. The moisture in her eyes told the story of the anguish she'd suffered.

"And as far as the money, if you want to know what God thinks of money, look at the kinda people he gave it all too."

She wrapped both arms around his waist and let out a long

breath. "I'm just happy you're safe and here with me now."

He leaned on her shoulder. "You can thank Black Eagle for that."

"Joseph Young told me a bit about that!" She looked up at him. "He told me a lot of things while you were sleeping during those thirty hours."

"Right now, I just want to talk about you and Georgie."

"I knew many of the wives and children of the men whose lives you changed." Her voice caught. "Most of their families lived in Park City."

Tom, breathing heavily, stopped on the trail to rest and share a drink of water.

"Are you okay? If you want my advice—"

"I'm okay," he interrupted.

"Listen, when I ask if you want my advice, it's just a courtesy really. I plan to give it either way." She looked at him with concern. "I think maybe we should go back."

"I'm fine!" Tom paused, shifting his weight. "Annie, I was scared." His voice cracked. "But what could I do . . . I couldn't stand by and let those men and their families starve because of one bully's unbridled greed."

"Some say there is no greater sacrifice than to risk your own life for another." Annie paused, emotion rising. "Constance Cohen would be proud of you."

"Mrs. Cohen was an insightful woman," Tom soberly acknowledged. "I've become a believer. But it was you who set the example, Annie. My experiences of late just pushed me over the top." He smiled as he looked down into her eyes. "Despite the danger all around me, when I saw the rekindled light of hope in the eyes of hundreds of men standing before me at Rockport, it brought an indescribable feeling I hadn't expected but didn't want to let go of." He paused. "I was slow to learn your patient lessons. I realize now darkness can never drive out darkness. Only light can do that. And maybe the true measure of a man is not found in worldly successes, but is more a measure of what he gives of himself to his friends. What he does to meet his commitments to his family.

Annie could see something had changed behind those eyes, shining amber in the soft light of a fall afternoon. And there was something in the set of his jaw, in the softness of his countenance. Something confirming that a life was not a thing unalterable. This was an older, wiser, calmer man whose hot blood had cooled with time and trial. This was a confident, secure man, at peace with himself.

"In the past few months, I've learned a bit about anguish, pain and humiliation—the refining influence it can have on our soul."

"I was sore afraid, I trembled at the very thought of losing you. I will never again take for granted the priceless gift of hope. It was my comforter. It was only hope that brought any brightness against the darkened fear in my soul—that you were alive, that you would come back to Georgie and me." Annie's voice caught. "But deep down below the fear, I was proud of the courage it must have taken to risk it all for those who had put their trust in you."

"Hmm." He recalled the harrowing weeks on the run. "I was afraid, lying in the mud near death. I wondered if I'd made the biggest mistake of my life."

Annie wrapped her arms around his and leaned her head on his shoulder.

"I left the despicable Doc Durant standing beside his train tracks with more money in the back of my wagon than I could spend in a dozen lifetimes . . . and all I could think about was freeing myself of the burden, getting it to its rightful owners, and coming home to you."

"Oh, Thomas." She thought of Martha's last words to her and knew they would forever remain fixed in her heart: *Thomas may not fully see it just yet, but someday he will see that you are the completion of him.*

Tom paused for a moment to compose himself. "I'm afraid it will be a long time before we can buy that piece of land of our own." He pulled in a deep breath. "I'm sorry, Annie."

Annie lifted her eyes to gaze into the depths of his, a crevasse she now knew to its greatest reaches. "I love you and I don't suppose I could ever find a way to untangle my heart from yours. From the moment we met, I was placed on a train with that destination. It was not of my choosing, but once on, there was no possible way I could get off." Annie said no more as they took their few remaining steps to the crest of the hill overlooking the valley below. Tom's comforting arm was around her shoulders, his breathing running deep and heavy. More than anything else she wanted to be held by him, to have him never again let her go.

⊱ • ⊰

It was late afternoon as they stood at the plateau overlook. The northern half light of autumn cast its long shadows over the valley. Endless evergreens, seamless cottonwoods, and quaking aspen cascaded down the hillsides in a rugged blaze of fall colors, blinding orange, splashes of gold, and garnet. And stretched out below, nestled amid the trees, was a stunning pastoral scene, a quiltwork of verdant meadowland. A wide stream slowly wound its way through the lush, spreading meadow of sweet-smelling wildflowers.

Tom breathed in the clean smell of crisp mountain air. Putting his arms around his wife and son, snuggled safe and asleep in his papoose. Tom pulled both in close, listening to the first song of the evening dove drifting on a light breeze through the trees.

"Breathtaking!" He gasped in awe. He turned to look at Annie's face glowing golden in the late afternoon sunshine. Her rosy cheeks, primped hair, and determined expression. He couldn't help but marvel at how confident and strong she had become. She was much like the unspoiled surroundings of this new land. It fitted her. "Aren't these untamed wildlands magnificent?"

"It's called Chalk Creek," she said, seeing his eyes light up at the sight of the shimmering, crystal clean flowing water of the whispering stream that meandered under a majestic canopy of scattered oaks, willows, and cottonwoods. "And yes, it's full of trout ready for the catching."

"Now you can even read my mind." He beamed. "It looks more like a river . . . stunning."

"I often come here on my walks with Georgie. I hear that every spring, Chief Black Eagle and his ever-dwindling band of Shoshoni pass along its banks on their way up to their summer hunting grounds. But I suppose you're familiar with that now."

Tom stood quiet with his young family, staring in astonishment at all that lay before him. "I can see why you brought me here. It's incredible, like a dream come to life. Someday, Annie . . . Someday, we'll have our own land, maybe even like this!" A wistful look across his face, an excitement for their future together as he stared down on the beautiful sight.

She hesitated just long enough for him to turn and face her. He could see in her eyes an understanding of his wonderment for this hallowed ground, his almost sacred love for the land, yet there was something more there.

"What?" His questioning eyes locked onto hers.

She started to speak, but her voice caught. Turning away from him, she wiped at her eyes, then turned back and whispered, "It's ours, Thomas."

He continued looking down at her, the meaning of her words not yet registering.

Annie waited patiently, in excruciating silence, while the message wound its way from his ears to his head and then to his heart.

"What are you saying?" In fear of breaking the spell, he turned back to the dream that had so long held his heart hostage.

"As soon as I saw it," she began, "I knew we must have a piece of it. It was exactly as you had described, only better." She ran on nervously, clearly hoping to get it all out before emotion caught her up. "I was reading about the Homestead Act passed by Congress. Captivated by the thought of it, in a moment of lunacy I was seized by a wild hope of owning a piece of it. So, I rode ol' Dixie down to Salt Lake intent upon meeting with Governor Brigham Young."

"That's more than a hundred miles through these rugged mountains!" Tom stared in astonishment. "In winter?"

"It was crazy, irrational. Not at all like me. But then, I was pregnant, and you know what they say about the impetuous thoughts of a pregnant woman." She smiled, trying to hold back the tears. "But Thomas, Brigham met with me! Though in the end, he told me it would be impossible. I never heard from him again, until yesterday. When you were sleeping, Joseph and I talked for a long time. He gave me this note."

"He's Brigham to you now, huh?" Dazed, overcome by admiration, his heart was caught in his throat and he could say nothing more.

Annie smiled. "Ah yes, Brigham and I are on a first-name basis." She raised crossed fingers. "This close! It was Brigham who gave me the engineering journal and Central Pacific's report on nitroglycerin to give to you. It was Brigham who let Joseph know where you were and what had happened to you."

"You're something else!"

"My good qualities are under your protection, sir, and you have my permission to exaggerate them at every opportunity."

A wide smile slowly crept across Tom's face as he looked down at her.

"Brigham seems to have his fingers in a lot of pies." She shrugged.

"So I've heard."

"Read it." She handed Tom the letter.

※ · ※

Dearest Annie and Tom,

Rubies, diamonds, and silver dollars are not gifts, but only apologies for gifts. The only true gift in the Kingdom of Heaven is the gift of oneself in the service of another; only the unselfish acts of the giver who forgets himself and earthly treasures in the offering is truly deserving of the Lord's greatest blessings.

In thanks to you both for your selfless acts of service to those in need, I am pleased to offer you this deed for the most beautiful 160 acres ever touched by the hand of the Almighty. And an offer to be the new Director of Operations for the Weber Coal Company and its recently acquired site for the proposed Wasatch Mine.

Good luck to you both and God bless,
Brigham

※ · ※

"Thomas, it's meadowland from the trail along its easterly boundary down to and including Chalk Creek running through it." Joining Tom in gazing out at the land, she pointed to the boundaries. "And you're right, for much of the summer after the snow melts, Chalk Creek is more like a pristine river. It's our meadow! It's our creek! It's our land as long as God will grant us breath to live in these magnificent mountains."

Tom stood silent, looking out in wonder.

"Joseph told me thanks to General Dodge and President Grant, Brigham's investment and contractor fees owed by the Union Pacific are to be paid in kind. Train tracks, all the materials and supplies needed, coal cars, caboose, and two first-class engines." Annie looked into Thomas's eyes as he stared at her in awe. "He plans to ensure the construction of a railroad spur taking coal from the new town of Coalville just down Narrows Canyon to the Salt Lake Valley. The Wasatch Mine is to be the largest supplier of coal in the eastern territory, to be locally owned and operated by the managing members of the Weber Coal Company." She paused, waiting for the message to sink in. "You now have an ownership interest in the company... If you take the position offered, that is?"

"Really!" Who was this remarkable creature standing beside him? With her indomitable spirit! A woman who could do anything she put her mind to. A woman of substance.

He leaned down, put his arms around her and their little one, and kissed her. "How lucky am I you chose me?"

"Very lucky indeed, sir!" She looked at him with a solemn expression. "Oh, I missed you so, Tommy." She wiped at her eyes. "Oh, how I missed you."

"Never even met Brigham Young."

"He clearly knows you," she said. "We have a title certificate for all 160 acres, signed by the US patent office. All we have to do to finalize our claim is build a house on it."

Tom just stood there looking down at her.

"And I want a brick, stone, and timber house, with a white veranda all the way around, and blue painted shutters."

He smiled. "You're too much." Then he looked at the written

offer. "This is more money in one year, than . . ."

"That Brigham knows talent when he sees it!" Annie grinned. "Joseph says, 'Best get ta hiring right away.'"

"Things are different in America. Suppose there are a few men around here who wouldn't mind working for me?"

"You have no idea, do you?"

He looked at her quizzically. "What?"

"Want 'em or not, you've got more friends around here than you can shake a stick at."

"Really?"

"Really! Hundreds of them." Annie smiled up at him. "When the fires swept through Park City, most were burned out of their homes. These families lost virtually everything. They would have been destitute, but you changed all that. You risked your life for those families, those husbands, fathers, brothers, sons, most of whom relocated here after the fire. They credit your sacrifice with saving their lives. But for the grace of God, it would have been your ultimate sacrifice." She paused, adding in earnest, "They will never forget it."

"I don't know what to say."

"Over the past day and a half while you were sleeping, word of your arrival spread. I've had to turn away dozens of well-wishers wanting to offer their heartfelt gratitude. I insisted they give you some time, but don't be surprised if they plan one grand celebration for your return."

"So, we'll be going to a picnic or two, will we?"

"Just leave it to me, honey. Unlike you, I've learned to love socializing."

"It's not a wise man who questions Annie Dale Wright!" He swiped at his runny nose, shifting his weight to ease the pain. "Just when I think I know the best of you . . ."

"Excellent observation, my husband," she chided. "As Captain Preston advised, it will do you well to mind your p's and q's around me!" Annie paused. She would never be a fragile beauty, she thought, but maybe a big-boned, Amazon woman, as the butcher's wife had once described her, was not such a bad thing. "It's always been my intention to astonish you, sir!"

He reached down, taking their son from her arms. Soberly, he held him to his chest, his large hand patting his little boy's back. "You know, I thought of you every night while I was on the run," he whispered. "I imagined you on our last night together. The sight of your strong, hard body, in your long white linen nightgown standing before the firelight." He soberly remembered the smell of sandalwood. How her mouth tasted of fresh peaches. The feeling of her skin against his, her beating heart against his chest and the sound of her breathing in his ear when he made love to her. How she looked when he left her in front of that cabin—capable, confident, her hard body strong from overcoming the rugged life of these mountains. "I missed you, but I knew you felt as alone as I did."

"I still have that nightgown!" she whispered, her eyes glistening.

Together, as a family, they gazed out at nature's showcase: the mountainsides covered in evergreens, the aspen groves the color of autumn, quaking in the fall breeze. Patches of reeds caught red pools of light reflecting the butterscotch glow of the waning sun.

"When I first saw it, the red, gold, purple, green, and blue spring wildflowers had just burst across the meadowland, with Chalk Creek running through it under the canopy of spreading cottonwoods," Annie said. "Even then I knew we must spend the rest of their lives here."

High overhead, they watched a majestic bald eagle spread his wings wide to sail effortlessly in a light breeze. Unfettered by gravity, he seemed to reign supreme over these rugged mountains, soaring in perfect balance with nature without the slightest perceptible movement of his wings.

"Magnificent!" Tom breathed the air in as he stood transfixed. The great master of the firmaments looked down upon them, then on a sweep of streaming air, the eagle streaked across the sky, the wind beneath his wings breaking the silence in a picture of majesty. And when the air was again still, Annie and Tom were left to gaze in awe at the empty space in the heavens where he had once been.

"Apparently, this is his country too!" Annie mused.

"One of God's many miracles," Tom supposed.

In a way, the phenomenon of flight, defying gravity, slipping the bonds of earth and entering some indescribable realm above it all—this was not so unlike shedding the cords of bondage to live free, to embrace their God-given liberty in this country of unimaginable beauty. Tom thought that if man could but endure the downward pressures of life and invite the uplifting wonder of God and nature, maybe man, too, could soar to great heights.

Annie threaded her arms with his and leaned her head on his shoulder. "Can you see the giant cottonwood just beyond the pooling pond?" She pointed toward the great tree with an enormous nest atop its branches. "I've sat here for hours watching Mrs. Bald Eagle caring for her chicks, waiting for her doting husband to return with dinner and relieve her for a time." Both looked on, spellbound. "They tell me bald eagles will remain devoted to each other for their entire lifetime, twenty years or more."

"Fascinating," Tom said in awe. "As so much of the natural world is!"

"Hmm."

"Annie, do you mind if we call this place Spring Hollow?"

"I would love that," she whispered.

Tom thought of their future here, living as a family, intertwined with land and nature. He slid around behind his wife. And with great solemnity, wrapped his arms around her and their son, dropping his chin to her shoulder. Touched by the sweet rush of songbirds singing in celebration at the close of this magnificent day, he was overwhelmed with serenity in his soul.

"What choice do I have but to love the woman you have become?" he whispered into her ear. "I don't suppose I deserve you!"

"Probably not. But then you must learn to be happier than you deserve. For like Mrs. Bald Eagle, I intend to be forever yours."

"This is my miracle—my family," Tom murmured. The proud father looked into his son's eyes. "And you, Georgie, my perfect little one, the first in our family to be born free in America!" Tom paused. He felt overwhelmed with gratefulness for his family and this country, the Almighty's gift to all of us. Tom couldn't help but smile to himself. He was happy.

He kissed his wife's cheek. He reached down and touched Georgie's creamy complexion, glowing fresh and healthy in the mountain air. "Our lives have just begun. So many roads to choose from."

"Including those less traveled." She paused. "You must promise never to leave me again."

"Never!"

"It took us a long time to get here." But it was clear now to both, once here they had become the completion of each other. Annie's words brought a warmth and a calm to the tumult in Tom's soul. Starting tomorrow they would begin to put their family stamp on this new land where eagles flew free. They would sink their roots deep into the dark, rich soil.

As far as Tom was concerned, for as long as the waters flowed and the grasses grew, there would never be a clear separation between the natural beauty of this sacred place and the hallowed ground of religious expression. Spring Hollow and Chalk Creek running through it would be forever woven into the fabric of their lives and the future generations of their American heritage. Far more than the land belonging to them, they would belong to the land, until eventually the land and their family would merge together into one.

Epilogue

⋟ • ⋞

FROM THE 214-YEAR-OLD SHIP'S FOOTLOCKER, neatly tucked away in a corner along with Martha's most precious things, I found a letter. It was from Thomas to his mam. I opened the brittle, yellowed envelope, pulled out the delicate 150-year-old parchment, carefully unfolded it, and began to read.

⋟ • ⋞

July 1, 1874

My dearest Mam:

Anna Judah surprised us with a visit in June. Riding for the very first time on her husband's ribbons of steel, she arrived here one fine summer afternoon to fulfill George's final request. She escorted him home to us that he might rest in peace by those he loved most. George had come full circle to where he always wanted to be, forever close to family. We buried him on the hill not far from our new home overlooking Chalk Creek and the meadow filled with wildflowers. With the help of a traveling builder, George Dunford, we built our beautiful brick, stone, and timber home, with a white veranda all the way around and blue-painted shutters. I only hope it will stand for generations to come, as solid as the land upon which it is founded.

Mr. Dunford, an interesting Scottish fellow, travels the Rocky Mountains practicing the age-old art of masonry and timber construction. He taught me a skill I'm sure I'll cherish for a lifetime: fly-fishing! The split bamboo fly rod is eight feet in length and wrapped with red and green silk thread for strength. It weighs only four ounces. When I hold the rod out in front of me, it trembles with my beating heart. Out of ignorance I suppose, an unsuspecting soul called it a fishing pole one afternoon, at which point Mr. Dunford gave the fella a look of utter condescension, as if he had referred to the living Christ as a mere mortal man.

At first, for some exasperating reason, I found it almost impossible to transport the vision of casting the fly onto the water I held in my mind—lift the line, leader, and tied fly off the water and put it back down again onto the eddies and pooling ponds along Chalk Creek. And if the business was done improperly, the wily trout quickly saw it for what it was—a ruse—then burst out in laughter, soon gone in search of the real thing.

It took hundreds of tries before I could consistently get that rod to do its appointed task. But, as with everything worth having in this life—time, patience, and careful practice are required. I am learning the art of what I'm sure is to become my lifelong passion. Each evening after work, in the cool northern half-light of Spring Hollow's long summer days, I unwind by fishing along the banks of Chalk Creek until dark falls. I find fishing in the bowels of nature does indeed restore the soul! It has a spiritual cadence about it. And I have come to believe that only by picking up this cadence can I gain the full appreciation of the power and beauty of being one with the Almighty and the natural beauty of Spring Hollow.

The great brown trout live in the deep pools, the rainbow

among the rocks covered in moss. Cut-throat, native only to these waters, flourish in the eddies and are found in abundance in the more turbulent rapids. Like men, each are different in their own right. Patiently, I work to better appreciate the natural beauty and hallowed ground of this sacred place while mastering the art of casting the fly into the pooling ponds, eddies, and rapids running under the Weeping Willow, meandering through the quaking aspen and around the spreading cottonwood. Each carefully placed cast brings a warmth to the soul. It helps me better understand the fundamental truths of God, man, and nature.

Now, while my little ones Georgie and TF are too young to master the art of the fly rod, I let them use worms to fish the creek. But in the years to come, I suspect that on these long summer evenings, I will slip away from my work in the late-afternoon sunshine to have an early supper with family. Then I'll take my boys down to the creek for a quiet evening spent as father and sons, learning the art of casting flies to settle on the water. I've learned fly-fishing doesn't solve my problems, but it does bring them to the surface. And I suspect, there by the creek, my boys and I might learn from each other that the greatest treasures in life come from serving our friends and those we love.

I thank the Lord every night for the lessons learned from you, Annie, and George, and the art of fly fishing. As the poet Henry David Thoreau said, "Happiness is like a butterfly, the more you chase it, the more it will elude you, but if you turn your attention to other things, serve the people you most care about, it just might come and sit softly on your shoulder."

Thank you, Mam. Thank you for everything.

Forever your loving son,
Thomas

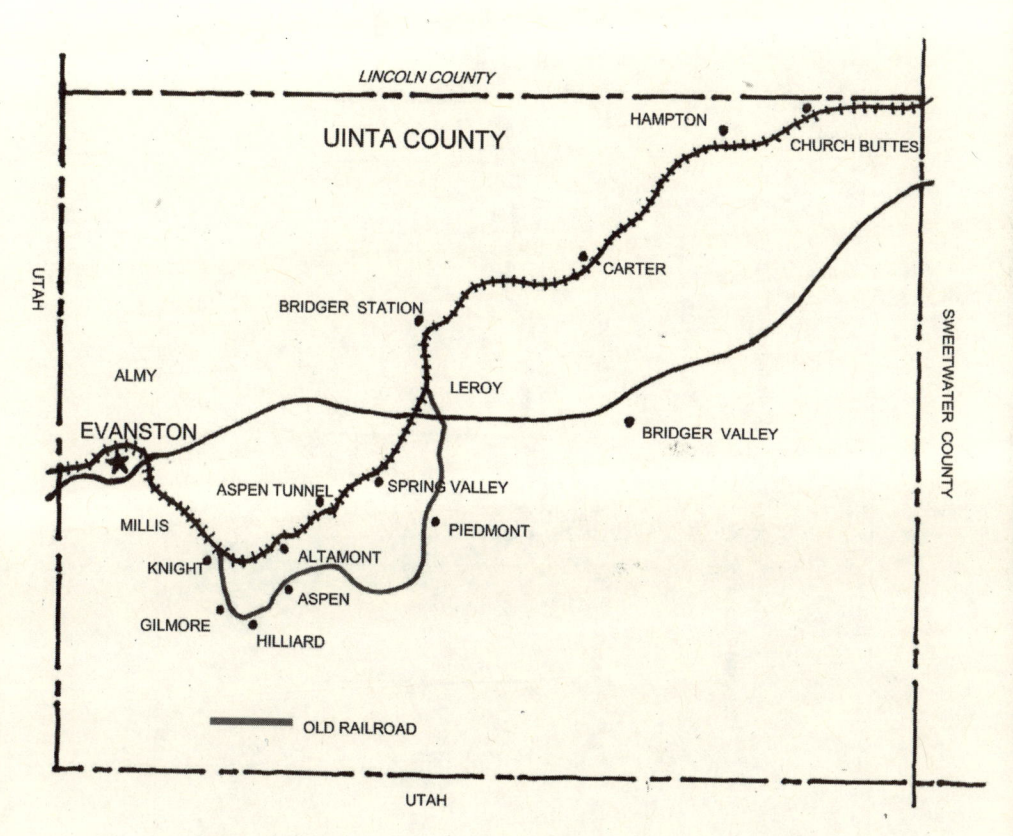

Courtesy of the Uinta County Museum, Evanston, Wyoming

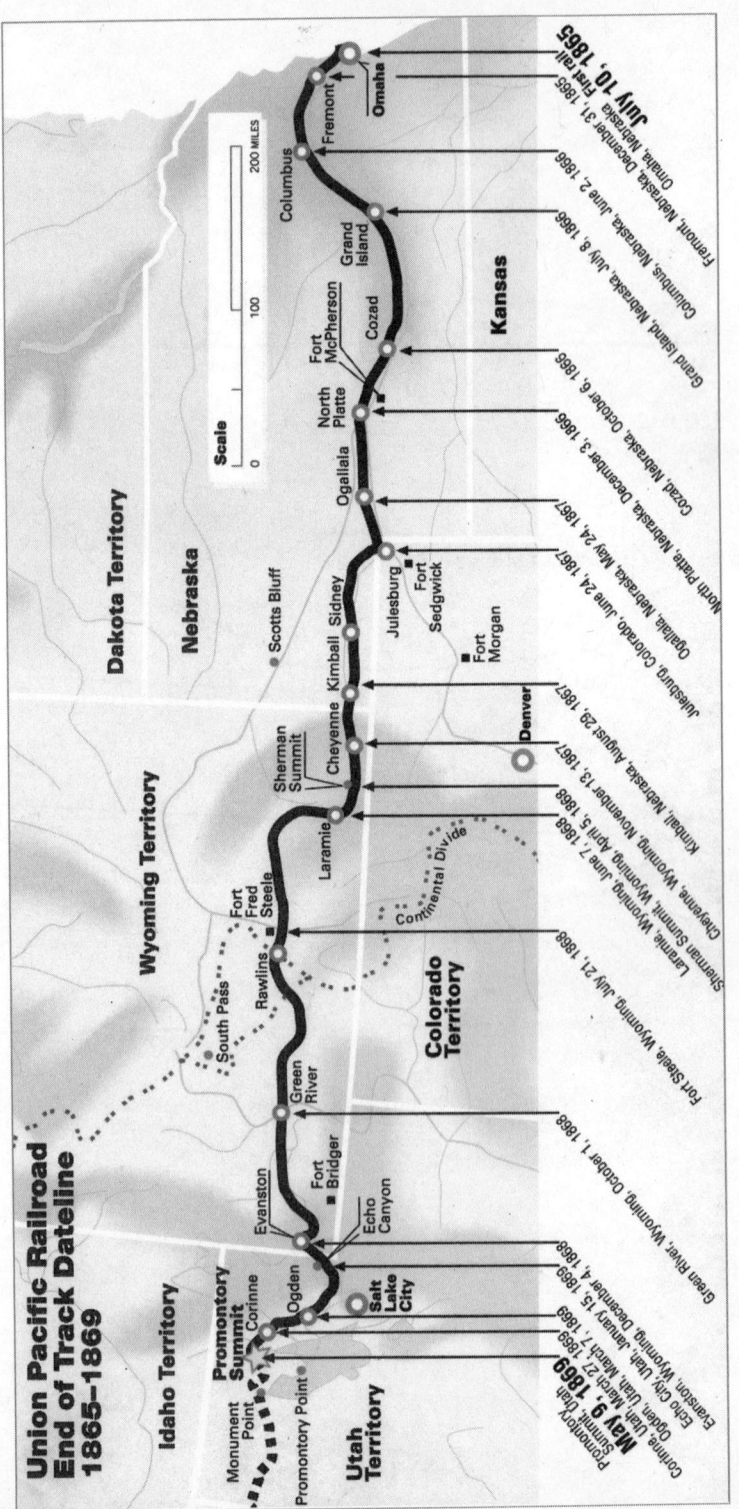

David A. Jacinto

Union Pacific Railroad End of Track Dateline 1865-1869

Omaha, Nebraska, July 10, 1865
Fremont, Nebraska, December 31, 1865
Columbus, Nebraska, July 8, 1866
Grand Island, Nebraska, June 2, 1866
Cozad, Nebraska, October 6, 1866
North Platte, Nebraska, December 3, 1866
Ogallala, Nebraska, May 24, 1867
Julesburg, Colorado, June 24, 1867
Kimball, Nebraska, August 29, 1867
Cheyenne, Wyoming, November 13, 1867
Laramie, Wyoming, June 7, 1868
Sherman Summit, Wyoming, April 5, 1868
Fort Steele, Wyoming, July 21, 1868
Green River, Wyoming, October 1, 1868
Evanston, Wyoming, December 4, 1868
Echo City, Utah, January 15, 1869
Ogden, Utah, March 7, 1869
Promontory Summit, Corinne, Ogden, Utah, March 27, 1869
May 9, 1869

Courtesy of the Uinta County Museum, Evanston, Wyoming

Author's Note

⇾ • ⇽

THE 1860S WERE A TRANSFORMATIONAL decade in American history. What transpired during those years would change the face of America more than any other decade in its history. That course correction would pave the way for tremendous economic progress, vast territorial expansion, and a population explosion that set America on the path to make it the greatest country the world had ever known. Thomas and Annie Wright were emblematic of many of the immigrants who left the old world to come to the new just after the Civil War's hostile fulfillment of the promises of the Declaration of Independence and the American Covenant.

Tom, Annie, and the rest of the Wright family in this two-book series, reflected in the family tree exhibit, arrived while America was experiencing the growing pains of transformational change. The personal and historical events, dates, and places depicted are generally accurate, although timing was sometimes collapsed for the purposes of the story. Martha's 1810 trunk, Annie's larger trunk with letters referenced in the bibliography, and many of the artifacts referenced in this series are still in existence today.

Martha taught her children well. All thrived in America. George did become an American journalist until he died young of unknown causes. The family voyage across the Atlantic including all the family members listed did occur, but the tragedies, storms, and diseases were taken primarily from George's journal on the brigantine sailing ship eight years earlier. Annie did lose her first and second child. The Great Chicago Fire occurred only three years after Tom met with the *Tribune* editor in search of George. It would burn 17,000 structures to the ground, including the *Chicago Tribune* building and the Tremont House across the street, where Lincoln spent a lot of his time and Mary Lincoln stayed after his assassination.

Most everything written about Brigham Young, and virtually every significant quote attributed to him, has been corroborated by multiple sources. Even some of the quotes and mannerisms in Brigham's meeting with Annie are taken from reports of his opinions on the subject. His son Joseph's company, Sharp & Young, were responsible for the Utah Territory portion of the transcontinental line construction under the direction of General Grenville Dodge. The Able family, as described, were one of the early families that followed Brigham Young to Utah.

The massacre at Haun's Mill and the events in Nauvoo, Illinois, were taken from actual historical records corroborated by multiple sources, although a composite of individual atrocities was attributed entirely to Daniel McArthur's family for purposes of the novel narrative. Missouri's Governor Boggs did put out an extermination order on all Mormons to drive them out of this pro-slavery state, primarily because of their support for the abolition of slavery and Indian rights that led to armed conflict in Jackson County, ultimately the flash point of the Civil War, as predicted by Thomas Jefferson. The federal government refused to interfere, citing states' rights, which trumped civil rights in the US Constitution's Bill of Rights until that summer of 1868, when Lincoln's thirteenth and fourteenth amendments to the constitution were ratified three years after his assassination. In 1844, while running for President of the United States on an abolitionist and Bill of Rights platform, the Mormon leader Joseph Smith was assassinated. After that, many Mormons were killed, their property seized, and virtually all the rest were driven from the region, ultimately settling out west. The details of the Indian wars and atrocities committed against the Indians, including the massacre at Bear River and other events depicted in *Where Eagles Fly Free,* are largely true. The Indian attack on the train crossing the plains did occur, and all those working for the railroad were killed. President-Elect Ulysses S. Grant, Dr. Thomas C. Durant, William Tecumseh Sherman, General Grenville Dodge, Leland Stanford, Charles Crocker, Brigham Young, and others did meet at Fort Laramie and Benton City at the same week Tom and family were there. There were eight deaths in accidents crossing the Green River that September in 1868, described in a similar fashion to that of the Stone family, but the Gabriel and Rachel Stone family are fictitious characters.

Jim Bridger was married to the daughter of the chief of the Shoshoni Nation, Washakie.

I followed the mountains of historical documents regarding the Youngs, the Judahs, Abraham Lincoln, General Grenville Dodge, and of course Doc Durant, the Ames brothers, and Crédit Mobilier, as well as many other characters and details involved in the building of the railroad and four Castle Rock tunnels.

Tom and Annie's involvement in the historically significant events depicted in this novel are not entirely accurate. This is a novel after all, and like any extraordinary historical fiction, this story has been told with the requisite embellishments worthy of such a tale. While it is true that they were participants in those generally accurate historical events referenced in this two-book series, I sometimes allowed them to play more integral roles for the purposes of the novel.

Tom did work on the railroad leading forces as an expert in logistics and the technology of the day. Nitroglycerin, mixed with diatomaceous earth to later be widely used as dynamite, was used successfully for the first time without casualty in building the Castle Rock tunnels. The 775-foot tunnel, the longest on the UP line, was one of four tunnels in the Echo Canyon area, all complicated engineering projects on arguably the greatest technological achievement of the nineteenth century. The transcontinental railroad, championed by Abraham Lincoln, was maybe the greatest sociological and political achievement in American history.

As with many works of historical fiction, the most outlandish events are often the true ones. The firing of General Grenville Dodge by Doc Durant did happen, in part because he strongly advocated paying the Utah Territory crews, but the intervention of President Grant overturned it. The hijacking of Doc Durant's presidential car on the way to the golden spike ceremony is substantially accurate. Thanks to the help of Windy Peterson, whose family has owned the property where the hijacking occurred since 1867, and careful review of historical records, we were able to unravel the most likely scenario and site conditions that made the three-day hostage crisis possible. It is unclear exactly how much money in total was sent after General Dodge and Mr. Dillon's message demanding the $500,000 be wired (presumably to Omaha then transported from there by train), but the ransom paid made an enormous difference in the lives of over three hundred workers and their families. Some of the language passing between the hijackers, Doc Durant, General Dodge, the train engineer, and others is documented. General Grenville Dodge despised Doc Durant and was personally insulted when the railway workers in the Utah Territory were not paid. His position on the matter seems to help explain, at least in part, why the hijacking was successful. The Devil's Gate Bridge over Weber River was taken out, and because of the high flood waters, the Fort Douglas cavalry was forced to abandon their rescue attempt. The Fort Bridger army troops were redirected at the Piedmont switching station away from the hijacking by workers dressed as UP employees. The hijacking and Devil's Gate Bridge repair did delay the driving of the golden spike by two days, with most of the world's celebration occurring on May 8, 1869, instead of May 10, when the actual gold and silver spikes were hammered down in front of a diminished crowd. Durant and Stanford did actually have to rely on a railway worker standing by to help drive the spikes into the ground. Apparently, the Fort Laramie cavalry was delayed from tracking down the hijackers until well after the hijackers had left the scene.

The community of Rockport was surrounded by a high impenetrable wall constructed for protection during the Black Hawk Indian wars in the 1860s and out of the fear of invasion by the US Cavalry. Much of the town is now under reservoir water behind the present-day Wanship Dam. Since Tom was working on the railroad at the time and no one knows exactly which workers were the beneficiaries of the hijacking, I took the liberty of making Tom the lead hijacker for purposes of the novel.

It is interesting to note that Doc Durant, the Ames brothers, and Crédit Mobilier were later convicted of conspiracy to defraud millions from the US government, bribing senators and government officials along the way. Thanks to General Grenville Dodge and the influence of President Grant and a humiliated Union Pacific Railroad, Brigham Young's final investment payoff was ultimately made "in kind." He received all he needed to build railroad spurs to Salt Lake and the new town of Coalville, which became a thriving center for mining coal, the lifeblood of America at the time, and the adjacent Park City silver mines, where many Chinese people had settled. Within five years of the railroad's completion, the robber baron

Doc Durant had been prosecuted and convicted of defrauding the government and lost his remaining millions in the great depression of 1873 to1879. Left almost penniless, he died in 1885, mired in legal battles.

The Wrights did acquire a 160-acre land grant, assisted by de facto governor Brigham Young. They called it Spring Hollow. And at Brigham Young's urging, Tom Wright became the director of operations for the Weber Coal Company and Wasatch Mine, also acting as a consultant to other mines in the area, including the Park City silver mines, where a statue of his nephew, Emmett Wright, now stands on Main Street.

This historical fiction encompasses one of the most pivotal eras in America's history. The Wrights' story is an example of the thousands of men and women who came to America's shores searching for liberty and land after the Civil War. Within the ten years of the 1860s, slavery was abolished with Abraham Lincoln's Emancipation Proclamation, codified with the Thirteenth Amendment to the US Constitution and ratified just before the Wrights landed in New York Harbor. The equal application of the Bill of Rights (ensuring life, liberty, property, and civil rights; freedom of religion, speech, assembly, press, and privacy; the right to bear arms; the right to equal protection; legal and voting rights, etc.) was granted to all men through the Fourteenth Amendment, also championed by Abraham Lincoln, which was ratified not long after the Wrights arrived. The extension of those God-given rights to every state and to all individual citizens bolstered equal opportunity and protections and helped drive expansion of America from sea to shining sea. And eventually the Fourteenth Amendment led to making women, black citizens, and other minority citizens equal under the law. Of course, the full implementation of those rights and freedoms remains an ongoing struggle and the subject of considerable debate by many, with some who would prefer to limit those individual rights, including suppression of free speech.

Despite these great leaps forward in human rights during the 1860s, the American Indians, who were not citizens of America, were driven from their lands and slaughtered indiscriminately. To tame the Wild West, the 1862 "forced" Indian treaty and the Homestead Act were used to push the Indians off the land and offer this hostile frontier to desperate city dwellers and immigrants. Sometimes the brutal taking was done with massacres like the referenced Bear River to strengthen America's hold on the continent and provide land ownership opportunities for families like the Wrights and thousands of other American settlers across the western frontier. Chief Black Eagle fought back, leading the Shoshoni rebellion of 1878 to 1879 against the US government in their fight to retain their ancient heritage. He was killed in the battle of Salmon River by the US Cavalry in August 1879. Brigham Young and many who followed him were ostracized for their sympathetic relations with the Indians, as were others in the territory, like the Wright family. As a result, they were considered unsuitable for military service. Chief Pocatello and several hundred of his followers were baptized into the Church of Jesus Christ of Latter-Day Saints in 1875. And in 1880, the Shoshoni Nation's Chief Washakie and 310 of his followers were baptized into the church by Amos Wright. The Washakie township was established by the church and there, unlike the government reservations or other religious reeducation centers, the Indians were free to govern themselves and to honor their own cultural traditions. In the delicate balance between white man and Indian, the Washakie township would thrive for over a hundred years. Tens of thousands of Shoshoni, Navajo, Bannock, Cheyenne, Ute, Sioux, Delaware, and dozens of other American Indian tribes converted to the Church of Jesus Christ. Most, like foreign-born Americans, were eventually integrated into the surrounding communities, education systems, and cultural life of Wyoming, Utah, Colorado, Arizona, California, Oregon, and Idaho.

Because of the public outcry over Brigham Young's polygamist ways and his unwillingness to bend to the dictates of what was deemed appropriate governance by Washington, DC, seven attempts were made to replace Brigham Young as governor in eleven years. This book makes no attempt to address, condone, justify, or excuse the plural marriages of Brigham Young or the 5 to 15 percent of the affluent church leaders engaged in that practice at the time. Most of America felt strongly that the practice of plural marriage for all the public to witness was abhorrent and degrading to women, an unconscionable and diabolical abuse of Christian values. Some ministers described Brigham Young and his church as "even worse than the Irish Catholic Church, the Whore of Babylon." This rhetoric, Washington politicians, and mainstream Eastern newspapers inflamed public opinion. For the most part, that feeling has not changed in America, and there is no doubt the criticism was entirely warranted in many cases. Nevertheless, it is interesting to hear what Brigham Young actually had to say about women. "Women can do more than sweep floors, wash dishes, make beds and raise babies," Brigham Young argued. "They are just as capable as men in mathematics, accounting, and the sciences. . . . They too should have the privilege to study these branches of knowledge, stand behind the counter, study law, medicine and run the counting house, to enlarge their sphere of usefulness to the benefit of society."

Many women in the Deseret territory took Brigham at his word and did just that. Eliza R. Snow was an internationally acclaimed writer and poetess, publisher of one of the first women's magazines, and head of the largest women's philanthropic organization in America, intended to help families like Artist Able's during the territorial depression of 1866–69. With the help of suffragettes Elizabeth

Stanton and Susan B. Anthony, Eliza led the charge to give women the right to vote in the territory.

In 1869, the Utah/Wyoming territory was the first to give women that right, fifty years before the rest of the country. Eliza Snow was the plural wife of Brigham Young. Three decades earlier while living alone in Jackson County, she had been gang raped by a Missouri mob in a horrific attack on the Mormons, preventing her from ever having children. The attractive, petite, and brilliantly confident Eliza, while pursuing her career of choice, often traveled across the country lecturing on what she considered the virtues of plural marriage, sometimes into the lion's den of Washington, DC, and even Europe. "Women living in mean accommodations on the frontier work 16-20 hour days through brutal winters and blazing summers in a dangerous wilderness, just to survive," she said, "and if they lose their men, which many do, life is untenable. . . Plural marriage makes possible alternatives for women." This was all without birth control.

There were many other plural wives who, surprisingly to most all across the country, joined Eliza's chorus of advocacy. Dr. Martha Cannon graduated from the University of Utah (Deseret University) and, with four other Mormon women, attended Michigan Medical School to graduate in a class of 406—all but fourteen were men. The women were often forced to sit in the hallways during lectures. While head of obstetrics at Deseret Hospital, Dr. Cannon's polygamous husband was prosecuted and jailed. Dr. Cannon was pregnant when she escaped to England. She would return years later to run for senator in the Utah Legislature on a platform of equal rights for women and equal pay for equal work. Dr. Cannon was the first woman in America to be elected to a state senate, decades before women in the rest of the country even had the right to vote. As a Democrat, Dr. Cannon was victorious over her husband, who ran for the same seat as the Republican nominee. To celebrate her victory, Judge Cannon took Dr. Cannon out to dinner with her three sister wives. Then, as now, this confusing arrangement left the rest of the country reeling. It should also be noted that at the time of this novel, there were few children born out of wedlock or single-mother households in this inhospitable frontier, where the majority of the members of the church were women. In contrast, for the rest of the country in the late 1860s after 25 percent of the young men had been casualties of a civil war, a large percentage of women remained unwed and hundreds of thousands of children were forced to be raised in vulnerable single-mother households with few opportunities for employment and no government support for either mother or child.

To the surprise of almost everyone in the country east of the Mississippi, when the US Congress passed increasingly stringent laws to extricate women from the chains of plural marriage, the most virulent outrage came from the plural wives themselves. The practice was officially abandoned in 1890.

Each new appointed governor intended to replace Brigham Young was charged with reeducating the residents of the territory to the proper order of things. All gave up in frustration, some after only a month. Washington even tried to bring the territory to heel with military force, but in the end, an exhausted invading Johnson's Army succumbed to Brigham Young's cunning tactics and harassment by Porter Rockwell and his men, without a single loss of life in battle.

They would enter Salt Lake City in a snow storm, near starving, to be fed and lodged under Brigham Young's protection. Even during the years Brigham Young wasn't actually the governor, he was the de facto governor in virtually every way. He controlled the legislature and was ostensibly the face of governance in the territory of Deseret, which in the 1860s not only included Utah but Wyoming, Idaho, Nevada, Arizona, and previously parts of Colorado, Oregon, and California. It was John Marshall, sent to California by Brigham Young, who was the first to discover gold at Sutter's Mill in 1848. Sam Brannon, another Mormon leader, marketed that find and ushered in the rush of forty-niners to the California gold fields. Brannon would become California's first millionaire, and he sent much of his wealth to Salt Lake City.

Out of frustration, a disillusioned *Cheyenne Daily News* wrote, "There is more political strength and influence united in Brigham Young than any other one person in America, including the President." Seymore and Reed, the New York City attorneys and UP directors sent to Salt Lake to convert Brigham's "YES" telegram into a contract, said of him, "It was one of the most difficult negotiations I've ever encountered." And when Brigham Young set up a bidding war between the UP and Central Pacific RR, a shaken Leland Stanford told his Central Pacific partner Mark Hopkins, "It's been very difficult navigating . . . I've been devilishly close to the breakers several times." In the end, Brigham Young negotiated some of the highest wages in the country for seven thousand workers on the UP and five thousand on the CP. General Grenville Dodge said of these workers, "Tea-totalers to the last man, tolerate no gambling, quiet and law-abiding, say grace at meals, some speak better English than I do, and unlike those damn Chinese, eat real American food . . . they work hard, building the finest grade on the line . . . Despite their religion, they deserve to be paid every penny for their work." Renowned historian Stephen Ambrose said of the controversial leader and entrepreneur, "Had it not been for his generally feared religion, Brigham Young, quite possibly could have been President of the United States . . . and maybe a good or even great one . . ."

Public policy opposing plural marriage, inflamed by Eastern newspapers and political rhetoric, led Washington to advocate scorched earth policies to rid the country of Brigham Young and his followers. A savvy Doc Durant took advantage of this opportunity to defraud these workers who made the momentous achievement of building the transcontinental possible, and their desperate families.

Like all of us, the characters in this book were products of their times, with prejudices, flaws, and shortcomings that Americans of today might find entirely unacceptable, but all were intimately involved in the making of America. Tom and Annie were self-educated immigrants, both strong, morally conflicted, gritty survivors, complicated in many of their views and failings, as most people are. Both strived to improve their lives and their relationship with each other, their fellow man, and their God, growing in many ways along life's journey. They were determined people, heroically devoted, capable of tremendous sacrifice, not untypical of the American immigrant of the early years of this country. Their story is intended to shine a light on the lives of our forefathers drawn to America to escape the tyranny of Europe's aristocratic overlords and oppressive governments. Because America was a country that championed the individual, with land available that families could aspire to own, they came by the thousands, then the millions, and are still coming. These rugged individualists hacked out lives of their own choosing in the sometimes hostile and lawless Western frontier wilderness.

Spring Hollow, the Wrights' family home of high mountain pastures, rugged yet beautiful landscape, with cascading forests, still remains in the Wasatch Mountains. It has changed little in the past century and a half. With the help of a traveling builder, George Dunford, Tom and Annie did indeed build their impressive brick, stone, and timber home, with a white veranda all the way around and blue-painted shutters as Annie had requested. Their home would be the grandest along Chalk Creek for more than a hundred years. Joseph Wright would build his humble home and church next door. He was to be a religious leader in the community for forty years. For almost a century, this family compound was the center of life and the heartbeat of the social fabric of the entire community, living side by side generally in peace with the Indians. Frequent picnics, special events, and gatherings drew hundreds of friends and family and sometimes included Black Eagle, his family, and others of his tribe. And today one of those first homes on the property and Joseph's small Spring Hollow church building are being preserved in perpetuity as historical monuments. Work on the small church building is not yet complete, and much of the proceeds from the sale of *Where Eagles Fly Free* and *Out of the Darkness* will be used to help complete this renovation.

Bibliography

⊱ • ⊰

Ambrose, Stephen E. *Nothing Like It in the World: The Men Who Built the Transcontinental Railroad, 1863–1869.* Simon & Schuster, August 29, 2000.

Bancroft, Hubert Howe. *History of Utah.* The History Company, 1890.

Barney, Lewis. Papers. Archives. Church of Jesus Christ of Latter-Day Saints Library, Salt Lake City.

Bracken, Jeanne Minn, ed. *Iron Horses Across America.* Discovery Enterprises, 1955.

Carson, John. *The Union Pacific: Hell on Wheels!* Press of the Territorian, 1968.

Clark, Rebekah. "Dr. Martha Hughes Cannon, First Female State Senator." Utah Women's History: The Women, https://utahwomenshistory.org/the-women/marthahughescannon/.

Clark, Thomas Curtis, et al. *The American Railway: Its Construction, Development, Management, and Appliances.* Scribner, 1889.

Dillon, Sidney. "Historic Moments: Driving the Last Spike of the

Union Pacific." *Scribner's Magazine*, August 1892.

Dodge, Grenville M. *How We Built the Union Pacific Railway.* Reprint, Monarch Printing, 1997.

Farnham, Wallace D. "Grenville Dodge and the Union Pacific: A Study of Historical Legends." *Journal of American History* 51, no. 4 (1964).

Gordon, Sarah. *Passage to Union: How the Railroads Transformed American Life, 1829–1929.* Ivan Dee, 1996.

Grant, Ulysses S. *Personal Memoirs of U. S. Grant.* Volume I and Volume II. Charles L. Webster & Company, 1885–1886.

Hamblin, Jacob. Journals and Letters to Jacob Hamblin. Manuscript copies prepared by Brigham Young University Library, 2004.

Hanks, Ted L. *Benton, Wyoming.* TL Hanks, 2002.

Judah, Anna. Papers. Bancroft Library, University of California, Berkley.

Kyner, James H. *End of Track.* Caxton Printers, 1937.

Meese III, Edwin. "The Meaning of the Constitution." The Heritage Foundation Political Process Report, September 16, 2009, https://www.heritage.org/political-process/report/the-meaning-the-constitution.

Reeder, Clarence A. "A History of Utah's Railroads." PhD diss., University of Utah, 1959.

Reeder, Jennifer. "Eliza R. Snow, Zion's Poetess." Utah Women's History: The Women, https://utahwomenshistory.org/the-women/elizarsnow/.

Rosewater, Andrew. "Finding a Path Across the Rocky Mountain Range." *The Union Pacific Magazine*, January 1923.

Union Pacific Railroad. *The Union Pacific Railroad Across the Continental West from Omaha, Nebraska*. Pamphlet published by the company. Omaha, 1868.

Wheat, Carl. "A Sketch of the Life of Theodore Judah." *California Historical Society Quarterly*, 4, no. 3 (September 1925).

Wright-Trietsch, Norma Jean. *They Came from England: The Wrights of Coalville, Utah, 1860–1972*. Published by the author, 1972.

Acknowledgments

The telling of this story would not have been possible without the work of special people who had a great influence on me:

My great-aunt Norma Jean Wright-Trietsch, who spent the first half of the twentieth century in a Herculean effort to meticulously comb through and organize genealogical records, old letters, journal entries, news clippings, and documents, and who interviewed countless relatives with connections to the nineteenth-century lives of the Wright family.

Ramona Pace, who is currently working tirelessly on the historical building renovation at the Spring Hollow site.

Margaret Moore and the many others who helped with the research.

Uinta County Museum in Evanston, Wyoming, whose staff provided exhibits and, together with many others, shared information on the transcontinental railroad line.

Michela Miller Dickson, a delightful young woman who spent countless hours going through this manuscript with me and engaging in long conversations to make sure I got it right.

Michael Levin, a brilliant writer himself and winner of multiple awards, who coached me through this process. And of course, Jane

Ubell-Meyer, Ed Bajek, and my editor Salvatore Borriello and publicist Javier Perez, who helped me put it all together.

I couldn't conclude my acknowledgments without mentioning my family: The main characters, Thomas and Annie Wright; Thomas's parents, the invincible Martha Wright and her husband Joseph; Thomas's brothers and sister, George, Joseph, and Edith Wright; my daughter Rachel, for slogging through the first draft of the manuscript and offering valuable suggestions; and my wife Anne, for reading the last draft and adding her suggested changes.